Also by Rufi Thorpe

Dear Fang, With Love
The Girls from Corona del Mar

The
Knockout
Queen

Rufi Thorpe

The
Knockout
Queen

Alfred A. Knopf   New York   2020

Library of Congress Cataloging-in-Publication Data
Names: Thorpe, Rufi, author.
Title: The knockout queen / by Rufi Thorpe.
Description: First edition. | New York : Alfred A. Knopf, 2020.
Identifiers: LCCN 2019012529 (print) | LCCN 2019012983 (ebook) |
ISBN 9780525656791 (ebook) | ISBN 9780525656784 (hardcover)
Classification: LCC PS3620.H787 (ebook) |
LCC PS3620.H787 K59 2020 (print) | DDC 813/.6—dc23
LC record available at https://lccn.loc.gov/2019012529

Jacket photograph by Robert Jones/Arcangel Images
Jacket design by John Gall

Manufactured in the United States of America
First Edition

For my mother

You're born naked, the rest is drag.

—*RuPaul*

It is insufficient to say that power and violence are not the same. Power and violence are opposites; where the one rules absolutely, the other is absent.

—*Hannah Arendt*

The
Knockout
Queen

1

When I was eleven years old, I moved in with my aunt after my mother was sent to prison.

That was 2004, which was incidentally the same year the pictures of Abu Ghraib were published, the same year we reached the conclusion there were no weapons of mass destruction after all. What a whoopsie. Mistakes were made, clearly, but the blame for these mistakes was impossible to allocate as no one person could be deemed responsible. What was responsibility even? Guilt was a transcendental riddle that baffled our sweet Pollyannaish president. How had it happened? Certainly he had not wanted it to happen. In a way, President Bush was a victim in all this too.

Perplexingly, the jury had no difficulty in assigning guilt to my own mother as she sat silently, looking down, tears running and running down her face at what seemed to me at the time an impossible rate. *Slow down, Mom, you'll get dehydrated!* If you have never been in a criminal courtroom, it is disgusting. You have seen them so often on TV that seeing an actual one is grotesque: the real live lawyers, all sweaty, their dark mouths venting coffee breath directly into your face, the judge who has a cold and keeps blowing his nose, the defendants who are crying or visibly shaking, whose moms are watching or whose kids are trying to sit still in the back. It's a lot to take in when you're eleven and even just a few months prior you were making an argument that not receiving a particular video game for your birthday would be "unfair."

The town to which my little sister and I were relocated after a brief stint in foster care was a suburban utopia a la Norman Rockwell, updated with a fancy coffee shop and yoga studio. We moved in just before the Fourth of July, and I remember being shooed into a town fair, where there were bounce houses and hot dogs being sold to benefit the Kiwanis club. What the fuck was the Kiwanis club? I was given a wristband and ten dollars and told to go play. A woman painted a soccer ball on my face. (All the boys got soccer balls, and all the girls got butterflies; those were the options.)

Bordered on the west by the sea, on the north by a massive airport, on the east by a freeway, and on the south by a sprawling, smoke-belching oil refinery, North Shore was a tiny rectangle. Originally built as a factory town for the oil refinery, it was a perfect simulacrum of a small town anywhere in America, with a main street and cute post office, a stately brick high school, a police department with predictably brutalist architecture; but instead of fading into rural sprawl at its edges, this fairy-tale town was wedged inside the greater body of Los Angeles.

My aunt's place was one of those small stucco houses that look immediately like a face, the door forming a kind of nose, and the windows on either side two dark, square eyes. She had a cypress bush in the front that had turned yellow on one side, and many pinwheels planted on the border of her lawn, the bright-colored plastic sun-bleached to a ghostly white as they spun in the wind. North Shore was a windy place with many hills, and I was shocked that people could live in such a wonderful climate without smiling all the time. The air pollution from the airport and oil refinery were pushed inland by the sea breezes. Even our trash cans did not smell, so clean was the air there. Sometimes I would stick my head into them and breathe deeply, just to reassure myself that trash was still trash.

On either side, my aunt's house was flanked by mansions, as

was the case on almost every street of the town. Poor house, mansion, poor house, mansion, made a chessboard pattern along the street. And the longer I came to live there, the more clearly I understood that the chessboard was not native but invasive, a symptom of massive flux. The poor houses would, one by one, be mounted by gleaming FOR SALE signs, the realtor's face smiling toothily as the sign swayed in the wind, and then the FOR SALE sign would go away, and the house would be torn down and a mansion would be built in its place.

If there were people living in the mansion to the right of our house, I never saw them. Their trash cans did not go out, no cars parked in their drive, except a gardener who came like clockwork every Tuesday, who always gave me a nervous but friendly wave. In the mansion to the left of our house, there lived a girl and her father, a girl who, though I would never have guessed it from looking at her, so young and unsullied did she seem, was my own age, and with whom I would go to school for the next seven years. Her name was Bunny Lampert, and she was the princess of North Shore, and somehow, almost against my will, I became her friend.

One thing that Bunny and I had in common, besides being next-door neighbors, was an unusual lack of adult supervision. North Shore being the paradisiacal bubble that it was, many children walked to school or rode their bikes. But I noticed that Bunny and I were never scooted out the door by parents who rushed to remind us of lunches or fetch lost backpacks, but instead climbed out of houses empty and untended, checking our belongings ourselves, distracted as adults about to set out on the morning's commute. Perhaps it would have been natural for us to walk to school together, but this did not occur. I was invisible to Bunny, and so I came to know a great deal about her before she learned anything about me.

The first year I was in North Shore, we were in sixth grade, but even then Bunny was tall, the tallest girl in our year, but also taller than the tallest boy. I'm sure there are people who would tell you who the most beautiful girls in our school were, and Bunny would not have been found on any of their lists, and yet I loved to look at her. Not for any arrangement of features or gifts of figure, but because she was terribly alive. Like a rabbit or a fox. She was just right there. You could see her breathing, almost feel the blood prickling in her skin, her cells gobbling the sunlight.

I think, as we headed into middle school, it was this vital, translucent quality that kept boys her age from having crushes on her, crushes that required a more opaque surface that they could project onto, that evoked different things than life itself. They were interested in girls who reminded them of movies, or who seemed older, or who seemed innocent, or who seemed smart. Bunny didn't seem. She didn't remind me of anyone. I liked to walk behind her for the cute way she would pull a wedgie from her butt, the way she would sing to herself, always a little sharp, the way she ate an Eggo waffle from a paper towel as she went, careful to throw the paper towel away in a trash can when she got to school.

Her father, though I hardly ever saw him, I saw everywhere. It was his wolfish grin on almost every dangling FOR SALE sign in the town, his arms crossed over his chest, his white teeth showing in a friendly laugh. He was on FOR SALE signs, but he was also on banners at our school, where he sponsored a seemingly endless number of fund-raising events. He was on the city council and so his name was further attached to every fair, carnival, rally, or Christmas parade. Ray Lampert was inescapable.

I had seen him at that first Fourth of July fair, a huge sign with his headshot on it at a booth where a pretty blond woman gave out picnic blankets with his company's logo stitched on one side. Two Palms Realty. I was afraid to take one of the blankets, even though the pretty blond woman manning the booth told me they were free. In my child gut, I believed they were sewn with some kind of voodoo that would ensnare anyone who touched them.

I often passed by his office, which was on Main Street. He was never in there, though I grew used to seeing the blond woman I had met at the fair, wearing her headset, tapping keys on a space-age-looking computer with a monitor bigger than our TV at home.

Because our houses were next door to each other and on rather narrow plots, the bedroom windows were directly across from one another on the second story, and so I had a literal window into Bunny's life, although I could not see her without being seen myself. When she was home, I kept my blinds carefully closed, but when she was not at home, I would look into her room and examine its contents. In fact, I looked in all the windows of their home, which was decorated with a lavish '80s decadence: gilt dining chairs and a gleaming glass-topped table, white sofas and white rugs over dark, almost black, mahogany floors. The kitchen, which I had to enter their backyard in order to properly examine, was a Grecian temple of white marble, though they never seemed to cook and what was obviously supposed to be a fruit bowl was filled instead with junk, papers, and pens and keys.

They had no dogs or cats, no hamsters, not even plants. Nothing lived in that house except for Bunny, and presumably her father, though he was never at home. As to what had happened to Bunny's mother, I knew only that she had died and that there had been some air of tragedy about it, a suddenness, not a prolonged illness, and I was in high school before I learned that it was a car accident. I found this explanation disappointingly mundane. Why had a simple car accident been so whispered about, so difficult to confirm? My informant, a glossy, sleazy little imp named Ann Marie, the kind of girl who is incessantly eating a sucker or popsicle in hopes of being seen as sexual, giggled. "That wasn't the scandal," she said. "The scandal was that her mother was fucking a day-care worker at the Catholic preschool. Mr. Brandon. And he was only like twenty at the time." Where was Mr. Brandon now? He had moved, had left town, no more was known.

I often walked by that little preschool, attached to the Catholic church, which was a lovely white stucco building on a corner lot with a playground and red sandbox, and wondered about Bunny's mother and Mr. Brandon. No one could tell me what he looked like, but for my own reasons I pictured sad eyes, too-low jeans, ice-cream abs begging to be licked. Perhaps I imagined him so only as a foil to Bunny's father, whose salt-and-pepper chest hair exploded from the collar of his dress shirt in that ubiquitous head-shot. Everything else about Ray Lampert was clean, sterilized, the bleached teeth, the rehearsed smile, the expensive clothes, but that chest hair belonged to an animal.

The gossip about Bunny's father was that he drank too much, and specifically that he was a regular at the Blue Lagoon, a tiki bar tucked a few blocks off Main Street, though he was what was referred to as "a good drunk," beloved for his willingness to spring for pizza at two in the morning and listen to the tragic stories of other sad adult men. There was further supposition that his incredible success as a real estate agent was due to his habit of frequenting drinking holes, making friends with anybody and everybody. Having spent many years observing their recycling bin, I can attest that such a justification would be a bit economical with the truth. Ray Lampert was turning his birthday into a lifestyle, to quote Drake. Each week there would be two or three large gin bottles, and then seven or eight wine bottles, all of the same make, a mid-shelf Cabernet. Perhaps he bought them in bulk. It was difficult to imagine him shopping, wheeling a cart filled with nothing but Cabernet and gin through the Costco. How did someone with such an obvious drinking problem go about keeping themselves supplied? Or rather, how did a rich person go about it?

In my experience, addiction was messy. A pastiche of what you bought on payday as a treat, and what you bought on other days, convinced you wouldn't buy anything, then suddenly finding yourself at the liquor store, smiling bravely, like it was all okay. What did the cashier at the 7-Eleven make of my own father? Did he note on what days my father bought two tall boys and on what days he bought the fifth of cheap bourbon as well, and did he keep a mental tally of whether he was getting better or worse, like I did? Or did everyone buy that kind of thing at 7-Eleven? Perhaps my father was so unremarkable in his predilections as to avoid detection at all. And what was happening to the children of all those other men? Buyers of beef jerky and vodka, peanuts and wine? What did a 7-Eleven even sell that wasn't designed to kill you one way or another?

Most scandalous to me, and yet so alluring, so seductive, was the possibility that Ray Lampert felt no shame at all. That a rich man could stroll through the Costco, his cart clinking with glass bottles, and greet the cashier smiling, because she would just assume he threw lavish parties, or that he was stocking his wine cellar, that these dark bottles were just like shirts for Gatsby, talismans of opulence, but whatever it was, even if it was weird, because he was rich, it was fine.

The first time I met Bunny, or what I consider to be our first meeting, because we did encounter each other at school from time to time (in fact we had been in the same homeroom for all of seventh grade, and yet never had a single conversation), we were in tenth grade, and I was discovered in her side yard. I had taken to smoking cigarettes there, and I kept a small bottle of Febreze hidden behind a piece of plywood that was leaning against their fence. The side yard itself was sheltered from the street by a high plank gate, and then was gated again before it led to their back-yard, and because it ran along the side of their garage, there were no windows, making it a perfect hiding place. Bunny and her father kept their bikes there, but neither of them seemed to ever ride, and I had been smoking in this part of their property for years now without having been detected, so I was startled when she opened the gate, already wearing her bike helmet, which was pink.

She was surprised to see me and she jumped, but did not yelp, and swiftly closed the gate behind her. She tipped her head, made comically large by the helmet, and looked at me. "What are you doing here?" she whispered.

"I smoke here," I said, bringing my cigarette out from behind my back.

"Oh," she said, looking around at the fence, and the side of her garage. "Can't people see the smoke as it rises above the fence?"

Her first concern seemed to be abetting me in my secret habit. She was neither offended nor concerned that I had been breaking into their property and hiding in their side yard.

"So far as I know," I said, "no one has. But usually I kind of crouch with the hope that it dissipates. And I always figured people would think it was you."

"Your name is Michael," she said with concentration, dragging my name up through the folds of her memory.

I nodded.

"My name is Bunny," she said.

"I know."

"I'm just getting my bike." She started to walk toward her bike, which was just to my right.

"The tires are flat," I told her, looking down at them. They had been flat for almost a year now, and I wondered what had possessed her today of all days to take a ride. There was a gust of wind then, and the fence groaned a bit, and we could hear, rather than feel, the wind rushing over the top of the fence, making a sound like scissors cutting through paper.

"Oh."

"Where were you going to go?" I asked.

"To the beach."

"By yourself?"

She nodded. "You know, I could put a chair out here for you. Like a camp chair."

"That's all right," I said.

She put her hands on her hips then, and twisted her torso with such strength that I could hear every vertebrae in her spine crack. She was perhaps five inches taller than me. "Do you want to come in?" she asked.

"To your house?"

She took off her helmet. "No one's home." There was a baby-ish quality to Bunny's voice, perhaps because it seemed too small for the size of her body, and she spoke as though her nose was always a little stuffed. Of course, I wanted desperately to see inside her house up close, and so I put out my cigarette and hid it in the Altoids tin that I also kept behind the plywood, and she watched as I spritzed myself with Febreze, and then we let ourselves out the back gate and into her yard.

"This is our yard," she said. "There's a pool."

I said, "Oh wow," though I had swum in her pool several times when she and her father had been on vacation. I had climbed the fence from my aunt's yard and dropped down into hers, which was dark, since no one was home and the outside lights seemed to be on a timer, and the pool, instead of being a lit rectangle of blue, was a black mass of reflected stars, and, shaking, I had taken off my clothes and slipped naked into the warm water and swum until I felt erased.

She opened one of the French doors that led onto the patio, and we entered the hushed cathedral of her living room. She closed the door behind us, as though it could never be left open. The outside, with its scent of grass and sway of water, its gauzy light and chafing winds, would destroy the interior, the careful, expensive furniture, a pretend world that had to be exactingly maintained.

She gave me a tour of the house, showing me her father's office, with its many bookshelves filled with leather-bound books I doubted he had ever read, and the marble kitchen. She offered me a Pop-Tart, which I declined. She opened one of the crinkly metallic packages for herself, and then, to my horror, spread the two Pop-Tarts with butter and slicked them together as a sandwich.

She led me upstairs, taking bites of her Pop-Tart sandwich along the way, and showed me the spare room, decorated in an Oriental style with a disturbing red satin bedspread embroidered with cranes, and the connected bathroom, which had a shiny black vanity and sink, a black toilet, and black floors. They were ready for Madame Butterfly to commit suicide in there at any time. While the house was uncluttered, I noticed that it was also not exactly clean. Gray trails marked the highest traffic routes on the white carpet, and the sink in the all-black bathroom was spangled with little explosions of white toothpaste.

She gestured at a closed door and said, "That's my dad's room," and then took me into her own bedroom, which was done up, as I already well knew, like a much younger girl's bedroom, with a white canopy bed and a white dresser that had been plastered with My Little Pony stickers. There was a small white mirrored dressing table with a pink brocade bench. Where there should have been makeup and bottles of fancy perfume, Bunny had arranged her schoolbooks and papers. There was a bookshelf that contained not books but trophies and medals and ribbons, all so cheap and garish and crammed together that it looked more like installation art than a proper display. On one wall, there was a bulletin board that I had not been able to see before as it was on the same wall as the window. At first, it appeared to be a Hydra of female body parts, but as I looked closer I could see that they were all women playing volleyball, and then, as I looked yet closer, I could see that they were all the same woman playing volleyball, carefully trimmed from newspapers and magazines.

"That's my Misty May-Treanor altar," she said. "She's a volleyball player."

"Not creepy at all," I said. I would have asked her why she had invited me in, or why she had shown me around with the thoroughness of a realtor, except that I already knew, for her loneliness was so palpable as to be a taste in the air. I had been many places in my life. Apartment buildings where babies free-ranged, waddling down the halls with dirty hair and diapers needing to be changed; houses like my aunt's, where everything was stained and reaching between the couch cushions to find the remote left your fingers sticky. Bus stations, and prison waiting rooms, and foster-care homes, and men's cars, and men's houses or apartments where there was sometimes only a mattress on the floor, and none of them had scared me quite as much as being in Bunny's silent, beautiful house.

"I've never had a boy in my bedroom before," she said, a little apologetically, and she sat on the bed, as though she expected that I would fuck her right there on her white eyelet duvet.

"I'm gay," I said, my affect as flat and casual as I could manage. I had never spoken those words to anyone before, not in that way.

"Well, I've never had a gay boy in my bedroom either," she said, and flopped backward, finishing the last of her Pop-Tart sandwich, licking the butter off her fingers. She contemplated the ceiling and I began to wonder if I could simply leave. I was fascinated by Bunny and I liked her, but I was beginning to realize I liked her more from a distance than I did close up. It was too much, being in her room, smelling her smells, hearing her breathe.

"You probably think my room is stupid," she said, still staring up at the ceiling, her legs, in their athletic shorts, agape on her bed in such a casual way that it was almost lewd, even though technically nothing was showing.

"It's a room," I said. "I'm not the room judge sent to adjudicate your decor or whatever."

"It is stupid," she said. "My dad keeps saying we should redo it. But I like it. I like it just like this."

"Well, thank you for showing me around," I said, trying to indicate that I would like to leave, when we both heard a door slam downstairs. Bunny sat upright on the bed, and I froze as we listened to the thumping of feet on the carpeted stairs. And then there he was, a man I had only ever seen in photographs, his giant head wedged between her door and the wall. "You're home!" Ray Lampert cried, giddy. "And you have a friend! I thought we could get Chinese—do you feel like Chinese?"

"Ugh, I'm starved," Bunny said. I, who by fifteen was already a neurotic counter of calories, almost gasped at this statement, having witnessed the 700-calorie Pop-Tart sandwich.

"And you'll join us, obviously," Ray Lampert said, turning to me. He was substantially fatter than in his picture, and while there were dark puffy bags under his eyes, the rest of his skin tone was so peculiarly even that I could have sworn he was wearing makeup. His blue dress shirt was unbuttoned a scandalous three buttons, and he was wearing a ratty red baseball cap. It occurred to me that I had probably seen him dozens of times and had just never realized that it was the same man as in the photograph.

"This is Michael," she said. "Were you thinking Bamboo Forest?"

"No, I want good, really good, egg drop soup. Bamboo Forest is so watery." He turned to me. "Don't you think it's watery?"

What I thought was that I didn't know anyone was such a connoisseur of egg drop soup. To me it just came, like napkins and forks. "I should probably get home," I said.

"You don't really have to go, do you?" Bunny said with sudden, cloying desperation. "Say you'll come with us!"

Ray reached out and squeezed my shoulder. "He's got nothing better to do, right, son? Don't tell me you're one of these overscheduled kids that's got back-to-back tutoring and chess club right before you off yourself because you didn't get into Harvard."

He had found me unattended in his daughter's bedroom; I stank of cigarettes and was wearing a Nirvana T-shirt and eyeliner, and I had a septum piercing. My hair was loose and went halfway down my back. It was unclear to me if his remarks were meant ironically or if he was actually blind. "Let's make it a party!" he said, slapped me on the back, and headed downstairs, shouting that he would meet us at the car.

Bunny turned to me and said in a low voice, "My dad's kind of weird, but I promise it will be fun."

And I thought: If Ray Lampert was one of the men I met on Craigslist, I would be too scared to ever get in his car, because he was the kind who would lock you in a closet or put a gun in your mouth and then cry about his ex-wife. Bunny took my hand and twined her fingers through my own. And she looked at me with eyes so hopeful that I nodded.

Honestly, I probably would have let her take me anywhere.

2

I did not often leave the narrow cove of North Shore, as my aunt Deedee possessed neither the material means nor the disposition to take us out to dinner anywhere, and since my mother had been released from prison and my little sister had returned to living with her, my continued presence at my aunt's house depended almost entirely on my being around as seldom as possible. My aunt was a difficult woman to know because her personality was almost entirely eclipsed by exhaustion. She worked at the Starbucks inside the Target and at the animal shelter, and between those two jobs she was still barely able to pay our ever-increasing rent. For her, the mansions that encroached daily were a constant reminder that her life was untenable, and that, as she rapidly approached fifty, she had nothing to show for her labors and would soon be forced to move to a less nice (read: less white) part of the city. She was holding on as long as possible, determined to get her son through high school in the good, rich town before collapsing.

I shared a bedroom with her son, Jason, an effortlessly masculine and unreflective sort, who was neither bad nor particularly good, and who often farted in answer to questions addressed to him. How he always had a fart ready to go was a mystery to me, but I knew that if I became annoying enough to him, he would complain to his mother so persistently that it would leave her little choice but to evict me.

When my mother had been released from prison for good

behavior after serving only two years of her sentence, my sister moved back in with her while I had remained with Aunt Deedee under the pretext that my mother could not "handle" both of us, though whether on a financial or an emotional level was always vague. It was easy for her and my sister to share a queen-size futon in her tiny studio apartment, but where would they put me, with my adolescent male body? It was as if they were afraid that when they opened a cupboard my secret erections would all come tumbling out.

There was a further bizarre line of reasoning that because I was the same age as Jason, but slightly smaller of build, I could wear his hand-me-downs, thus making my upkeep "practically free." It "just made sense." It was "easier for everyone." While I did nurse this rejection by my mother and sister as a core psychic wound upon which my entire personality was founded, I also breathed a sigh of relief. As much as I wanted my mother to want me to live with her, I didn't want to actually live in that tiny, airless studio apartment, and I think I even told Aunt Deedee as much.

Really, I suspected there was another reason I remained with my aunt, and it was because almost immediately upon her release my mother had taken up with a new boyfriend who was so exactly like our father it was comical, and Aunt Deedee and I both knew without having to ask or look for clues (the first time I met him he was wearing a shirt that said CONQUER YOUR INNER BITCH; who needed to know more?) that he was probably homophobic. While I had never come out to my aunt, one day in ninth grade, when I had been struggling in the bathroom, she came in and said, "If you are going to wear eyeliner, let me at least teach you how to put it on so you don't look like a sad clown." And she had taken the cheap black pencil I had purchased at Rite Aid, explained to me that it was useless, and opened her own makeup bag to me, showing me all of its wonders: tiny arched brushes and tubes and palettes of colors and primers and luminizing sticks and other products I had never heard of. "Go to a MAC store," she told me. "They'll love you in there, sweetie."

Her sympathy did not extend to my septum piercing, which she said made me look like a cow. "A bull," I pointed out. "At least it's a boy cow!" But she tolerated it and me, though I did not want to test this tolerance, which I intuitively felt was jerry-rigged from moment to moment, a rope tossed casually to me as she rushed from one shift to another, yelling over her shoulder, "I think there might be tater tots, make something."

But whenever I went over to see my mother and Gabby, Aunt Deedee would examine me, inspect me. She would make me turn in a circle. Sometimes she would suggest I change my shirt. If I had dared to wear eyeliner, she would tell me to take it off. She requested that I put my hair back in a gross ponytail that made me look like I bred iguanas. But it made me look less gay. And that's what she was doing. De-gaying me before I went over there. We never talked about it, she never said those words. But that's what she was doing, and I suspected it was part of why she let me stay. She was protecting me, shielding me in North Shore. When my mother and Gabby moved into a two-bedroom with her new boyfriend, no one even asked if I wanted to go with them. By that time I was in high school, and it was such a good high school, it would have been a shame not to let me finish. Or that was what was said out loud, anyway.

Meanwhile, the older Gabby got, the more pensive and chubby she became. She was, and I say this with love, a total Pokémon-loving, nerdy Trapper Keeper–clutching sad sack. Mopey in a most unsympathetic way. Not only was she not making jokes, she wasn't laughing at the jokes of others. To me at the time, this was a heinous offense, a grievous wrong. What else were you supposed to do with pain but polish it until it became something pointy and pretty?

Every time I saw Gabby on one of our forced monthly family dates, which usually took place in a Denny's that was right next door to a Goodwill on Hawthorne Boulevard, at which, over the years, I purchased many a natty men's shirt, she seemed less alive, more grayed out. Once I cornered her in the hallway outside the bathroom of the Denny's and asked if Mom's new boyfriend was molesting her, but this seemed not to be the case. She became so offended she refused to speak to me for months and would sit through our meals silent and bored as my mom gave me the latest gossip from the hair salon where she had gotten a job. The new boyfriend had sent her to cosmetology school. Fancy fancy.

When I brought up to Aunt Deedee the possibility that all was not right in that house, that Gabby was officially failing to thrive, Deedee swatted the air in front of her face as though there were gnats, and said, "Some things you just have to accept." I did not know if she meant that my little sister should accept my mother's craving for love alloyed with violence, or if she meant that I should accept that my sister and I were now on separate trains on diverging tracks, experiencing different childhoods that would lead us to different adulthoods, and were helpless to do anything other than wave through the window as we passed each other. "Gabby wanted to move in with her. Viv's her mother. Can't do anything about that."

Latent in this observation was the fact that my mother had a legal right to my sister and was exercising it in a way she had chosen not to exercise it over me. Whatever conversations my aunt had had with my mother I had not been privy to, so I did not know if my aunt had begged for me to stay with her, or if my mother had begged her to keep me.

Regardless, my time in North Shore had not included many excursions to the neighboring towns, and I had rarely been to Manhattan Beach, even though it was only five minutes by car, and I was shocked that a place could be even more visibly affluent than North Shore. The main drag was crowded with boutiques and gastropubs, every house was built up two or three stories, every square inch of the lot covered, and the only cars on the road were BMWs, Mercedes-Benzes, Bentleys, Maseratis. Everything glittered. Mr. Lampert's car smelled of leather and stale french fries as we glided through the dusk. Bunny and I both sat in the back as though he were our chauffeur, but mainly because the front passenger seat was covered in trash, papers, and fast-food contain-ers, and maybe as many as thirty empty Muscle Milk bottles.

Ray kept up a steady patter, talking to Bunny about his busi-ness dealings, and asking me questions about myself that I found alarming. In interactions with my own parents and aunt, I had perfected a series of what I thought of as "prey behaviors" that included careful lack of eye contact, silence, and unobtrusiveness bordering on invisibility, but none of this deterred Ray Lampert, who had questions about my shirt (Did I know that he had actu-ally been to a Nirvana concert back in the day?), whether I played sports (You should, everyone should, even if they weren't good at it, because it taught you about life), my eyeliner (Young people were so much more free these days, and wasn't that a good thing? He, for one, supported my wearing eyeliner if I chose to).

Bunny did not react to any of this as though it were unusual and looked placidly out her window at the lighted facades of glamorous homes flashing by, though she did reach her hand out again and lace her fingers through mine. While this gesture was unquestionably overly intimate, my little sister had also been a hand-holder, and so I squeezed Bunny's hand in little pulses as I had Gabby's, and she squeezed mine back, though otherwise we did not address each other but spoke only to her father as he quizzed us about our teenage lives.

The Chinese restaurant, casual and merrily chintzy in a way I found deeply reassuring, was almost empty, and we took the largest corner wraparound booth, even though we were only a party of three. I did not know what to order and felt anxious about pronouncing things correctly, but Ray Lampert was the kind of man who loved to order without consulting others, and he gave the waitress a long list of dishes, ordered a Tom Collins for himself and two Shirley Temples for Bunny and me. I had never had a Shirley Temple before, though as a child I had coveted them, and, while it was so syrupy it made my teeth itch, to possess one now caused my stomach to continually rise within my torso like a helium balloon bumping along the ceiling.

"I've been reading," Mr. Lampert said, "about the founding of the Jet Propulsion Lab at NASA, and you know, back then rockets were considered sci-fi, and basically they were just these three guys, amateurs, who were obsessed with rockets. They spent two years just trying to launch a rocket, you know, but they had to invent rocket fuel basically, in order to make a rocket. And they wound up working with this expert at Caltech, who said, you know what, you guys are going about this in the right way, I'll help you and you can use some of my grad students. They used to call themselves the 'Suicide Squad' because the open joke was that they were probably going to blow themselves up. But they did it, they successfully launched a rocket, about the size of a soda can, and that was that, and they got absorbed by the Department of Defense. But none of the generals would take seriously anything with the word 'rocket' in it, because it sounded too sci-fi, so they became the Jet Propulsion Lab, because that way they could get funded. Then after the Second World War, the government said: Do you want to be a defense company or do you want to join this new thing we're starting, called NASA? And they opted for NASA."

"Wow," Bunny said, though she was clearly bored and not really listening.

"Can you imagine that?" Ray Lampert said, and ordered another drink from the waitress before continuing, "Just three guys obsessed with rockets, no background in aerospace, and they wind up part of NASA? Just monkeys shooting shit at the moon. Wild, you know?"

"Wow, you're like a little museum in person form!" I said, because I didn't know what else to say, though I did find it genuinely interesting.

"Oh, not really," Ray said, waving away what I'd said as though it were a compliment. "I never went to college, you know that? But no one, I mean, aside from the founders, but I'm saying in contemporary times, I've had a really unparalleled influence on the town. I mean, I really can't think of another single individual who has more directly influenced the development of the town in the last twenty years. I got the new high school built, I got the building code changed so now we finally have some development. Did you know I'm behind that new Italian place that opened up on Main? I convinced the chef to move there, I said, 'Screw L.A., I've got rich people who don't want to drive to get decent pasta, live the good life, put your kids in decent schools,' you know what I mean? Were you born in North Shore?"

Even as he asked me this question, he was loading his plate with fried rice and cashew chicken and some kind of honeyed shrimp, and his eyes were roving the restaurant as though he was looking for someone he was expecting to meet. "No," I said, "I moved here when I was eleven."

"See?" he said, and smiled at me. "Everybody's moved here. Nobody is from North Shore because everybody wants to move here, I mean, except her mother." He gestured at Bunny with his thumb. She sipped from her Shirley Temple, sucking hard on the straw, then grew frustrated, pulled up the straw, showed us the cherry stuck on the end of it, and laughed like a kid.

Her father continued, "They were from here, very serious people, her dad was a machinist for Boeing. Used to have this huge shop in his garage, the guy could fabricate anything."

It took me a moment to track that we were discussing Bunny's mother's father, Bunny's grandfather. "Is he still around?" I asked.

"He passed," Ray said. "But he lived a good life. Yeah, he passed when Bunny was, what were you?"

"Nine," Bunny said.

"Helluva thing, being able to make things with your hands. That's a real loss in the digital world, I think. Making things. Don't you think so?"

The dinner continued on in this vein, Bunny occasionally queuing up her dad to tell an interesting story, almost as though he were a jukebox and she were playing me her favorite songs. Occasionally she would try to steer him away from dangerous topics: "I'm not against immigrants, but I'm just saying they should come here legally—" and she would pipe up, "Tell him about the pool, tell him about the pool you're going to put in," and he would seamlessly switch tracks and begin telling me about the Olympic-size swimming pool he had convinced the city council was vital to the town's growth. "I mean, think about it, how are we going to have kids that grow up to be Olympic swimmers if we don't even have a damn pool for them to swim in?"

Both Bunny and her father were putting away shocking volumes of food and drink, and I thought perhaps this was normal for them, the way that André the Giant could drink forty beers with dinner. She had given him a pleading look when he ordered the fourth Tom Collins, but he had ignored her, as though he could not feel her eyes boring holes in the side of his face as he told me about a guy he had known in construction who had a pet chimp, and wasn't that incredible? It used to wear little overalls.

Aside from that single warning look Bunny had given Ray, she appeared to be at ease with the situation, and Ray's conversational alacrity had never ceased, so I was disoriented when he was visibly weaving as we made our way out to the parking lot for the car after dinner.

I looked at Bunny, who would not meet my eyes. *Oughtn't we not allow him to drive? Shouldn't we suggest that we taxi home?* But she was already casually getting into the car, as though everything were fine. I could not fathom a polite way to decline, and so I got in and buckled my seat belt nervously. Perhaps he would be somehow more able to drive a car in a straight line than he was able to walk in one.

"A funny story about Bunny's grandpa," he said, looking over his shoulder as he backed out of our space, when suddenly the car lurched forward and we slammed into a pole. The force of the impact was surprising, considering that we had been at a stop. He must have had his foot slammed on the gas, and the car in drive instead of reverse. I was breathing hard and the backs of my hands were prickling with adrenaline.

Ray Lampert popped the car back into park, yanking on the

gearshift. "Fucking bloody shit hell fuck motherfucker," he said, and got out of the car to look at the front bumper. Bunny and I stayed in the backseat, and she turned to me and said, quite casually, "This is not the first time he's done this," and then laughed.

Outside the car, he was yelling and kicking the tire of the car repeatedly, but the noise was hushed by the expensive car, almost as though we were sealed in some kind of space pod. I could see the spittle fly out of his mouth, lit up by the streetlight. Mostly, I was confused. My entire childhood had been a training exercise in alcohol tolerance mathematics, and it didn't seem to me possible that Ray Lampert could be this drunk from only four cocktails.

"Best to wait," Bunny said. "Until he wears himself out."

She reached over and held my hand again, and we watched her father kick the car some more. I had assumed the damage could not be much, considering that we couldn't have been going very fast, but it seemed the bumper was more seriously dented than Ray Lampert wished it to be. Finally, as Bunny predicted, he seemed to tire out, and then he just sat on the hood of the car and stared up at the stars.

Finally, Bunny decreed him calm enough and opened her door and popped her head out. "Do you want to just cab?" she said, since this was before the days of Uber.

"What?" He swung his head toward her, surprised, and I realized he was in such a blind drunk that he had not remembered we were in the car. "Sure, sure, honey," he said. "I'll call you a cab."

She got back in the car and we watched him as he did things on his phone, and when that seemed to be concluded, he lay down on the hood of the car, put his hands behind his head, his phone resting on his belly, and then fell asleep. Had he called a cab through some sort of web form? At first I was not sure he was asleep, except for the incredibly slow and steady rhythm of his stomach rising and falling, the phone balanced precariously on top of it. I kept expecting the phone to slide down and hit the windshield, but it did not.

"Do you think the cab will find us?" Bunny asked me. I had

no idea. We waited for perhaps twenty minutes, during which time Bunny became visibly more anxious. She kept apologizing. "This is so embarrassing," she would whisper as we watched her father sleeping on the hood of the car. "I can't believe this is happening. I'm so sorry. I thought tonight would be fun."

Finally, she felt she should at least check his cell phone, and so she carefully cracked her door open and crept around the car. But when she leaned over to snatch the phone off his belly, she was forced to put some of her weight on the crumpled bumper and it sheered right off the car with a tremendous clang, causing her to jump back and Ray Lampert to sit bolt upright, already yelling a kind of Viking war cry without words. He looked around frantically and saw Bunny with her hands up, cringing.

"What the hell were you doing?" he asked.

"I was trying to get your phone," she said, pointing to his phone, which had fallen off his belly when he sat up and was now wedged against the windshield.

"Get your own fucking phone," he said. "I'm going home." And then he slid, awkwardly, off the hood of the car, grabbed his phone, and fumbled with the driver's-side door. I scrambled to unbuckle myself and get out, and I went around to where Bunny stood by the lost bumper of the car and the lamppost we had hit.

"Daddy, don't," she said. "You're not good to drive."

He started the car.

"Daddy, don't!" she said again, both hands up at her mouth like a little mouse gnawing a crumb, but she was not little, she was already almost as tall as her father.

He rolled down his window. "Get in," he said.

"No," she said. "I won't let you drive Michael like this."

"Get in, Bunny Rabbit," he said. His left eye was only half-open, but the right one was functioning normally.

"No, Daddy," she said, and actually stomped her sneakered foot.

"Fine," he said, and backed out of the spot and then drove away. We watched him as he exited the parking lot and turned onto the street without so much as jumping a curb, and then he was gone. Bunny covered her face with her hands, breathed in and out, then turned to me and said, "My purse was in the car."

"That's not good," I said.

"Do you have any money?"

I admitted I did not. I had about seven dollars in my wallet, but that would not get us a cab back home.

"We'll have to walk," she said, which sounded crazy to me. I had no idea where we were or how we would get home, and I could not understand how she was being so calm about it.

"It's not hard," she said, "we just need to go north, and the ocean's right there, so we just go that way." She pointed into the darkness.

And so we wound up walking the four miles from Manhattan Beach to North Shore, taking Highland Street, which wove along the coast beside the sea.

"I'm just so embarrassed," Bunny kept saying as we walked. "He must have been drinking before he even picked us up."

"Don't be embarrassed," I said as we puffed up the big hill that led out of Manhattan Beach.

"How can I not be embarrassed?" she asked.

"My dad was a drunk too," I said. "Nothing new to me."

We walked some more, and the ocean came into view, its oil tankers glittering with pinpricks of light off the shore. Suddenly we could hear the crash of waves.

"Was?" she asked.

"Oh, he's still alive," I said. "I just don't see him anymore."

"Is that why you live with your aunt?"

And so I told her, even though I had never told anyone in North Shore what had happened, and was so unused to telling the story I wasn't exactly sure where to start. What was hardest for me to ever adequately explain was how collaborative my father's violence had been, how we had all conspired in it, to hide it from him, to hide it from ourselves, to edit out the frightening sequences from the filmstrips of memory. The way when I was five and we were at some family barbecue, I had frustrated him, begging for candy or something, and he had grabbed me so suddenly that I fell and scraped my back on a tree root, and how for days we all wondered aloud where I had gotten that scratch on my back and each concluded that we didn't know where I had gotten it. I really wasn't sure how I had.

Or when he was too drunk to hold my baby sister and he dropped her, badly, and how she cried all night, screamed, and yet no one took her to the doctor, and then how my mother observed the next day that she seemed to be fine and she wondered what that had all been about. And I had told her, quite innocently, that the baby had fallen, that my father had dropped her, surprised that she didn't know because she had been in the room at the time, and she had said, "Oh, I don't think she was crying because of *that*."

The crux of the problem was that my mother was in love with my father, and while he was terrifying when he got too drunk, when he was only a little bit drunk he was so much fun, and when he was sober he was profoundly depressed. Because we were poor. Because raising little kids is hard. Because he hated his job as a line cook at a seafood restaurant. And so my mother, without ever consciously realizing it, did not want him to get sober. What she wanted was for him to drink without getting too drunk, in part because she drank too, and her own drinking was indispensable to her as a coping mechanism. The scarier her life became, in fact, the more she needed it, and the less able she was to suggest that either of them should be steering toward the shores of sobriety. But it was impossible to keep the worst episodes from happening, and so the easiest thing to do was to pretend they weren't happening at all.

I told Bunny all of this as we walked, and she listened without offering sentimental interruptions or reassurances, and I was grateful for that, was so tired of earnest social workers telling me it hadn't been my fault, or my sister's fault, when I wanted to scream at them and tell them it was all our fault. Every single one of us participated in it. I loved my father when he was drunk. I could always tell when he was the good kind of drunk and I would run to him and climb him like a monkey and he would tickle me and body-slam me into the mattress and tell me I was a good boy. How good I was, how strong, how handsome, how smart.

I could tell these things to Bunny only because they did not strike her as scandalous but as factual. And Bunny's very unfamiliarity with guile, her inability to dissemble to even the slightest degree, somehow gave me permission to be my unadorned self as well.

"Did your mom fight back?" she asked.

"Yeah," I said. "They were like alley cats, it was crazy, it would just explode and he would be hitting her and she would be hitting him, and we would just hide in the bathroom or lock ourselves in the bedroom and watch TV."

"My mom didn't," she said. "Fight back."

"So he hit her?" I asked.

"Not really. I mean, I'm sure he did, I'm sure some amount of hitting occurred, but it was more like he would just keep explaining to her that she didn't love him, and then he would take her favorite vase and smash it and say she loved the vase more than him. He would stay up all night, just torturing her like that. Setting up, like, these psychological tests. He would get kind of stuck in a loop and wanted to have the same upsetting conversation over and over again. I think part of it was that she had grown up very middle class, like, safe and nice, but nothing fancy, and he had grown up much poorer than her, and I think his parents were really, I don't know, I never met my dad's family, he was estranged from them and he didn't even go to his mom's funeral when she died, but I think he got it in his head that to make my mom happy he had to earn all this money. And then he did, he earned this crazy amount of money, and it was really like he made it all appear out of nowhere, but then he hated her for it and he hated the money even though he loved the money. I don't know. I was just about to turn eight when she died, so a lot of this is just putting pieces together and guessing."

"Did she love the money?" I asked.

"I don't think she did. I don't think she gave a shit about the money."

"How did she die?" I asked, though I already knew.

"Car accident," she said. "Unrelated. To the drinking."

"And your dad still drives like that? Drunk like that?"

"I never really thought about it, but I guess that is kind of weird."

We were quiet then, walking along a long stretch of road that bordered the oil refinery. Every now and again, a car would rush by, blinding us with its headlights and making us dizzy with wind, and we would pause. I had a terrible blister developing on my baby toe from where it rubbed inside my shoe, and she laughed at me when I mentioned it. "Wuss," she said. "Want me to carry you?"

"You can't carry me," I said, and to my surprise she picked me up and swung me into her arms like I was a bride crossing the threshold, and walked easily with me like that, even as I kicked and yelled at her to stop and put me down. When she finally did, I was breathless and a little thrilled. I was so confused by her. By her naïveté mixed up with her worldliness, by her beauty that was so unattended by vulnerability.

"So what happened? Why did you move in with your aunt?" Bunny asked.

"Oh," I said. This was the part of the story I had been most dreading, since it was the sharpest fork in our diverging experiences. "Well, one night they were fighting, and she just stabbed him, in the chest, with one of the kitchen knives, not a big one, like a little fruit knife? So she went to prison."

"Oh my god," Bunny said. I worried she would think I was trashy or low-class for having a mother who had been to prison. I myself was very ashamed about it. It seemed an inherently shameful thing to me.

"He didn't die or anything, he just had to get stitches, but she got three years for it."

"So that's when you moved in with your aunt."

"Uh-huh," I said, unable to look at her, certain that now she would think differently of me.

"It's such a shame we didn't become friends earlier," she said, grabbing my hand. "All this time, we could have been friends. Doesn't that just seem so sad?"

But I was glowing, electric, so happy I could not even feel regret for those lost years. I had made my first friend in North Shore. My first best friend in my entire life really. And we were walking by the sea, a little lost and holding hands.

3

I had first begun finding men to meet on Craigslist when I was thirteen. I had not intended to reply to any of the ads, I was just window-shopping. While we had grown up poor, in many ways I had been sheltered, and I did not feel myself to be street-smart enough to handle myself well in such an encounter. But I did want, desperately, to find out if there were other gay men in my town and what they did and what they wanted and how they acted and the kinds of things they said to one another, and the easiest way for me to do that was by looking at the M4M postings on Craigslist. Our town was listed under the greater South Bay area, but there were a surprising number of salacious invitations within a fifteen-mile radius. The ads there were mostly terrifying to me, but I read them with absolute fascination, frantically decoding acronyms and learning lingo that seemed to me an indispensable code for gaining access to the world I would one day need to inhabit.

There was one other boy at my school who I could tell was also gay, but he was a quiet and obviously feminine sort, and I dreaded the episodes of *Glee* he would presumably insist we watch, as we drank, I imagined, Capri Suns purchased by his accepting mother.

During those late elementary, early middle school years, I was in crisis. I knew that I was gay, but I did not want to be gay-gay. I did not want other people to know, but I also had a culturally acquired prejudice against queen-y mannerisms for their own sake. That was a popular take when I was growing up, among the post–*Will & Grace* generation: Fine, do what you want in bed, but do you have to talk in an annoying voice? I did not want to be annoying, I did not want to be wrong, I wanted to be right. And yet I knew that something about the way my hands moved betrayed me, the way I walked, my vocabulary, my voice. I did not consciously choose my eyeliner and septum piercing and long hair as a disguise, but in retrospect that is exactly what they were. I knew I could not pass as straight, but I thought perhaps I could pass as "just weird." No, I wanted nothing to do with that fey boy who accepted himself, and it pains me now to wonder how my life would have gone had I been psychologically sound enough to have made friends with him and begun so much earlier the hard work of attempting to love myself. I probably would have really loved *Glee*.

The first ad I ever responded to on Craigslist was from a "20yo Shy Boi" who said he had never been kissed, and wanted his first kiss to be on the pier at Redondo Beach. The ad was sweet and stammering, and before I could reconsider, I hurriedly wrote back that I also had never been kissed and would love to share his first kiss with him on the pier.

We set a date and time, and I took the bus down to Redondo Beach, a halting, galloping ride down Sepulveda that took nearly an hour and a half, though the actual mileage was scant, and I made my way out onto the pier, a massive U-shaped expanse, where seafood restaurants served slabs of grilled fish on sheets of newspaper and gelato shops spilled neon light, and I waited and waited, until finally a fat ginger-haired boy came up to me. I could see at once why no one had kissed him: His skin (pale), his lips (chapped), his hair (bowl), his shirt (Super Mario Bros.), all were nerd. Even the air around him seemed to nerd. I did not find him attractive, but I could in no way stomach the thought of turning him down now, so brutally, in such a carnival atmosphere, not to mention the wasted bus fare, and so we stood together for a long time by the sea, not saying much except that we were both nervous and that I was younger than he thought I'd be, and then he lunged at me.

The kiss was wet and squirmy and terrible, but it was over soon enough, and we did not repeat it, though we did sit on a bench side by side, I think both of us scanning our surroundings to reassure ourselves that skinheads were not going to rush out of the arcade and push us into the sea for being homos. When we finally parted after some truly painful conversation about the video game *Halo 3,* we hugged, though the term "hug" does nothing to evoke the awkward frozen grip we used, unable to relax, unable to let go, both of us shuddering every time we breathed in or out. When this intimacy became unbearable, it became so in unison, and in magical concord we released our grip, thanked each other, and departed, going opposite ways on the U-shaped pier. We never spoke to each other again.

It was then that I understood that these encounters were fundamentally about loneliness, flashes of intense intimacy so awkward and fragile that they had no place in real life. The men I met online were not secret initiates into a world I could take part in, but refugees from the world I already knew too well.

I did not initially tell Bunny about these encounters, even as they became ongoing and dominated more and more of my mental field of play. In part, she seemed to me to be from another world where such things simply didn't happen. But I also had a sense that I could continue with my actions only if they were entirely unexamined, and I needed desperately for them to continue, even if my interactions with these men were unfulfilling and bizarre. I once had sex with a man in a Starbucks bathroom at ten o'clock in the morning on a Tuesday. I can still remember vividly the electric thrill of going to algebra afterward.

I spent a great deal of time in the apartment of a man named Ed, who was Chinese and tall and worked in finance, whatever that meant. What indefinable loveliness, to feel the mountain of him shaking beneath me. To learn his smells, the vaguely sour yeast of his balls, the sweet and dark smell of his bum. It did not matter to me at all that though he was in his forties, he seemed to have the emotional maturity and insight of a teen girl, and not even a real teen girl, but the stereotype of a teen girl. Sometimes he would say shyly, "I think you're really cool." He was insecure about the size of his cock. "Everything else about me is big," he said in a gloomy Eeyore voice, clearly expecting to be told that no, his penis was fine, was average. "I'll have to punish you for having such a puny cock, then," I said. And I made him lie down across a big black leather chair in his living room, and I spanked him with a whisk I found in the kitchen.

How could I tell Bunny I did these things? I could scarcely admit to myself they were happening. Where had the impulse in me to hurt Ed come from? Why had I enjoyed it so much, making his muscular little ass red and welted? Was it related to watching the way my father had once spanked my sister with a hairbrush? What was wrong with me? It was much better not to investigate it at all.

In every other sense, my relationship with Bunny became one of intimate confidences, though we avoided each other at school, where she belonged to a flock of similarly sporty girls who carried great duffel bags of kneepads hither and thither, and where I belonged, however peripherally, to a group I had privately begun to think of as the "Revolting Youth" (do you like the pun?) that included goth girls and stoners and metalheads and also some guys who just really enjoyed Magic: The Gathering. But in the evenings, or on the rare afternoon she didn't have practice, Bunny and I convened in her empty house to watch *RuPaul's Drag Race* — which, to my surprise, Bunny had loved even before I met her.

Drag queens for me glittered the same way all queer cultural artifacts did, with an intoxicating, radiant, ultraviolet dust that indicated they were secretly for me. For Bunny, I think the allure may have been the deconstruction of the artifice that is cultural femininity. As often as I was failing to pass as a straight boy during those years, Bunny was failing to pass as a girl. She was built like a bull, and she was confident and happy, and people found this combination of qualities displeasing in a young woman. She had no mother or sister to teach her how to do her hair, or how to dress, or how to do her lipstick, what was "too much" and what was "just right," and so she felt like a clown attempting any of it.

I became her confidant as she explored the girliness she had been too shy to explore on her own: face masks and what to do about her cuticles and how to pluck eyebrows. And she became the one person in my real life, my regular life, my non-Craigslist life, around whom I could practice being gay. *RuPaul's Drag Race* was oddly central to all of this, and we culturally appropriated the shit out of those drag queens. Every catchphrase, every piece of slang, we immediately fell in love with and began using as our own, not with other people, but only between ourselves. It was like a secret code that expressed everything: who we were, and who we wanted to be.

After watching *RuPaul's Drag Race,* we would usually go for a swim in her pool. Bunny was a terrific swimmer, and she liked to roughhouse in the water, which scared me, and several times she almost drowned me. She liked to lull me into a false security by claiming she was going to swim some laps, and then, when I was floating peacefully on my back, she'd suddenly surface directly under me and grab me by the middle and drag me down and roll me around like she was an alligator. Every single time she did it, I swore I would refuse to swim with her ever again, and every single time she promised she would never do it again, and then of course she would.

At first I wondered if Bunny was gay, given the obsessive cutting out and arranging of images of female athletes into collages and scrapbooks, as well as her general size and disposition, but her heterosexuality was so fervent and tender that it caused her much pain. When would she get a boyfriend, would she ever get a boyfriend, what was wrong with her that no one wanted to be her boyfriend? Once she asked me to look at her naked and tell her what I thought.

I had just finished plucking her eyebrows and her entire fore-head had turned bright red, the blood rushing to the surface at having been so assaulted.

"I don't need to see you naked," I told her. "You're a sixteen-year-old athlete. Your body is unfathomably perfect. There is nothing that seeing it naked could tell me that I can't see when you're in a bathing suit." (This was a weensy lie: There was some-thing overdeveloped about her abs that made her look like a Ninja Turtle, in my opinion.)

"I think my nipples are weird," she said. "I think the areolas are too big and, like, pale."

"Your areolas are fine," I said.

"You haven't seen them."

"Even if your areolas were purple and covered with hair, boys would still want to suck on them," I said, and I considered it to be true.

"Do you watch porn?" she asked.

"Of course," I said. "Do you?"

She nodded. This surprised me.

"Well, at first it was scary," she admitted. "But then I figured out how to really only see the kinds of things I liked."

"What do you like?" I asked, even though I wasn't entirely sure I wanted to know. That was a character trait of mine, the kind of curiosity that killed so many cats. I was always sniffing rotten food in the refrigerator too.

"Bigger girls," she said, unable to look at me. She squinted her eyes shut and forced herself to go on. "Girls who look more like me. Just having, like, normal sex. That isn't, well, mean. With, like, gagging or choking or hitting. I don't like that stuff."

Oh, Bunny, I thought, *of course you don't.* And I pictured her, alone at her computer, so desperate to understand sex, so desper-ate to have it, to touch and be touched, and then to stumble across videos like that, where women's heads are hoisted by their ponytails in blow jobs so violent they gag and throw up. Or who were throttled, their faces turning red and ugly, or who were spit on, or who were slapped. And brave, quizzical Bunny, wondering: Will I have to do that? Is that what I am supposed to do? To be?

I was jealous, too, that there was something so healthy in her, so vital and pure, that she saw those images and knew not to like them. I had been stunned, but not surprised, by the first man who hurt me while we were having sex, and I learned quickly to hurt others. Ever since, against my will, images of a more sadistic nature had been appealing to me, and sometimes I could click and click and click until I was watching things that gave me nightmares afterward.

And so I told her what maybe I should not have told her, which is that it would be older men who wanted her, men who were more confident, less cowed by her physical strength and size. That to a man even in his twenties, her youth itself would be enough to flood his mouth with saliva.

"Like how old?" she asked excitedly.

"No," I said, "this is not an endorsement of you trying to find perverts to fuck you."

"But like how old?"

"When you're in college," I said. "Boys then won't be so scared. Someone will be lucky to date you."

"Do you think a college guy would date me now?" she asked.

"Bunny, you could be a fucking camgirl if you wanted, it's not about that, it's about finding someone to have a real relationship with. Who will value you. Who will understand how insanely incredible you are."

She let it drop, but I knew she wasn't satisfied.

One of the terms we stole from *RuPaul's Drag Race* was the concept of "realness." They would say, "Carmen is serving some working girl realness right now," and a lot of the time it just meant passing, that you were passing for the real thing, or that's maybe what the word began as. But there were all different kinds of realness. In

Paris Is Burning, which we must have watched a hundred times, a documentary about New York City drag ball culture, there were drag competitions with categories like Businessman or Soldier. Realness wasn't just about passing as a woman, it was about passing as a man, passing as a suburban mom, passing as a queen, passing as a whore. It was about being able to put your finger on all the tiny details that added up to an accurate impression, but it was also about finding within yourself the essence of that thing. It was about finding your inner woman and letting her vibrate through you. It was about finding a deeper authenticity through artifice, and in that sense it was paradoxical and therefore intoxicating to me. To tell the truth by lying. That was at the heart of realness, at least to me.

I made Bunny play realness games with me all the time. I tried on her clothes. She tried on mine. We wore the same size shoes, as it happened. We practiced walking like boys, we practiced walking like girls. We did impressions of specific people. I was particularly good at imitating Ann Marie, a girl on Bunny's volleyball team, but I could also do a convincing Principal Cardenas.

The thing about these games is that Bunny was absurdly bad at them. She couldn't do it. She always seemed like a child overacting. When she tried to act feminine, she careened into strange Blanche DuBois territory. When she tried to act masculine it was all mid-'90s LL Cool J lip-licking weirdness. All her accents quickly devolved into Australian. And the thing about these games was that I was great at them in a way that scared us even as it made us laugh.

"Do my dad," she said one day, "ooh, do my dad!"

I turned to her, finding almost immediately the way Ray held his mouth, the lips a little pooched, the way he raised one eyebrow higher than the other, the way his cheeks were a little flabby so they made his consonants too plosive, his vowels a bit sticky. "Bunny Rabbit," I said, and I was prepared to go on, to say something like "And I'm not a racist, I love black people, but—"

Bunny screamed and leapt up to stand on top of the bed and began bouncing. "That was too good, that was too weird, oh my god, that was so weird."

I laughed and said, "Really?"

"No, it was scary good."

I tried to stop smiling, closed my eyes, and found him again in my mind. "Bunny, goddamnit, Coach Creely called because you're failing trig, is that true?"

Bunny was jumping on the bed, squealing, "Oh my god! Oh my god, put on his clothes!"

"What? No," I said, though I was fascinated by the idea, and it was not long before we had entered her father's bedroom and dressed me in one of his shirts, unbuttoned too far, and with a small pillow from the couch as a paunch. I put on one of his ratty baseball caps, and we drew purple bags under my eyes with a plum lipstick Bunny had bought but never been able to pull off. We examined me in the mirror of the black Madame Butterfly death-suite bathroom.

"It's perfect," she said. "Now the hands."

"What, this?" I asked, as I crossed my arms up high over my fake belly so that it looked like I was fondling my own armpits.

"Oh my god," Bunny said. "Oh fuck. How do you do that?"

"Do what?" I asked, and then I did his laugh and she screamed.

I lost it and we both laughed with our real voices as we watched ourselves in the bathroom mirror. Who were we? I wondered.

Who was anyone?

I often wondered who Bunny would be without volleyball, it so dominated every aspect of her life. And while the dream had been set for her by her father—Ray who had seen her height and her strength and decreed her a star, Ray who plotted her course to Olympic fame (it was always, always assumed by her father that the Olympics were the goal)—volleyball was also something Bunny genuinely loved. She had done basketball too, when she was younger, and she had liked it, but the decision to focus on volleyball had in large part come from her, even if her attachment to her female coach seemed to me obviously psychologically unhealthy.

Coach Creely was cold and mean, her approval hard to get and stingy when it came, and to watch Bunny slave and slaver, seeking comfort and love from this false mother figure, was at times a bit much for me. Overall, the psychodynamics of the entire situation were undesirable, and yet the game itself was the one good thing in Bunny's life. She was happiest on the court, where all her instincts were the right instincts, where she didn't have to second-guess anything, where she and her body were fused and single. She was, quite literally, an animal on the court, and I sometimes marveled at the easy violence of her playing.

She made varsity in tenth grade and had a stellar year, but the summer before junior year, she began to grow. At first she was excited. She was already tall for her age, but there was no "too tall" for volleyball. But then she kept growing. By Christmas she had grown five inches, which hurt her, her legs in particular ached constantly, but which also disorganized her coordination. I only ever occasionally attended her games, both for scheduling reasons and because I found most sporting events boring, even if I knew someone personally involved. But she reported them all to me at excruciating length, and I was aware of every missed dig, every embarrassing fall. In fact, she fell just walking around the house. She was constantly hitting her head getting into cars, misjudging curbs, suddenly stumbling over her feet. It was comical at first, and then less so. "I think we should take you to the doctor," Ray finally said, but he put off scheduling it.

That year, her team made it to the state playoffs, and Coach Creely benched Bunny for the entire game, though the team lost anyway. Sitting on that bench had shamed Bunny more deeply than going stag to every school dance had done. She had also happened to be on her period, and Bunny's periods were horrific, tidal affairs that she was prone to discussing in the goriest language she could conjure. After the playoff game, she had texted me that she was depressed and could I come over, her father was not home. Aunt Deedee was working late that night—she had recently been fired from the Target Starbucks and was working nights at a bar in Culver City, which meant more money but even fewer hours of sleep. I had never seen her so gray and flattened, and sometimes I worried she would just drop dead. I told Jason where I was going, and he farted at me, and I went next door, where I found Bunny still in her uniform, purple short-sleeve jersey, "buns" (the adorable name for the black panties they pretended were shorts), kneepads down around her ankles, a heating pad on her stomach, eating gummy worms.

"Dude," she said, "you want to know the grossest thing about having a period?"

"No," I said. "I do not."

"When you take a shit and you wipe, it looks like peanut butter and jelly."

"And we wonder why you don't have a boyfriend," I said, stealing a gummy worm from the bag in her lap.

"Ugh. I know exactly why I don't have a boyfriend," she said. "Because I'm fucking eight feet tall. I'm a monster."

"You're not a monster. You have charisma, uniqueness, nerve, and talent, and you know it."

"I'm never going to have a boyfriend. I'll probably be, like, a forty-year-old virgin, all wrinkled from too much sun, and I'll get stocky and thick, and everyone will just assume I'm a lesbian."

"That's pretty insulting to lesbians," I said.

"I wish I *were* a lesbian," she said.

"It's never too late! Are you attracted to girls?"

She seemed to think about this, chewing thoughtfully on a gummy worm. "I think they are so, so pretty. I like to look at them. I think they look pretty naked. Is that enough?"

I wasn't sure. "Does looking at them make you hungry, like, I want that, I want to squeeze that, I want to shove my face in that?"

She laughed. "No."

"Then you are probably not fit to be a lesbian."

"Do you feel that way about guys?"

"No comment," I said.

"Can I tell you something?"

"Obviously you can."

"Penises kind of freak me out."

"In what way?"

"Like, they look like they don't have enough skin. They look like naked mole rats, have you ever seen those? And they are all vulnerable and pink and everything, but then, like, hard and long and pokey? Sometimes just looking at a dick, like, if it's alone, actually kind of makes me sick to my stomach, like one of those videos where they pop a big zit?"

Her honesty gave me the giggles. "If it's alone?" I gasped.

"Yeah, I mean, like, not in the context of a porno, but like, just a dick pic, like just, wham, right there, erect penis, no context. That doesn't gross you out at all?"

"Not really," I said. But it had once. I could remember getting queasy when I first started cruising Craigslist. I had known enough to expect, even at thirteen, that I would see penises. But there were so many kinds, and sometimes they had weird veiny knots in them, or oversize heads on tiny staffs, or they were too pink, or so black I didn't know they could be that black and shiny, slick purple, almost eggplant. But it had been the pictures of anuses that had been most alarming to me. Some of them were so well bleached and manicured that they looked like doll parts, but some of them were dark brown and hairy and scary looking. But I still felt very compelled to look at them, and gradually they had become less and less frightening to look at, but the fear and the excitement went together, were almost one thing.

"I wonder why sex is so terrifying," Bunny mused. "Like, why is it this great big thing and so full of pleasure, but also, like, very, very frightening?"

"I don't know," I said.

"I was so embarrassed sitting on that bench, it was like I couldn't even look up. I couldn't look at anyone, or I would start crying, you know? It was like a public shaming or something. What were those things called? Where they would lock your hands and head in a piece of wood in the town square?"

"A pillory."

"Yeah, it was like I was pilloried."

"I'm sure nobody but you thought of it that way," I said.

"Do you think there's something wrong with me?" she asked.

"What do you mean?"

"Michael. I'm taller than all the students, but I always kind of was, or at least the second tallest. But I'm"—she sat up, leaned in, almost whispered—"I mean, Michael, I'm taller than the teachers. I'm taller than my dad." Her eyes begged me to understand the unnaturalness of this, the constant pain of it. And I knew. I knew she had to lean down to hear her friends talk. I knew that if we went anywhere besides North Shore, where they were used to her, she would have to answer endless questions: How tall are you? Are your parents tall? Do you ever wear high heels? Do you have a boyfriend? People would ask her that, just, like, at the mall.

"I don't know, Bunny," I said.

"I mean, do you think there is something genetically, biologically wrong with me that I'm this tall?"

"Do you think there is something genetically, biologically wrong with me that I'm this gay?" I said, keeping her gaze, even though the more I looked at them, the weirder her eyes seemed to me, too large and shiny, the dark brown of her irises glossy and slick as melted chocolate.

She burst out laughing, belting out hee-haws so improbable that at first I thought she was faking it.

That winter, Bunny didn't join the swim team as she usually did. She didn't do anything. Ray had finally taken her to the doctor, and he wrote a note exempting her from even regular P.E. She was still growing too fast.

While Bunny had never been good at school, there was no sign she had the developmental delays one would expect with DNMT3A overgrowth syndrome, and a DNA test confirmed this. The concern was that there might be a tumor in her pituitary gland causing an excess production of growth hormone. Her hands had grown so much that the joints ached, and her jaw had become heavier, more manly. While these changes filled Bunny with despair and self-loathing, there was now an androgyny to her looks that I found fascinating. I had an impulse to grab her long, thick throat and push my fingers into that jaw and turn her head this way and that. She was beautiful.

Was there something wrong? Not on the ultrasound of her pituitary gland. She was taken for X-rays, where they studied her bone plates to see how much more she would grow. She was given blood tests for which she had to consume a sugar drink she described as tasting like liquefied Smarties.

This drama unfolded slowly over that winter and spring. After two ultrasounds and an MRI, it was decided that her pituitary gland was normal, and still she grew. They X-rayed her bone plates again. Her endocrinologist promised she would stop soon. She grew another inch. By the end of junior year, she was six foot three, and an even two hundred pounds. And she felt like a complete monster.

4

The very moment I turned sixteen and could work legally, I had gotten a job at the local Rite Aid, mostly because it was only seven blocks from our house. To have a job, to earn money, to be able to afford my own food and clothing, was essential, but it was apparent that no one was going to teach me how to drive or give me a car to learn on, and so my employment options were geographically limited. I applied to the Starbucks, to the Rite Aid, and to the North Shore Fish Company, but the Rite Aid was the only one that called me for an interview, and when they hired me, I considered myself lucky, even though the job was painfully boring and going to work without makeup on, with my septum piercing tucked up invisibly inside my nose, caused me to feel vulnerable and nude.

As it happened, I fell immediately and hopelessly in love with my manager, Terrence, a soft-spoken father of four and former high school quarterback with floppy blond hair, who was perpetually both gentle and stoned. I loved him impersonally, abstractly, like a character in a book who, by virtue of their very distance from you, their belonging to a different world that you may never yourself enter, enflames your longing all the more. I didn't want to fuck him exactly, though I would have (quite enthusiastically) if asked, but I was borderline obsessed with him. He carried a one hitter in his pocket, and I feared that something tragic might happen to him, specifically that he might commit suicide, though there was nothing definite that led me to believe he had plans to do so. His wife was bossy and exuberant, his four children happy and demanding, and certainly loud when they visited the store, but I got the sense that, even though he was overtly grateful for his life, he could see that he was lucky to have them and to have a steady job, he was also someone who found life's beauty inextricably mixed with sadness. He was devoutly Catholic, and it always seemed to me that this informed the development of his personality, the way he liked to clasp the hands of the staff as we said goodbye, as though the hands were the conduit through which blessings could be communicated.

Whatever it was, it made Terrence kind, so patient with his staff that it bordered on the saintly, and he would ask old women filling their prescriptions or buying stool softeners about their days and then he would listen, listen so intently that they felt pierced by him, and I got the feeling that he really did find their days interesting to hear about, and that he loved them, loved all of us, even as, at the end of the day, as he folded his long legs into the driver's seat of his pale blue minivan, which was always covered in dust, he found it all a bit too much, too hard to take, and he would fumble with his one hitter as though the smoke were medicine, an asthma inhaler that would force his lungs open and allow him to keep sipping the air amid the pandemonium of the living.

One night in July, during the summer between junior and senior year, I was working the register when I saw Bunny and another girl come in with two boys. It was around seven at night, which was a busy time for us, even on weekdays, because we had excellent prices on liquor and wine, and the line for the register looped around the front of the store, with mostly men and some women holding cases of beer and multiple wine bottles awkwardly in their arms like cold, abstract babies. It had come as somewhat of a surprise to me how pervasive alcoholism was, even in our picture-perfect town. On the one hand, it was a relief to know that what had happened to my own family was not singularly shameful, but I was also taken aback to learn that the majority of people found their lives so dreadful as to need to enter a near stupor every night in order to continue living it. It did not give me much hope about my own adulthood.

I hadn't been seeing Bunny lately because she was doing a volleyball intensive at Cal State Fullerton for the summer, and she often didn't come home until eight o'clock at night, and then was so tired she just collapsed after sending me a few weird gifs and strings of heart emojis. I did my best not to resent her unavailability because I also knew this summer was a turning point for her. She had finally stopped growing, maybe, possibly, at least it was thought by her doctor and repeated frequently by Ray Lampert that she had stopped growing (Ray was always strangely gleeful about Bunny's size, like she was a 4-H project or an Amazonian orphan he had adopted from Themyscira; he told anyone who would listen that his daughter, his baby girl, was taller than him now), and whether this was true or not, her growth had at least slowed enough to allow her to regain her coordination, and she was learning her "new legs," as she called them. She could now jump vertically twenty-nine inches in the air, which was better than most pro football players. Even as boys seemed more out of reach than ever, the Olympics had come back into view, and she seemed psychologically able to handle this exchange.

So I was surprised to see her, and I was even more surprised to see her with two boys I didn't know well, and the girl, who I vaguely knew was named Samantha because she had been in my biology class freshman year. I disliked having to ring up people from my high school. It was a small town and a small school, and while I didn't know everyone's names, I always knew them by sight and they knew me, and it was awkward that they were buying things and I was selling things, that they had money to spend on items they didn't need, and I needed money so badly that I was wearing a blue smock.

As I continued to ring people up, I watched them move through the store. I couldn't tell if they were stoned or drunk, but I knew they were not normal, were giggling and looking around the store like it was an alien planet. Bunny had picked up a stuffed toy, a lion Beanie Boo with huge plastic eyes, and was cuddling it even as one of the boys was prying it from her hands and putting it back on the shelf. "Ooh, gum!" the dark-haired girl said. "Gum sounds amaaazing right now."

I watched them as they got in the long line for the register, as they pawed through the items lining the display, picking up miniature-size hand sanitizers as though they had no idea what they were, examining alien writing on packages of candy. They were each buying a soda and a variety of snacks, and Bunny had picked up the toy lion again. "I can't believe you're buying that," the girl said to her.

"Look at his eyes," Bunny said, and smiled into his plastic eyes as though she could see real emotion there, some enchanting vulnerability. "I mean, I have to."

I did not like any of this, and I was extremely anxious not to be the one who rung up their purchases, but I was relieved to see that when their turn came they each paid separately, and Bunny hung back, timing it so that she could come to my register. Terrence, my manager, was in his office, so I was relatively unobserved, and I skipped the canned lines I was supposed to say to her: "Did you find everything you were looking for?" And started with: "What the hell are you doing here—are you high?"

"I don't know," she said, and I saw that her pupils were huge, and I knew whatever she was on, it was more than weed, more than vodka pilfered from someone's mom. "Ryan asked me out on a date and then we went to the mall and then we all took these pills, and I feel amazing, but now I'm really scared. Am I okay? Is everything okay?"

"You need to go home," I said. "Just tell them you have to go home and then walk there—*do not drive*. Just walk home. I get off in two hours, I'll come take care of you."

"I don't know how," she said. I had rung up her items and bagged them, and there was a limited amount of time left for us to talk without holding up the line.

"What do you mean you don't know how? You're at Rite Aid. It's seven blocks. You've walked from here to your house a million times."

"I think I would get lost," she said.

"It wants you to swipe your credit card," I said.

She fumbled with her wallet and swiped her card.

"You are not good to be hanging out with boys like this. Do you understand? You need to go home. Bunny, are you listening?"

She nodded, and I could tell she was on the verge of tears. "How long have we been in this store?" she asked me.

"Ten minutes," I said.

"Oh good," she said, "I thought we had been in here for hours!" And then she laughed, and I knew she was not going to go home. "There is," she said, and paused, "some kind of shadow on your face."

"There's nothing on my face," I said.

"You look so sad!"

"Take your card and fucking go," I said.

"Why are you mad at me?" she asked, but she took her card and put it back in her wallet. Her friends were waiting for her by the exit, holding their bags, cracking open their sodas, giggling.

"Just go," I said, so angry I was getting tunnel vision and my heart was pounding.

As soon as she left, I felt guilty for getting angry at her, and guilty for not doing more to protect her. And yet, I knew that this was the world. I knew that this was what teenagers did. I knew that Bunny was so desperate to be seen as sexually attractive that she probably would have had sex with one of those boys stone-cold sober, even if they had Cheeto breath and there was bad lighting. I had no reason to suspect those boys had drugged her in order to get in her pants, no reason to imagine them ignoring her protests as they took it too far, no evidence that she would wind up scared and missing pieces of her memory the next morning. Bunny didn't need my protection. She could probably pick up one of those boys and throw them. And I had no knowledge of those particular boys and whether they were a good or a bad sort. I knew only that one of them was on the wrestling team and they both took Spanish. I hoped that they would all go to someone's house and eat too much candy and watch a movie whose plot they couldn't follow. I hoped they would get lost staring at someone's fish tank, saying things like "Isn't it crazy that fish exist?"

Still, I must have been visibly perturbed because toward the end of my shift, Terrence put a hand on my shoulder and squeezed the muscles there and they twanged under his fingers like guitar strings. "You poor thing," he murmured. "Do you want me to see if Lisa will close for you?"

"Uh, no, it's okay," I said. I had already texted Bunny several times and she had not texted me back.

"Is something wrong?" he asked.

"Just worried about my friend. But I'm sure she's fine."

"You're such a good guy," Terrence said, and I knew he was more stoned than usual, and I felt like I was in a nightmare where everyone was on drugs but me. Except that it was not a nightmare, it was quasi-factual, because everyone present in that Rite Aid, every one of my coworkers and customers, was, if not already drunk or high, planning on becoming so within the next few hours.

Was I a good guy? Was Terrence a good guy? In many ways he was the kindest person I knew, but I also was aware that he was nothing but a sad, doped-up manager at a small-town Rite Aid, and that if he was the best guy I knew then there was really no hope at all for anyone.

"It's fine," I said. I wanted to work the extra hours. I needed the money.

When I got home, there were no lights on in Bunny's house. I knocked on their door, rang the bell. It had been a hot day, but now the air was cool and the wind was picking up. I texted her from her front porch. I was still sitting there when Ray Lampert suddenly materialized in the darkness, having evidently walked home instead of driving.

"Michael, my man!" he cried. And I regretted all of my life choices leading up to that moment so intensely that I felt I was internally collapsing.

"Come in, come in," he said, fumbling with his keys.

"That's all right, sir," I said, already standing and trying to edge past him down the steps to the sidewalk. He grabbed me by the shoulder and shook me like I was a dog toy. "Get in here," he said. "Don't make me spend the rest of the night alone. I'm not ready for it to be over! It can't be over. You know why? Because we won't let it be over!"

And it was exactly like when Bunny would grab me in the pool like an alligator and pull me under, only now, instead of drowning, I was inside a gaudy living room, watching Ray Lampert fumble with his phone trying to put a Patsy Cline record on the Bluetooth sound system, as he told me about how it had been stand-up comedy night at the Blue Lagoon and some comics had come from L.A. and that was something he had always wanted to try: stand-up comedy. I could not imagine anything more horrible than Ray Lampert doing stand-up.

"Where's Bunny?" he asked, as he poured himself a glass of wine.

"I don't know. She didn't answer my texts, so I'm guessing she's asleep." It was always best to sprinkle your lies with truths.

"We'll let her rest, then," he said. "She's so tuckered out from those practices. It's a long day, she's there from seven to seven just about." His pride in her caused his face to become beautiful, and for several seconds I could see him as a younger man, the kind who would marry the prettiest, well-brought-up, good and sweet girl he could find, determined to earn her, to make a place for himself in this world, to build this house for her. The kind of man innocent enough to think that an all-black bathroom was compelling and chic. I had come to understand, somehow, over the years, that it was Ray and not his wife who had decorated their house. His touch was everywhere, in the grandiose marble and the gilt end tables, the oversize art reproductions in bold colors hung on every wall as though they were real paintings. He had tried, with a teenage boy's imagination, to conjure a rich man's house, and then he had made it a thrilling reality in every detail.

"Hey," he said, "you wanna see pictures of Bunny as a baby?"

I had already mentally imagined at least a dozen ways this night could go, but I had not imagined Ray would suggest something I would actually want to do. "Of course!" I said.

He paused, gave me a smirk I couldn't interpret. "You want me to pour you a glass?" He gestured with the wine bottle.

"Oh, that's all right," I said.

"C'mon," he said. "I won't tell if you don't." And he got down another jumbo wineglass and poured enough red wine in it that a goldfish could have comfortably swum around in there. I felt ridiculous, though I accepted the glass. I had no intention of drinking any of it, but I did not wish to be rude. "That'll put hair on your chest," he said. Before I could think about it, I said, "What I've always wanted—chest hair."

I was worried this would offend him, but instead he laughed uproariously and clapped me on the back.

He led me to his office, that wonderful wood-paneled room that no one ever seemed to spend time in, and pulled down from the shelf two fat black leather-bound photo albums. We sat, he on the big brown tufted chair, I on the ottoman, and he opened up what seemed to me another world. No one my age had printed photos, our childhoods were on memory cards, but Ray Lampert must have been a man who liked real cameras and developing film. The pictures were of an overexposed, brightly sunny, '90s world I could hardly recognize. He skipped hurriedly past the photos that interested me most, which were the wedding photos and early pictures of Bunny's mother before Bunny was born.

There was one large photo of Bunny and her mother that hung in the upstairs hallway, a posed portrait with a black background that must have seemed modern at the time. The woman I saw there was a pretty ice bitch: small features, pearly skin, glossy brown hair, an oatmeal-colored sweater. Bunny was dressed in a white T-shirt, both of them were wearing jeans, and they stared at the camera with a certain smugness, like they were members of a select club. But these more candid photos showed Bunny's mother, her name was Allison, to be silly, goofy even, mugging for the camera, making the west side sign with her fingers. She had a tattoo on her upper arm, though he flipped by too fast for me to properly see what it was; I thought a flower, something delicate and faded. In their wedding photo she was wearing a simple white cotton dress and holding a bouquet of Technicolor daisies, so happy she seemed delirious, and I had the overwhelming impression that she was some kind of white witch.

And then there was Bunny: a large, fat, potato-y baby, so big it looked like her mom was holding a Christmas turkey. She was often dressed in weirdly Victorian clothes, and even as a baby they had put black patent-leather Mary Janes on her tuberous little feet.

"She was such a funny little girl," he said. "You might think she was a tomboy, but no, it was princess princess princess." There was Bunny in a pink swimsuit and clacking plastic Minnie Mouse high heels dripping water all over the foyer. There was Bunny frustratedly peeling an orange at some kind of picnic table. There were Bunny and her mother, safe and rocking in a big white hammock, some beautiful, exotic-looking locale in the background. I saw that her mother had been a gardener, and their yard, assuming it was the same house, which perhaps it was not, had been a wonderland of plants before the pool was put in. I saw Bunny, perhaps five, pulling a carrot from the ground. On her head was a hastily twined crown of wildflowers that clashed with her red T-shirt.

The older Bunny got in the photos, the less interested I became. By the time she was in middle school the only photos of her were taken before, during, or after games. There were no images of her not in some uniform or another. But those early photos of her fascinated me, and I wished I could go back and really look at the divide in her life: before her mother's death, and then after. When she ceased to be part of a scene that her father was documenting and began to be posed artificially, always on her own. Was I imagining the sadness I saw in her smile? Or was it an effect of the camera flash, the glossy way the photos had been printed, that made her seem trapped in those images, sealed in and suffocating behind the plastic sheeting of the photo album?

"Thank you for showing these to me," I said.

"Aw, thank you for looking at them! I don't have many people to share these with." While I objected to almost everything about Ray Lampert, in that moment I was able to really like him, to feel I knew him. His skin had the clammy sweet smell of my own father's when he was drunk, and for a moment I missed my dad so intensely I became light-headed. The night my mother had been arrested, they didn't let us go to the ER with him, maybe because he was so drunk. The squad car, my mother handcuffed inside, drove off; the ambulance, my father recumbent inside, glided into the dark, sirens like the call of a robotic whooping crane; and I assumed that Gabby and I would stay in the house. We had been alone in the house so many times, I didn't even think about it, and I was horrified when I understood that we were going to be taken, against our will, somewhere else.

We were driven to some lady's house in Torrance. She was a retired nurse with a mastiff named Cookie. We stayed with her for three days and no one came to get us. Why didn't he come then? He could have waltzed in, flashed his photo ID, and legally claimed our lives. But he didn't. What did he do during those days? Did he sit in our empty house and think about things? What did he decide?

After the first seventy-two hours, we were moved to another house, this time in Inglewood, a house full of kids, the oldest of whom was named Renaldo and who stole my pajamas. I was involuntarily extremely attracted to him, and I can still viscerally recall what it felt like to be that mad and humiliated and turned on at the same time. I found out later that Aunt Deedee tried to come get us in those first three days, but she didn't have the right paperwork to prove she was related to us, and she had to wait until our detention hearing. But at the detention hearing, dear old Dad suddenly showed up. And the judge had to decide who to put us with: him or Aunt Deedee.

What did she say? What did she dare say in front of him, to his face? Had she seen the bruises on Viv's neck? Had she noticed the way Gabby flinched when someone moved too quickly? I imagine him getting redder and redder—he was always angriest when he was ashamed—and blurting out, "This is bullshit, Your Honor, this is fucking bullshit." He was like an eighteen-year-old who one day woke up in a thirty-five-year-old man's completely fucked-up life. Whatever she said, it was enough. The judge awarded her custody, and set a jurisdictional hearing where my father would have a chance to defend himself and regain custody. But he never showed up at the court date they set, and I had not seen or heard from him since. I knew that if I did see him now, he would take one look at me and know that I was gay, and his shame and disgust would ignite in a whoosh, and all the love that had ever been there would be gone.

Bunny was lucky to have Ray as a dad. That's what I was thinking when Ray's phone rang. He checked the number. "Shit, I gotta take this. Business."

I was surprised that business should take place at what must be past ten o'clock at night, but more surprised when he picked up the phone and began speaking in what I could only guess was Mandarin. He spoke a few phrases of greeting and then spoke in English again, all in a happy, reassuring, genial tone even as his face remained frighteningly blank and intense. The result was like bad dubbing in a movie.

"Very soon, yes. So grateful for your business. As always. Yes, old friends. Hahaha, yes. No, I sent them to your office. Cassie sent them. I'll double-check, but I'm certain she sent them. All right." He followed this with a few more phrases in Mandarin, then hung up, and without looking at me dialed again.

"Cassie, did you send Mr. Phong the blueprint files? Uh-huh. Did the wire transfer go through? Yeah, go ahead and send them, he's waiting on them. Sorry to wake you up. All right. Catch you later, doll."

And then he hung up and looked at me and giggled like a teenager. "I cannot possibly begin to tell you, Michael, how deeply fucked I am."

"Is that right?" I asked, so nervous that when I crossed my legs, I sloshed some of the wine onto the Oriental carpet. "Oh shit, I'm sorry," I said, leaping up, the red wine dripping down my hand and along my arm to the elbow.

"It's all right, it's all right, I spill wine on it all the time," Ray said, but he looked tired suddenly, and I knew that the night was over. I brought him a roll of paper towels, and I tried to help him sop up the mess, but he shooed me away, and I left him there, crouched in the dim office on his hands and knees, scrubbing at the rug.

5

Really, it was a confusing summer. I was working full-time at the Rite Aid, or as close to full-time as Terrence could manage for me. Bunny was always gone at her volleyball intensive. I began hunting flies in my aunt's house. The screens were torn, but we would have baked without the windows open since there was no air-conditioning. My aunt said daily that she needed to go by the hardware store and order new screens, and the problem was always framed as a scarcity of time and wherewithal, but I knew it was a scarcity of money. I was unwilling to spend my own hard-earned cash to have new screens fitted, but I was willing to spend two dollars on a flyswatter and spend hours a day hunting flies. To narrow the scope of my mental activities to the tracking of a single aerial point in three-dimensional space was deeply soothing to me. I drove Jason half-insane. "You need to stop," he would say, "you've been killing flies for like an hour."

But I couldn't stop because I was profoundly anxious, not because of Bunny's weird Ecstasy date, for which she apologized the next day, assuring me that nothing terrible had come of it except that she'd had to feign flu and miss a day of volleyball. She was excited, thinking that now this boy Ryan would be her boyfriend, but the relationship did not materialize. Ryan returned her texts with one-word answers and then not at all, creating a sticky wound that eventually crusted over with bitter acceptance and shame. I could hardly bring myself to pay attention to this, so consumed was I by what was transpiring in my own life.

By the time I was sixteen and I got my first phone, I switched from Craigslist to Grindr, lying about my birthday and claiming to be eighteen. But as I aged, so did my Grindr profile, and now that I was seventeen, my digital representation was almost twenty. I tended to steer clear of younger men, afraid they would ask me questions about college, or notice cultural points of reference I did not share with them. A young man can tell the difference between a seventeen-year-old and a twenty-year-old in a second. But to a man in his forties, all the young are awash in a golden haze.

On Craigslist, the ads tended to spell out what the encounter would entail: "You come to my clean apartment and fuck my hairy ass. We watch porn and j/o with some edging, no kissing." The ads were insanely specific, age, height, weight, dick length, cut or uncut; these statistics were displaced from sentences and laid out cold, separated only by the tiny knives of commas. They were clear about what they wanted in return: "You can have a small dick if you have a bubble butt, but if you have no butt, you must have monster cock. You must be 18–23 ONLY!!!" People advertised that they were "neg" and "on prep." If they were offering massage, they were prostitutes. If they said they just wanted a friend, they were ugly. It became easy to navigate, and an ad that I was willing to respond to was practically a unicorn. I did not have a computer of my own, nor did I have a phone back then, so I was mostly browsing on my aunt's computer after everyone went to bed. In short, Craigslist was like a massive yard sale, a flea market of sexual opportunities, most of which you definitely didn't want, but you always knew what they were. Do you want this fat hairy man to fill you with cum? Do you want to stroke it with this insanely buff Nigerian dude at precisely 2:15 in his garage?

But then I got a phone, and the very first week I owned it, I got on Grindr, where there was less to go on. Almost all profile pictures were headless torsos, almost all profile descriptions were half a sentence of acronyms. Creating my own profile was terrifying. I had never had to for Craigslist, had always been an anonymous stroller through the bazaar. Realizing I would have to become one of these headless torsos, I took the bus to the mall, where I camped out in the dressing room of a Zara with a men's section for forty minutes trying to find a good angle in the full-length mirror. With a little editing and cropping, I turned myself into a flesh violin like all the others and placed myself on the marketplace, uncertain how to say the things I needed to say: I can't host, I have no car, I have no money, I have little experience and what experience I do have is weird and scary, I am a ball of nerves, I am terrified, no one knows who I really am, I think about killing myself daily, I like to read books, please don't murder me.

Honestly, I was afraid of most of them, these floating photographs of dicks and hard-bodied torsos. Hey cutie, hey sexy, you ready to bend over? It was not a place where I expected to find love. Indeed, I was not allowed to have a boyfriend, even if I had somehow managed to find one. My aunt had once stopped me in the hallway and said, haltingly, "I don't think I need to say this, but I'm saying it: No boys. No boys in the house."

At bottom, I thought she was right. It wasn't even because I was gay that my love, my body, my touches, needed to be contained. It was because I had been born of a woman who could stab a man in the chest with a fruit knife at three in the morning because she had run out of other ideas for how to make it stop. Maybe there were some truly clean people in the town. There seemed to be. But I suspected most were like me, were like Ray Lampert, were like my aunt even, chasing after a middle-class dream that would have spit her out like a seed. To live in North Shore was to be committed to pretense. Committed to this beautiful, fake, wholesome dream, because even though it was a dream, it was so much better than anything else.

There was a certain category of man on Grindr, in his forties or fifties, who was looking for the validation of youth, no strings attached, but was not an official daddy, would not expect to buy me or control me. Men who wanted a golden hour with a young man so that they could remember something about themselves. So that they could feel a way they used to feel. And who couldn't understand that? Far from being the kind of person who requires his conquests to be physical perfection, I was instantly reassured by their sagging bellies, their imperfect mouths and receding hairlines. I preferred to be the beautiful one in these fragmentary encounters.

Some of them were acting out something in their own lives that caused them to be casually mean to me. "You should go to the gym more," one guy said when we were done. "Your hips make you look like a fucking woman." All of that hate and abuse heaped on young gay boys, where does it go but into the gay boy? Where it stays, and becomes a kind of pattern, like a crystal, causing other psychic material around it to conform to its structure. No one has ever said things as casually cruel to me as gay men, online or in person. That is how I, too, learned to be cruel, and while I try to contain those impulses, to quarantine those patterns, I can feel them growing in there in the dark.

But for the most part my lovers were kind, if somewhat detached. Sometimes they even claimed to love me. When I broke up with dear Ed of the tiny penis, he told me I was breaking his heart, and the idea that his heart had ever been involved struck me as so absurd I accidentally laughed.

But that summer I began to see someone seriously. The relationship was obviously doomed; he was forty-five, I was seventeen. I could not imagine what his life was like or how I fit into it. I suspected he was married because he wore a ring, but whether to a man or a woman I wasn't sure, and I was hesitant to ask too many questions for fear of puncturing the flimsy skin of whatever dream contained our goings-on.

His name was Anthony, and he was long-limbed with shinbones so bony and unpadded they looked like the bottoms of canoes. His hair was already mostly silver gray and he wore it in a late-Pierce-Brosnan quiff. Honestly, he was a snack in a dad-core way, radiating the confidence of a man who knows how to bandage a skinned knee. He was easy to smile, quick to compliment, as un-coy as it is possible to be.

He said he dreamed about me, that he couldn't wait to see me again, that I was perfection. He called me Adonis, he called me Butterfly, such ridiculous and extravagant pet names that I blushed. He wore jeans from Costco. He was wild about wiener dogs and would cry out whenever he saw one. He loved sports and was always asking me if I had caught a particular football or basketball game, and when I told him I didn't like those things, he was never offended, in fact, my lack of interest seemed to delight him, and he would say, "Of course you don't, of course." He was a corny, corny man, and he appalled me, and I loved him, the deal clinched in my heart before I could object.

We first met at a park, at night, the big one in the center of town, where the baseball and soccer fields were. Even though it was full dark out, the stadium lights of the fields kept the park weirdly bright, and as I walked to meet him, my shadow followed me in triplicate. I didn't normally meet dates in North Shore. I liked to meet up in a neighboring town where there was less chance of being seen. But I also liked the safety of a public space and being within walking distance of home, so when he proposed meeting at the park, I said yes. He was already there, sitting on a bench, and I recognized him from the pictures he had sent me.

The first thing he said to me was: "I am so nervous to meet you, I don't think I've been this nervous in years and years."

"Oh?" I said, sitting down next to him, not too close, but not too far either.

"So I have to thank you for that much already. What an experience. To meet a beautiful young man at night in a park. I mean, wow."

I laughed. "You not get out much?"

"No," he said, and smiled at me. "I do not get out much."

I think that was when I noticed the wedding ring, or maybe I only noticed it later. The memory has become so romanticized and blurred in my mind that I tend to remember him as I knew him later. But at the time, I think I worried he was somehow deranged. He smiled so much. He was wearing a truly ugly sweater, color-blocked cashmere in shades of dog poop and amber.

"Are you nervous to meet *me*?" he asked. "You probably do this all the time. I don't mean to say—well, not all the time! But you have done this before, this internet dating."

"Of course," I said. I thought of telling him about the time I met up with a date only to realize we had already fucked each other once before and not liked each other much. "Oh, it's you!" we said. And then we fooled around, even though we didn't really want to.

"It feels like it's happening completely outside the bounds of normal life," he said, excited. "I had no idea they kept the park this bright at night! I think that may be adding to the surreality of this encounter for me, if you will forgive me for going on and on like this. I'm so sorry. How do these things normally go?"

"There's no script," I said.

"See? No script!"

"None!" I laughed.

"You could say anything to me. I could say anything to you."

"You could," I admitted.

He screwed up his face like he was thinking hard, an eight-year-old in a spelling bee. "Oh, man, I can't think of anything good," he said. "Wait, did you know there are different sizes of infinity?"

"Isn't that impossible?"

"Precisely not. Okay, imagine the first infinity, the regular one, just one, two, three, four, and on and on to infinity."

"Yeah."

"Now, in your head, circle all the prime numbers. If your first list goes on infinitely, then your list of primes would also go on infinitely, even though it is a smaller infinity than the infinity of the original set."

He smelled like clean laundry. "You could make, actually, an infinity of subset infinities," he said.

I felt then this wild, jerking, insane hope that manifested as an intense desire to get his pants off, to press him into me, to seal the cosmic deal, but really it was some buried healthy part of me that saw that he was kind and good and smart and thought he could save me.

"I like your nose ring," he said. "Very brutal looking."

"Thank you," I said. "Do you want to go to your car?" I asked. A jogger ran past.

"Well, that had been my plan insofar as I had a plan," he said, "but now that I've met you, I think we need a new plan."

"Oh," I said, stung. It was a measure of my inexperience that I had never been turned down before, and my first reaction was not sadness but rage that fizzed behind my closed mouth as though I were a shaken soda can.

"You are so young, and I knew that, but I just, you know, twenty looks a lot younger than I remember it being."

"I'm not some innocent," I said.

"I realize, I realize," he said. "I just want to take my time. I want to replace everything I imagine about you with something real that I know about you," he said. He thought for a moment. "That's what I want."

"Okay," I said. And maybe if I were the me I am today, I wouldn't have found that so compelling. But the idea of someone wanting to know me, to know the real me, to see me as I was when I was so invisible and so dedicated to my own invisibility—it was everything I'd ever wanted and always assumed I would never have.

"Can I take you on a date?" he asked. "A real one?"

—

The next day, I called in sick to Rite Aid. Anthony picked me up in his Porsche and took me to a lunch place in Santa Monica so fancy it made me queasy. I didn't know what to order, I felt I had waited a beat too long to remember to put my napkin in my lap, I was having a full out-of-body experience, I squeezed lemon in my water and it squirted in my eye, blinding me. Anthony laughed and laughed. "Now you're the one who's nervous! Oh, I am so sorry. This was the wrong place. I don't know why I thought this was the place to take you."

I had my cloth napkin, which I had dipped in my water glass, pressed to my eye, but the pain was not abating. "This place is lovely. This place is like a dream of where a guy would take me."

"That's what I was going for!" he cried, and after that the lunch was easier. When we had finished and were driving back to North Shore, he asked if I had anyplace that we could go. Aunt Deedee would be at home sleeping before her bartending shift. But Bunny had given me the key to her house. While Ray was hardly ever home except late at night, and while Bunny's whereabouts were dependably easy to track, she was at that volleyball intensive from seven to seven, there was always the risk that Ray, who spent his days going from house tour to house tour, from meeting to meeting, might swing by for something he needed or had forgotten, and it was a measure of my insanity that I took such a risk so confidently.

I let Anthony into Bunny's house and showed him around. I did not mention that the house was not mine. I wanted Anthony to think I came from a place like this. "This is the living room," I said. "This is the kitchen."

"Who's that?" he asked, pointing at a picture of Bunny.

"My sister."

I led him to the spare bedroom, or as I liked to think of it, the "Madame Butterfly Suicide Sex Suite," and I jumped on him and pushed him down on the bed. I loved how large his rib cage was, and I could feel his big lungs inflating and deflating in his chest, his big heart hammering inside him. I wanted to get his shirt off, so I could get as close to his skin as I could.

"Hold on, hold on," he said, "I want to look at you." He slipped my T-shirt over my head. He unbuttoned my pants, and I shimmied off my jeans. He marveled at my calves as he peeled off my socks. "Every inch of you is perfection," he said.

"Stop," I said, laughing, because the idea that I was perfection was ludicrous. My leg hair was thin and weird-looking, my skin Mariana-Trench-pale. His chest hair was a sparse constellation of tight little curls and he had two small moles on his neck, and I liked to rub my cheek on them. His skin smelled yeasty and good, and I wanted to drag my face across every inch of him.

The most disconcerting part of it for me was that I had never had the experience of being both sexually turned on and happy at the same time. I kept thinking something was wrong. I kept breaking out giggling. "What?" he would ask.

"I just can't believe we get to do this," I would say. "I can't believe it is allowed for something so wonderful to happen."

When we had tired each other out, and I was lying cuddled up to his chest, and he was running his fingers up and down my biceps lazily, he said, "Whose house is this?"

"Mine," I said.

"I don't think it is," he said. "You're telling me you picked out this bedspread?"

There was no way I could claim I had picked out this bedspread. It was maybe the first lie in my life that I had decided I couldn't possibly sell. I didn't know what to say and could only blush.

"It's okay!" he said. "It's okay."

I think he realized I was going to cry before I did. "Oh, Michael," he said.

I was so embarrassed. Embarrassed to have lied, embarrassed to be crying. "I don't know what's wrong with me," I said.

"Not a thing is wrong with you," he said.

And then the truth spilled out, and I found it was all easy to say. That this was my friend's house, that I lived next door, that I lived with my aunt because my mother had been to prison.

"What about your father?" he asked.

"What about him? I mean, he didn't even show up at the hearing to get us. I think that bridge is pretty well burned."

"I wouldn't be so sure of that," he said. "A father's love for his son—it's not such an easy thing to throw away."

In retrospect, so much seems obvious, but it was not obvious to me at the time. I fell head over heels in love with Anthony. We saw each other twice a week. Sometimes more. I was in a fever.

Anthony sent me a Frank O'Hara love poem in an email, and I mistakenly thought that he had written it, and that he loved me, but then he hadn't written it, and I got embarrassed that I didn't even know who Frank O'Hara was, and so I didn't know if he did love me or if he was just sending me a beautiful poem.

Anthony didn't want to do anything dark sexually, and the one time I placed his hand on my throat, hoping he would choke me, he withdrew it as though I had burned him, and said, "I hope it's all right with you, but I'm not that sort of fellow." He was always saying old-fashioned things like that, and when he gave me presents they were usually novels. He gave me *Giovanni's Room* and *Maurice*. He gave me *Mrs. Dalloway* and *Sons and Lovers*. I read these books in such a fever that I have feared to ever read them again, lest the golden, irradiating magic they held for me be replaced with dusty, actual words.

Still, every time I saw Anthony, I was filled with dread. Dread that he would tell me we shouldn't see each other anymore, dread that he would do something to hurt me, dread that I would accept it, dread that we would be discovered, dread that I was doing this at all, that I was so hungry, so desperate for love that I would do anything to continue to meet a grown man I knew nothing about and then treasure my memories of the encounter, playing and replaying them inside my mind, so I walked about my daily life as a zombie, there but not there, a hollow vessel filled with only the charmed air of potentiality those borrowed novels granted me. One night I killed seventeen flies, and Jason ripped the flyswatter from my hands, marched downstairs to the kitchen, and cut the swatting part right off it.

It was also the summer that Donna Morse and her son, Spencer, were murdered. Surely there must have been other murders during the time I lived in North Shore, but those were the first and only ones that I was aware of, and for weeks it was all we could talk about, not just Bunny and I, but the whole town. Waiting for your drink to be made at a Starbucks, whoever was standing next to you would suddenly say: "What a shame about Donna Morse, eh?" And then you would be talking about it with someone you didn't even know.

Donna had gone to North Shore High, but several years ahead of me and Bunny, and we did not know her directly, though we knew of her, mostly in the sense of a negative example because she had gotten pregnant and then married and dropped out of community college. North Shore could have been a launching pad for her, but it was not, and like my aunt she was a vestige of a poorer past, clinging to the town like it could save her. She was overweight and her hair was dyed bright red, like a Raggedy Ann doll's. Aunt Deedee told me that Donna Morse had been hooked on drugs, but got sober when she got pregnant with Spencer. Now she nannied around for families who didn't mind if she brought Spencer along.

Our main source of info about the murders besides the local paper was, of course, Ray Lampert, who, being a fixture at the Blue Lagoon, was a sponge for gossip. And so it came to be that we heard every detail of what happened from his gross lips as he sat hungover at the breakfast bar in the kitchen, trying to choke down a microwave burrito to keep from throwing up. That was something that happened during those high school years: Ray's stomach started to go. He was always throwing up, and Bunny was always telling him to go to the doctor, but he never would make an appointment.

According to Ray, Donna Morse had gotten a divorce from Spencer's father, Luke, because of domestic violence. "He wasn't so much a puncher as a grabber," Ray said, wiping bean splatter from his chin with a paper towel. "He would just grab her and go. Smash her into things, like bash her head into the microwave, wham, wham, wham. Her cousin said the worst was when he threw her against the furnace and one of those metal screws, like, cut her face open. That's why she had that scar."

I did remember the scar. It ran down her cheek like a pink tear trail. I would see her and Spencer come into the Rite Aid all the time, and I remember I used to judge her because she would buy him full-size candy bars, even though he was only three.

"Why was he even over there?" Bunny asked. "What the fuck was Spencer doing at Luke's house if he was this violent turd?"

"Court mandated," Ray said. "Visitation."

"It makes me so mad!" Bunny shouted. "I hope whatever judge granted him visitation has nightmares for the rest of his fucking life."

"We're all gonna be having nightmares for the rest of our lives," I said. That was how young I was. I thought I would never forget. I didn't know how things faded, became simple facts, until they were things you hardly thought of anymore.

On a Saturday night that August, on a weekend Spencer was court mandated to spend with Luke, Donna got a call from Luke's cell phone. She heard Luke's voice in the background, "Tell her." And then her son's shaky little voice, "I'm gonna die tonight, Mommy," and then she heard the gunshot. But she didn't believe Luke had killed their son. Many times in the past, Luke had baited her, pretending to kill himself on the phone in order to get her to come over. The idea, however, that he was firing a gun in the same room as her son made her blood run cold, and she called 911 as she set out on foot to his apartment complex, which was only a few blocks away. She did not own a car.

They played the 911 call on the local news. She argued with the dispatcher, who told her to go back to her home. "The police are coming, ma'am, they are on their way." "I can't wait. I can't wait out here when my baby could be in there hurting, please, I can't." "You must return to your house." But she didn't return to her house, she went into Luke's, and she screamed as she saw her three-year-old boy bloody on the carpet, his face and most of the right side of his head missing. They did not play the rest of the 911 call because it was too graphic. Luke didn't shoot her with the gun, though he still had four rounds, but he beat her to death by slamming her head into the kitchen counter over and over again. When the police arrived, he had just finished shooting himself in the head. They heard the gunshot as they broke down the door.

It was so terrible that it seemed to be from another world. I remember, too, a quote from the medical examiner that wound up in the paper, describing Donna's skull as not just fractured but turned into a "mosaic of bone chips." The violence was otherworldly. We couldn't understand how someone could have performed it in a place that was so familiar to us.

"Doesn't it seem weird," Bunny asked one Sunday afternoon, a rare one that I wasn't working at Rite Aid, as we sunned ourselves on her back patio, our skin glistening from the pool. "Doesn't it seem weird that it was *Donna Morse*?"

I knew instantly what she meant. Donna, who was neither beautiful nor smart, who had not said one interesting thing as far as either of us could ever tell, seemed an unlikely object for such all-consuming desire. That was what we thought somehow. That all of this violence was *over* Donna, was, in essence, her fault, as though Donna were the gunpowder and Luke a helpless cannon, a series of mechanical pieces inexorably igniting her. If she had been beautiful or capricious, mysterious or charming, we could have understood how someone could have fallen so in love with her that it drove them to murder.

"It's like, just get another girlfriend," Bunny said.

"They had a kid together," I said, but I wasn't even sure what such a bond entailed. My own father had seemed to find it easy enough to let us go. They had gotten divorced while my mom was in prison, and he had certainly never contacted me again. Whatever life he lived he must have found sufficiently distracting to forget us. And as a child I had felt his love as physically as the heat of the sun. So where had it gone?

"Phh," Bunny snorted. "Like he loved the kid."

Did fathers love their children? It seemed only some of them did. Others were immune somehow, or they could turn it on and off, and we assumed that because of Luke's violence, or perhaps because of the tattoo of a giant angry moon on his calf, or perhaps because he wore a beanie even in summer, that he was the kind of father who felt nothing for his offspring, or who felt the wrong things. We saw him often enough at the dog park, which was right off our street. He had a sandy-colored pit bull named Pecan. But even Hitler had a dog.

"She should never have let Spencer go with him," Bunny said. "She should have fought harder in court to keep Luke from getting visitation."

"She should have listened to the 911 dispatcher and stayed out," I said. "Spencer was already dead. She couldn't save him. She was already too late."

Donna Morse had not been smart.

If she had been smarter, she would have succeeded in not being murdered.

Bunny and I were smart. Something like that could never happen to us. We would never let our own murderous fathers get out of hand. Our murderous fathers were more refined, confined themselves to smashing vases and brief bouts of strangulation.

Bunny was especially hung up on why Donna hadn't fought him off harder. "How could you let yourself be slammed into the kitchen counter like that? I mean, after the first few times, aren't you like, enough, get off me?"

"Maybe he was stronger than her," I said.

Bunny shook her head. She couldn't imagine it. She couldn't fathom it. What it was to be physically weak. To be overpowered.

"I think she was waiting," she said. "I think she assumed he would stop. That it would be like all the other times, and he would slam her head once, twice, but not keep going. But she'd seen the kid already. How could she not know he was going to take it all the way? She thought she could calm him down. That was her mistake."

Donna made false calculations. Donna had failed.

There was no discussion of whether Luke had been smart or not smart. There was no discussion of what Luke should have done. Luke was, somehow, not a person.

We needed to pretend violence was something we could control. That if you were good and did the right things, it wouldn't happen to you. In any event, it was easier for me then to demand that Donna become psychic and know how to prevent her own murder than it was for me to wonder how Luke could have controlled himself. It was easier for all of us that way.

When school started, I was mostly concerned with how I would continue to see Anthony, since we could meet only in the daytime due to my housing situation, and we could not meet at his place because of his marriage (I presumed; he never actually said as much). Still, we often talked of ways we could sneak away, a fake camping trip with a fake flyer I could show my aunt, though I did not mention to him that my aunt would never believe that I wanted to go camping. We would go, he said, to the Hotel Angeleno, which was a round turret with windows on all sides so that every room had a balcony overlooking Los Angeles, and we would go to the Getty, he said, and look at the art together.

It was senior year, and for all my classmates the specter of the future loomed, but for me the questions, over where I would live, what I would do, whether or not I would go to college and how, were kaleidoscopic and overwhelming. The relationship with Anthony had unseated me from my usual pragmatism and suddenly anything, even impossible things, seemed like real possibilities. Maybe I would get into college and get a free ride and live in some kind of idealized dormitory setting, and Anthony and I could go on dates, and maybe he would take me to the symphony, and maybe we would fly to Paris together, and after brief, wrenchingly beautiful sodomy, we would eat croissants and notice together a stray cat *dans la rue.*

Maybe I would become homeless and begin to prostitute myself in Inglewood and eventually be murdered. Maybe I would go to community college and continue living with my aunt and working at Rite Aid and would stop seeing Anthony altogether and my life would go on much as it had. All of these futures seemed equally possible to me, and I spent my days lurching from one scenario to another, and so I did not exactly notice that some kind of vicious gossip was going around the school until the third or fourth day of the year, when I saw a fat, ruddy-faced boy named Scott, who was on the wrestling team and who was rumored to have absolutely chronic ringworm, snap his jaws at Bunny in the hall and growl, "You can bite me anytime, girl."

Bunny stared at him, as expressionless as a mannequin, and then slowly rotated toward her locker and opened it.

"What was that about?" I asked her.

"Nothing," she said, but I noticed that her head was wobbling on her neck oddly, as though the muscles had given out and she was having to keep her head perfectly balanced upon the nub of her spine. She seemed, if anything, not upset but ill.

"Did he say you could bite him?"

"Yes," she said, and closed her locker and walked away from me, her head still carefully balanced on her neck as though it might tumble off.

A few carefully posed questions throughout the day provided

me with the rest of the story. It was regarding Ryan Brassard and the night I had seen them together at the Rite Aid in July. In none of the stories I heard were drugs ever mentioned. In none of the stories were the other boy or the girl, Samantha, mentioned. In one, the setting had been Ryan's bedroom. In another, it had been Ryan's car. In all of them, Bunny had behaved somehow inappropriately. She was a slut. She was begging him for it. She jammed his hand down her pants, or she had stuck her too-large hand down his. She had writhed like an animal, she had squealed or made noises like a pig. In all of the stories, the crescendo of the action was that she had bitten him on the ear, nearly drawing blood, or in some versions actually drawing blood. Ryan had gotten scared of her and dropped her at her house. In one story, he had not even done that, just told her to get out of his own house, slamming the door in her face. She was disgusting. She was a whore. One boy speculated to me that Bunny must have a huge vagina, and he would like to see it, as he imagined it was the size of a cow's vagina.

I texted her repeatedly, but she did not reply. I knew she had volleyball practice after school, and so I went to my shift at Rite Aid but asked Terrence if I could leave early, and since I rarely made such requests, he complied, and by seven p.m. I was knocking on the door to Bunny's house desperately, pounding really, forgetting altogether that they had a doorbell, as though I were afraid to find her murdered inside.

When she swung open the door, I almost fell. She stared at me with some confusion, her face blank and pale, her lips almost white. Her hair was pulled back in a sweaty ponytail. She was still in her gym clothes, her kneepads pushed down around her ankles, and she didn't say anything, just stepped back so I could come inside. I could see she had been watching TV, and spread out on the coffee table were Cheetos, cookies, what looked like part of a muffin, a can of AriZona iced tea. She had not been crying. She had been eating.

"Are you okay?" I asked.

"I'm fine," she said, and threw herself on the couch.

"What happened?" I asked.

"What, with Ryan?"

"Well, yes. And, I mean, everything! Bitch, do you want a hug?" I asked, standing there, not knowing whether I should sit down or where.

"No, thank you," she said. Her eyes were glued to the TV.

I didn't know what to do. Wasn't I her friend? Didn't I have the right to expect to be her confidant? I sat down on one of the pretty French armchairs. "Did you bite him?" I asked.

She shut her eyes.

"Bunny, what the fuck happened that night?"

"Whatever he said happened, apparently." Her eyes were still closed. I heard the air-conditioning click on. I got up, stood over her on the couch.

"I am your friend," I said. "I don't care if you bit him! I'm not going to judge you! I just want you to let me in, and—" I must have been shouting at her, though I hadn't meant to, because her eyes snapped open and she lunged at me, pushing me so that I fell awkwardly over their coffee table and then she was on top of me, sitting on my stomach, pinning my hands to the floor above my head.

"I don't want to fight you," she said, "but I really do not want to talk about this. I thought it was normal, okay? I read it in *Cosmo*."

I could hardly breathe; she was so heavy on top of me. I gasped, nodded.

"I got carried away and I bit him on the ear, but I did not make him bleed, I just bit him too hard, okay?" She was shouting down into my face.

I nodded. Tried to take a deep breath so I could talk. "It is normal," I said. "People do bite each other's ears when they make out."

She looked at me quizzically. "They do?"

I nodded. "I can't breathe," I said. "Could you?"

"Oh, sorry," she said, and clambered off me, grabbed the sad bottom half of the muffin, and began peeling its wrapper as she sat back on the couch. "All day long I've been cursing that fucking *Cosmo* article, like, why put something in there if it's not true? I mean, some of that stuff always made me wonder, like about licking balls, do guys like that? Licking balls?"

"Some guys," I said, sitting up.

"Or, like, they said to put an ice cube on a guy's dick."

"That sounds pretty terrible," I said.

"That's what *I* thought!" she cried. She finished the muffin and threw the limp, crumb-covered liner on the coffee table like it was a used tissue. "It's all just fucking bullshit, you know? And he didn't act weird that night! I mean, he said ow when I bit his ear, and I said sorry, but we kept kissing after that! So I don't get how it was some big deal!"

"Was that your . . . first kiss?" I asked.

"Yes. Yes," she said, "that was my first goddamn kiss and I was, like, I don't know if that pill was really Molly, but I was loopy, and I thought he, like, loved me, like we had this soul connection, and I told him stuff, stuff I totally shouldn't have told him, and I'm so stupid, I can't believe I was that stupid."

"What did you tell him?"

"Like about my dad throwing up all the time and how scared I sometimes was that he would crash the car like my mom and then I'd be an orphan, and you know, I don't even spend that much time thinking about that stuff, but somehow I was just talking all about it." She shrugged, shoved another handful of Cheetos into her mouth.

"Oh, Bunny," I said.

"Don't say that," she said, raising an orange-dust-covered finger at me and shaking it. "I am not a victim. It's not like they put a gun to my head and told me to swallow that pill. I knew it was drugs!"

"I know, but this really isn't your fault. I think Ryan is making a really big deal out of something that seems pretty normal."

She seemed to grow calmer, and she began licking the cheese dust off her fingers.

"So it *is* normal to bite someone's ears?"

"Yes."

"This is so frustrating! I thought it was! Why did he get so freaked out, then?"

I didn't know. I had my guesses. "So how did that night end exactly?"

"Well, we were making out in his car, and I don't know, there was this other part where we were all in the park, him and me and Samantha and that guy Steve, and then I don't know where they went, only the idea was that they were going to do it, like, the big joke was that they were leaving us because they wanted to go do it, and so Ryan said he would take me home and then we were kissing in his car, and I bit his ear and said sorry, and it was fine, and then I got out and we were just outside my house, and I snuck in and went to bed."

"And that's it?" I asked.

"Well, yeah."

"Did you, I mean, was there any other stuff that happened? Like sex stuff?"

"No!" she shouted. "Are you crazy? But, I mean, like, I was very handsy. I felt like a cat being petted, it felt so good to touch him and be touched, and I kept touching his hair which maybe bugged him?"

"And then what happened? Did you text him the next day?"

"No, well, he called me the next day, and he said he couldn't be my boyfriend because I terrified him. Which, I was like, 'In what way do I terrify you?' But he just kept saying, 'You're not the girl for me, Bunny,' and I was like, what do I do with that? I didn't get it. But I must have—there must have been something about me, some way I did everything wrong, that just—just grossed him out."

I was both angry and sad that she had not told me any of this before. She had never shown me the texts she sent him or anything, but I could distinctly remember her saying, "Gosh, I texted him like five times and he hasn't responded. Isn't that rude?" It had seemed humiliating enough to me, but now to discover that this had been a face-saving lie to cover an even more painful reality made me want to bite Ryan Brassard's ear off myself. "What a fucking limp-dick loser," I said.

"What do you mean?" she asked.

"You just—you intimidated him!"

"I did not," she said. "I scared him."

"Bunny, nothing is wrong with you. You didn't do anything wrong."

"Well, obviously I did."

"No," I said, and I reached out and squeezed her naked calf in my hand. "Do not eat this. Do not take this in as information about yourself. This is not valid data. This does not mean you are bad at sex, or you are gross, it means only that Ryan Brassard is a scaredy-cat, limp-dick, manipulative little shit who wants a girl who will just lie there quietly while he excites himself."

Bunny laughed. "I don't know. I mean, it's pretty ballsy of him to have asked me out in the first place. He's only five nine. Like, you have to at least give him credit for that."

"Maybe he got scared by how turned on you made him."

"Why would that scare him?"

"Maybe he's secretly gay and he was freaked out because he thought you figured it out."

"That's only slightly more believable," she said. And she took in a deep breath, blew it out, then said, "Wanna go swimming?"

And so we did, and I even let her almost drown me in an effort to buoy her spirits.

6

As it turned out, it was Ann Marie, Tyler's girlfriend, who had spread the gossip about Bunny biting Ryan Brassard. Ryan and Tyler and Steve were all on the wrestling team, and Ryan had told them what happened, but the gossip might have been contained to the world of ringworm-infested wrestlers had Ann Marie not been in the car when the story was told. Ann Marie was a special kind of being, small, cute, mean, glossy, what might in more literary terms be called a "nymphet," but only by a heterosexual male author, for no one who did not want to fuck Ann Marie would be charmed by her. She was extra, ultra, cringe-inducingly saccharine, a creature white-hot with lack of irony. She was not pretty, but somehow she had no inkling of this fact, and she performed prettiness so well that boys felt sure she was. She had brassy golden hair and freckles and blue eyes slightly too wide set and bulging. Even though she was short, she played varsity volleyball with Bunny.

In a town like North Shore, where everyone had known everyone forever, there were many points of connection, and before I relate what happened next that fall of our senior year, I feel the need to enumerate each point of connection we shared with Ann Marie, or else the story simply makes no sense.

Bunny and Ann Marie had known each other since they were two years old because Bunny had attended the Catholic preschool that Ann Marie's mother ran. (This was, of course, how Ann

Marie, my sleazy imp of an informant, became aware that Bunny's mother had been having an affair with Mr. Brandon.) Ann Marie's mother, otherwise known to the children as Ms. Harriet, was the principal, and so as a two-, three-, and four-year-old, Bunny was disciplined by Ann Marie's mother, and Bunny's memories of her were vivid. What was most interesting and most frightening about Ms. Harriet is that she never said what you were expecting her to, and she was completely unmoved and unfrazzled by tears, fits, tantrums, and violence. She was calm not in a way that was kind, or soft, or in any way jiggly, Bunny said. Hers was a calm made of stone. Ann Marie's mother loved no one and hated no one and was surprised by no one. She and Ann Marie's father were divorced and divorced early. Ms. Harriet was well done with bullshit even by the time both girls turned two. Bunny could still remember one comment Ms. Harriet had made, quite calmly, to a boy named Liam, who was prone to hitting. "Do you like to be hit?"

"No," Liam had said.

"Do you love people who hit you?"

"No," he had said. How old was he? Three? Maybe not even that.

"So who is going to love you if you keep on hitting? Who is going to love someone like that?"

"No one," the boy said, tears sliding down his cheeks as he studied the tile floor at his feet.

"That's right," Ms. Harriet said. "So you've got some thinking to do and some decisions to make. You can hit. Not anybody in this world can really and truly stop you if hitting is how you want to be. But if you do, you're risking all that love that you could have. Because nobody, nobody, nobody, is going to stand around all day for you to hit just hoping to give you love in return."

And then she ruffled his hair.

That was the thing about Ms. Harriet, Bunny told me. She was always almost right, but a little bit wrong in a way that was scary.

What must it have been like to be Ms. Harriet, watching her

own daughter grow up side by side with Bunny? What did she notice about the two girls? What judgments was Ms. Harriet forced to make about her own daughter after seeing her so clearly among her peers? Most parents wonder, are all children like this? Is my child special and wonderful? Is my child awful? But Ms. Harriet knew what all children were, she knew what normal was, and she was horrifyingly lucid about the strengths and weaknesses of her only progeny.

As a little girl, Ann Marie had been whiny and sticky, not naturally moral or empathetic, prone to being quite mean actually. She was the kind of little girl who taunted, who teased, who grabbed a toy from your hands and then ran off with it, and when you chased her, burst into tears and told the teacher you attacked her. In short, she was the sort of child other children disliked, and Ms. Harriet was daily aware of this. Bunny's commentary was, "I always got the feeling Ms. Harriet liked me more than Ann Marie, and that made me feel so bad that I was always extra nice to Ann Marie so we became friends even though I never liked her."

From preschool through about third grade, Bunny and Ann Marie were best friends. If Bunny had been a dog or a horse, what she possessed would have been termed "a good temperament." But there is not a precise category for this kind of personality type in humans, one characterized chiefly by tolerance and a kind of good-hearted obliviousness. Mean jokes and pranks slid off her, and she was untroubled and unaware that she was not popular and that her friendship with Ann Marie made her even less so. As they grew older, she was aware that Ann Marie wanted to continue playing with dolls long after Bunny and other girls had stopped, but she felt only pity for whatever fever seemed to clutch Ann Marie when she looked into the inert face of a doll. Once, Ann Marie had told her that she believed dolls came alive when you weren't looking or when you were asleep. She was the kind of girl who continued believing in Santa too long, who didn't get the memo about the tooth fairy. A true literalist, she once informed a boy at school that he was definitely going to hell because his family didn't go to church and that Satan was going to press hot skewers into his body. "You're gonna rot," she said, her eyes lit up with excitement. "You're gonna burn!" (While the preschool was Catholic, Ms. Harriet was not, and she and Ann Marie attended the evangelical church that was pleasingly located across the street from the donut shop, and hell seemed to interest them a lot more than heaven.)

But Ann Marie was not all bad, Bunny was quick to point out. When Bunny's mother had died when the girls were seven, Ann Marie had said nothing at all about Allison going to hell, even though Bunny's family didn't go to church either. If anything, Ann Marie was swept up by the tragedy of it, crying more orgiastically at the funeral than even Bunny herself. She suggested to Bunny elaborate ways that they might mourn together, and wanted to contact Bunny's mother's ghost using a scented candle and one of Allison's old scarves that still smelled of her perfume. She made them black armbands that they wore for weeks.

In third grade, however, something shifted. One day on the monkey bars, Ann Marie pointed out to the other girls that Bunny's legs were unshaven. "Look," she said, "her legs are hairy like a man's!" And the other girls had laughed. Bunny had not been aware that everyone had begun shaving, and she dutifully went home and asked her father for a razor, which at first alarmed him, but when she explained about the teasing, he quickly acquiesced. Ray Lampert was nothing if not keen to the necessity of fitting in, even if it meant sexualizing the legs of his eight-year-old daughter.

But even once she was shorn, Ann Marie liked to point out that Bunny's stubble was thicker than the other girls', that Bunny's throat was too thick, that Bunny walked like a boy. Bunny, in fact, did not walk like a boy. She walked like a girl who was naturally 90 percent fast-twitch muscle fiber and who was already a head taller than the tallest boy. She walked like a girl who could, and sometimes did, lift up the entire end of the living room couch to scout for change underneath. She walked like a girl who could dangle one-handed from a monkey bar while she ate an apple with the other hand. "They shouldn't have named you Bunny," Ann Marie said with a laugh, "they should have named you Monkey!"

When the break came, it was quick and tawdry. Ann Marie and the other girls had a sleepover to which Bunny was not invited, and the mother of the girl whose house it was drove them all to Bunny's house—she said it had to be the house of a friend, someone who would know they weren't doing it to be mean—and she let them TP the entire front of Bunny's house.

Ray Lampert was furious. He didn't care what PC cant that mother had been spouting, Ray Lampert knew that you TPed the loser kid's house, and this TP on his front lawn meant that Bunny, and himself by extension, were losers. Bunny was never to see Ann Marie again, Ann Marie was not to come to their house, she was to be entirely blacklisted. (Everyone had agreed on the fact that it was Ann Marie who had come up with the idea of TPing someone's house and also the one who suggested they do it to Bunny Lampert.)

Bunny felt two ways about all of this. On the one hand, she was righteously angry. Ann Marie had made her father angry, and to Bunny there was no greater transgression. She took off her half of the best friend necklace and never put it on again. But she was also somewhat relieved. She had disliked Ann Marie for years but had suppressed this knowledge, and now she found great joy in not spending hours and hours being criticized and bossed around. (Ann Marie was the kind of kid constantly instructing other kids: "No, color it like this. Use this marker. No, you're doing it wrong, it's not supposed to be like that.") Bunny decided at that point that girls were simply too complicated to be friends with, and she began playing basketball with the boys, who accepted and adored her immediately. After school she went skateboarding with them.

They liked to travel in herds, buying candy and going from one of their houses to the next depending on which video game they wanted to play. It was heaven.

But by sixth grade, coincidentally the year I moved to North Shore, the other girls had figured out that Bunny had cornered the boy market, and these girls wanted the boys to be their boyfriends, and so they started playing basketball too. Bunny argued that they shouldn't be allowed to play. They were girls. "But you're a girl," the boys replied, confused. They knew the girls would ruin the basketball game, but they were now more interested in the girls than they were in the basketball. And so Bunny's paradise was ruined. Dates, which were nothing more than a group of boys and girls going to the mall together, began to be arranged. She would sometimes go on these, paired off with a boy who made it very clear to her that he was not really asking her on a date but wanted to include her out of friendship. She watched as Keith Moore spent money to buy sunglasses for Michelle, and this spending of money worked everyone into a froth, because it meant that Keith Moore maybe even loved Michelle, or else it meant that he had bought Michelle and now Michelle would have to kiss him or do whatever he wanted and be his slave.

As it would happen, Bunny began volleyball at around the same time, and so it was easy to let go of one world and dive into the next. Practice was a better place for her to be than at the movies platonically holding hands with a boy who told her about his crush on someone else. All of those girls, who had once been her best friends, and all of those boys, who had once been her best friends, were no longer her friends at all. And she entered high school mysteriously friends with nobody at all, despite the fact that she was well liked by everybody, and considered popular by dint of her father's omnipresent quasi-celebrity.

In high school, Ann Marie found true ascendancy. All of the things that had made other children dislike her, the overly high spirits, the bossiness, the meanness, suddenly made her attractive to both boys and girls. Her preening, always fussing over her hair, her clothes. When she complained that her mother had bought her the wrong socks and these ones looked cheap, every girl around her looked down at her own feet and realized she was wearing the wrong ones. Ann Marie took herself so seriously that even the smallest, most pedestrian details of her life were charged. You had to be careful because Dr Pepper Chapstick was actually chemically addicting. Your underwear should be at least as expensive as your shirt. Using vanilla scented products made you irresistible to boys because subliminally they wanted to eat you. This sense of drama, the momentousness of the mundane, was intoxicating to the teen girls around her, and even if they didn't believe everything she said (she was aggressively pro-enema, for instance), talking to her made them feel important. Ann Marie was a creature specially adapted to the unique and fleeting habitat of a white, suburban high school.

By tenth grade she made varsity volleyball and became again a daily presence in Bunny's life. She also began dating Tyler Jenkins, who was on the wrestling team, and she liked to ask other girls in the locker room for water so she could take her teeny tiny birth control pill, just so everyone knew she was taking it, which meant she and Tyler had sex, which meant she was desirable and queenly. And while Bunny disliked Ann Marie, and disliked a world that saw fit to worship her, she also took comfort in the fact that Ann Marie was only five foot six and unwilling to work very hard. She was coordinated and mean, and this had taken her far in the world of high school athletics, but it would never take her where Bunny was going. How could Bunny, then, begrudge her this tiny kingdom, if that was what Ann Marie wanted? Queen of lip gloss, queen of fucking boys, queen of being at the right parties. She would never win a gold medal for that.

And so Bunny found it in her heart to ignore Ann Marie and treat her with a distant respect. She was, after all, part of the team. In the meantime, Bunny had made friends with a girl named Naomi, the only black girl on the volleyball team, who was extremely reserved and stone-faced, but who could really spill the tea once she trusted you and was wickedly hilarious and mean. Naomi was also tall, and also great, and also going places, and also naturally repelled by Ann Marie. "That girl is trivial" was all Naomi had to say about the matter, and so she and Bunny cemented a bond based on being serious about the correct things, and ignoring everything else, though Bunny was never quite as good at the ignoring part as Naomi.

Naomi didn't play with boys. Naomi did schoolwork, church, sports, and not one thing else. She didn't even watch the TV you were supposed to watch. She didn't even help her mother with the cooking. Naomi didn't like me, though I found her intriguing, and I was rarely able to get more than a drowsy "hello" from her in the halls. If pressed about how she was doing, she would always answer the same, "Just getting through it." Bunny and I both wished we could be more like Naomi, and we often spoke about her, wondering where her steely discipline had come from and why we didn't have it. Naomi didn't care if the socks she wore were the "right" socks or the "wrong" socks. Naomi didn't care if not one single boy had a crush on her. And it wasn't just pretense, at least so far as we could tell. She literally gave not two shits about any of us really. She was biding her time. Her real life, she seemed to imply, would begin shortly, and she would dust us completely when she got there.

All things considered, for Ann Marie to be the one to spread the story of how Bunny bit Ryan Brassard was part of a much larger narrative in both of their lives, which made it both worse and better. Bunny assumed that the gossip would die down eventually the way it always had, even though this wound felt so much more personal and terrible than Ann Marie calling her monkey or pointing out her legs were hairy or even TPing her house. But it was not world ending, and it was especially tolerable because in volleyball things were taking an extraordinary turn. They had a new assistant coach, Coach Eric, who was a volleyball player at UCLA forced to take the season off due to a shoulder injury, and he was warm and praising where Coach Creely was cold and withholding. He had dark hair and blue eyes, which made him look slightly malevolent, like a Siberian Husky, even though he was overtly friendly. Of course Bunny had a horrible crush on him; he was six foot seven and she had to look up into his dreamy blue eyes (barf). But it didn't interfere with her playing. In fact, quite the opposite. It was almost as if her hypersensitivity to his gaze supercharged her from moment to moment, causing her to vibrate at an unusual new frequency.

Bunny had her new legs, and Naomi was lit from within by the cold, hard light of securing a college scholarship. It was the only thing Naomi had ever cared about: getting the fuck out of here. Naomi lived in Hawthorne but had secured transfer into North Shore through a series of careful lies. (What was hard was not transferring into our district, but getting Hawthorne to relinquish her and the $60 a day the school would receive for her attendance. If she had to forge a letter saying her mother worked in North Shore for an aerospace company, so be it.) But coming from our (more highly ranked) high school with a 4.23 GPA, making varsity volleyball, varsity basketball, and varsity track, Naomi wasn't just interested in going to college: She was interested in ripping the face off college and fucking its throat. She was interested in burning the whole rigged system to the ground. Once I asked her who her favorite teacher was and she said, "I don't have a favorite."

"You don't like any of them?"

"To be totally honest, I hope they all die," she said.

To say that I adored Naomi would have been an understatement.

On the court, the two of them were a dazzling pair, and I began attending their games, which they couldn't seem to lose, just to watch them. I even dragged my little sister, Gabby, to a couple under the mistaken illusion that she might see in Bunny and Naomi a possible future for herself, but she was unimpressed with the way the girls looked strung like puppets, so smoothly and perfectly did they move in unison. She couldn't feel the power radiating off them, or see the way the entire team was oriented by the guiding pulses their bodies sent out. I took an abstract interest in the concept of sports at that time, maybe because of Anthony's enthusiasm, but I viewed them through my own sociological filter as a vestige of our primordial past.

Part of the reason that man was such a social animal had come from our need to hunt large game together; our ability to work as a group, silently communicating to achieve a goal, was an ancient skill. Of course, plans were made in advance, strategies were devised, huddles had. But once they were on the court, those girls shared a special collective mental space, and in that wordless place, Bunny and Naomi were queens. Every turn of their knee, every flick of their eyes, every twitch of their shoulders was part of the reality they were weaving together in which the team existed. Their power was great enough that it didn't matter to Bunny and Naomi, that at bottom, Ann Marie was their enemy. And that had always been the function of this kind of space, in the hunting party, and in its natural extension: the war party. To insist on the primacy of our social connection. To create the bedrock for morality and society itself. We needed to be able to murder together, and that was exactly why we had to learn to be good to one another, no matter our disagreements or grievances.

The team was greater than the self, and so while Ann Marie prattled to anyone who would listen about how Bunny was a biter, and made jokes like "I thought rabbits were vegetarian!" (*so funny I could scream*), Bunny remained ultimately neutral toward her, and when they were playing, Ann Marie was a dutiful member of Bunny's conquering army.

And conquer they did. They were Division 1, the best in Southern California, and they had already won enough games to secure a spot in the semifinals of the state championship, which was scheduled for November 7.

To review: Bunny's date with Ryan Brassard was in July, Donna Morse's murder was August 28, the first day of school was September 6, the semifinals were going to be November 7, the anniversary of Bunny's mother's death was October 25, and Bunny's eighteenth birthday was October 28.

Bunny once told me about the day her mother died. This is what she said:

"I was in second grade, and I got pulled out of class and taken to the principal's office. I thought I'd done something wrong, but no one would tell me what it was, no one would tell me until my dad got there. I remember he was wearing sunglasses and he didn't take them off, even when he was inside the office, even as he signed me out he kept them on, so his eyes were just shiny black bulges, like a bug's. And everyone looked so sad, but I still didn't know, I still didn't know why, until we got out to the car, and I could smell the new leather of his car, getting in that hot car, and he didn't turn on the engine right away, and I kept thinking: Please turn it on, turn on the air, roll down the windows. But he turned to me, and he still had his sunglasses on, and he said, 'Your mother's been in an accident.' And for ten minutes after that, I still thought she was alive, because he was making it sound like that. I assumed we were going to the hospital to go see her, and I kept asking how bad it was, and he said, 'Bad,' and I kept asking, but he just said, 'Bad, Bunny.'

"But he didn't drive us to the hospital. He drove us to McDonald's, and he bought us milkshakes. We were sitting on a bench outside by the play area, which is a place we had spent a lot of time, and I wanted to go play but I knew I couldn't, and I felt so creepy because I knew all of this was staged. He was taking me somewhere and making it be a certain way. He had planned that he would buy me a milkshake and tell me here, but I still didn't know what he was going to tell me. As soon as he finally told me, I felt this strange hiss of release, because now they wouldn't fight anymore. Now there would be quiet in our house.

"And I knew that wasn't the reaction that I was supposed to

have, and that I was being watched carefully, that I was supposed to have a reaction and it needed to be the right reaction, because he had set up this whole scenario, this whole space that was designed to hold my reaction, but I had no idea what it was supposed to be. They had been fighting so badly for so long that I worried he would think I was siding with her if I cried, but of course I was devastated at the loss of her, I mean, she was my mother.

"I know that's stupid now. Obviously, he was expecting me to cry. I was seven, well, almost eight, but I was a kid. That's why he had bought me the milkshake. That's why he had tried to take me someplace happy. But at the time, I thought it was some sort of secret deal he was offering: If you accept her absence, then everything will be milkshakes between you and me. If you let go of her, then I will love you, and I will be fun dad, and everything will be okay. And honestly, it seemed like a great deal. A scary deal, but one I could not afford to pass up. So I snuggled into his arms and I asked him if Mommy was in heaven, and he said yes.

"And the older I got, the grosser my reaction seemed to me. My mother had died, and I thought it was part of the war between my mother and father? And I had better side with the victor if I still wanted to get milkshakes. Because. You know. Look what had happened to her.

"I had always thought that, on some level. That he had caused her to die. Not literally, like he had arranged the accident. But mystically. Psychically. Like the force of his personality had bucked her off like a thrown rider, to say: Life is for Ray Lampert. You must go elsewhere.

"And every year, all day long, when it's the day, when it's her day, I feel like I'm trapped in that hot car, begging him to turn on the engine and start the air. So, yeah, that's why I don't really like Halloween or my birthday."

Indeed, Bunny hated Halloween. She hated everything about it. She hated the day itself, she hated movies about witches, she hated pumpkin carving, she hated costumes of any kind, she hated haunted houses, she hated fake teeth, she hated fog machines, she hated the song "Thriller." She even hated the color orange. Because that year, her mother not yet buried, Ray Lampert took her trick-or-treating, and kept asking, "Are you having fun?"

And Bunny had said yes. She'd said, "Yes, Daddy!" Because that was what she thought she was supposed to say.

Sometimes I wonder: Did Bunny really say all of that to me? I have presented it here in quotations. But the memory is years distant now. I feel I can recall it so clearly. But was she really that insightful? Sometimes I wish she wasn't. Sometimes I wish she was just a big dumb cow that all this happened to.

7

On October 28 I knew it was Bunny's birthday and so I had gone to Starbucks early and gotten Bunny's order, which was a caramel macchiato and a pumpkin scone. (Bunny could not get fat no matter what she ate, and honestly, it was disgusting to watch.) I brought it to her house and rang the doorbell and she popped out, like she always did, and she was happy I had brought her a treat. We walked together, then parted ways at school: she had Spanish; I had AP English. "Don't worry," I told her, "soon it will be over," and she nodded. The span of time between the anniversary of her mother's death and Halloween was absolute torture each year, and she always felt like she'd escaped something if she made it to the first day of November.

I saw her in the hallway before lunch, but she said she was going to the library because she had to finish her homework for sixth period, and I didn't press it.

About three p.m., right as I was leaving AP French and was going to head home and get changed for my shift at Rite Aid, I saw an ambulance pull up in front of the school. I had time, I wasn't in a rush, and so I waited to see who the ambulance was there for. The paramedics took their gurney and scurried toward the gym. I thought one of the girls had probably passed out or something. That happened last spring when there was a heat wave, a girl had passed out during band practice because she stood with her knees locked for too long. When the paramedics came back, they were trotting and the girl lying there had the oxygen mask on, but her face was unmistakably bloody and already swelling in a way that looked fake. Her nose was under her left eye like a cubist painting. She was not awake or moving. It was Ann Marie.

Half the volleyball team was trotting after her down the hall, and Coach Creely was working her way past them, yelling at them to go back to the locker room and finish getting showered and to go the hell home, except then Principal Cardenas, who wore a lot of pencil skirts and pendant necklaces, came out of the office and into the hall and said that no, all the girls needed to stay because they were going to be interviewed by the police, and she ushered them into the reception area of the main office, a fishbowl-style room paneled in glass. There weren't enough chairs in there to hold them all, and the volleyball girls were all unusually tall and big anyway, so they looked positively crammed in there, a herd of giraffes. I kept waiting, thinking Bunny would come, or that she was already in the fishbowl and I would see her, but I didn't.

Then Naomi came, walking up the hallway all by herself.

"What happened?" I asked her. She shook her head, like she couldn't talk, wouldn't. Like if she opened her mouth a frog would push out.

"That was Ann Marie, right? What happened, I mean—did she fall? Like, off something? Or?"

"Bunny hit her."

"No."

Naomi had reached where I stood in the hall and she closed her eyes and bowed her head and let out a big sigh. "Jesus, that was crazy, Michael. That was some of the craziest shit I've ever seen."

"What happened?"

"We were changing, and Ann Marie was, you know, just talking talking talking, and I guess Bunny had enough because she—still in her bra and panties, hadn't even finished changing— just goes over there, and grabs her, starts smashing her head into her locker. Boom, boom, boom. Sounded like celery wrapped in meat, like, just *crunching*." Naomi's face was screwed up tight at the memory of this sound. She shook her head again.

"Nobody could get her off, I mean, nobody tried, it all happened fast, and then she had her on the ground, and we were all yelling, stop, stop, you know? And it looked like she wasn't going to, and she was just going to kill her? But then she suddenly leapt off, like, wham, she was off her, like Ann Marie's body was electrified and she got shocked. And she starts going, 'I'm sorry, I'm so sorry, I'm so sorry, oh god, what happened?' Like she didn't even know. So." Naomi shrugged.

"Where is Bunny now?"

"She's still in there with Coach Eric. I mean, I think they're gonna let her shower before they arrest her or whatever."

"But what was it about?" I asked. "What was Ann Marie saying that made Bunny lose it?"

"Honestly, I wasn't paying attention. I pretty much just tune that girl out, and I was thinking about this calc test I took earlier." Naomi shrugged and then did an uncharacteristic thing, which was spit on the floor. "I hate this place," she said to me very seriously and calmly.

I did not ask Naomi to clarify, even though her comment bewildered me. What did her hatred of high school have to do with this sudden display of violence and what could only be a very bad outcome for our mutual friend? I did not understand, did not have the tools, the lenses and filters for understanding how all of this seemed to Naomi. Our collective whiteness. Our glistening safety. Our innocence displayed, as though it were a virtue instead of a collective cosseting. A sniveling softness. Children, wandering around in adult bodies, swiping their parents' credit cards to buy sugary drinks at Starbucks. The kind of place Ann Marie could be queen of. The kind of place Bunny could be fool enough to lose.

—

I didn't want to barge into the girls' locker room, but if it was just Bunny and Coach Eric in there, it seemed like my only chance to talk to her. I hesitated at the door, my fingers just touching the metal curve of the push-bar, listening. Did I hear voices? I heard something, but it sounded like a machine, rhythmic and low, like a pump system or a vacuum being pushed in a repetitive pattern. I pushed the door open a crack, and I could see down the hallway of lockers that led to the showers.

I saw Coach Eric. I saw Bunny. She was in her bra and panties, and she had blood on her chest and on her stomach. She was sitting right next to Coach Eric on a bench. There was a puddle of puke on the floor between her feet. She was barefoot, and her feet were spread far apart to keep from getting in the puddle of puke. He was rubbing her bare back, up and down, up and down, with his big hand, and murmuring to her, like they were lovers. Bunny was the one making the noise I had heard, a kind of labored breathing in between sobbing and hyperventilation. *Havroom, havroom.* Like she was scraping something clean inside herself.

Coach Eric was the one who saw me. "Hey, kid, get out of here!" he shouted. Bunny didn't even look up, just puked again between her legs, her knees and ankles splaying dramatically, almost balletically, to get out of the way of her own bile. I jerked away from the door and ran down the hall, my shoes squeaking on the tile, as though I had been caught at something truly shameful.

I called Ray Lampert and left a message, telling him what I knew of the situation. I called Bunny's cell phone and left a message, begging her to call me. As I left the voicemails, my legs continued to carry me, walking on autopilot through our town, past houses where boats and RVs blocked the driveway, where giant trampolines took over the front yard, where happiness was a garage full of camping equipment and bins of children's cleats in every size. Before I knew it, I was in front of Rite Aid, though I still wasn't sure if I should go in, or if I should call in sick somehow in case Bunny needed me.

I remember there was a massive magnolia tree across the street, like this was some other place, Georgia maybe, and not Southern California at all. That's when I realized something odd. There were no palm trees in North Shore. The newer city plantings were slightly more adapted to the climate: orchid trees and succulent beds. But most of the plants and flowers were East Coast transplants. Deciduous trees providing the illusion of autumn. The thick almost-painted-looking leaves of cannas borrowing the humidity of southern summers left behind. And that's when I started to feel really creepy. Because North Shore was a fake place, a manufactured town. I had always liked that about it, thought I accepted it. But now it was creepy the way a stage set is creepy after the show has ended. The way an empty costume is creepy. And I kept thinking of Bunny puking between her naked legs, Ann Marie's blood drying brown on her belly, and about Naomi spitting on the floor, and about the mosaic of bone Luke had made out of Donna Morse's head.

I texted Anthony. I typed: *I'm in love with you. Please say you love me too. Please just say those words because I need them.*

I saw that the message was read almost immediately. And there were three dots, which meant he was typing, and then they went away, and then the message came:

I am wildly, passionately, truly, and deliriously in love with you, Michael.

I texted: *Oh fuck, thank god.*

He texted back a smiley face.

And then I went to work.

The first sexual fantasy I ever had, I developed when I was maybe eleven years old. I had known I was gay for some time by then, and I had crushes on boys, but I could not fantasize about them, and I had not yet figured out masturbation. I would just try to go to bed and develop a hard-on and sort of roll around, squirming, for hours. I did not dare to picture kissing one of the boys I liked at school. When I tried to imagine kissing one of them, they inevitably shoved me away or laughed at me. Instead, I imagined some kind of alternate reality wherein all men were gay and used other men as sex objects, almost in the same way that men use women in this world, only, for whatever reason, in my childish brain, I imagined the men being used as sex objects as being inside furniture. We were inside chairs and desks and tables and bookshelves, and there would just be holes cut out so that men could have sex with us while we were inside the furniture.

That was the most I could picture for myself.

Halfway through my shift, I got a text from Bunny. It said: *At home now. I'm so sorry. I made everything worse. I know you can never forgive me.*

My first reaction was almost to laugh. Of course I would forgive her. I mean, wouldn't I? How could I not forgive her? She was my best and only friend. We had made ourselves sick eating Funyuns and doing impressions of Johnny Depp together. We had written extended ode-like text messages about our favorite drag queens. I had let her meet Gabby and my mother. Just once, and for about twenty minutes, but it had occurred, locking us together in an overlap of worlds that could not be easily undone.

Don't be silly, I texted, hiding in the bathroom at work. *I will come by after my shift.*

You really want to see me?

I was baffled by this, but I knew I couldn't keep hiding out in the bathroom forever, I wasn't even on break, and so I didn't respond, and just slipped my phone into my pocket. Toward the end of my shift, a kid I didn't recognize, who was older, maybe in his early twenties, hissed "Faggot" at me as he left the store. I hadn't even been the one to ring him up, I'd just been standing there, organizing my cash drawer so that when I had to count out it would go faster. Truthfully, I had never been called "faggot" in that kind of menacing fashion, though I had imagined being called "faggot" in such a way many times. It seemed almost like it was a common occurrence, so often had I mentally prepared for it to happen, but for it to actually happen seemed purely bizarre and theatrical to me. Like seeing someone dressed up for Halloween on a regular day.

Terrence came up behind me.

"Did that kid say something to you?" he asked.

"No," I said.

At Bunny's house, it was a bit like being let into the control room. They had their supplies and they were hunkered down. Ray had a glass of scotch going and seemed to be eating an entire pizza by himself. Bunny had an array of ice cream and chips around her on the coffee table, and there was an empty liter bottle of Mountain Dew next to the couch. The news was on at full volume, CNN, so national news, and its purpose seemed to be either to distract or else to just project an air of gravitas. They couldn't watch a sitcom and accidentally laugh or have a moment of pleasure. On her stomach was a heating pad, and on her hand was an ice pack. Her hand was already swollen to almost twice its normal size and a weird magenta color. "I'll go to the doctor in the morning," she said.

My impulse, since I was her friend, was to act as if this were something that had happened to her, instead of something she had done. "Your poor hand!" I cried, as though she had not hurt her hand bashing a girl's head in.

"I can move all the fingers," she said. We both looked up as Ray answered a call on his cell phone and went into the kitchen to pace and talk.

"How is Ann Marie?" I asked, because I didn't want to ask why Bunny hadn't been arrested. Or perhaps she had been and had already been let out on bail. I didn't know how those things worked. We had not been able to afford bail for my own mother. In movies it seemed like the kind of thing you could do in a day, but movies were terribly inaccurate regarding the banalities of the court system.

"She's okay. My dad went to the hospital and kind of smoothed things over."

"Oh yeah?"

"Yeah, basically he is going to pay for her nose job, because, you know, insurance might not cover the very best plastic surgeon, so he promised to hook them up and cover the difference and all her medical bills and all that."

Bunny looked a little bit green.

"Well, that's good," I said.

She nodded, not looking at me, and I realized she was about to start crying. "He told them he'd get them a house. He told them he'd make sure they got a house for below market. They've been trying to buy for like two years. And, basically, like, he bribed them. He fucking bribed them not to press charges. And I feel so sick, I keep thinking I'm asleep. Like, I can't keep track of what's real."

"So you didn't get arrested or anything?"

"No, well, the DA could still press charges. So I still have to go to the police station tomorrow morning. But that was basically the whole afternoon. Dad's lawyer was over here prepping me."

"Prepping you in what sense?"

"How to lie. Essentially. What to say."

"What are you supposed to say?"

"That I went to hit her and then I fell and she fell with me and bonked her head and I crashed on top of her and she hit her head again on the bench on the way down."

"And that's not what happened?"

"Well, I mean, I don't know." She looked at me blankly.

"What do you mean you don't know?"

"I don't remember most of it." She was playing with the pendant of her necklace, a tiny silver hippo no bigger than her pinky nail, scraping it back and forth across the chain on her neck. "I remember being so mad at her and walking over to her, and then it was like waking up, I just sort of came to on top of her."

"What happened anyway?" I asked. "I mean, what triggered it?"

The tiny hippo went scrape, scrape, scrape on the chain at her throat. Bunny's eyes were unfocused and I didn't know if she was thinking about how to answer or if she was completely zoned out. "Fucking hell," we heard Ray Lampert yell in the kitchen and then a horrible clatter, like pots and pans falling from high up, and then glass shattering. We ran in to him, and then ran out of the kitchen just as quickly. He was taking plates out of the cupboard one by one and sending them sailing across the room to shatter on the marble floor. He swept the metal fruit basket filled with junk to the floor. He threw a full bottle of wine. We waited, crouched and panting outside the door of the kitchen. Just as suddenly as he began, he seemed to stop. "Fucking hell," he said again, but this time slower and sad.

"What is it, Daddy?" Bunny asked from the doorway in her best good-girl voice, still too afraid to enter the kitchen.

"Ann Marie has a bleed in her brain."

The CT scan Ann Marie had in the emergency room had shown a concussion but no hematoma, but then, just as they were getting ready to discharge her, she'd started slurring her words. Gotten real sleepy.

The result of the second CT scan showed a very small subdural hematoma in her occipital lobe. The result of the third CT scan a few hours later showed a slightly larger subdural hematoma in her occipital lobe. The bleed was growing and it was putting pressure on her brain. They were rushing her to surgery to drill a hole through her skull to try to relieve the pressure. And then she would be put in a medically induced coma.

Battery on school property was Section 243.2 in the California penal code. Even if Ann Marie's parents didn't want the DA to press charges, and who knew if Ray's magical house promise would still stand in the face of a brain bleed, the state still could. It would all depend on the mind-set of the prosecutor. Prosecutors, Ray's lawyer had explained, had almost unfettered discretion in which cases they prosecuted.

Their decision would depend on the seriousness of Ann Marie's injuries, which were growing more serious by the second. And Bunny would be tried as an adult because the crime had been committed on her literal eighteenth birthday.

"I can't fucking be here," Ray Lampert said, looking around at the kitchen filled with broken glass. "I'm gonna go to Charity's. I'll call you as I hear stuff." He shuffled through the glass in his slippers, trying not to pick up his feet or get cut. "Jesus Christ," he said, before walking out the front door, still in his bedroom slippers, a glass of scotch in his hand.

"Who is Charity?" I asked.

"I don't really know," Bunny said. "I assume he's dating her."

Without Ray in the house, we were able to function more smoothly. We muted the news and began to sweep the broken debris in the kitchen into piles as we talked.

"I just feel so, so sick," Bunny said. "What do I do? Do I go in there tomorrow and lie? How on earth can that be the right thing to do?"

"But if you tell the truth, what will happen?"

"I'll probably go to jail. I don't know. I don't have any priors."

All I could think about was my mother. I pulled out the trash bin from its built-in cubby and began to ferry the bigger pieces of broken glass and porcelain into it. Everything was dripping with wine. "Bunny," I said, "judges don't like violent women. I don't know how to say this. My mom cut my dad superficially with a fruit knife and she got three years. If a man had done it, if it was just a regular domestic violence dispute and the woman who got stabbed, he probably wouldn't have even seen the inside of a jail cell."

"You think?"

"I don't know," I said. "Maybe that's an exaggeration. But that's what it seems like. I mean, look at Luke and Donna Morse. How was he not in jail for beating her all those times? My mom said it's different when it's the woman who's violent. It strikes people as abnormal. Like, it's natural for a guy to just 'lose his temper,' but if a woman does the same thing, then it's a sign of something deeper wrong, like psychologically or almost metaphysically."

Bunny continued sweeping. The broom's bristles were getting stained by the wine and it seemed like maybe we were just making a bigger mess.

"But I deserve to be punished," Bunny said.

"Listen, I trust you. I trust you to be punished. I trust you to learn from this and move on and make it right, and I trust you to accept and live through whatever winds up happening. What I don't trust is for the system to deal fairly with you, because the system—well, the system will just not deal fairly with you."

"So you think I should lie?"

"I think you should follow the advice of the lawyer you are lucky your father retained for you."

"And I should allow my dad to bribe Ann Marie's parents?"

"Could you stop him?" I asked.

Bunny laughed. "That's the real joke, all these years I thought I was somehow 'keeping him in line,' like I was the one running everything. Like I had any control over what he did or didn't do."

"Okay, if we get the big pieces in, then I'll get the dustpan for the little pieces, and then where's the mop? We should mop because the wine is seriously gonna stain this white marble."

It was only as we were saying good night that I found out.

We were on her porch. It was late and cold and the town was hushed enough that you could hear the Pacific in the distance, roaring as it hit the shore. Crickets chirruped. "I'm just so sorry," Bunny said, twisting up her hands inside the sleeves of her sweatshirt. "I know my heart was in the right place, but I wasn't thinking. Obviously. I mean, I just wanted her to shut up, I wasn't thinking about how my, like, attacking her would make it even bigger gossip."

"Don't apologize," I said. I thought she was talking about the gossip of her biting Ryan Brassard's ear. I thought she was talking about how now there would be two strikes against her, the bite and the attack, that she would be seen as a monster.

"Does your aunt know?"

"I have no idea," I said honestly.

"Well, just let me know how it all goes at home. I know she kind of knows you're gay, but I mean—I just assume if *I* didn't know you were dating someone, then *she* doesn't know you were dating someone."

It was like the moment in a dream before something terrible happens and the perspective shatters and you start seeing everything from three different camera angles at once.

"Oh god, you didn't know," she said. "I thought for sure you knew. I knew you saw Naomi and the team, and when I texted you I already thought you knew and I said I was sorry and you said don't be silly, so I thought you knew."

"Well. Obviously, I don't know."

"The reason I attacked Ann Marie was because she was talking about you."

All the darkness of the night was trying to get inside my mouth.

"I guess she saw you and some guy kissing in a car. And she recognized you, but she also recognized the guy. I guess he used to work with her dad at SpaceX and he's like sixty, and she was all, 'I went to that guy's retirement party! He's a fucking geezer, it's so gross.' And I just—I just wanted to shut her mouth. I just wanted to make words stop coming out of her mouth. She was calling him a pedophile and, like, how could you be into it, and I—"

I was nodding, rapidly, as though that could help the shame disperse more quickly through my bloodstream. I knew instantly that Ann Marie had been telling the truth—that she really did know Anthony. No part of me considered for even a moment that she was wrong, that she had been mistaken when she recognized him. It was a small world, a small town, a small piece of a big city. Of course he had lied to me. Of course he was older than his profile, just as I was younger than my profile. He had fucking gray hair for lord's sake! Of course that's why he was always available in the daytime. He didn't have a job because he was fucking retired. He was looking for something secret on the side because he was in the closet, probably married forty years. He probably had kids. He probably had kids older than me. That was the shame—that I had known and refused to know, and now someone had turned on the lights to reveal that I had been humping a doll, not something real, but something false, constructed by my own wishful thinking.

"I have to go," I said. "It's late."

"Michael," Bunny said.

"Are you going to be okay?" I asked. "Without your dad here?"

"He'll probably come back before morning," she said. "I mean, I assume he's not gonna let me go to the police by myself."

"Right," I said. And I walked to the sidewalk and turned up my own front steps, so upset and surprised that I was both blind and numb, barely able to work my key in the lock, horrified at the idea of talking to anyone, of anyone even seeing my face. I could just imagine it, Ann Marie laughing and saying, "What a fucking pedo!"

8

Probably I would have had a torturous night under any conditions, but to have to exist in my current mental state, which was essentially a strobe of shameful images, imagining Ann Marie laughing, imagining other kids at school making grossed-out faces as they heard the story, imagining Bunny slamming Ann Marie's head into the lockers over and over again, hearing Naomi's voice, *like celery wrapped in meat, like, just crunching,* imagining Anthony kissing his children on the head, imagining Anthony attending his children's high school graduations, imagining Anthony having sex with his wife, imagining Anthony teaching his kids to drive, buying them cars, when I would never learn to drive, and I would never be able to afford a car, and I would become a bus person, and I would not be saved; to imagine all of this in a fast-forward phantasmagoria while also sitting in the same room as my farting, burping cousin Jason, who was playing *Call of Duty* on his computer late, late into the night, wearing headphones, so all I could hear was his gross voice talking to his buddies through his headset and the plastic creaking of the controls as he hammered them, pretending to shoot imaginary people, was creating such a high-pitched distress inside my body that it seemed impossible that I could continue to lie there unmoving, scrolling through my phone.

I was obsessively monitoring the Instagram and Facebook accounts of everyone we knew. I wanted to know what was happening to Ann Marie, but I also wanted to know if anyone was talking about Anthony and me. If the gossip spread far and fast enough, it would enter my household, and I was genuinely uncertain if I would still be allowed to keep living there once Aunt Deedee knew that my sexuality was no longer merely theoretical (and therefore clean, sympathetic even), but now actual (and therefore dirty, saturated with human fluid, dangerous).

In the same way that certain brands of toothpaste house the component colors of the toothpaste in separate chambers before a compression pump unites them on the brush, my mind seemed to contain two contradictory paradigms that nevertheless existed simultaneously: 1. The gossip might stay contained to the world of high school, and there were pretty even odds of whether or not Jason, who would no doubt hear tomorrow that I was gay and making out with grandads in cars, would tell Aunt Deedee. After all, he told Aunt Deedee nothing else that went on. And even if he did tell her, couldn't I deny it? The only person who had actually seen me was now in a medically induced coma. I could pretend it was just a vicious rumor. Maybe she would even feel badly that I was being bullied at school. I made good grades, I worked a job, I paid for my own clothing and food, and last month I had even paid her electric bill because she was a month behind. She wasn't going to just kick me to the curb. 2. Her face would go dark when she found out. Jason would tell her immediately, and her reaction would be visceral. Hadn't she told me? No boys in the house. And didn't we both know that it meant: No boys? Sure, I hadn't brought a man home, but I had behaved so foolishly that now the entire town knew I was thirsty for seniors. Jason would refuse to share a room with a "known homo."

I had been living in a careful system of Don't Ask, Don't Tell and I had violated the agreement, and now the bonds of family and obligation would be null and void. In such circumstances, returning to my mother's household would be out of the question. Just yesterday, I might have fantasized about running away with Anthony, but now that idea seemed flimsy and childish. Really, the best outcome I could possibly see would be if Ray Lampert would loan me the money to put a deposit down on a studio apartment and quit school so I could work full-time. And if he wouldn't lend me the money, then perhaps Terrence would. And if Terrence wouldn't, then perhaps I would live in a shelter. Didn't they have shelters? Or maybe I could buy a beater car and just live in the car? I didn't even know how to drive. The one thing that was tripping me up was that I couldn't imagine staying in North Shore. I would have to get a new job. I would have to start entirely over. It was too much to think about.

And so I scrolled and scrolled through my phone. Ann Marie's accounts were silent, obviously. She wasn't well enough to post dramatic ER selfies.

I checked Kelsey's Snapchat, another girl on the volleyball team, best friends with Ann Marie. There she was, in the hospital waiting room, looking somber in a selfie. She had put crying-face emojis over it and the text running across the bottom in a stripe said: "Praying for my best friend." Then I checked the Snapchat stories of the rest of the team. Half of them were in that hospital waiting room or had spent some portion of the evening there. Even Naomi was there. She had taken a picture of Ann Marie's mother, Ms. Harriet, her shoulders hunched, staring off into space, sitting under a TV she wasn't watching. Her face looked numb and frozen, as though if you pinched her it would feel like chicken breasts that hadn't thawed all the way. The text Naomi had chosen said: "Psalm 34:19." I didn't know the Bible, had never been to church even as a child, and while I knew Naomi went to church every Sunday I had not given this considerable thought. It was just something she did, the same way she did her homework. In my defense, so many of her opinions were openly blasphemous that a display of sincere religiosity caught me off guard.

I googled the Psalm, and it said: "The righteous person may have many troubles, but the LORD delivers him from them all."

Was Ann Marie the righteous person? Was that how it seemed to Naomi?

I couldn't imagine what she meant, although there was

something about the word "righteous" that did ring a distant mental bell. Almost as though you didn't have to seem right, you had to actually be right. Straight and unbent. True. Inside yourself, the circuitry untangled and clear.

I looked at the picture of Ann Marie's mother and I understood that her baby girl had been attacked, her face mutilated, her brain damaged. And she might die tonight.

For the first time that day, I understood that it was real. That Bunny had done this monstrous thing, and that none of it could ever be undone.

When I woke up in the morning I had a text from Anthony. It said:

> *Sometimes I am terrified of what we are doing. I read these lines by Jack Gilbert last night and thought of you: A feudal world crushed under / the weight of passion without feeling. / Gianna's virgin body helplessly in love. / The young man wild with romance and appetite. / Wondering whether he would ruin her by mistake.*

I read the poem almost numb, and I could feel one part of my brain go down the familiar track of sympathy and delight, that Anthony felt these big feelings, that Anthony framed his life so metaphysically, and I was interested in this "passion without feeling," what a phrase. What did that mean: to have passion without feeling? Some kind of numb, ecstatic frenzy! And wasn't the young virgin to be pitied? And wasn't the young man wild with romance and appetite to be pitied? And weren't all these big dramatic feelings to be pitied and explored and charted and indexed and treated with the same reverence an astronomer feels toward the stars?

And on the other hand, I thought: You fucking pathetic piece of trash. Send poetry to your wife. Stop finding children to explore your romantic feelings with. Because really, what was he saying? He was saying I was the young virgin Gianna, and he was the young man wild with romance and appetite. Wasn't that it? But he wasn't a young man wild with romance and appetite. He was a sixty-year-old man who had made a mess of his life by refusing to be honest with himself. And it struck me as boring and gross. As boring and gross and sad as the fact that I had been having sex with adult men since I was thirteen years old because I was so ashamed of myself, and so terrified, that I didn't think a boy my own age would be interested. I didn't think I was worth something more normal. I didn't think the happiness I saw all around me was on the menu for me.

I texted back, *I don't have time to go through this right now, I'm going to high school, talk to you later. By the way, do you have grandkids?*

And I hit send, cruelty flushing through my veins like adrenaline, energizing my limbs with an eerie cold.

Bunny was not in school. Ann Marie was not in school. Naomi was in school, and even though we sometimes ate lunch together with Bunny, when I saw her in the cafeteria, sitting with the rest of the volleyball team, she wouldn't meet my gaze, and I understood that she would not be sitting with me or being seen with me or associated with me in any way. And it made sense. She was going to jettison Bunny as quickly as a sandbag falling hoists a piece of scenery out of view in a play. Naomi was here to win. An association with Bunny would only harm her standing on the team and more largely in the school. In fact, without Bunny, she was the uncontested star player of the team and would stand out even more strikingly to recruiters. I also think Naomi was truly disgusted by Bunny's behavior. And why shouldn't she be?

In thinking about all of this, I realized that no matter what happened, even if all charges were dropped, even in a best-case scenario, there was no way that Bunny would be allowed back on the team. Her volleyball career was effectively over. It appeared that now she would be six foot three for no particular reason.

I wondered how things had gone at the police station, or if perhaps she was still there. I wondered whether she was under arrest. Or getting her hand X-rayed at Urgent Care. Or sitting at home watching RuPaul and understanding piece by piece that her life was ruined. Maybe that was a dramatic way of putting it. She was still a young white woman after all. There was still that marble kitchen, though we had not been able to get up the wine stains, blurry rust-colored splashes that we had coated in baking soda because the internet told us to. Her father would undoubtedly be able to afford to send her to college. Though her grades were bad. That had never seemed to matter because of the volleyball, but now it didn't seem good. But she could go to community college.

Unless she was in jail. Though she probably wouldn't go to jail. She had no priors. Her father was rich and powerful. So much depended, I realized, on Ann Marie.

I wondered how her surgery had gone.

When I got out of school, I had a text from Anthony. It said, *I wonder why you would say something so hurtful to me. No, I do not have grandchildren. Why would you ask that?*

I read the message over and over as I walked, and I didn't know what I wanted to say back. I wasn't sure why I was so angry at Anthony. It wasn't really that I was angry with him for lying. The issue was not trust. I didn't trust anyone, and the idea of expecting to trust someone and then being miffed to discover I could not seemed a luxury so laughable I could have spit on the floor like Naomi. No, it was not that Anthony had betrayed my trust. It was simply that he was older than I thought he was and that made him seem pathetic to me, and it made me feel pathetic for loving him, and I did love him.

So gross, Ann Marie's voice said helpfully in my mind. *What a pedo. He could be your granddad.*

How can you touch his wrinkly old skin?

What does he even smell like? Like old sweaters? Like talcum powder?

I realized that what was unworthy in Anthony, what was so deeply uncool about being old, was that he was closer to death. And we disdained death, didn't we? The glossy young. We looked at death and wrinkled our noses, rolled our eyes: yuck. We would have shiny hard penises forever. We would cuddle only the most velvety vulvas. Our cells would always have perfect plump walls. Our mitochondria would gush ATP like limitless fountains. We would stay young by fucking young, and we would never fuck the old, because that was how death got in—through your skin. Through your heart.

I got to Bunny's house and rang the doorbell, but there was no answer. I opened her side gate and went around the back and peered in the windows, but I couldn't see anyone. I had texted her several times throughout the day with no response. It didn't seem like a good sign. I turned and looked at her pool, and I had the instinct to swim, but it was too cold. I looked up the bus routes instead. It would take two hours to get to Cedars-Sinai, where Ann Marie was.

I sat on Bunny's patio furniture, examining my motivations. It wasn't exactly that I wanted to spy on Ann Marie so that I could report to Bunny on her medical condition, though, of course, I was desperate for any new information so that I could adjust my own internal Vegas odds on how things would play out legally for Bunny. Goodness knows I did not expect to speak to Ann Marie herself, since she was supposed to be in a coma. If anything, the fact that she was in a coma made visiting her more appealing. I was not sure I could have handled an awake Ann Marie, not least because she wouldn't be at all glad to see me. But I did not want to go home and run the risk of having some kind of conversation with Jason or Aunt Deedee. I would delay opening that envelope for as long as I could.

I suppose what I wanted most was to see Ann Marie's mother, Ms. Harriet, and bring flowers, and try my best to indicate that whatever Ann Marie had said about me, she hadn't deserved this.

I boarded the 625 bus on Main Street, holding the outrageously overpriced flowers I had bought from the local florist. As gouged as I felt by the price, the experience of buying the flowers had been nice. The woman who ran the shop had a black cat and he sat regally, as though it were a throne, on a child's armchair arranged artfully in the window of the shop, surrounded by buckets and buckets of flowers. She had picked out yellow and pink tulips and tied them up with scraggly brown string that looked like a thousand women's Pinterest wet dreams.

The bouquet looked strange to me, in my own hands, as I boarded the bus. How weird it was—to cut off the sexual organs of plants and give them to each other. I hoped Ms. Harriet would not see the stamens tucked inside the tulips as tiny penises the way I did. I hoped they would look like regular flowers to her, and I would look like a regular boy.

I had not anticipated how restrictive the visitation policy would be, and I was surprised, when I finally found Ann Marie's floor in the Saperstein Critical Care Tower, to speak to the nurse at the front desk and be told that I could most definitely not enter. "I brought flowers," I said. "Maybe I could just leave them?"

"Sure you can," the nurse said.

I frowned. I did not have a card, or even a piece of paper on which to write my name or explain whom they were from. I had ridden two hours on three different buses to get here. The nurse was jarring to me in her calm casualness. After all, she was at work. This was a regular day for her, and here was a kid hemming and hawing with flowers, and she didn't have time to deal with him, did she?

Then Ms. Harriet, Ann Marie's mother, appeared and saved me.

"My lord, it's Michael Hesketh," she proclaimed in that low voice of hers. "Come here and hug me, son," she said. "Oh, you brought flowers. Bless your heart. Don't tell me you think this was your fault."

I walked toward her in the hall and she folded me up into a fierce hug. Her arms felt like iron bars through her sweater. "I was going to the cafeteria, care to join me?"

I walked with her to the elevators, still carrying the flowers she had not taken from me, grateful to be in the sway of her powerful and practical energy. Ms. Harriet had the peculiar ability of collapsing things flat. Of turning shades of gray back into black and white. As soon as the elevator doors closed on us, she said, "I want you to know, before we continue any further, that I'm deeply ashamed that Ann Marie was picking on you like that. Not that it excuses Bunny Lampert, obviously, but I want you to know, I did not raise my daughter to be a homophobe or a gossip. I don't hold with that."

I blushed and stared down at the floor of the elevator. "Oh, gosh, Ms. Harriet, you don't have to—"

"You know the part of this I still cannot fathom?" Ms. Harriet said. I looked up at her to meet her gaze and realized that her blue eyes were half-insane. "That it was Bunny. I just—you know, I helped raise her. She always seemed like such a good egg to me. Which just goes to show—" She gestured wildly with her arms in the elevator and I had no idea what it went to show.

"It just goes to show," Ms. Harriet said, as the doors dinged open on the busy scene of the cafeteria, "it's always the preacher's son. Doesn't matter what you teach them, it's what's in them at the start."

I nodded and followed her as we entered the line to order.

"Look, they have chili," Ms. Harriet said. "I wonder if it's good."

While it felt surreal to be expected to genuinely provide insight as to the quality of the hospital chili, Ms. Harriet's only child was upstairs in a medically induced coma, her brain so swollen they'd drilled a hole in her skull. I myself had seen her nose pushed under her left eye, like a Picasso. Ms. Harriet had carte blanche to say whatever the fuck she wanted.

"What are you getting?" she asked me.

"Probably just this banana," I said, holding it up.

"Get some real food," she urged. "Get the tuna melt, and that way if my chili is mediocre, then I can have some of yours. My treat. Oh, but look, they have taco bowls."

In the end, we wound up ordering all three entrées, as well as a Diet Dr Pepper and a large black coffee. We settled with our food at one of the tables. The cafeteria furnishings were nice, but there were no windows and the light was bad and bright in a way that reminded me of the Rite Aid.

"I just—I kind of wonder if she had some kind of break."

"Bunny?" I asked.

Ms. Harriet was blowing on her chili, looking expectantly at me. I did not want to give too much away, wasn't sure if I should play into or deny such a break. There was too much at stake legally.

"I have no idea," I said. "I don't know how that stuff works."

"Her poor father," Ms. Harriet said.

"Yeah," I said, though I found this surprising. I would have thought a person like Ray Lampert would be anathema to a practical being like Ms. Harriet.

"I mean, he worked so hard to make her mother happy. You should have seen. Night and day, that man went around, rearranging life itself to make opportunities where there were none. He built this town. He really did. And he worshipped her. Would have done anything for her." She tsked. "Maybe Bunny was more like her mother than I thought."

"I never knew Allison," I said. "I moved here after she died."

"Oh, well, she wasn't unlikable or anything. But still. You know. Apple doesn't fall far from the tree. And don't think I'm speaking ill of the dead, I'd say the same thing about my own daughter. I've always said Ann Marie has too much of her father in her. Got his golden hair and his utter disregard for other people's feelings. Can't fake that kind of thing. It's in you or it's not." She stabbed her plastic spoon repeatedly into her chili, as though the beans needed loosening.

"Do you feel Allison had some kind of moral failing?" I asked.

"Listen," Ms. Harriet said, "I don't gossip. Okay. I don't. Your business is your business, and my business is my business. But when you bring your business into my workplace? It becomes my business."

"Are you talking about Mr. Brandon?" I asked.

"That poor boy," Ms. Harriet said.

"I never heard that story," I said. "I don't even know what happened."

"Nothing happened," Ms. Harriet barked, laughing. "I mean, a lot worse could have happened! Those two were carrying on, and at first I thought it was just a flirtation. Everybody has that, a joke or a smile at pickup or drop-off. That kind of thing is harmless for most people, and I assumed that was how it was for them, though to me personally Brandon was a little bit young for a grown woman to be flirting with to make herself feel better, if you know what I mean. But anyway, that's what I thought it was. And then one day, I find them making out like teenagers in the church basement. Brandon was supposed to be on his lunch break. I was like, all right, all right, not here. I don't want to see it, I don't want to hear it, I don't want to know about it, as far as I'm concerned this never happened. What I should have done was fire him. Right then and there." She shook her head, ate several more bites of chili.

"But I didn't. To be honest, I liked Brandon too. He was such a handsome kid, and sweet in this sleepy way, and so patient with the kids. He was valuable to me. It's good for kids to be taken care of by men as well as women, helps them be more balanced, and believe me they follow the rules better for men too! I always like to have a man or two around, but it makes parents nervous, so you have to really find the right kind. Anyway, I didn't fire Brandon, and as far as I knew it had petered out, but then when she killed herself like that."

"When who killed herself?"

"Allison," Ms. Harriet said, giving me side-eye like I was slow.

"I thought she was in a car accident," I said.

"She drove into oncoming traffic stone-cold sober in the middle of a weekday," Ms. Harriet said.

"But, I mean, did they rule it a suicide?"

"Whatever you want to call it," Ms. Harriet said, "the fact is that woman was stone-cold sober and drove into oncoming traffic on a Wednesday. Call it what you want."

"So, wait—I'm just trying to get the timeline straight. Because what reason would Allison even have to go to the preschool, wasn't Bunny in school by this point?"

"Exactly, though. Exactly my point. She would drop off things for him, bring him cookies she baked, and I'm like, lady, you don't even have a kid here anymore!"

"And then what happened to Brandon when she died?"

"He was hurting," Ms. Harriet said, nodding emphatically. "He couldn't talk about it, but he was hurting. Like the whole world just faded to black and white. All the magic just went out. Wham. And I kept saying, Brandon, the Lord has a plan for you! The Lord always has a plan. But he was too far gone. I couldn't reach him."

She shook her head sadly, as though she could have or should have been able to reach anyone, as though she saw herself as that kind of person. For myself, I could not imagine anything worse than being at a low point in my life and then interacting with Ms. Harriet. To discuss one's innermost feelings with Ms. Harriet would be like allowing one's eyeballs to be abraded by a scouring pad soaked in bleach.

Had Ann Marie turned out to be such a lying, conniving sociopath because her father had handed down douche-genes, or because her mother had never loved her? Though of course Ms.

Harriet thought of herself as a loving mother. Ms. Harriet lived in a world of doing, where her actions were as clean and formulaic as a sheet of Lego instructions. To clothe the child and feed the child and teach the child is to love the child. Those actions are the same as the metaphysical state for a person like Ms. Harriet.

For instance right now, hadn't she rescued me in the hallway? Wasn't she feeding me, comforting me? I was sure I would wind up in her evening prayers that night, and I was sure she would look back on the way she had absolved me, forgiven me, "Don't tell me you think this was your fault," and she would feel pride. She would never perceive herself as using even this meager opportunity to spread damaging, toxic gossip about a woman long dead. She was being so kind as to extend her sympathy to Bunny, who had obviously lost it or had some kind of "break"—whatever it was, it was obviously not normal, it was obviously sick and pathological and other and monstrous, and obviously we could never look at Bunny the same way, could we? No, we could never see her the same way, the same way we could never look at her mother the same way, for what Allison had done was also disgusting. A younger man. The selfishness of the affair compounded by the selfishness of the suicide. She was not a proper woman, not a clean and godly woman, and hadn't we all known Bunny was not a proper girl either? I mean, she was too large, wasn't she? We had all known when she grew too big that there was something wrong with her, and we should not be surprised now that the something wrong had come to light, and that the monster had been exposed for what it was.

"He never should have let that girl play sports," Ms. Harriet said, out of nowhere.

"Bunny?"

"It's what made her violent, I bet." She stared off into the middle distance, as though her own daughter did not also play sports.

That was the thing that was turning out to be most difficult about being a person. The people I had the most sympathy for were almost never the ones everyone else felt sympathy for. I should have felt sympathy for Ann Marie. Everyone else did. Everyone else took selfies in the waiting room with crying-eye emojis. Everyone else saw in her homely features and glossy blond hair something vulnerable and sweet. But I had never liked Ann Marie and I could not start now, even if she was in a coma. And I had always liked Bunny and I could not hate her now, even if she was a monster. Nor could I hate Allison for whatever she had done with Mr. Brandon. Nor could I hate my mother.

I knew that sometimes people found themselves in a moment. They found themselves pressed up against themselves inside of a claustrophobic moment. And you couldn't see how it really was from the outside. You could talk all day until you were blue in the face about what Donna Morse should have done to not get murdered, or about what my mother should have done to get us out of there. But sometimes when you are in a moment, it's so close to your face, reality, it's pressed up so close to you, that you just flinch, you react, and then your fate is decided, and all you have done was what you couldn't help doing, and yet your fate is decided. You've done something that can't be taken back. You've kissed Mr. Brandon, or inserted the fruit knife into the pectoral muscle, or suddenly woken up on top of a girl whose nose was under her left eye. And there was something about me, but I always seemed to be right next to the kind of people who wound up making such decisions. I always seemed to be right there, loving the wrong person, betting on the wrong dark horse.

9

I have always loved buses. They carry their own unique enchantment called forth by the pneumatic squeak and whoosh of their doors and the drone of their massive engines as they lumber about the city carrying individuals who are daydreaming, all together, each pretending to be alone. On the bus home from Cedars-Sinai, as I was thinking about Bunny and about violence, I accidentally stumbled into a kind of reverie about my mother. I had not intended, exactly, to think about her, and then suddenly I was plunged into the deepest, darkest part of the water.

I suppose it had been triggered by a selfie my sister, Gabby, had posted. I monitored her Instagram and Facebook accounts much more often than I spoke to her. There was some kind of awkwardness between us, some kind of bad blood that I couldn't seem to find the source of. When we met up, I would ask her questions about her life or about school and she would roll her eyes at me. The most I knew about her was what our mother told me. She would always give a little recap at the start of our Denny's dinners. "Well, Gabby got a B in pre-algebra," or, "Gabby has become obsessed with Lil Wayne and I think I'm about to lose my mind." My senior year of high school, Gabby was in eighth grade. Is there a darker night of the soul than eighth grade? In the last year or so she had suddenly veered from potentially plump, otherwise known as "Wisconsin Skinny," to damn-is-that-girl-dying skinny. Her thigh gap was a handbreadth. Her skeleton was iconic. In the particular selfie I was obsessing over, she and my mother were both dressed in weirdly slutty outfits, black bras under white wifebeaters, ripped denim shorts, too much eyeliner, and they were staring at the camera unsmiling and serious as court reporters. It was captioned "Cat got your tongue?"

I should have seen it coming. That my mom and sister would become friends, subtly excluding me the way that my mother and I had always subtly excluded Gabby. It was the age difference really. I had always been the old one, the reasonable one, the one who could be talked to, my mother's confidant. I had been her bestie. And I had been relieved when she went to prison and this intimacy had ended, so I was unprepared for the flash of intense jealousy that sliced through me when I saw this picture of my mother and sister together. And all sorts of things came flooding back.

I had sat in the courtroom during my mother's trial, which took two days. There was something about the way the prosecutor spoke to her that alarmed me. He spoke quickly, as though he were trying to trick her or make her look stupid by asking him to repeat himself. He was a white man with brown hair and a brown beard and lips that were very pink and a vein in his forehead that was tremulously violet. In every way he looked at my mother, spoke to my mother, referred to my mother, there was a careful detachment that bespoke visceral disgust. Of course, at ten years old, I had no words for what I was witnessing. But what I knew was that to this man, there were one hundred other things my mother could have done besides stab my father. Why had she been so stupid as to not think of them? It would have been so easy not to stab my father, this man seemed to suggest, that for my mother to have done so indicated some kind of violent fixation on her part. Why hadn't she called the police, for instance? Why hadn't she gotten the children into the car and left, even if it was to drive around the block until she could think of what to do? Why hadn't she locked herself in the bathroom? Why hadn't she left my father years ago, for that matter?

I was a child, and I had thought that the law would be concerned with doling out moral judgments. Honestly, I had thought we would be deciding whether it was my mother or my father's fault that all this had happened, and in my estimation, it was mostly my father's fault, and the idea that my mother would be held accountable for it—as though she wanted to stab him, as though she had put it on her to-do list: maybe stab Aaron for fun on Saturday!—was so absurd to me it bordered on surreal. The entire court scene was, to my eleven-year-old eyes, the Mad Hatter's tea party. I had no idea they were trying merely to ascertain: Had my mother stabbed my father? Yes, of course she had! But didn't it matter why she had done it? Wasn't there any pity for the fact that she had been reduced to this? Why hadn't she left him months ago? Because she fucking loved him and she loved us and she wanted her family to be okay, and that meant refusing to understand that her family was not going to be okay. Had they never lived life?

I wonder now why my mother didn't plead guilty and cop some sort of deal. Did they not offer her a deal? Did her lawyer think he could plead self-defense? Didn't her lawyer know that the only thing harder to win than a rape case is a woman defending herself in a domestic violence dispute?

"And where were your husband's hands during this exchange?"

"On my throat. He was choking me."

"With both hands?"

"Yes, I think so."

"Did you believe he would kill you?"

"I feared for my life," my mother had said. I can see now that they coached her to say that. I had not been in the room when this altercation occurred. I had been in my bedroom with Gabby watching *American Idol* on an old laptop, the screen of which was crusted so that Ryan Seacrest seemed to have a large mole on his face. But I did not doubt my mother. My father often strangled her, although he did not try to crush her windpipe, but simply cut off the blood flow through her carotids until she passed out, and then he would lay her on the floor, where she would splutter, almost instantly, back to life, just as mad as before, and he would say, *"Jesus Christ,"* like she was just too much for him and why couldn't she just stay passed out, just for a minute, just for once. Her relentless consciousness was galling.

"Had he ever strangled you before?" the prosecutor asked.

"Yes," she said, sure that this was the right answer. He had been bad, he had been bad two times, he had been bad many times! God, how many times had he strangled her!

"And the times that he strangled you before, had you ever feared for your life?"

"Yes," my mother said.

"And yet, fearing for your life, you would not call the police or separate from your husband?"

"Well, I'm sure that I did, but—"

"What about this time made you fear for your life so intensely that you picked up that knife?" the prosecutor went on.

But it had already happened. I could see it on my mother's face, she had lost the thread of her righteousness. She had never believed he would kill her. Not in the past, not in that moment. He would never have let her die. If anything, my father would have killed my mother by accident. But her body did not know he wouldn't have killed her. Her body was fighting for air and trying to get him to stop, and her body picked up a knife. My poor mother did not have the vocabulary or wherewithal or ability to try to make such a distinction in that courtroom. It was all happening too fast. She was too intimidated by the prosecutor and his glossy brown beard and his purple forehead vein. I still remember he applied cherry ChapStick. The ChapStick brand one. He kept one in his suit pocket and he applied it at least once an hour. I thought it was so weird. I had never seen a man wear ChapStick before, even though I understood it was normal. I had just never seen it before, and it stirred something in me. It seemed almost lewd, this man constantly bringing attention to his rosy lips.

In the end, my mother did not know why she had stabbed my

father. It was her body that had stabbed him, but not her. Even in that courtroom, she still loved him. And after her failure to be able to adequately explain this to anyone, she became withdrawn. She guessed too soon that the trial was already over, and maybe part of why she lost is that she stopped fighting. Her eyes glazed over. She didn't listen to the testimony. She looked bored, but also ashamed. And she was ashamed. Because she knew what the lawyers and the judge and the police and probably the jury thought she was, and she knew, too, that their thinking she was trash would make her trash. Her future didn't matter to anyone. Her love for her children was as theoretical and easy to discard as a bitch's love for her pups. Everyone but her knew what was best. And how could she argue? She loved a man who was bad and bad to her, and that was shameful, shameful the way loving food or drink that is bad for you is shameful. And so she let them. She let the trial happen. She let us move into foster care and then into Aunt Deedee's house. She let everything happen around her, like events were so many petals falling from a bouquet of flowers left too long in a vase.

The thing Bunny said after she met my mother was: "Wow, I had no idea she would be so much like you." We looked alike. We talked alike. We had the same blend of morbid and dorky in our jokes. Both of our mouths jutted with slight, uncorrected under bites. We had a joke when she kissed me good night, we would call them "piranha kisses" because of the shape of our mouths. We shared a flair for the dramatic in our language and our looks, pale skin, dark hair. She could get angrier at me than at my sister or even my father because she expected true friendship from me. I was her companion, her comrade.

If my father was too drunk, we would catch each other's eye. If my sister was being a glutton or a brute, we would tease her together, mercilessly ganging up on her until she cried. Gabby was a brash, fat, and happy baby, uncomplicated and selfish. We both envied her, loved her, coddled her, and hated her. Why couldn't we be more like her? we wondered. Why couldn't we be like my father, for that matter, drunk and demanding and happy and charming? Why were we always watching, afraid to speak in the moment, thinking up clever replies days later? Why did we need, so badly, to paint our stubby nails with black nail polish? Why were we so drawn to books and movies about witches? Why were we destined to be neurotic prey, trembling rabbits clamped between the hot jaws of larger, better, more vital animals?

For me, watching my mother give up during her trial and fall into the depression that consumed her throughout her prison sentence was a betrayal of such epic proportions that it became one of the great before-and-afters of my life. I learned something deep about myself, about her, about love, and it was a lesson that could not be unlearned. I remember being a kid and thinking it was kind of fun when someone broke their arm, jealous even that they got to wear a cast and have everyone sign it. And then I remember being with my mom after my dad broke my little sister's arm, which of course we hid completely (the official story was that she fell jumping off a swing), and standing next to my mom, fingering the sleeve of her sweater as the doctor explained the odds of the fracture healing well, and understanding that Gabby's arm would never be the same, never be as good as it was before. It was that kind of lesson, the lesson I learned during my mother's trial. Maybe it would have been easier for me if she and I had not been so much alike.

But we were.

Now I think I have assembled something, fragile and piece-meal as it is, that might be called understanding, but when I was seventeen to even think of my mother was to enter a world of memories I could get lost in for hours, and even if I set out to remember or understand just one thing, for instance, I was always trying in those days to conclude whether my mother was a good person or a bad person, I would find myself almost drowning in remembered details: how trash collected in her purse, and how she would have to empty it every few months, the dense mat of receipts and gum wrappers that settled in the bottom, how her face looked as she was listening on the phone, the way her mouth was always slightly open to accommodate her underbite, giving her a look of expectant excitement, her short, bestial-looking thumbnails, her love of overpoweringly sweet perfumes. She was intensely dyslexic and she couldn't spell anything, would get lost spelling the word "Wednesday," but she was also a kind of genius. She had an extraordinary memory, though her encyclopedic knowledge was limited to music trivia and pop culture. She knew every nuance of Britney Spears's life, for instance, and talked about Britney as though she were, if not a close friend, then perhaps a saint, someone whose story could be consulted for guidance as one moved through one's own life.

And so it came to be that I missed my stop, still staring at the picture of my mother and Gabby ("Cat got your tongue?" Jesus!), and rode on the bus all the way down to Manhattan Beach and then had to wait for another bus to take me back to North Shore, and by the time I got home to Aunt Deedee's house, I was exhausted and disoriented and so sad it felt like my very being was saturated with it and had begun leaking, causing dark stains on the air around me. Aunt Deedee and Jason were in the living room, and when I opened the door they looked up in unison. There was a plastic tray of Oreos on the coffee table. The TV was on, some kind of sports game show with an obstacle course, but it didn't seem they'd been watching it. I thought Aunt Deedee was going to be mad at me for being out so late, but instead she looked sad and worried. *Oh,* I thought. *It's going to be bad.*

"Hey, homo," Jason said.

"Jason!" Aunt Deedee said. He was not going about it in the way she had thought they would. She needed, in order to be able to do this to me, for it to be clean, dressed up as decent.

"What?" Jason said, standing up and then sitting down again. "He's the one living some secret life!" He took off his hat and began curling the bill in his hands, squeezing and squeezing it, like it was a cow's udder.

"Come here and sit down," my aunt said, tucking the escaped

wisps of her ponytail behind her ears. She looked very tired and her ponytail was sad and straggly. She was wearing a peach-colored sweatshirt with a large white bleach stain on the shoulder in the shape of a kidney. I had not really thought she would kick me out. It felt like the molecules of my body were dissolving like sugar in a glass of water, nothing was stable, everything was melting. I just had not thought she would really, really do it. But I looked in her face, and I thought: She's going to do it. She's already reassured Jason that she will do it, and now she has to carry through, and she's realizing it is going to be harder than she thought, but she'll do it. I sat down on the ottoman of the chair by her, trying to take up as little space as possible, trying even to float slightly above the ottoman.

"Michael," my aunt said, and she said my name with so much love and kindness that I couldn't stand it. "Jason has heard some really disturbing things from some of the boys on his water polo team, and we were hoping to talk to you."

I looked at the pink carpet. Pink as the inside of a conch shell. I had always been so embarrassed of the carpet in our house, but what was embarrassing about it? Why shouldn't carpet be pink?

"You're moving out," Jason said.

"Jason!" Aunt Deedee snapped at him.

"What? He is. Better to just put it out there. I'm not fucking sharing a room with him!"

"And I respect that choice," Aunt Deedee said, "but—"

"How much time do I have?" I asked.

"Back up—hold on, both of you, this is not what I wanted. Just back up, we need to back up a few paces, and start over."

"Mom," Jason said, furious now, "I'm sorry, I just don't want to see two guys kissing *in my bedroom*. Okay?"

Aunt Deedee got angrier at this than I had ever seen her, and the words seemed to leap right out of her throat. "Oh, Jason, grow a pair! He's not kissing people in your bedroom, and even if he were, Michael's had to watch straight couples kiss in every movie ever made, so I think you could probably handle seeing two men kiss each other without the hysterics." She smoothed the light denim of her jeans on the tops of her thighs, as though that were that, and she appeared to be thinking about something.

"Part of what concerns me about what Ann Marie said, and god, I hope she's okay, is that she had seen you in a sexual position with a man who was much, much older than you, and—"

"A sexual position?" I said.

"She said they were kissing, Mom," Jason said, irritated. He was in no way on my side, but even he thought calling kissing a "sexual position" was a little unfair.

"All right, kissing. Can I just ask, how did you meet this man?"

I was not sure what the right answer was. If I said in real life, wouldn't that insinuate an even more advanced and evolved secret life? What if she thought I was part of secret societies where we had orgies with antlers strapped to our heads and made burnt offerings to the moon? And yet, I dreaded even uttering the word "Grindr"; it seemed so cheap and childishly obscene. "Online," I said.

"Meeting people on the internet, Michael—it's just not safe! And you don't know—older men, they will expect things from you, and they might take advantage of you, and—"

"I'm not a virgin," I said. "If that's what you're talking about."

"Oh," Aunt Deedee said, and she seemed suddenly wildly sad, almost despondent. "I feel I've done such a really terrible job as your guardian," she said. "I should have talked to you about all this so much earlier—I just never thought—"

"I'm not fucking living with him," Jason said.

"That's fine," I said. "I'll figure out a place to live."

"Where?" Aunt Deedee said. "Where would you go? You can't go live with your mother, even aside from the fact that she doesn't have room, I won't have it. I won't have you living there. Are you talking about living with— your man friend?"

"No," I said, "I was thinking I would look into staying at a shelter until I could save enough money to rent an apartment."

"Oh, Michael," Aunt Deedee said, her hand raised to her cheek like I had slapped her.

"Well, where did you think I would go?" I shouted.

"I don't fucking care where he goes," Jason said.

"Calm down, Mountain Dew," I said, but Aunt Deedee was already shouting him down.

"What the good goddamn is wrong with you, Jason Clark? I mean, for heaven's sakes! He's your own cousin. And you don't care where he goes? You want him to live in a shelter? Shame on you. I can't believe I raised you. I should have taken you to church more because you don't know the first thing about how to be a decent human being."

"Yeah, they teach that a lot in church, how to love faggots," Jason said.

"Go to your room," Aunt Deedee said, pointing at the ceiling.

"You're being ridiculous," he told her.

"Go."

He went. She sat back in her chair with a great sigh and idly smoothed her pants again.

"I'm just so tired," she said.

"Your shoulder okay?" I asked. Aunt Deedee had something vaguely wrong with her left shoulder. She'd never been to a doctor about it. But it had to do with being on her feet too much and being too tense and lifting things that were too heavy, and I often rubbed her back for her. I got up behind her to do so now and I could feel her relax under my hands as all her quivering little bird muscles, in her neck, in her shoulders, webbing her spine to her scapulas, almost hissed with release.

"I can't let you move into a shelter," she said. "I can't have you live with Jason. He's too—"

"Annoyed," I said.

"Hateful," she said.

I was beginning to come around to the idea that Aunt Deedee was going to let me stay, even though it made me feel servile and weak. There was something daring and beautiful about the idea of storming out, packing a single bag of my things, going to a shelter and quitting high school and starting my own life. I had even been fantasizing about it on some level. But when the reality of being kicked out had been so naked in the room, I found that I was terrified. If Aunt Deedee had kicked me out that night, I would have simply gone to Bunny's house like a child playing at running away. I would never, it occurred to me, actually have gone to a shelter. I would have been too scared. And now, as I rubbed Aunt Deedee's back, the nodes of her vertebrae so unpadded with fat that they felt like sharp rocks through her skin, I was willing to do anything to stay.

Aunt Deedee put her face in her hands and breathed in and out. "I have to give Jason his own room. The question is where to put you where you'll be as comfortable as possible. You could room with me?" she said, but the look on her face was reluctant.

"Oh, no, no," I said. "I don't think that would be—I mean, I could sleep on the couch."

"I don't want you sleeping on the couch," she said.

I made a sympathetic sound as I thought: I'll get to keep going to high school. Even the sense memory that flooded me of the odor and weight of my textbooks seemed like sweet ambrosia.

"I'll think of something," she said, and patted my hand on her shoulder, a signal that I could stop rubbing. But I didn't want to stop, I didn't want her to think of some way of fixing it later because I was certain she would change her mind.

"I could just sleep on the couch," I said. "Really."

"For tonight that's probably best," Aunt Deedee said.

"No, I mean, like, until I graduate. And then I could get out of your hair. I'm already practically full-time at Rite Aid."

Aunt Deedee motioned for me to return to my seat on the ottoman, and then she took hold of both of my hands and she began to speak to me in a manner so earnest it seemed old-fashioned and at first I almost got the giggles. "Michael, I need to tell you something that I don't know how to say, and I may fail, but I will never feel quite right again if I don't at least try to say it, which is that there is something absolutely beautiful in you. I'm not sure what it is, if it's your brain or if it's your soul, but it reminds me of your mother and what was so beautiful in her when she was a girl, and I don't know if she ever spoke about this, but she is profoundly dyslexic, and back then it wasn't talked about, it wasn't known, what it was, and so the name for it was—just being dumb. And she would cry about it, about thinking she was retarded, and her teacher telling our mom that she was learning disabled and that she would never be able to go to college or have a job that involved reading or writing, and, well, it would mean a great deal to me if you were to go to college."

Her brown eyes were set at a hawkish angle in her face, and the dark circles under her eyes made her seem tough in the most fragile way possible, like a person who has tasted the poison and is speaking the truth even as they are succumbing to death.

"To college?"

"Jason will go to a few semesters of community college and that's fine. Maybe he'll join the army. He'll do something. But you. I mean, when is the last time you even got something lower than an A?"

"I got an A-minus in chem last year."

"An A-minus is an A," she said.

"Oh."

"Michael, you have to go. I never went. Your mother didn't even finish high school."

"She didn't?" I asked, scandalized by this idea.

Aunt Deedee shook her head. "Our parents didn't go. You will be the first one. And you might be the only one. And so if I need to fight with Jason, I will fight with Jason. But what I need from you are two things."

"What?" I asked. We were still holding hands, which was weird, but I didn't want to let go.

"I need you to keep up your grades and apply to colleges, a lot of them, state schools, out of state, spread a wide net. I don't even know what the options are, but you go to someone who knows—maybe Ray Lampert can help you—and you figure out what the other rich kids know and you copy them. And you get in, and you graduate. Okay?"

"Okay," I said, hardly able to breathe.

"And then the second thing is I need you to stop with the online stuff. Any profiles you have, I need you to cancel them. And I need you to end things with the man you've been seeing. Completely. No contact."

"Can I write him to tell him I'm ending it?"

"Of course," Aunt Deedee said. "But I want you to close all your other accounts tonight. And if I hear that you're still messing with all this, then it's over. You're out. Okay?"

I wasn't sure what had happened, but I felt tricked. I had practically broken up with Anthony already. And yet I had the feeling that Aunt Deedee's vulnerability had been a disguise, and now I was finding myself at her mercy. Did she see something beautiful in me? Could she? Did she know enough of what was authentically me to see something beautiful there? And if she could, how could she think that the subterranean taproots I had been sending out all these years, through the internet and down into the casual embraces of men, through lives strange to me that turned my life strange, through kisses and bruises and jokes and cruel remarks, how could she behold the entire domain I had built for myself in the dark and decide it should be amputated? The portal closed.

I felt then that no one would ever know who I was. No one, I thought, was even capable of seeing another person clearly, let alone loving them. Aunt Deedee was merely clacking beads on a moral abacus together. College + no sex = safe + good.

They were unspoken equations that propelled her as surely as physics equations could explain a ball's arc through the air. I had watched my mother keep trying, and failing, to live by her own moral equations. Being nice to husband = being a good wife. Making husband angry = being a bad wife. Suddenly, blossoming in me like food dye dropped in a water glass, was a memory of his voice, angry at her, saying, "I need you to be fucking available by phone. Why is that so hard? Are you fucking nuts? You're my wife, you're taking care of our children, you should have your phone on you at all times." She had taken us to the park, one of the rare days when she was in a good enough mood to want to go outside, and her phone had died, and she had been nervous about that, but she'd taken us to McDonald's on the way home for ice cream anyway. I remember telling her, "Don't worry about it, he probably hasn't even called. He won't notice. He's at work, why would he call?" But he had called. How old had I been? Seven?

"What?" I said.

"I don't want you involved in things like that," Aunt Deedee was saying.

"Things like what?" I asked.

Aunt Deedee looked sad, but also frustrated because she wasn't allowing herself to speak plainly. Finally she said, "I hope you've been very careful."

She was talking about condoms. She was talking about AIDS.

"I've been careful," I said. And I hated her so completely that it seemed to me that I would never love her again.

"Oh good, Michael." She squeezed my hands. "So sleep on the couch for tonight. Tomorrow, we'll figure out a more permanent place for you."

Tomorrow, I imagined her saying, we'll figure out a more permanent place for your disgusting, diseased, morally frightening body, which is too much for my son to handle, my son, who is eighteen years old and who may soon enlist in the army because he is willing and able to kill people, but I will refuse you the comfort of your normal bed, on this, one of the worst nights of your life, in order to appease his bigotry and coddle his feelings of superiority to you.

What is wrong with you? I thought in the dark, after she had gone, as I listened to the fan in the refrigerator cycle on and off, over and over. *Why can't you accept that this is what love is like?*

10

For the following weeks, Bunny was in a kind of limbo. She had been suspended from school, initially for thirty days, which was far in excess of the normal suspension for fighting on campus, Ray Lampert liked to point out. He'd thrown a fit in the principal's office, Bunny told me. "I thought he was gonna pop! His face was bright red, and he said, 'You're telling me this is how you would handle two boys getting in a fistfight in a locker room?' And Principal Cardenas was like, 'This was not a fistfight, this was an unprovoked assault.' And he said: 'Hate speech against a fellow student doesn't count as aggravation?' It was so, so embarrassing." (I had already had a deeply uncomfortable sit-down with Principal Cardenas where I had declined an offer of school counseling for the effects of said hate speech.)

As for the beating itself, Bunny was processing what had happened about as well as a congressman responds to a school shooting. She kept returning to two ideas, one of which was: "I would never do that." In other words, the awake, normal Bunny would never choose for what happened to have happened. She also phrased this as: "If I had known it would hurt her so much—I just didn't think—" She felt terrible that Ann Marie was in a coma, so terrible that she had panic attacks and at one point even threw up in a potted plant at the mall, but she also never took true responsibility for her role in Ann Marie's injuries. She had not meant to do that, and therefore she was innocent of the consequences.

The other idea she kept returning to was that there was "something wrong" with her. She found the fact that she had only fragmented memories of the fight to be deeply embarrassing, and together with the fact that she had bitten Ryan Brassard's ear, each contributed to a narrative she was developing about herself, that she was "crazy" or "out of control." She associated these problems with her height, with some way she was a "monster" or a "freak."

In later years, I've spent a lot of time thinking about those words, "monster" and "freak." They are very different words. "Monster" is from the Old French *monstre,* from the original Latin *monstrum,* meaning a portent, or a warning. A monster was something malformed, afflicted by God's wrath, and was a warning to the community to examine their moral standards. "Freak," on the other hand, was a much jauntier word of much less certain origin, thought to have derived from Middle English *friken,* "to move nimbly or briskly," from Old English *frician,* "to dance." It is a wild move you unexpectedly bust out, a sudden change in tempo, and so a "freak of nature" is more a jaunty deviation from the norm than a sign that God is mad. In other words, I had always looked at Bunny as a freak, a beautiful, exciting, pulsating freak. But now Bunny worried she was a monster. Because on some level she had always seen herself that way.

She was deeply, morbidly ashamed. But her shame never managed to lead her out of herself and toward empathy for others, but instead led her into self-involved circles. Why had she been unjustly made this way? Why had this fate befallen her? She had no agency, it seemed. The question was not: Why had she done this? The question was: Why had God done this to her? Not that she believed in God either.

Perhaps I am being unfair. I think it astonished her that her friendship with Naomi had popped like a soap bubble. Where had it gone? It had seemed so tangible. Those girls had spent hours and hours together, took Spanish together, ate lunch together, went to practice together. And then it was all gone, vanished as if it had never been. Naomi had been straightforward about it too. The very first time Bunny texted her after the fight, Naomi had texted back within minutes: *I'm sorry, I can't be friends anymore.* Donezo.

At school, almost especially because she wasn't there to make them feel awkward, kids spoke about Bunny freely, their disgust bright in the daylight. They had always known there was something wrong with her. She was sick. They hoped she got help, but they also hoped she never came back to school again. And wasn't it weird she didn't have any real friends? Besides being a star athlete? Not that that could be helped when you were built like that. Poor Ryan Brassard, everyone agreed. In retrospect, he had been lucky to get only a bite on the ear.

I heard all kinds of things. I heard one girl volunteer that she knew for a fact that Bunny didn't wrap up her used tampons in toilet paper but put them in the trash at school all bloody and exposed. I heard girls agree together that she had a weird way of scratching her boobs after she took off her sports bra. One girl posted a picture of the volleyball team on Facebook that went viral, in which, because of the perspective of the photo, Bunny, who was closest to the camera, seemed nearly twice the size of her classmates. Overnight, Bunny had gone from being the princess of North Shore—happy, popular, a varsity athlete, and daughter of one of the most influential men in town—to being a disgusting pig everyone agreed they had never liked.

I seethed. I wanted to scream, "Yeah, well, I remember when you went to her fifteenth birthday party and you certainly fucking liked the full-on carnival her dad put on in the backyard, and if I recall you threw up cotton candy right into their pool, so take your corny, basic, lip-kit idiocy right back to the YouTube channel you came from." But I did not say things like that. When you are seventeen, no one demands moral continuity of social bonds. Everyone was trying on new personalities all the time, weren't they? Innocent enough, wasn't it? And this was just another one, a phase that they would remember when they were older:

Remember when we were all united during senior year by hating Bunny Lampert?

And why shouldn't they? Their friend Ann Marie was on a ventilator, in a coma, and her gel manicure was starting to grow out in an upsetting way. (Why was it so upsetting that Ann Marie's fingernails kept growing? But it was!) Bunny was practically a murderer because Ann Marie could seriously die, and if she didn't, then that was just luck. Bunny might as well be a murderer. In essence, her peers felt, she already was.

Bunny, who had never cultivated her social standing or even understood that she had any, that the friendlessness she had occasionally experienced before was far from rock bottom, was bewildered by this change of affairs. I, of course, did not report to her with blistering accuracy the things being said about her at school, but she found out soon enough. It was a small town. Kids crossed the street in groups so as not to pass her on the sidewalk. If she approached a group of girls at the Starbucks they froze, pretended not to see or hear her. "Hey, guys!" she would say. "Guys!" And they would exchange a look and then walk away from her.

She cried about it. A lot. I held her while she cried about it. I bore the brunt of those misplaced tears, and I found myself often bored, exhausted by the expanse of her anguish, burned by the heat of her skin, her cheeks red as if slapped, her lashes webby black with salted tears. If anything, it seemed that Bunny was more upset by losing all of her friends and her life and her future career as an Olympic volleyball player than she was over the fact that Ann Marie was in a coma and the swelling in her brain was not going down, not going down, day after day, not going down. But perhaps that is only because the shunning by her peers felt more immediate, less abstract. Perhaps it was because at the end of the day, she was a teenage girl to whom being liked means everything, or almost everything.

Legally, Bunny was still waiting, and the district attorney was waiting, to see if Ann Marie would be waking up. We were all waiting for Ann Marie to wake up. (Or since it was a medically induced coma, I guess we were really waiting for the swelling in her brain to go down enough that they could bring her out of the coma, but for some reason no one referred to it this way, and we all spoke of Ann Marie magically waking up as if on her own, like Sleeping Beauty with no prince.) Ms. Harriet had called Ray Lampert herself and said as much. "I don't believe in an eye for an eye, and I am not in any way interested in making life harder for Bunny than it needs to be, however if there are medical bills beyond my ability to cope with, then of course I will have to address that. This is life. Things happen. I'm not trying to paint Bunny as some kind of villain. Although I do think maybe counseling would be a good idea. I'm just saying, let's be realistic. Your kid hurt my kid. My kid may never be the same. So I can't promise what I will do. I will have to do what seems to me the most correct thing to do in the moment, and if you would help us buy a house maybe we can work on that when all this is over."

And while they waited, Ray got tired of Bunny sulking around his house and eating everything in sight, and so he put her to work in his office. At first this disturbed his assistant, Cassie, the blond woman who had offered me that Two Palms Realty blanket on the Fourth of July all those years ago. She was devoted, pathologically, to Ray Lampert, and she took any attempts to help her as an insult to her ability. She assigned Bunny to put doorknob flyers on every house in North Shore, made her hand-collate photocopies, told her to relabel all the already labeled files so that the font of the labels would all match. "We want a united look," she said. As though customers were looking through the files. As though the united look would be observed by anyone other than Cassie herself. Eventually she relegated some of the more annoying computer work, keeping all the postings active on the various websites, uploading endless virtual tours, but even this mindless busywork, Cassie seemed to believe, was almost sacred in its importance.

Bunny told me about all of this when we would get together,

usually every three or four days, in the weeks after her assault on Ann Marie. We didn't see each other more often than that, and I'm not sure why. My aunt, while expressing a certain apprehension about my friendship with Bunny "all things considered," had not vetoed it. If I had wanted to, I could probably have spent every evening hanging out with Bunny and Ray Lampert. I could see the lights of the TV flickering inside their house. Considering that Aunt Deedee had emptied out what was literally a walk-in closet and put a twin-size bed in there and called it "Michael's room," it wasn't like hanging out in my own house was great. But I didn't want to go over there too much. In fact, every time I saw Bunny, I felt more and more distant from her.

The first moment I noticed it, I didn't even know what it was. The feeling was caused by an offhand remark that Ray had made. Her father had mentioned to her that perhaps she should take up boxing, since it was somewhat unusual for a woman to have the upper body strength necessary for a knockout. I was not aware in the moment that this remark bothered me, and I did not experience distaste per se, but the comment did get lodged in my head and I would think of it randomly even weeks later. Imagine this being Ray Lampert's takeaway. That his daughter was specially gifted, but this time, as a boxer.

I was similarly perturbed by the fact that Ray Lampert had arranged for the assistant coach, Eric, to work with Bunny three or four times a week to "keep her sharp, just in case." He told me this as we were all eating pho together on Main Street on a Saturday afternoon. "Just in case?" I asked.

"In case something changes," Ray Lampert said, as though this were the most reasonable thing in the world. As though the school would magically reverse its decision and reinstate Bunny just in time for her to play in the championship game. Bunny slurped her pho, nodding, like it all made perfect sense. She was on lunch break from her new job at her dad's office. They were open even on Saturdays. She was wearing professional clothes that Ray had bought for her in a spree at Target, ruffly, cheap, polyester chiffon things that fit Bunny absurdly. On Bunny, a knee-length skirt was practically mid–thigh. "Things could change!" Ray Lampert said, and laughed. "Life is a fickle bitch."

In fact, things were changing. Ms. Harriet was changing. She called Ray Lampert at ten o'clock one night when Bunny and I were watching a movie in their living room. Ray picked up the phone, and we knew by the way he greeted her that it was Ms. Harriet. Through wrenching sobs, she told Ray that her baby was never gonna wake up again, that he stole her baby, that everything he touched turned to shit, that there was a curse on him and black evil that poured off him and she had seen it in Bunny as a baby.

When Ray finally got her off the phone (and one did have to commend him, he kept his head admirably and was responding with much kinder, floofier BS than I could have summoned: "Oh, Harriet, I hear you are so upset. I hear your grief"), he told us verbatim what she had been saying in a cruel impersonation of her voice. He and Bunny laughed, and I knew it was nervous laughter, but it disconcerted me anyway. "Ann Marie's not going to die," Ray Lampert said, as though Ms. Harriet were being absurd. He had spoken to his friend who was a doctor, who said a medically induced coma could be necessary for days, even weeks. There was no reason to believe Ann Marie would die based simply on the length of the coma. They understood how Ms. Harriet could be afraid of that, of course they could. But they were more distant from the problem. They could be more objective. Ray had done some research online. And the odds were good.

There was no humanity in them. Or perhaps there was too much humanity in them.

I had been supposed to break it off with Anthony, and I told my Aunt Deedee that I had, but somehow I could not do it. Instead, I ghosted him. But I could not bring myself to block his number, and so his texts leaked through, blooming like blood through a bandage. And I read them.

He wrote:

Probably you are wise to be ignoring me, and I imagine it is because you have learned something about me that displeases you, and probably you are right to do so. There is something in the geometry of your upper lip and the way the skin connects to the cartilage of your nose and the thicker flesh of your lips that dissolves my moral ability into a series of snapping synapses. I look at your blinking eye and I do not know who I am or what I am allowed to have, and I feel joyful and guiltless like a child. It is difficult not to believe I have a right to this feeling. It is difficult not to believe that every creature under the sun has a right to something as simple and honest as the pleasure I feel hearing your voice as you talk, climbing a series of ideas as a young boy might climb a tree, innocent of how far he could fall.

He texted:

I am so sorry to keep texting you. I do not want to be this whining, childish person chasing after you and insisting on explanations. But I do wish you thought enough of me to be willing to explain. I suppose I am afraid also that this might be some sort of test, and if I persist and show you that I am willing to debase myself, to text you every hour, to beg to hear your voice or kiss your knee, then perhaps you will relent and our relationship can come into itself even more fully than before. Perhaps you need me to prove myself.

The anguish caused by not answering his texts was physical in nature, as though someone were pressing with their thumbs on my eyeballs until they ached. I got a C-minus on a calculus test and felt that I might soon perish through the intensity of my emotions.

One day, Anthony texted me a picture. It was a little boy, perhaps four years old, handsome, with dark curly hair. The boy was laughing so big that you could see the pink roof of his mouth.

This is Hank, he said. *This is my son. He's twelve now, but this is one of my favorite pictures of him.*

The next day he texted me a picture of a middle-aged woman who was not unpretty. She was blond from a bottle with her roots growing out, and she had downy cheeks and tortoiseshell glasses. She was making a peace sign at the camera and sticking her tongue out. He wrote:

This is my wife, Laura. I married her when I was forty and she was twenty-five. She does not know that I have relationships with men. Despite this, our marriage is happy and I love being a father. Hank is my world. Laura is my best friend. I'm not willing to give them up. This means that the kind of relationship I can offer you is necessarily limited, and I am so sorry. I am so sorry because I wish I could offer you more. I am so sorry because I understand now that to have withheld this fact of exactly how limited my ability to enter your life was going to be was unethical. It was wrong. I can only say that at the time, I thought you were young and would tire of me anyway. Life would pull you down its road, and you would not have time for old men like me.

The next day he texted:

I am sorry for lying about my age on my profile. I told you I was 45, but I am 56. I have told you many lies. I told you I was in love with you, and I believe this to be true. What other name can I possibly give to this feeling? How is it that I feel I could die from your silence, yet I am not willing to alter my course or offer you more? Is it that I have chosen my own death?

I didn't know what to tell him. I was weirdly relieved that he was fifty-six and not sixty as Ann Marie had claimed, but what was the difference really? His son, Hank, looked like him, was beautiful in an easy smiling way that reminded me of him. His wife, Laura, looked nice. Maybe it worked for him. Who was I to make proclamations about adult life, the compromises worth making, the joys of parenthood compared to the joys of erotic love? I was not confident enough to tell him what I myself barely knew, which is that being true to yourself, even if it makes everyone hate you, even if it makes people want to kill you, is the most radical form of liberty, and when you make contact with something as electric and terrifying as the unadorned truth of yourself, it burns away so many other smaller forms of bondage you weren't even aware of, so you find yourself irradiated and unencumbered. That there is something holy in that kind of stubbornness. That's what I wanted to say to him. But I didn't know how to text that. And I didn't know why I should even try or whether I was an idiot or what there was to live for now that the greatest intimacy I had ever known had been shown to be so cheap and tawdry.

"Look at this place," Bunny said. She'd had me meet her at a house her father was selling. It was on the other side of Main Street, and I had never had a friend on this part of Oak Street, never spent any time over this way, which was odd. To find a part of your incredibly small town that you are not familiar with. It was a huge house that had been added on to repeatedly with an utter disregard for a centralized design, and so as you moved through the rooms you felt like you were in a dream where doors kept opening onto new doors. The front door opened onto a small living room and open kitchen, but then a door on the left opened into a library with a full bar, all of the woodwork intricate and custom. "He was a finish carpenter," Bunny told me. Through the library there was another living room with a fireplace, as well as a large bedroom and bath. All of the walls were painted hot pink. Santa Fe chic, Bunny called it. "Look, he built in hidey-holes everywhere. I guess he was some kind of gun nut." She showed me how panels in the library came away and secret compartments could be accessed. Upstairs there were another two bedrooms, and in one of the bedrooms there was a flight of stairs in the middle of the room that led up to a half-size door. It was the most peculiar thing.

"What's up there?" I asked.

"Come on," Bunny said, and scampered up the steps, having to hunch to stay low enough to open the tiny half-size door. She crawled through into the darkness and just as I was following her on my hands and knees into the dark, she snapped on the lights. The attic had been converted into what could only be described as a child's library and office space, with child-size built-in desks, bookshelves, track lighting. It was the kind of space one would have killed for as a kid or even a teenager. Neighborhood children would be inexorably drawn to this space. All it needed was a couple beanbag chairs and a lava lamp or maybe a fish tank. It boggled my mind that anyone had ever been lucky enough to possess this room, and then, as I realized that the retired carpenter must have built it himself for his children, I was undone by the concept of a parent who would spend the time and money to build something like that for their kids, and for some reason I thought about Anthony's son, Hank, and his big open smile and I felt like I couldn't breathe and maybe I needed to leave.

"What is Ray having you do here?" I asked Bunny.

"Weird, but kinda fun. We have to put a pee smell somewhere."

"He wants us to pee in here?"

"No, it's down in my car, it's coyote urine. I'm thinking we put it in the master bedroom."

"Why would he want to make the house smell like pee? Isn't that like the opposite of what would make it sell?"

"Well, so, Mr. Mitchell retired, and then, like, dropped dead, very sudden, last year, and right before they were supposed to go on a cruise. So Mrs. Mitchell was utterly bereft, and he basically built this house, all the woodwork was his, so Mrs. Mitchell didn't want to stay here. She moved in with her son and his wife in Arizona so that she could be closer to their kids and be grandma and everything. But she needs the house sold really bad because

Mr. Mitchell didn't have life insurance or anything, and I think she was counting on his Social Security for their retirement to work or something. Anyway, her one thing was she didn't want to sell to someone who was going to tear it down, so my dad priced it high so that it would sit, so she would change her mind."

"What?"

"Well, he priced it about a hundred grand above market, so it's just been sitting here for like almost a year, and finally Mrs. Mitchell got really mad and demanded he have another open house, so he wants it to smell like pee, and for me to try to make it seem sort of weird, like we rented too-big furniture to make the rooms feel smaller—did you notice that downstairs? Because he doesn't want anyone at the open house to make an offer."

"But why?" I asked, starting to be truly alarmed.

"Because his friend Toby is going to buy it. After the open house, he'll go to Mrs. Mitchell and say, I'm so sorry, there were no offers, and then a few days later, he'll go to her and say, I did finally get an offer, but it's only for X amount, and it's from a developer. But she'll be so desperate at that point that she'll just take it."

"That's fucked up," I said.

"I know!" Bunny said. "It really is. But I guess that kind of thing goes on all the time. Because, like, then the developer guarantees my dad that once he remodels it, he'll list it with my dad, so my dad gets commission on both sales. And usually some kind of kickback to boot. And also, the development drives up property values all around, so my dad winds up making more on every other sale, and on and on."

"Your dad is . . ."

"Utterly cold-blooded. I know. It's interesting. I had no idea. I'm not positive if the things he does are illegal, but they are definitely immoral."

"What other kinds of things does he do?"

"Oh, like he bribes inspectors and stuff."

"He bribes inspectors?"

"Yeah, when you buy a house, the buyer pays to have it inspected, and usually people don't know house inspectors, like off the top of their head, so they ask my dad, who do you usually use? And he says, 'Oh, use these guys, they're the best!' And so then the inspector is getting all his business from my dad, so he'll generally pretend everything is okay with the house even without my dad paying him, though sometimes he has to pay them if there is something really, really wrong."

"Wrong in what way?"

"I don't know, like a heat pump leaking carbon monoxide or something. Black mold."

"Yeah, I'm definitely guessing that's illegal."

Bunny shrugged. "Everyone does it, he says."

"Right," I said. I didn't know what I was so upset about. I had always known Ray Lampert was not some upstanding guy. I'd known he was a shark, that his teeth were fake-white, that he cared more about the way things looked than the way they were. Why was I so surprised?

Bunny was lying down on the brown shag carpet, her arms and legs spread out like a starfish. "This room is just so cool," she said. "I almost wish I could be a kid again just so that it could be mine."

"You don't feel guilty?" I asked. "Helping him."

Bunny sighed, then rolled over onto her stomach and looked at me. "At first, I really did. But, Michael, just—if everyone already thinks I'm bad, then why not just be bad?"

"That's the most idiotic thing you've ever said," I told her.

"Look, what I'm saying is, my dad—he can be terrible. I mean, he's selfish, he's manipulative, he has delusions of grandeur, he compulsively lies, even about things he totally doesn't need to lie about. He'll even lie about having seen a basketball game he didn't catch! But there's good in him too."

"Everyone has good in them! Jesus!"

"He's my dad," she said. We were still lying side by side on the carpet, looking at each other. I could see the vein in her neck bouncing with her pulse. I could hear it when she blinked her eyes.

"I don't want to be good anymore," she said. "I think it's a rigged game."

"What does that even mean?"

"Like, think about your mom. I looked it up, and there's a whole pathology and strangling is the last stage before domestic violence turns into murder. Your mom was one hundred percent right to stab your dad. She's probably still alive because of it. You're probably alive because of it."

"My dad would never have killed us!" I said, furious with her, with her internet wisdom, her "whole pathology."

"People kill people," Bunny said. "Anyone could commit a murder if they were just put in the right situation. Right and wrong are just these labels people use to oppress each other."

"You are fucking crazy," I said.

"There is no justice in the world, Michael," she said, composed as a baby vampire. "My father is the worst person I know, and look at him. He's fucking rich."

At least that much was true.

"Coach Eric kissed me," she said. "When we were practicing."

Of course he had, I thought. That rotten, blue-eyed, Disney-villain-looking creep.

I did not stay and help Bunny pour coyote urine in the closet of the master bedroom. But I find myself now, years later, unable to discharge from my memory that house. I can remember every room, every detail of its odd layout. I think about Mr. and Mrs. Mitchell and everything they built together, that library with its built-in bar, its secret compartments. I imagine Mrs. Mitchell had a book club and that they felt special meeting there, and maybe Mr. Mitchell played bartender, and maybe he was even hokey about it and pretended to have an Irish accent as he served the ladies Guinness or something. And their children. Imagine having grown up in that house. Imagine trying to describe it to someone else. There had been so many amazing spaces, even beyond the child's library in the attic. There was a huge deck off the second story with a hot tub inside a screened-in gazebo. There was an artist's studio with built-in rolling storage because Mrs. Mitchell had liked to paint. There was a two-thousand-square-foot garage filled with machinist equipment worth thousands of dollars where Mr. Mitchell had done his work. You could have parked eight cars in there. There was a tiny pond with a little bridge over it in the side yard, and there was a turtle still living in it. Bunny and I saw him, basking on the edge. Did the developer know to get the turtle out before he tore it down?

Did adults even give two shits? It was hard to believe they did.

I remain, in some way, in love with that house, tortured by it, even though it no longer exists. I think it may be the most perfect thing I have ever seen. Better even than the Sistine Chapel or the Taj Mahal or the Palace of Versailles.

11

I used to believe you could cross a line. And once you had crossed it, you would never be the same. Metaphysically. If you stabbed someone. If you killed someone. If you ate someone. If you fucked someone. I remember after the first time I had sex, examining myself in the mirror afterward. Was I different? Or was I exactly the same? I was horrified to see my face there, my piranha under-bite, my blackhead-seeded nose, the exact same, too-tender pink eyelid skin. Nothing, I suddenly knew, nothing could ever truly change me. All magic vanished from the world with a hiss.

So why was I so uncomfortable with Bunny hitting Ann Marie in the face? Why did the thought of her kissing Coach Eric make my stomach clench? Why was I so incredibly angry that she had soaked that house in coyote urine?

Why did I still refuse to talk, really talk, to my mother, even after all these years?

I was walking home from my shift at Rite Aid, deep in an internal reverie, when a car door popped open right beside me and I almost screamed, sure I was about to be murdered.

"It's me, oh god, I scared you! Can we talk?" It was Anthony. He was sitting in the driver's seat of the dark car and he looked like hell. The bags under his eyes were fat as change purses.

"I shouldn't," I said, knowing that I would, that I wanted to get in the car and that I was helpless before that want. The most I could do was delay. "My aunt has forbidden me from talking to you or seeing you," I said, as dryly as I could. "Or she'll kick me out." I shrugged in my coat. It was cold from the night sea breezes and I could feel my own saliva chill on my lips. My neighbor Mrs. Cowan's black cat, the one with no tail, meandered down the road ahead of me.

Anthony visibly deflated. "Oh, I'm so sorry," he said. "You poor fucking kid. I'm so sorry."

I had never heard Anthony swear before, but here he was using no-no words. It felt good, how bad he looked, how rattled he seemed. Like all this had been a big deal for him too. Like I mattered.

"I don't want to get you in trouble," he said, looking out his windshield into the middle distance, like he was on a highway, was driving through a forest of things that were just shitty. That's what his face looked like. Like when he looked at the world, all he could see were things that were stupid and shitty. I swung myself into the passenger seat and slammed the car door behind me. My book bag was in my lap. It was suddenly awkward and quiet in the car; we could hear each other breathe.

"I realize I am behaving like a psychopath," he said. "I—I'm not trying to stalk you. For whatever myopic reason, it did not occur to me that continuing to contact you could be putting you in jeopardy. That's very helpful to hear actually. It makes your silence less personal."

That wasn't what I wanted him to say, but I wasn't sure why. I didn't say anything in response. I wanted to press my silence into him like a knife. I wanted to hurt him with it. I cleared my throat.

"I see," he said.

And then I couldn't stand it anymore, because somehow, frighteningly, I could not remember why I was mad at him in that moment, and yet I still felt all the physiological sensations of anger: the prickling in the throat, the hammering heart. I wanted to make him say he loved me, and I wanted to hear his voice, just unspooling, saying more and more in the darkness. "You lied to me," I said. That seemed like the clearest of the transgressions. It was the place to start, even though I knew it wasn't why I was angry with him. I had lied to him just as often. I lied to everyone. I assumed that most people lied to each other, constantly, habitually. *This soup is delicious, I love your earrings, of course I've read Proust . . .* Civilization itself was a lie, North Shore was a lie, clothing was a lie, language was a lie.

"I did," Anthony said, and nodded.

"I'm not an excuse for your midlife crisis. I'm a person," I said. "I'm not a convertible you buy when you figure out you're going bald." I was getting shrill. I tried again, more reasonably toned. "Or maybe this has been an ongoing thing? Maybe you've been cheating on your wife this whole time with different boys?"

"No," Anthony said, "you were the only one."

"I just don't get it, are you gay? Or?"

"I think I'm bi," he said.

"Jesus," I said. "I can't believe you fuck women." I had wanted, as different as we were in age and background, in this one way for us to be the same.

"The fact that you think it's disgusting is one of the reasons I've always shied away from dating men," he said.

"Vaginas are disgusting," I said. "So many folds, and the smell." I had never seen a vagina in my life, but I felt confident I never wanted to.

"No one's body is disgusting," Anthony said quietly.

"You watched your wife push a baby out of that thing and you still want to fuck it? Color me confused is all, not my cup of tea."

"Or maybe," he said, "it's easier for you to joke that your sexuality is about hating vaginas, instead of the fact that it's about loving cock. Maybe being mean about women makes you feel better about the ways people are mean to you."

"Don't fucking psychoanalyze me." None of this was going how I wanted or needed it to go. Why had I even gotten in his car? I just wanted to be by myself and cry. I didn't want to fight, or explain myself, or understand. I just wanted to cry with no one watching me and then smoke a cigarette in a bathtub. It seemed insane that such simple desires were so impossible to fulfill, and yet it would be years before I would have my own space, my own house, and be allowed to smoke in a bathtub.

"I cheated on my wife with you," Anthony said, "but that doesn't make my entire life a lie."

"Doesn't it, though?"

"No," he said, his voice resounding. He squeezed the leather of his steering wheel until it squeaked under his huge palms, and then he suddenly released it, raked his fingers through his hair, shaking with rage. "What the fuck am I doing here?"

"You tell me," I said.

"When I was your age," he said, his nostrils flaring, his rage contorting his face into something beautiful and strange, "I fell in love with my friend."

The way he said the word "friend" hurt me, and I knew already the kind of story it would be.

"And he loved me. And we kissed each other, touched each other, all of it was a secret. It was so secret it was almost a secret from ourselves. We didn't know what we were doing because we couldn't afford to know. It was so dangerous just to be ourselves that it seemed dangerous to see, to feel, to be. It was like a dream where one thing morphs into another, and what maybe started out as a fear that we were not like other boys, that we were attracted to men, became a fear that our deepest selves in every particular were blasphemous, and that if we ever truly communicated with anyone the world would end. It was another time, there's no way you can understand what it was like."

"I understand," I said, and I thought I did.

"My mom, she didn't grow up watching *Will & Grace*. It was— I'm sure you have some stereotype in your mind about what the world was like before Prop 8 was struck down, but you will never understand what it meant for it to be that way, the kind of—the kind of deformity of consciousness that takes place. The way you can pretend you aren't thinking certain things, refuse to notice that you notice what you notice. Anyway, I will never know exactly what happened or why, but word got out at school. I don't know how someone found out. But the bullying was . . . was so tremendous that I had to leave the school."

"My friend," I said, my voice nervous on the word because it meant so much and it meant so little. Bunny was my only friend, but she was not my friend in the way that Anthony had used the word. She was not my lover, and yet, in some way I knew I loved her more than I had ever loved anyone before, more even than I loved Anthony. "Not a boyfriend, just a friend, beat up another girl because that girl saw us making out. In your car. And she was telling. And now the girl is in the hospital in a coma and she might not wake up. And my friend might go to jail, or else maybe nothing will happen. Her dad is really rich, so."

"You weren't out," he said, a guess instead of a question.

"I mean—I wasn't *not* out. I wore makeup and I had my little piercing and my sass. I'm sure people knew. But no, I was not *out* out."

"Sometimes I wish I could have grown up in your generation. Just the freedom. Gay, bi, poly, queer—you could—I know it feels like the world is ending now, but coming out won't end your world. You'll see—it will be—"

And then I was so angry that the words ripped out of me just like the string on a FedEx envelope shreds the cardboard, unzipping myself, exploding with thoughts I didn't even know I had inside me until I spit them into the close air of his car. "You tell me, 'Oh, you don't know what it was like, you could never understand the past, it was so hard'—well, you can't fucking understand the present. You don't know what it is to grow up in a country that has only ever been at war. To do active shooter drills in fucking kindergarten. To grow up knowing you'll never make a living wage. You'll never own a house. That the whole game is rigged, and you'll work your whole life and have nothing to show for it.

"Sometimes I look at all these houses. These mansions. Sometimes I walk through this town and wonder: Who needs a house like this? Who needs a three-car garage? Who needs a master bedroom big enough for a couch by a fireplace? Who needs fucking LaCantina doors that slide so the whole front of your house is open? And the answer is: Everyone. Everyone wants their own personal fucking mansion, and everyone is willing to do whatever it takes to get one. We're like rats at the feeding machine, pushing the lever, confused when all we get are shocks. And sometimes I walk around this neighborhood and I wish that everyone in it would die and all the houses would turn to ash and fall down in piles of clean black powder like sand, and everything that has ever been done could be undone."

"God, I love you," Anthony said, looking at me with his wet brown eyes, pure and beautiful as the eyes of a deer. I felt I could see him as he had been at every point in his life: as a hopeful little boy, as an arrogant teenager, as an earnest college student, as a tired father, as a man, a brave man, a man who chases after his own vitality and refuses to give up on what is right even when it's wrong.

Reader, I fucked him in his car.

Part of the fallout of my conversation with Aunt Deedee was that I had been relocated to the tiny room that had been a walk-in closet on the first floor, and so I no longer had a window into Bunny's bedroom. I no longer had a window at all. Jason had our old bedroom to himself, which delighted him. Whenever we encountered each other in the house, he would address me as "faggot." "Good morning, faggot!" he would say. "Would you like some cereal, faggot? There's milk left."

I think Aunt Deedee had hoped that the small victory of kicking me out of his room and forcing me into a literal closet (!)

would pacify him, and he did seem happy about it, but he did not seem satisfied. A fire does not stop after consuming a single log. I knew he would keep trying to get me out, but all I had to do was get through senior year. I could outlast him. For me, the situation was also a kind of improvement, since I had a new solitude in my tiny room, where I was free to watch porn or makeup tutorials without censure.

In retrospect, it seems clear that I should have had more of a reaction to being treated so uncivilly in my own home, a space where I was supposed to be, at least in theory, safe. But I had never been safe in my own home. Not even as a child. In fact, I had been much more alarmed when my own father commented that he thought one of the bag boys at the Albertsons might be a "poof." I had no idea what being a poof meant, but I knew it was dangerous. I didn't immediately associate it with sexuality, at that age, around six or seven, I associated the word with a makeup poof, something soft and pink. Jason calling me a faggot and thinking it was funny or rebellious or interesting to do so was disgusting, yes, but also pathetic and childish. A bit of the moron doth protest too much, methinks. So I would answer him: "Hey, dudebro, why don't you go drink some ranch and swim with your shirt on?"

"Go suck a cock, homo," he would say when he saw me getting home from school.

"Your pussy is way too dry to be riding my dick like this," I would say as I shouldered past him into my room.

And I think my rage felt as good to me as his rage felt to him.

The only place it was tolerable to exist in my house was in my tiny, windowless room, which was fine for studying or sleeping, especially at first, but as the weeks wore on, I found myself spending more and more time at Bunny Lampert's house, even though I was still finding Bunny extremely hard to take. For one thing, she had begun wearing her mother's (very large) sapphire engagement ring on her right hand. This, together with her ridiculous new office wear, made her feel elegant, causing her to use her arms and arch her torso in new, oddly artificial ways. Maybe she wouldn't even finish high school, she said, languorously stretching. Maybe she would get her GED and go to work for her father. Maybe she would marry Coach Eric, who was still coaching her three times a week. It would be nice, she admitted, to play volleyball for the sheer joy of it. She had gotten so narrow in her thinking, focused on the wrong things. "I mean," she said, leaning in conspiratorially, "it's just a game!"

The Coach Eric business was extremely distressing. He had kissed her at the end of one of their practice sessions on the beach. There were several volleyball courts down at the beach, free for anyone to use, and mostly they remained unused except in the height of summer, but Eric and Bunny spent an afternoon down there three times a week. That Friday they had stayed to see the sun set; the sun was setting earlier and earlier as winter settled in, and they'd sat, sweaty and exhausted in the sand, their bodies too close.

"I could hear his knee creak when he moved it," she said to me later, rapturous. And then he had kissed her, and, as she put it, "smashed her down on the sand." I took this to be the most unromantic description of dry humping I had ever heard, and I did not ask questions, desperate to have no further particulars root themselves in my imagination.

"This is," I said as brightly as I could, "a super-bad idea! And you should stop! Immediately! 'K?"

"Phh," Bunny said. "Says the king of online hookups."

I had lost credibility with her.

The next time they met, he told her it was a horrible mistake, never to be repeated, that she must not tell anyone, that they must go on as before, that he would hold himself in check. But of course it proved "difficult to control himself" around her, and Bunny for her part was doing absolutely anything she could to break his resolve, from wearing her shortest, tightest shorts to accidentally spilling water all over her breasts. She was a comically large Lolita. Coquettishness was also not something that came naturally to Bunny; "on the nose" was her flirting style in toto.

"So then I said that having a nice butt was like my number one quality that I was looking for in a husband, and he kind of did this thing with his eyebrow, like, did you just say that? And then I said, 'And you have a nice one!' And he blushed!"

I mean, I was fish-mouthed, just blinking, trying to take it all in.

She would say things to him like "Dang, I hope I don't get sand in my cootch, I'm not wearing any underwear!"

It was madness. It was lunacy. She was a child bull in a china shop of adult social norms. I didn't think I could handle hearing about it for even a single day more.

After Thanksgiving, there was a long weekend to endure, and I was dreading seeing her, but spending time in my own house was out of the question. Jason had friends over and the living room was a miasma of farts, Axe body spray, and cultural appropriation. "Na, son," they crowed to one another, bouncing on the balls of their idiot feet, "she a trap queen!"

I was expecting to find Bunny ebullient with her latest frontal-assault flirtation, but instead she was somber and preoccupied. Ann Marie had been comatose for more than a month, and I realized, looking at Bunny as she chewed her thumbnail on her father's white sofa, that she had lost quite a bit of weight in that time. Her cheekbones were more prominent, giving her face angles that made her look more like her mother. "Will you look at something for me?" she asked. She got out her backpack, which was white canvas and covered in small black hearts. She pulled out a wad of opened mail, handed me the clump, and went back to chewing the skin around her thumbnail. "What do those look like to you? I mean, do you think I'm reading them right?"

I opened the first one. They were letters from the IRS. Some were notices of deficiency, some were notices of examination. They spanned, in the tax years they referenced, almost a decade, and the amounts they listed as owed were staggering. For 2007, they claimed Ray Lampert still owed $107,000 in back taxes. For 2009 he owed $65,489. There was a notice of a tax lien placed against their house. There were notices explaining that his bank account had been frozen. What was most confusing, as I sorted through them, was that there was not a clear escalating time frame. The notice claiming his bank account had been frozen was from five years ago. The lien on their home was new.

"Where did you find these?" I asked. "I'm guessing Cassie doesn't know about this."

"I don't know," Bunny said, rubbing her eyes with the palms of her hands. "That bitch would die for him."

"So how did you get these?"

She sighed. "They were in his office here at the house. I mean, they weren't even hidden. They were just on his desk. I was never curious about what was on his desk before, but I got the mail today and there was a notice they were putting a lien on the house, and so then I went looking and found the rest."

"I don't understand," I said, "he's been making money hand over fist, so why not pay his taxes? It just seems so weird!"

"He's been overextended," she said. It was such a Ray word, such a typically grandiose euphemism, but for what exactly?

"Upstanding city council member and tax dodger," I said, in a game show–host voice, but she didn't laugh.

"What's going to happen?" she asked me.

"I mean—I guess, eventually, he'll have to pay?"

"He doesn't have the money to pay," she said, "I mean, obviously!"

"Bullshit," I said, "he has this house. I'm sure he has other investments. He's just living in some kind of system of cycling delusions where he thinks he can catch up. But he'll figure out that he can't, and he'll settle up with the IRS and maybe you'll lose the house, but you'll be fine."

Bunny began to cry. "Where will we go?" she asked.

"Jesus Christ," I said, "you'll rent an apartment!"

She nodded, wiping her tears.

And then a young woman whom neither of us recognized opened the front door of their house, and Ray Lampert came in with a bandage wrapped in a thick halo around his head and bruising of Technicolor plum in perfectly symmetrical triangles under his eyes and on the tops of his cheekbones. Something was wrong with his eyes and he seemed to be blind, or his eyes seemed to be stitched shut—in any event, they were swollen and something was deeply wrong with the skin above them. The young woman led him to one of the pretty French armchairs and helped him heave himself down onto it. "Hello," she said in a singsong voice, "I'm Charity!" She was wearing all black: tight black pants and a black lace shirt over a tank top. She was delicately pretty and had pale, milky skin.

"What happened?" Bunny asked.

"It's not as bad as it looks," Ray said, which led both of us to continue in our assumption that he had been in some sort of fight. "I had to get it done before we went to court and you never know when that's gonna be."

"Okay, baby," Charity said, "I'm putting your meds in the kitchen. He should not drink on these pain pills! Okay, Bunny? Don't let him drink. I gotta go to work."

"You're the best," Ray said.

"Wait, w-what?" Bunny stammered.

"It's a simple surgery. In, out, bing, bang," he said. I noticed there was something wrong with his speech, some thickness to his consonants that I assumed was from the head bandage or the drugs.

"What surgery?"

"Just a little stuff," he said.

As I examined him more closely, I began to understand that his eyelids were scored with crescents of black stitches in their swollen folds. I gasped and covered my mouth with my hand. "He's had his eyes done!"

"It was a forehead lift," Ray said, "but it really only makes sense to do the eyes at the same time."

Bunny, beside me on the sofa, got up into a half crouch and was shaking with rage. Everything she said came out in a half yell. "You got plastic surgery? We're about to lose our house and you got plastic surgery? What is wrong with you? And who is that girl? Is she the hostess from La Trattoria? Because she looks like the hostess from La Trattoria!"

La Trattoria was the fanciest Italian restaurant in town.

"Charity is a friend," Ray said. "Who was kind enough to drive me to the doctor."

He said this as though Bunny had failed to be kind enough to drive him to the doctor. She sputtered for a moment, then cried, "I mean, how much did this even cost?"

"It's fine," Ray said. I was beginning to understand what was wrong with his lips as well. He'd had them pumped full of collagen.

"Really, because I found a bunch of letters from the IRS saying they are going to take the house, and it doesn't seem like it's fine!"

"My lawyers are on it. Don't worry. I'm sorry you were scared, but really everything is fine, Bunny Rabbit!" He looked at her through his squinty swollen eyes. Bunny was frozen on the couch, trying to decide whether or not to believe him. "You know me, Bunny. You know I'm the king of this kind of stuff."

"Then why haven't you paid them?"

"Because I don't owe that money! The only way you can contest disagreements is by refusing to pay—if I pay but then say I didn't owe that, I'll never see the money again. They nickel-and-dime you every step of the way, you have to fight to get a fair shake!"

Bunny visibly softened, and I was astonished his pants didn't burst into flame. I felt sick as I watched, even though, or perhaps because, I understood. She wanted everything he said to be true so badly that she would ignore all evidence to the contrary. "Jesus, Daddy," she said, "you should tell me about these things!"

"I didn't want to worry you with a bunch of bullshit."

"And this surgery? Why would you have plastic surgery?"

"It's an investment," he said. "For the business. You have to look young, look good, you know, plus with the forehead lift, it's interesting, they basically cut away a strip of your forehead at the hairline, so it hides that you're balding. It's like a two for one!"

"But couldn't you have told me you were getting it?" she asked.

"Honestly, I didn't understand it would be this big a deal. I mean, look at me. I look like shit! I thought I could turn in early and you'd never notice. Wear some makeup, what's it called, concealer, for a couple days!" He smiled, shook his head to show what an idiot he'd been about it.

"You do look really horrible," she said.

"I look like they messed up a Raggedy Ann doll!" he said, and they both laughed. "Let's order a pizza!"

And they ordered a pizza. And I stayed, and I ate it with them. Somehow, the night was weirdly fun. Pizza grease and red wine got on the IRS letters. Ray convinced us that he could have just one glass of red wine with his pills, and Bunny said we should get to have a glass if he did, and for some reason I drank it with them. I held the glass in my hand, and I couldn't believe I would really drink it, because not crossing this line had been a deep part of my self-identity. I took a sip. It tasted exactly like it smelled. I was ready for a whole new world. I was ready to be a different person. A terrible person.

After the first glass, I understood why every, or almost every, adult I knew did this. I felt amazing. My body was like rippling water, full of energy, nothing hurt, and everything was funny, even me, especially me. I couldn't stop the things that came out of my mouth, and at one point I made Ray laugh so hard his eyelid suture tore a little and he started bleeding.

"Stop," he moaned, holding a Domino's napkin to his bleeding eyelid. "Stop!"

"Mr. Lampert," I said, holding out an imaginary microphone, "why did you feel the need to do this terrible thing to your face?"

"I don't know," he gasped, still dabbing at his eyes.

"Was it a fear of death?"

"Eh, death. I mean—I don't love the idea of dying, but no, I don't think it was death."

"Then was it fear you would no longer be able to attract the pussy?"

"Jesus!"

"Answer the question, sir."

Bunny was clapping, laughing, delighted with this game.

"Honestly, yes. I mean, it was terrible. I mentioned to Charity about maybe getting work done, and I'm expecting her to say, no, no, you don't need it, but right away she chimes in with 'That's a great idea!'"

"Do you love Charity?"

"No, but she's a freak in bed," he said.

"Well, you know what they say about a woman who'll eat ass—don't marry her, but keep her in your phone."

Ray laughed at this like it was the funniest thing he had ever heard. "You are too much, Michael," he said.

"Next question, marriage equality: Were you for or against?"

"For!" he cried.

"Hallelloo, hunty!" I said.

"Gay people should be able to do whatever they want. Except maybe teach little kids."

"Wh-what, now?" I said.

"Well, I don't know, I just—teaching preschool or something. Or even elementary school teachers. That doesn't seem right to me."

Bunny's mouth was literally hanging open and her eyes were bulging out of her head. She couldn't believe her dad was saying this. But I could.

"Yeah, you think gay teachers can turn little kids gay? How do they do it? Pheromones, or like pixie dust, or do you actually think that we're all pederasts who want to fuck little boys?" I was still pretending to speak into the imaginary microphone for some reason.

"Well, I don't know," Ray said. He was still smiling, like we were going to have some kind of interesting fucking debate.

"This isn't *Fox & Friends*," I interrupted him. "I don't care about your opinions, Mr. Lampert, because you are a cesspool of a human being with the moral compass of a gnat." He was squinting at me through his busted, swollen eyes, trying to tell if I was joking, if this was some fun read, hashtag the library is open. Bunny had both hands clapped over her mouth, just watching. "You think this town loves you, but have you noticed you don't have any friends? You've built a child's idea of a rich man's house and you live in it like you're the king, but what are you king of? Money you don't have? A daughter who doesn't like you? No wonder your wife drove into traffic, you're a fucking joke."

And then I got up, and I left, and no one stopped me.

12

I do not know where, in a genetic sense, my intellectual bent came from, but I can remember exactly when school began to seem less useless to me. I had always been a reader, and novels provided me much company throughout my boyhood, but school itself held no appeal. The adults there were using the same bad scripts as social workers, like they were telemarketers cold-calling the youth. All the lining up, all the tiny, incremental punishments, pull a green card, then pull a yellow card, but if you pull the red card . . . Or later in high school the elaborate demerit system: five tardies equal one unexcused absence, and three unexcused absences equal one demerit, and three dicks sucked equal one I couldn't care less about any of this. Even the schoolwork itself, the worksheets and Scantrons, textbooks instead of real books, it was all so meaningless and bizarre. Why were we all doing this together, and so obsessively?

But there was a day in early April of my junior year of high school when our biology teacher came into class on fire, so excited that he exploded at us, holding up a newspaper and stabbing at the text with his finger. What so excited him was a finger bone that had been found in the Altai Mountains in Siberia in 2008 had now been genetically analyzed and found to be neither Neanderthal nor Homo sapiens in origin. She, the study called her X-woman, was from a third hominid species, Denisovans, named after the cave in which the bone was found, who had diverged from our lineage about a million years ago, and her finger bone had been found in a cave where both Neanderthal and Homo sapiens remains had also been found, along with stone tools. More startling, while the modern Eurasian populations shared up to one percent genetic material with Denisovans, consistent with the theory that we shared a common ancestor, in Melanesian populations the figure rose to four percent, indicating more recent genetic exchange between Denisovans and Homo sapiens in that part of the world. In another study, bones found in Croatia indicated Homo sapiens and Neanderthals had interbred. The picture, hazy as it was, was that there had been many kinds of humans living, fucking, competing, and killing each other at the same time.

Our teacher, who was a young man, perhaps in his late twenties or early thirties, and who had some kind of rockabilly undercut, much too stylish a haircut for a teacher, was in a kind of rapture about this, and he kept interrupting himself, trying to explain to us why this was exciting. "It's such a deep assumption in our culture that there was this steady and inevitable march from ape to man, that it was this clear progression, but it was chaotic! I just think it says so much. And it really puts xenophobia in a different light, as some kind of possibly helpful mutation. I mean, we were in direct competition, but also interbreeding, with different species of humanoid animals. Doesn't that just blow your mind?"

It did blow my mind. And I connected it, rightly or wrongly, with a sensation I had often had with my own father, when he was drunk enough, where I would stop recognizing him. His face, or his eyes, would become too strange, and suddenly he was no longer a man I loved but one I wanted urgently to murder. The idea that this was a human impulse and not a moral failing on my part as his son but some kind of genetic adaptation, a holdover from a time when we decided whom to fuck and whom to kill based on whether they were the same or other, was deeply comforting to me and intellectually freeing.

Questions that had always bothered me, about slavery, about

the Holocaust, about the Armenian genocide and the Rwandan one, about the human ability to look at another human being and decide, nope, I think that kind of human is an animal, suddenly coalesced into a powerful shape of interdependent facts and observations. Human beings were murderous because it had been necessary for our survival. Human beings committed genocide because we had evolved to commit genocide. Human beings projected themselves onto animals, and then retracted that sympathy, and then projected that sympathy once more, confused about the line between what was like us and what wasn't, because for thousands of years we had been making exactly those judgment calls. Violence was not something that had infected us, some alien thing that could slip into our bloodstream and cloud our judgment via ideology or mechanization. It was not gray-eyed Athena tricking Ajax into murdering sheep. It was sewn in. We were violent, murderous animals, by design.

So I was not entirely surprised when a group of boys jumped me behind the Rite Aid as I was getting off my shift. I was tired, but I was excited because I was about to go meet Anthony. If we got caught, fuck it. I hadn't spoken to Bunny since that night in her house, and I didn't want to. I didn't want her to apologize for her father, to try to explain him to me. And I didn't want to have to apologize for myself.

While Matthew Shepard had been murdered when I was a child, it was still a story very much in the zeitgeist. In 2007, Ryan Skipper was found dead of multiple stab wounds and a slit throat, and his murderers had driven around in his blood-soaked car, bragging of how they'd killed him. So I understood that other men would want, and possibly would try, to kill me. But it had not occurred to me that it would happen in my hometown. In some sense, I think I viewed North Shore, even then, with the child's eyes with which I had first seen it when I was eleven. It seemed to me too good a town to harbor such violence, though I kept being proved wrong. Donna Morse's murder. Bunny beating Ann Marie. Yet I still assumed that if such a thing were to happen to me, it would happen to me in college, or in my adulthood, when I was living in a glamorous metropolis. I just hadn't imagined I would be getting off work at Rite Aid, still wearing my blue smock, lighting a cigarette.

The one I recognized first was Ann Marie's boyfriend, Tyler. "Hey, faggot," he called to me in the parking lot. And so I knew what they were there for, but I did not know how far they meant to take it. I paused, and perhaps because I was very tired, I sighed dramatically and said, "What do you want, honeys?" I had never let myself talk like that except in private, and it felt thrilling and dangerous.

"We wanna talk to you," one of the other ones said, a boy named Jonah whom I had taken English with sophomore year. I remember we read *The Great Gatsby.* "Just come here, we wanna talk."

I started toward them. "Listen guys, I—" But by then I was close enough, and Tyler socked me in the face. The pain was as sudden and real as when you bark your shin on a coffee table, and for a moment I could not understand what had possibly happened. He hit me again, and I went down.

Then I was on the ground, and they were kicking me, and they were shouting things and spitting on me and laughing. I had my hands wrapped around my head because my instinct was to protect my face, but this left my ribs and stomach open, though I was curled into a ball as well as I could. "Dude, I'm gonna pee on him," one of them said, but I don't think he ever got around to it. I was surprised by how much it all hurt. I was almost indignant that I was still so fully conscious, and that I was thinking things so calmly, wondering when they would stop, if there was anything I could do to hasten the end of this situation, hoping Terrence would come out, hoping Terrence would not come out because it would be so terribly embarrassing. Then suddenly, I heard his voice, and I knew that my cousin Jason was with them, and I thought: Oh god, they are going to kill me.

But then I must have really, finally, blessedly gone into shock, because I cannot remember the beating ending, only that I suddenly became aware that they were gone and I was lying in the parking lot and I should probably get up in case someone came and ran me over. But the idea of getting up seemed impossible, and I decided it was all right to lie there because I would see headlights if a car was coming. And then I think I slept, or something close to sleep, because I had the sensation of waking when Terrence found me.

"Oh boy, oh boy," he kept saying. "Sweet mother of god. Hold on, buddy, just hold on." I could hardly see his face because the streetlight was behind him, but I knew his voice, and I loved him, oh how I loved him. I knew he would call 911 for me, and I knew he wouldn't leave me, and I knew that he loved me, just as he loved all God's creatures, and in my head I pretended that I was a deer that had been hit by a car, and Terrence was the kind of man who would stop, who would pull over, and he was holding me because I was real to him, because my face, in its terrible nudity, demanded something from him. It was my otherness that so angered those boys, my unknowableness, my dangerous wrongness. They couldn't understand me and it made them want to extinguish me, and Terrence couldn't understand me and it made him want to save me.

And that was all it was: a difference, a genetic predisposition, some ancient snippet of DNA that made you want to fight what was different from you or else fuck what was different from you, and both strategies existed in our population. I pictured Terrence with a strange-eyed, unknowable Denisovan wife, and I pictured Tyler and those boys murdering his alien and wonderful hybrid babies, and I understood then about bashing infants on the rocks, about internment camps and gas chambers, about slave ships and plantations and shooting black young men on the streets, about all of human history, it seemed, and then I was gone for a little while and I wondered if, even hoped really, that perhaps I was dying, but then the ambulance came and it was like a dream ending, and I wished that I could have stayed in that parking lot with Terrence forever, just breathing and quietly bleeding while he held my hand.

I don't remember a lot of what came next, but I do remember how bright the hospital lights were and I remember big flurries of everyone doing a lot of stuff to me and then other times when I was left alone for what seemed like a long time. I remember over-hearing a conversation between two orderlies who were taking me from one place to another about how one of them had gotten a new dog, and they were so excited to meet the dog and I wanted to ask what kind it was, but when I tried to talk they weren't able to hear me and just went on talking as though I weren't there. We took what seemed to be four or five different elevator trips, and I couldn't imagine what kind of Escher-like design the hospital must have to require so many different elevators. When we finally got to my room, the orderly bent over me and said, so softly that only I would be able to hear, "You've gotta get out of here, buddy. This isn't a real hospital."

Adrenaline sang through my body, and suddenly I was in a large white room, but I was lying on the floor and I was by myself. I couldn't see anything else in the room, but I remember the floor was extremely cold and my back was aching from how cold it was, and I wondered if possibly I was simply lying on a sheet of ice, but somehow I knew I was not in a natural place, I wasn't on a frozen lake, I was in a building, but some kind of otherworldly building with nonreal characteristics, and that is when I became convinced that I had snuck in somewhere I was not supposed to be, and that eventually they were going to figure out I was in here and I was going to be in unimaginable trouble. When I tried to think about who "they" were, I realized they were some kind of angels or aliens, beings from another level of reality, and I was not supposed to be in their area, and they would send me away, and in being expelled I would most likely die. I wanted desperately to sneak out while I still could, but I could not move my arms or legs.

When I woke up, there was a nurse near me, and I cried, "I've been in a car accident!" I kept telling people that, because I thought if they found out that I had been beaten for being homosexual then they would refuse to treat me. But no one would talk to me. The nurses and doctors kept having hushed conversations with one another, but they never addressed me or told me what was going on. At one point, I was in a huge shopping mall going up thousands of escalators. I bought myself a blazer as yellow as the sun and one of the nurses tsked that I was selfish. And then I remembered the orderly telling me I was not in a real hospital, and I thought: Of course! What kind of real hospital has thousands of escalators and elevators in it and sells yellow blazers!

My aunt Deedee came to visit me and told me she was incredibly disappointed in me. I wanted to tell her that Jason had been the one who did this to me, that it had been him and his friends, but that I had pushed him to it by means of sickening shade, that it was my incredible, ingeniously sharp tongue that had done me in, that my wit was dangerous and second only to Oscar Wilde's or Dorothy Parker's. She cried and told me the TV would be watching me and then she left, and I didn't know what to make of that, and I became terrified of having the TV on because I thought the people inside it could see me through the screen.

Perhaps the most ridiculous part of all this is that Ann Marie kept coming into my room. She kept talking to me about Jesus and how he wanted to do this weaving in my internal organs, and how they were going to take a wire and put it in my veins and then explore my whole body with it, and Jesus himself was going to do this as performance art.

The sounds that I could hear from my hospital bed were extremely loud and I figured out that the nurses were Foley artists practicing making sounds. Crinkle, crinkle, crunch. Footsteps, footsteps, footsteps. They were working as nurses while they got their degrees as Foley artists so they could work in radio. There was going to be this big resurgence in old-timey radio serials because of podcasts. These nurses were so visionary! I rooted for them, but the sounds they made were also extremely annoying.

Anthony came at one point, and I became aware that my aunt Deedee was also in the room, and that shit was *tense.* "You guys are going to have to communicate via radio," I kept saying. "So you don't have to talk, but you can radio from inside your head, and then he can radio from inside of his head, like, *Roger that!*"

Anthony held my hand, and he kept crying, and he said he was sorry because he couldn't be with me anymore, that he had been very foolish, but he just couldn't risk his family and his marriage, he owed it to Hank. "I think that's really on point," I said. "You're gonna get an A."

I asked Aunt Deedee when she was gonna kick me out, but she said we could talk about it later. I asked her how it felt to be the mother of a murderer, but she said, "You're not a murderer." She seemed to have no idea Jason had killed me.

By the time Bunny came, I was feeling a lot better. Aunt Deedee had been gone for maybe days, and the only person who regularly came was Ann Marie. I asked her what she could remember of her coma and she said nothing. It was like being asleep. I was so jealous. It didn't seem fair that she could almost die so much more than me and yet have it suck so much less.

Bunny was so real in my room and for the first time in a long time I felt like I was awake. She touched me all over, she touched my face and I figured out I had bruises on my face because of the way it felt as her fingers skimmed the skin. She even sniffed my hair at one point. It was like she was a mother dog and I was her lost pup. "I know I shouldn't be telling you this, but I don't know what else to do," she said.

"You can tell me anything," I said. "I'm transparent as glass."

"My dad has basically stolen my identity." I thought for a moment she was saying that he was doing drag as her, and I thought that was so fascinating, but it was just that he had stolen her Social Security number. "He has like five credit cards in my name, and there is a bank account with thousands of dollars in it, and he took out a mortgage in my name. You know those apartments they are building up on Grand? I guess he wanted to invest in them with Mr. Phong, but he couldn't get a loan because of all the IRS stuff, so he used my stuff. He said the credit cards were to build up my credit, that it's actually a good thing, but it's like—Michael, it's like several hundred thousand in debt all told. And he's like, of course I'm gonna pay it off—"

"Lies," I said.

"Right?" she said.

"Your father sprouts lies, it's like he was cursed by a gypsy, oh my god, I bet that's what happened!"

"And then he said the apartment buildings were actually a surprise birthday present and he even made it seem like it was because of the Ann Marie stuff that he didn't tell me about it then. Which made me feel, just, just fucking awful about myself."

"What an amazing lie," I said. "He's so good at it."

"I just don't know what to do."

"Listen, I've been in a car accident, so I might not be the best person to help you with this. I think I might be dying and stuff."

"Oh, I promise you're not dying," she said. "Your surgery went very well and they say you'll make a full recovery."

"Really! Oh wow, that's such a big relief. Is this a real hospital and everything?"

"Yes," she said.

"I'm so overjoyed, I can't even tell you. Where's Ann Marie?"

"What?"

"She keeps coming in here," I said.

"Ann Marie died," Bunny said.

"No," I said. "I swear she hasn't. She's around here somewhere. She was just here." I was going to tell her about Jesus doing performance art in my veins but decided that would sound too weird.

"Michael," Bunny said. "I've been worried about those apartment buildings for a long time. And now it makes me just sick that they're mine. That my name is on the deed."

"Does it feel like a lot of responsibility?"

She was crying suddenly.

"It's just like your name, but in a different font," I said to comfort her.

"No, it's just my dad has been freaked out about those buildings forever. Construction is running way over budget and he got this shady electrician to do all the panels with parts he got from China and then paid off the inspector. And—it's probably fine! I mean, they're up to code in China! But what if it isn't fine? What if people move in there and it's not right?"

"The sins of the father," I said.

"If those fuse boxes malfunction," she said, "people could die."

"You can't stop people from dying, they do it anyway."

"What should I do?" she asked.

"You could burn them down," I said.

"The apartment buildings?"

"Yeah."

"What function would that serve?" she asked.

"Why, it would be poetic justice. I've always wanted to burn this town to the ground, did you know that?"

13

The next time I opened my eyes, I was looking at my mother, who was standing by the right side of my bed. I was in an incredible amount of pain in my midsection. Machines all around me were pooping jujubes of sound. Slow robot claws were being extended.

"He's up," she said. Aunt Deedee was on the other side of me, sitting in the single chair in my curtained-off enclosure, and I swiveled to look at her. She looked tired and numb and sad. She was holding my left hand, which had lots of tubes in it.

"I'm sorry," I said.

"Why are you sorry?" she said.

"For being so much trouble," I said.

"Don't be an idiot," my mother said, chewing savagely on her already short nails. "We're just happy you're not dead!"

"You have new bangs," I said. She looked at me and there was a flash, some kind of explosion of memory, an intimacy we used to share, a way we once were madly in love with each other, a world lost, a building engulfed in flames. "It looks good," I said.

"Well," she said.

"How did the car accident happen?" I asked. "I just—why was I even driving?"

"What, honey?" Aunt Deedee asked.

"I know I was in a car accident," I said, "but I can't remember it."

They looked at each other and for some reason I knew that Aunt Deedee had told my mother that I was gay. And then I remembered. The dark parking lot and the floating bright rect-angles of the streetlights overhead. The sound of their laughter, the smell of the asphalt and blood and then a waft of spearmint. One of them must have been chewing gum. I started crying. "I was supposed to tell her," I said. "I was supposed to get to tell her."

"Shh . . ." Aunt Deedee said.

"Do you know where you are?" a doctor asked me. His face was familiar and I wanted to tell him that yes, I was in a hospital where he had been my doctor for some days now and that I recognized his weirdly long upper lip. His cupid's bow looked like a tiny waterslide.

"In the hospital?" I said.

"That's right," he said. "Do you know what year it is?"

"2010."

"Okay, it seems like you're a bit more oriented, so I want to just go over with you what has happened, what your treatment plan is, and where we can go from here. You were admitted to the ER with internal bleeding, a grade two laceration to the spleen, minor lacerations to the kidneys—" The doctor saw my attention start to wander and put his face weirdly close to mine, said, "Stay with me here, I need informed consent, buddy! After this there will be some forms to sign. There was some bowel and mesenteric vessel injury, two cracked ribs, and a grade one hematoma on your liver. We were able to go in nonoperatively and halt the bleeding in your spleen."

"Nonoperatively?"

"Basically, in this case we inserted a wire into your vascular system through the groin and were able to stop the bleeding."

"That sounds super bad," I said.

"Actually, you're very lucky," the doctor said. "You're young. You've got that good protoplasm. You'll heal fast."

"I can't believe protoplasm is a real thing," I said. "I mean, what a crazy word!" I was also thinking that Jesus really had performed art through my veins, and I was suddenly anxious about how much of my other memories were real. Obviously the nurses were not Foley artists. But had Anthony come to see me and told me he couldn't be with me anymore? Had I told Aunt Deedee that Jason had been part of the group who attacked me? Had he even been there? I hadn't seen him at first, but I had heard his voice, and I swear at one point I had seen his face, heard his disgusting laugh. I didn't know how I would ever be able to trust myself enough to say for sure. A nurse had wrapped my fingers around a chubby plastic pen and was holding out forms for me to sign on a clipboard.

"Here," she was murmuring, "and here. Here. And this states you do not have insurance. Here."

"Wait," I said, thinking that I did have insurance, but then I remembered Aunt Deedee had been fired from Starbucks and so our health insurance was probably gone. "So what happens if you don't have insurance?"

"Well, honey, you're still seventeen, so we can probably get you retroactively into Medi-Cal, but even if we can't, you were the victim of a crime, so all your expenses will ultimately be covered by the Victim Compensation Board, as long as you cooperate with the police investigation."

I was still seventeen, so I got insurance. Bunny had turned eighteen, so she'd be tried as an adult. Of all the arbitrary boundaries in the world, I marveled.

"We're going to transfer you out of the ICU," the doctor said, "to a regular room. We're gonna hold on to you for a few more days, just to give that spleen some time to heal and make sure we don't get any clots or blockages in your urinary tract from those kidneys. I do think the police want to have a word with you, and they're out in the hall—are you up for it?"

"Uh, sure?" I had not thought about that at all, the legal side of my situation.

The doctor and nurse left, and a man and a woman entered my room. Some kind of switch flipped and suddenly I was sure all of this was fake, that it was part of some TV show or social experiment. These were not real detectives but people impersonating police detectives. It was so obvious. The man had mussed-up hair and was wearing a leather jacket over a button-down shirt that had a stain on it. The woman didn't know how to dress at all, and her outfit was so extremely basic that only a costume designer could have produced it. They were both beautiful and yet ordinary-looking, with eyes that were too shiny.

"Michael," the woman detective said, "I'm Detective Carmine and this is Detective Brown."

Even their names sounded made up.

"We were hoping you could tell us a little bit about what happened on the evening of Tuesday the seventh."

"Was that the night I got beat up?"

She nodded.

"Well, I was working, and then I got off work and I was in the parking lot."

"Going to your car?" the male detective asked.

"No, I don't have a car, I was just lighting a cigarette and I was about to walk home, when I saw a group of guys, and they called me over."

"Did you recognize any of them?" Detective Carmine asked. Her teeth were way too white. It was the little details that people forgot about, and it was forgivable on TV, but for someone to be trying to get away with it in real life was absurd. No detective would ever have teeth that white.

"I'm not sure," I said.

"Not sure if you recognized them?"

"I just—I'm coming to this place in my life where I'm not sure I believe in punishment."

The two detectives exchanged a look.

"I can't talk about this right now," I said.

"We just need you to tell us as much as you can," Detective Carmine said in a soothing voice. "Unfortunately, when you were admitted they were under the impression that you had been in a car accident and so no one preserved your clothes for evidence, so we have no fibers, no hairs, no actual physical evidence of any kind. Do you have any idea why someone would want to hurt you?"

"Well, because I'm gay," I said. "Which would make it a hate crime. Which is, can you see why I am hesitant to just accuse people of a hate crime?"

"That's something for their lawyers to worry about," Detective Brown said.

It wasn't that I didn't want those boys to be punished. It wasn't that I didn't believe they were bad. I was disgusted by them. The look on their faces, the way they had laughed at me as they did it. But I was confused about whether or not to say Jason was among them. And it didn't seem fair to name the others if I was going to refuse to name him. I remembered the nurse saying that my medical expenses would be covered so long as I cooperated with the police investigation, and I thought: They are trying to extort me!

"I just need to think about it a little bit more," I said. "Would that be all right?"

"In an investigation like this," Detective Carmine said, "it can muddy the waters. You don't want a defense attorney saying, look, he wasn't even sure he knew who attacked him, how can you know it was my client? If you won't cooperate with the investigation, then I'm going to be honest with you, it will be dropped. Most likely it will be dropped."

"Drop it, then," I said. I don't know why I was so angry, but I was furious. I felt that these detectives were questioning me in the wrong way, and I badly wanted them to behave differently. I wanted someone to say how sorry they were that this had happened to me, to ask me how I was doing, to make sure I knew what was real and what wasn't, to listen to my thoughts and feelings and fears without rushing me or telling me I was wrong. You weren't supposed to threaten a victim that unless he talked, he'd owe hundreds of thousands of dollars in medical bills. They were threatening me, even in the way they stood there. Wasn't I the victim? Weren't you supposed to at least be nice to the victim?

I thought about Bunny that day at the wonderful house on Oak Street. "I don't want to be good anymore," she had said. "I think it's a rigged game."

"How about this, we'll go downstairs, we'll get a coffee, we'll come back up. Would that work for you?" Detective Carmine said, and Detective Brown rolled his eyes as hard as any teen girl ever has.

"Maybe we should come back some other time and we can bring a social worker," Detective Brown said softly to Carmine. "'Cause we still need to get out to Santa Monica to talk to that witness. I'm just saying, there's gonna be traffic."

"We'll be right back," Detective Carmine said. "We're just going to get a coffee, you can think about that night, and when your head is clear we'll be back and maybe you can give us some idea of what happened. Because this isn't right. You don't need to worry about punishment, you don't need to worry about hate crimes, or what their lawyer is going to say or do or how they will be sentenced. All you have to do is tell us what you remember, okay? Nothing about that could be wrong. Okay?"

I nodded, and they left, and I waited and waited for them to come back but they never did.

I was moved to a regular room later that day, and they also removed my catheter. "Some blood in your urine is par for the course at this point," the nurse said. "Just let us know if you see big chunks."

After that, I peed with my eyes closed, terrified of seeing anything even remotely like that.

When they made me get up and walk for the first time, I understood how bad it was. My abdomen was so full of fluid that I felt like I was wearing a fat suit. My feet and ankles were swollen to the size of pug dogs, and when I stood, it felt like my ankle skin was going to snap and water would just gush out of me. I had thought I was dying so many times during my hallucinations, but nothing was as horrifying as understanding that now I would be living, and that it would hurt this badly. It wasn't even really the pain, it was the shame of it, the humiliation of the flesh, the sense that my body was disgusting.

Other than that, I liked my new room, which I shared with a darling old chap named Scottie. Scottie was there for pneumonia, but he was getting better now, and he let me put on *The Golden Girls* and laughed at some of the jokes. We both got excited when they brought pudding. I have always loved, and felt a deep affinity for, the elderly. People always go on about babies, but if I were to give birth to something, I would want it to be an eighty-year-old woman who loved to play bridge.

I began to be afraid of being released. As much as I had been unwilling, or even weirdly unable, to report Jason, I could not imagine continuing to live in the same house as him. I even felt like I remembered a conversation with Aunt Deedee in which she said I would have to move out, but I could not tell if that had been a dream or not. I wasn't sure when anyone had said they would visit me again either, but I knew it had been at least forty-eight hours since I had seen my mother or Aunt Deedee. Everything before that was in a kind of timeless miasma. I wasn't even sure when Bunny was coming back. For the first time, I wondered where my cell phone was, but there was no one to ask.

Ann Marie did not come to my new room, and I began to accept that Bunny was right, and that she was dead. For some reason the physicality of death, the mortification of the flesh, was very real to me, and whenever I would think of her I would viscerally imagine her corpse, and I often could not make these fantasies end and would find myself hyperventilating and nauseated. Ann Marie was dead, and Bunny had killed her. That was a fact.

But Ann Marie's corpse also felt like some kind of puzzle I was trying to solve. What did the inside of a person have to do with the outside? And were we all the same inside? Were our interior psychic organs all identical in the same way we each possessed a stomach and a heart and a spleen? Psychology seemed to be predicated on this assumption, that the psychology of one person would be comparable to the psychology of another. But what if it wasn't? What if there were no organs of the mind at all? And what if, in our rush to think of the inside of a person as a corollary to the body, we misnamed ourselves? And what if in that misnaming, we turned ourselves into something unspoken and unspeakable?

All the things you couldn't say! It seemed to me there were so many. And how were you supposed to get anything sorted if you couldn't talk about it? Wasn't language our best hope and our last stop before murder?

Bunny came sometime that night. I didn't know the time, but it was definitely dark outside my window and Scottie was asleep and snoring sweetly.

"You look so much better!" Bunny cooed as she sat down, scooting the chair up closer to my bed.

"Oh, thank you, darling," I said. "Being beaten almost to death does wonders for the skin." I fanned my face so she could examine my pores.

"Oh, oh, oh, you are back! You are fucking back!" she cried, a little too loudly.

"Don't wake Scottie," I said, "he's had a very long day. First, a *Golden Girls* marathon, and then a *Designing Women* marathon. We are exhausted, honey."

"Has the hospital made you gayer?" Bunny asked.

"Perhaps! Perhaps! Maybe I'm just less inhibited because of the vvvvunderful drrrrugsssss."

"Whatever it is, I like it."

"They say I could be released as soon as Thursday," I said.

"That's great."

"But I can't go home. Where the fuck am I gonna go?"

"Why can't you go home?"

"Ugh, because Jason."

"The farting?"

"No. He's much more hostile these days."

"He is?"

And suddenly I was crying. I covered my eyes with my hands, trying to wipe away the tears, but I could tell I was not going to recover and this was going to become a serious crying jag. "I'm so sorry," I whispered.

"Oh, Mikey," Bunny said, and climbed up into my bed. I had to scoot over painfully to make room for her, but her body was so big and warm and safe.

"Tell Auntie Bunny," she said, and kissed my ear, my cheek, my hair.

"Well, you know how it happened?" I asked.

"No, I mean, I know you were beat up, but when I asked you before you said you couldn't remember it."

"Oh, I can remember it," I said.

"Who was it?" Bunny asked, her voice so cold and serious I worried she would go out and murder whoever I said.

"Ann Marie's boyfriend, Tyler, and Jonah Anderson, and Riley Masterson, do you know him?"

She nodded. She knew them all.

"And then, well, I think Jason was there."

"You think?"

"I don't have a clear visual memory of his face, only his voice and his laugh, and he only came halfway through and by then I was really out of it. But they were debating whether or not to pee on me, and—"

"To pee on you?" Her voice was rippling with hate.

"They didn't, though," I said. "They decided not to." I tried to rearrange my hands on my stomach in a way that was more comfortable for my IV, and I felt like a prim old woman.

"Who else?" she asked.

"Bunny, you can't tell anyone," I said. "You can't go out and beat them up. You have to promise. I'm telling this only to you.

This information exists only within the sacred oasis of our friendship. I didn't even tell the cops."

"Why on earth would you not tell the police?"

I sighed. "I probably will if they ever come back; I just hadn't decided what to tell them about Jason. I can't—I can't guarantee he was there. I can't promise that my brain, during the horror of it all, didn't just insert him."

"So tell them that—tell them you're not sure, but you think you remember him."

I don't know why that wasn't the answer I wanted. "I don't like police," I said. "I don't like lawyers and courtrooms. I don't want those boys to go to prison! Prison would be the worst thing in the world for them. But if they never get caught and it's this horrible guilty secret they have for their whole lives that just, like, festers—I mean, I can just see that being better."

"They deserve to be punished," Bunny said.

"But prison isn't punishment," I said. "Look, the first weekend my mom was out of prison, you know what she did?"

"What?"

"She picked up me and Gabby and she took us to Target and she had us shove gift cards to Outback Steakhouse down my little sister's panties and then took us out to lunch there and explained how she needed us to help her panhandle for twenty bucks so she could buy some heroin to hide inside the ad card of a magazine, then seal it up in mailing plastic, and return-to-sender to a friend of hers on the inside."

"What?"

"Oh, it's like this whole scam—they don't search prison mail if it's from a corporate business, right? Like one of those magazines that is sealed in plastic? So her friend had given her a magazine addressed to her in the prison—look, none of this matters, suffice it to say that we spent the first weekend back with our mother on, like, a criminal scavenger hunt."

"I don't understand how this connects," Bunny said, nuzzling her head into the crook of my neck.

"Prison will not make them better people. Prison will make them worse people. No one should go to prison unless you just need them to never be with regular people again. Like, whoops, you're a terrible person, never coming back here, buh-bye. For everyone else, all prison does is make things worse."

"Okay," Bunny said.

"Okay?"

"I just, I see what you mean," she said.

"And maybe justice needs to be made manifest on earth, I can see the human impulse to try to make the world look like it should, where bad people are punished and good people succeed, but, like, sometimes it seems very weird and childish to me."

"I don't see how it's childish."

"I just mean, what you remember and what I remember—they will never be the same. Trying to re-create what happened and arrive at a definitive assignation of fault is so simplistic and idealistic that it seems like playing pretend. Like, sure, this person is 'guilty.' This person is 'innocent.' Isn't it weird?"

"What about DNA evidence, video cam footage. I mean, maybe our ways of knowing are imperfect, but if you add together everything we do know, you can arrive at something pretty close. I mean really pretty close."

"I get it, I do," I said, "I just—I just have no feeling for it. I'm not necessarily arguing it can't be done, I just personally, as a victim—it will do nothing for me and how I recover from this to see those boys charged and then a trial and all of that."

"What do you think would help you?"

"Well." I licked my lips. I really didn't know. "I mean, first of all, I would love to never see any of them again so long as I live."

"That's why you should have them arrested!"

"But that's the other thing, Bunny, who do you think everyone is going to hate? Them for attacking me, or me for jeopardizing their 'bright futures'?"

"No one is going to hate you, Michael," she said.

"Well," I said. "I guess we'll see."

—

When Detectives Brown and Carmine returned the following day, they were very obviously real detectives. I was in the middle of eating an impossibly delicious salad. Really it was just iceberg lettuce and ranch dressing, but the cold, sweet way the leaves hissed open between my molars was so life-giving I felt I would never want to eat anything else ever again. Scottie had been released earlier that morning and I was a little sad. His daughter, a fat, jolly woman, had come to get him, and Scottie had introduced us and had his wheelchair pushed up close to my bed so that he could "get a look at" me.

"You are a brave young man," he said to me. "You are considerate and kind and strong and brave and I just marvel that I've had a chance to meet you."

I had never had anyone say words quite like that to me, and it was surprisingly painful. My eyes stung. I wondered if he would feel that way if he knew I was gay.

"I wish my grandson would grow up to be a young man like you. He's only four now, but I hope someday he will be like you." He reached up his gentle hand to pat my bed.

"Scottie, thank you—for being a friend!"

And then we both burst into song: "Traveled down a road and back again! Your heart is true, you're a pal and a confidante! Thank you for being a friend!"

I could remember being eight years old, during the worst of it between my mother and father. I always thought of those years as the "Yellow Apartment Years" because we had moved into this extremely depressing complex that was painted a violent shade of marigold. And *The Golden Girls* would come on, two back-to-back episodes, on the Lifetime network, right when I got off school. Gabby and I would eat tortillas I microwaved with ketchup and Kraft Singles inside, and watch *The Golden Girls,* arguing about who was our favorite. She loved Blanche, but I loved Sophia. For her meanness. She didn't seem to need any of the others. She was complete in herself.

"Do you think you could tell us any more about that night?" Detective Carmine asked.

"Right," I said, snapping back into the present. And then I told them. It would have taken too much strange effort to refuse to tell them. And I did not wish to owe hundreds of thousands of dollars in medical bills in case I couldn't get into Medi-Cal. That wasn't justice, not justice for me. I did not, however, mention that I thought I had heard Jason's voice. I had decided that his voice had been a hallucination, something I made up, possibly even after the fact.

"But," I said, "I don't want to press charges."

"That's something that happens on TV," Detective Brown said. "You don't press charges, the DA does, and it all depends on whether there is sufficient evidence to prosecute."

"Oh," I said. It seemed wrong that I could be in a hospital for a crime there wasn't enough evidence for, as though I were Schrödinger's cat. I might be, but possibly was not, the victim of assault. Maybe four guys had gotten together and beaten the piss out of me, or maybe they hadn't? Hell, who could say in this wacky world! It didn't matter that I was bruised, peeing blood, that it hurt like fuck to laugh or sneeze because my ribs were broken. Just moments ago, when I had **thought** the choice was mine, I had wanted to make sure those boys would not be brought up on charges, but now that I knew I was powerless, I was furious that they might not be, and anxious about what it might mean in terms of my medical expenses.

"A social worker should be stopping by today or tomorrow to see you," Detective Carmine said. I was released the next day, and Bunny drove me to her house in her red Jeep Cherokee, and I dimly saw through the darkened glass Jason watching from our kitchen as she led me, limping, up the path into her mansion.

14

Bunny devoted herself to taking care of me in a way I might not have expected. The next morning, she showed up in my room. They had installed me in the Madame Butterfly Suicide Sex Suite, a place teeming with memories of Anthony, so that any surface my mind attempted to land on became a knife that cut me. She was carrying a tray: peanut butter toast, a bruised banana, and a shot glass holding a bug-eaten rose from their front yard. I had been worried after the way I drunkenly insulted Ray that I would not be allowed to stay with them, but Bunny had told me he was extremely sorry and embarrassed about it, and indeed Ray himself had made a speech to that effect immediately upon my entering their home, and at the end had even gotten down on one knee and grasped my hands. "I am determined," he said, "to become a better man." I looked at him, understanding that he was already very drunk. The bruising on his cheeks was gone now, I had been in the hospital for so long, but there was a hot pink seam at his hairline that I couldn't stop looking at. Really, all things considered, he did look much better, and it was amazing how completely the bags under his eyes were gone. He looked ten years younger. With his eyes open, you could no longer see where the stitches had been because they were right in the fold, but every time he blinked, you could see the hot red line where they were still healing. I did not believe he would become a better man, but

I was very grateful he was letting me stay in his house. When I thought of the things I had said to him, especially about Allison, I felt like a dog that had pooped indoors.

"Oh my god," I said, gesturing at the tray. "You're so Judy!"

"Well, you deserve it. I'm not going into work today," Bunny told me as I ate my peanut butter toast. She had thrown herself across the foot of the bed, having settled me with my tray, and was now examining her toes.

"I know I'm not allowed to mourn," Bunny said. "But I—"

"For Ann Marie?"

"Yeah. I just, you know, and I never, I just can't—" Her words were like a car that wouldn't start, an engine that refused to turn over into a full sentence.

"I know," I said. "Bunny, I know." What had happened was so big, and we were so used to considering our lives as trivial. We almost didn't know how to approach it. The largeness of what had happened, of what we had done.

"It was an accident," Bunny said, her chin crumpling. "I never meant. I never, ever, ever meant to—"

"Of course you didn't," I said. "I know that."

"I loved her. I mean, I hated her, but I also loved her."

Those two girls growing up in that red sandbox. Those two ponytailed heads turning at the sound of the ice-cream truck. Ann Marie's round ugly-cute face in goggles as they stared at each other underwater. They had braided each other's hair. They had slept in the same sleeping bag. Ann Marie had known Allison, could remember meals Allison used to cook. She knew how their living room used to look before Ray redid it.

"And then sometimes," Bunny said, "sometimes I'm just mad at her. Please don't ever tell anyone this because it's so bad that I even think these things, but like, of course Ann Marie would find the ultimate way to ruin my life with her crazy-fragile brain tissue. Like, how dare you die and pin all of this on me, and I even picture her, like, laughing in heaven or whatever. She was always so on about heaven. Who was getting in and who wasn't. Who God loved and who he didn't. And then I thought I saw her. At the Rite Aid."

"What?"

"I just fully hallucinated that this other girl was her! She was in the skin-care aisle, and I was so convinced it was Ann Marie that I was, like, creepily walking up behind her, about to tap her on the shoulder. And I just thought, oh thank god, it's all been a big mistake." She stared at me. "Am I going insane? How could I think that? How could my mind—and I just keep remembering stuff. Stuff we did as kids. Like we loved the game Concentrate. Do you remember that game?"

"No," I said.

"It was a really weird game, I don't even know how we learned it, but it was like a rhyming game? Where you were supposed to be hypnotizing the person and kind of simulating these experiences for them? You would hammer on their back with your fists and say, 'Concentrate, Concentrate, People are dying, Babies are crying, Concentrate.'"

"I have never heard of this game in my life."

"I swear, it's a thing," Bunny said. "Lots of girls played it. Anyway, you pretended to crack an egg on the person's head, and then you would pretend to stab them in the back and push them off a building, and they were supposed to imagine themselves dying and tell you what color they saw."

"This is insane."

"I know. Little girls are insane."

We sat there and Bunny didn't say more.

"What's going on with Eric?" I asked, later when we were out by the pool. I had taken a shower in her dad's ultra-luxury steam shower, and we had made cinnamon rolls from the can, and I was feeling woozy but good from the sugar.

"Well, we're definitely having sex."

"Shut the front door!" I said. I had not been prepared for this. I had stupidly been in the hospital and out of touch, unable to protect her or at least try to sway her from driving just straight into the rocks.

"Well?" I said. "How is it?"

"I mean, good?"

"How did it happen? You have to give me the entire scene. Go."

"Well. One day, I guess like ten days ago, after our practice, he asked what I was doing, and I said, avoiding going home for as long as possible, and he asked if I wanted to come see his new apartment, because he just moved to Hermosa Beach. So I was like, sure. So he drove us there, and he asked a bunch of questions about my dad, and was he super strict, and I was like, no, he doesn't know half of what I do, I don't even have a curfew, I've stayed out all night before and he's never even noticed. And he's like, cool, cool. So then we go to his apartment."

"What was his apartment like?"

"Oh, it was like boy stuff, like bro-y, he had a cheap leather couch from IKEA, but then no rug or coffee table or other stuff to make it look less sad. He did have a cat, though, which somehow made me feel safe. It's an orange tabby named Mayonnaise."

"That's cute," I said. I was already feeling yucky about this story and she hadn't even gotten to the juicy parts, but I was trying to be supportive and nonjudgmental. Stay focused on the cat.

"So he made us drinks, Cactus Coolers and tequila, which is yummy, turns out. And we were just being silly. I don't know, I remember laughing a lot, but I guess I got pretty hammered, which is kind of embarrassing, and then I don't have any memories at all."

"Wait—what?"

"But in a way, I'm kind of glad because I got it over with and I didn't have to be all awkward."

"So wait, you had sex?"

"I guess so, I woke up in the morning totally naked with him on top of me, like inside me, and I leapt out of bed and I was scrambling around, out of my mind, like crying and screaming and trying to hide in the bathroom." She was laughing as she told me this, making fun of herself. "Because I had no idea what was going on. But then he explained it to me, how I was the one who kissed him, how I gave him this whole speech about how I wanted him to be the one to take my virginity and then I burped in his face, which is embarrassing, but I was also like, that sounds about right."

"So were you upset?" I began rubbing at my knees where the sunscreen was refusing to soak in.

"I mean, no. I mean, like, yes, obviously, because also I was hungover so I felt like I was dying and I spent the rest of the day throwing up and then that was the day you got attacked, and it honestly felt like the world was ending. But we've done it since then. So, like, I have memories. That was important to me. Because I feel like it's not really your virginity if you can't remember it."

"Right," I said. In a way, I wasn't sure how to proceed, but honesty seemed like a good base layer. "So that was date rape."

"But does it really count as date rape if I wanted it to happen?"

"Admitted gray area," I said. "But it sounds like in the morning you did not want to have sex, and, like, he was having sex with your sleeping, passed-out body, which is gross and wrong."

"Please don't ruin this for me," she said.

"I'm not trying to ruin it! If you're into it, then I'm fully supportive, I just want to advocate for your boundaries."

"Thank you," she said. "Noted."

"Well, do you enjoy it? I mean, is the sex good?"

"I have no idea," she said.

"Do you cum?" I asked.

"I'm not sure," she said.

"If you're not sure, then you're not cumming."

"It's just so much going on, I mean, I certainly feel a building to something and then a kind of frenzy?"

"But is it like when you masturbate? Are you like, *nrrrr*?" I rolled my eyes up in my head and faked a small seizure.

"No. Definitely not. But it's still pretty painful so I'm not sure if that maybe has something to do with it."

One of the simplicities of being male was always definitely knowing whether or not I had orgasmed, so I found her answers maddening. I had chosen much more bizarre and, on paper, *bad* sexual partners, but I had always had my own erection as a kind of guide, a Virgil, if you will, to lead me through the inferno. And I had been occasionally freaked out by where it led me, but there was no faking it.

Women, however, had drunk so very deeply of the cultural Kool-Aid that they couldn't even figure out if they were cumming. Were they moaning right? Did their tits look good? How were they supposed to let go, get carried away? They were in deepest drag and they didn't even seem to know it. I felt bad for Bunny but also ill-suited to help, and a little bit grossed out. It just seemed unnatural to me. Not a man and a woman having sex, although that wasn't my favorite thing to picture, but someone not understanding or being able to detect their own sexual pleasure. It was like someone confessing they liked eating soap and dirt, that they couldn't tell what was food and what was not food.

"But isn't the pain," I said, trying to figure it out, "like, at first it hurts, and then it gets hot and it stops hurting?"

"No," she said, "definitely not, it hurts the whole way through."

"Like, pardon me if this is too intimate, but are you really dry or something?"

"I have nothing to compare it to," she said.

"Has he said anything?"

"He said I'm really tight, which is a compliment, right?"

"Yeah, but if it's causing you active pain, then not so much."

She took off her sunglasses and sat up on her lounger then, and she looked more sad than I had ever seen her, even after Ryan Brassard told everyone she had bitten his ear. "But it's supposed to hurt! That's like the first thing anyone tells a girl about sex is that it's gonna hurt and she's gonna bleed, but no one ever tells you when it will stop being like that. I don't even care," she said, "I would keep doing it except—"

She broke off and there was a wet sound in her voice like tears were coming, but then none came. She put her sunglasses back on and sat perfectly still, like she was killing someone far away with her mind.

"What is it?"

"He has a girlfriend," she said with a tremendous exhale. Sometimes I marveled at the sheer size of her lungs. They must be the size of grocery bags in her chest. "Which I knew! And I thought I didn't care, but obviously I do."

"Well," I said, searching for a bright side. After all, my boyfriend had a fucking wife.

"And I told myself I was fine with it, but he teases me about it. He'll be on the phone with her and start fingering me and keep talking to her, and when I pull away or get mad, he's like, 'Don't get all butt hurt.' Or he will make fun of me for being jealous. He says I'm irrational, he calls me his irrational little bull."

I hesitated, because calling Bunny an irrational little bull was both apt and kind of cute, but these were all still giant red flags, just waving in the lusty breeze. "I don't like this, Bunny. It's one thing to have a girlfriend but to call her in front of you and then try to finger you—that's power-tripping."

"I think he thinks he's just being funny," she said. "He says if he didn't know better he'd fall in love with me."

"What is that supposed to even mean?"

"I have no idea," Bunny said. "But I'm pretty sure it's supposed to be a compliment."

"That's the shadiest compliment I've ever heard."

"I don't know," she said, and shrugged. It struck me as perverse, a grown man treating such a majestic creature as Bunny Lampert this way. With her large hands and soft little titties, she was a Wagnerian fantasy of a milkmaid, a baby Valkyrie. Was Eric insane? Did he stomp on flowers and piss on kittens?

"Fuck that boy," I said.

She smiled. "Indeed, I already have."

"Walk on him in your heels, grind his face into the mud, honey. That boy is trash."

"You are sweet to me," she said, and picked up my hand, kissed my wrist. "But I don't think I'm the kind of girl who is going to get Prince Charming."

"What do you mean?" I asked.

"Nothing," she said. "Just nothing."

"It's not nothing," I said.

"Well, Michael, I'm a fucking murderer."

"No, you're not," I said, before I could think about it.

"But I am," she said, with such sureness I was terrified.

Because I was living with Ray and Bunny, I had front-row seats for everything that came next. We did not attend Ann Marie's funeral; Ray thought it would be offensive, and his lawyer advised against it. I was there when his lawyer, a man named Swanson, whose lips were too red and who wore truly unattractive glasses, little beady grandma wire-frame dealies that made him look ten years older than he was, swept into the house at ten o'clock at night, also drunk, demanding that Ray pour him a scotch and then getting angry at the quality of the scotch ("Swanson, I don't drink scotch! Forgive me, this was a gift from a client, blame him, not me!"), and told us that Ms. Harriet had called the DA and was demanding murder charges.

"There's no way," Ray said. "It's involuntary manslaughter at the most, which you yourself said was a wobbler. Misdemeanor manslaughter. That's the most they'll do."

"Ray, I'm telling you that the DA was making noise about going for second degree murder." I was beginning to understand the dynamic between Ray and Swanson. They were like frat boys, even though neither of them had probably ever been in a fraternity. Maybe Swanson had, but there was deep acne scarring on his cheeks and he was a pedant through and through, so I doubted it. The man had no style, no swagger, he'd been pretending to be forty his whole life and now he had finally grown into it. But together they were making up for the youths they'd never had, or something along those lines.

"How? How would that ever fucking fly?"

"He's saying she has a violent past. Some incident where she bit a kid."

"That's ridiculous!" Ray turned to us, the silent peanut gallery curled up under a fake-fur throw on the couch. "You never bit anybody, did you?"

"Uhh . . ." Bunny said. "Well, it was like—"

"Jesus fucking Christ," Ray said.

"I'm not a criminal defense attorney," Swanson said. "Ray! I can't take this to trial, you know I'm not a trial lawyer. We've gotta get you somebody else."

"It has to be you," Ray said. "I want you. You're the only one I trust."

"I know a great guy," Swanson said, sucking down the rest of his poor-quality scotch. "His name is Remi, and he's the best, he can sit in, and—"

"I don't want Remi, I want fucking Swanson! Because you're an animal, Swan! You're a fucking dirty, cheating, little animal and I want you in my court." The two men embraced. Ray was almost crying. Bunny was frantically chewing her nails.

"We'll see what happens," Swanson said. "Who knows. Some of those witness accounts, I mean, we could go in there and argue mutual combat."

"But she didn't hit me back," Bunny said. Both men looked annoyed with her for interrupting.

"I thought you couldn't remember anything," Ray said in a singsong parody of her voice.

"Maybe she did hit you back, you hit her, you didn't know your own strength, it was a hell of a punch and then she fell just the right way. These things happen. They happen all the time."

"But that's not what happened," Bunny said.

"It's not about what happened," Swanson said, waving his glass of scotch around. "There was no video footage. We have nothing but your word, a dead girl, and a bunch of eyewitness accounts that vary wildly."

"They vary?" I asked. This was the first I had heard of this. Bunny crossed her arms over her chest, pushed air through her nose.

"They vary substantially," Swanson said, turning to me, warmed by a new audience. "We have some people claiming the punching went on and on, Bunny was like a wild dog, no one could get her off the girl. We have some people claiming it happened in a flash, was like a scuffle, they became aware of it and it was over before they could look. No one agrees how many punches, no one agrees who started it, everyone agrees Ann Marie was running her mouth about that gay kid."

"He's the gay kid," Ray said, gesturing at me.

"Oh, sorry," Swanson said. "But you know what I mean."

"Do you think it would make any difference that I was later attacked?" I asked.

"What do you mean?" Swanson said.

"Well, the girl who Bunny hit, her boyfriend and his friends jumped me. I was in the hospital for a little over a week."

"No, no," Swanson said, "I think that might look bad, make Bunny look even more guilty. Everyone is going to forgive the grieving boyfriend for getting wild after his girlfriend kicks the bucket, I mean, come on. You got any food around here, Ray?"

I felt like I'd been hit in the head, dizzy and blind. *Everyone is going to forgive the grieving boyfriend for getting wild after his girlfriend kicks the bucket.*

It was like getting my heart broken, somehow. That what

happened to me could be framed that way, casually, to my face, in a house with Oriental carpets and marble.

Later, in her room, Bunny and I did face masks.

"It feels like fire ants are crawling all over my skin," I said.

"It feels like my skin is literally burning completely off."

"Oh, I love it," I said.

"The pain is how you know it's working."

We were quiet. Skin care was a bond between us because both of us longed to be beautiful, even as we feared we were not and could never be, even as we were suspicious of the urge to be beautiful in the first place. What was that power? You were supposed not to want it, not to crave it, not to pursue it. Beauty was just supposed to land on you like a butterfly, showing the world that you were special, worthy of love, attended by magical birds who folded your laundry. But here we were, trying to burn our skin off for that.

I could tell she was upset. How could she not be? The possibility of a trial, homicide charges. "Why . . ." I began, not certain what I was going to ask until I said it, "do you think that Ann Marie's boyfriend jumped me? I always assumed it was because I was gay, but maybe it was because I was your friend, and it was more because of Ann Marie."

"I don't know," she said. "Maybe because he was afraid of being seen as beating up a girl? So he couldn't beat me up directly?"

"Or he was afraid you'd overpower him."

"Or it was Jason who made it all happen and it *was* because you're gay."

"Or it's all of those things."

"Do you ever get freaked out because you do things without planning them?"

"No, I don't think so," I said.

"I mean, like, sometimes I'll reach to get an apple off the counter, and then I'll get freaked out because I didn't plan to reach out and grab the apple. I just did it. And maybe as I'm doing it, I have a thought like, mmm, apple. But I didn't plan it. And yet other stuff we do plan and then do on purpose, but it's like a small, small percentage. At least for me. And I get freaked out about that, and I get afraid that basically I'm sleeping even while I'm awake."

"I know exactly what you are talking about," I said. "And I feel exactly the same way."

And then we washed our faces and went to bed.

I texted Anthony: *So did you really break up with me at the hospital while I was totally out of it?*

He didn't text me back for three days.

Then he texted: *No, I don't remember breaking up with you per se, but I feel very guilty because I do think we should stop seeing each other.*

I didn't write back. I didn't want to seem weak by showing him my anger or my hurt. Yet I mentally composed texts that I refused to send every hour of every day. *I just feel ashamed,* I imagined writing. *Why? Don't feel ashamed,* he would say. *For having such a coward and Cyprian man, such a stretched-out, gaping old asshole, as my first love.* My rage was incoherent. I didn't even know what I wanted from him exactly. Probably for him to be someone else, and for me to be someone else, and for the situation to be an entirely different situation than it was. Probably something along those lines.

Meanwhile, I was afraid to leave the house. I didn't want to run into Jason or Aunt Deedee. Tyler and his friends had not been arrested or charged as far as I knew. I had gotten an unclear phone call from Principal Cardenas telling me to take as long as I needed before coming back to school, with no mention of any formal procedure for resuming my attendance, but I knew I was never going back. It wasn't exactly that I was afraid they would jump me a second time. In a rational sense, I didn't expect we would be playing Tom and Jerry, banging each other with hammers all over the town or something. But I did feel like if I caught sight of one of their faces without being braced for it, that I might lose my voice and never be able to speak again. Or perhaps go blind, or turn into a pillar of salt. If I saw them, even for an instant, I would lose the coherency of self, such as I still possessed it.

Aunt Deedee, in particular, was extremely miffed at me for moving out. I could not explain myself. I could not tell her that it was Jason, because I did not know for sure that it had been Jason. What if I were wrong? Or worse, what if I told her and she didn't believe me? I could not afford these realities. And so I told her that Ray Lampert had insisted, that they had a spare bedroom with an actual closet, that it "just made sense." And she let it happen because it made her life easier too, but she was still insulted. There she had gone, treating me like her own child, taking care of me like one of her own, and what did I do? Move in with a friend who had a pool, like I wasn't part of her family at all, like she wasn't the closest thing I had ever had to a mother. She had actually said that part. "I've been like a mother to you, Michael, and I suppose I would have expected a little bit of gratitude."

Did she think I had forgotten my own mother? My real mother? And even if she had been trying to be a mother to me, shouldn't she have done a better job? Was teaching me how to apply eyeliner and telling me "no boys" really enough? I had paid for my own food and clothing since I was old enough to get a job. I was living in, literally, a closet. But I said, "I don't mean to express a lack of gratitude. I am very grateful, Aunt Deedee, I really am. You know I love you."

"I love you too," she had gasped, and hugged me so tightly that I finally caught it, what was going on for her, what was at stake. She was upset because she knew she had failed me, and she could not, could not look at it. And I didn't want to make her look at it either. She really had done her best. She really was trying very hard. It was not fun to be Aunt Deedee. In fact, it was terrible and bleak to be Aunt Deedee.

For whatever reason, in these bizarre, timeless weeks, Bunny decided she needed to teach me to drive. We were always together. She had stopped working for her father out of moral disgust more latently, and need to "take care of me" more patently, and there were only so many shows to binge-watch and only so many blueberry muffin mixes to bake (she loved blueberry muffin mix, she loved to eat the batter raw; I had to positively claw the bowl away from her to make sure any of them got baked). And so we went to the DMV and I got my permit, and then she would take me out driving. We drove only in parking lots, especially at first because her Jeep was a stick shift, and I was a slow learner. I would scream every time I stalled the car. This made Bunny laugh hysterically each time we lurched, and I would say, "Shut up, shut up, I can't concentrate with you laughing like that!" and she would say, "How can you be so bad at something? I've never seen you be this bad at anything!"

The thing is, I was falling in love with Bunny again. She was so clumsy with artifice that she had no choice but to be absolutely and authentically herself, which gave me permission to be the same. And that had been part of it all along. That we were our truest selves when we were together.

That Christmas was a weirdly happy one. We didn't get a tree or do any of that, but we did order in Chinese and have a movie marathon. I hadn't gotten presents for Ray or Bunny, and I didn't think there would be any gift exchange, but then on Christmas Eve, Ray suddenly pulled two wrapped boxes out of the closet.

"Wut," Bunny said.

"You didn't tell me we were doing presents!" I said.

"We're not," Ray said. "Weirdest thing. Found these up on the roof. Wrapped up just like this. I think they're from Santa. He must have dropped them off early."

He set a box in front of each of us, and we tore into the paper like little kids. I couldn't imagine what was in a box this size, and then when I saw the packaging, that white packaging, I almost started crying. I was like one of those audience members sobbing after Oprah gave them a car.

MacBook Airs for both of us, silver and sleek and so expensive I didn't want to touch it and get finger grease on it.

"To take to college," Ray said proudly.

I had never known that a material possession could make me so happy, but my giddiness lasted through New Year's.

Of course, I could not help but think about, almost constantly, what Bunny had done to Ann Marie, and how it was different or the same as what those boys had done to me. I found myself observing her hands, thinking about the heaviness of her bones, the densely packed muscles in her back, in her buttocks, in her thighs. "Like celery . . . just *crunching*," Naomi had said. A mosaic of bone. Pulp. I could vaguely remember someone saying that in the deeper dream chambers of my hospital memories. *His spleen is pretty pulpy.*

But the difference was, at least to me, that Bunny had seen red. She had left herself, lost herself, in a kind of divine madness, almost like Heracles, who was driven mad by jealous Hera and tricked into killing his own wife and children. Madness personified gets onstage and brags: "Nor shall the ocean with its moaning waves, nor the earthquake, nor the thunderbolt with blast of agony be half so furious as the headlong rush I will make into the breast of Heracles."

In such a model, madness and violence both are seen as a loss of control, and the essence of good behavior is defined as a maintenance of control. There are a thousand versions of the same philosophy, from studies showing hypotrophy of the frontal cortex in murderers to treatment protocols for domestic abuse that advise against the consumption of alcohol, lest the batterer "lose control." (I wish I could have told them, drunk as my father was, he always seemed to know to hit my mother or the kids and never accidentally hit a cop.)

In some ways it made Bunny's violence more terrifying, more otherworldly. I remembered Naomi, how stricken she seemed afterward: "That was some of the craziest shit I've ever seen."

But the boys who had beaten me, pulped my spleen, cracked my ribs, had been laughing. They had been chewing gum. They were not in an ecstatic frenzy. They did not "know not what they did." They were talking to each other like they always did. I remember one of them made fun of another one for being out of breath from kicking me. They were perfectly in control.

And for me, that made their behavior much worse somehow, though I was hard-pressed to articulate exactly how.

At root, I seemed to be upset about the existence of physical power at all. That violence is nothing but another kind of touching.

I was also confounded by the existence of Ray Lampert as a ready moral corollary. He, an overtly bad man, a man who cheated his neighbors, who committed frauds both large and small, who abused his wife, who was venal and petty and drunk, was universally revered, a valued member of the community, a city council member. And Bunny, by virtue of her actions on a single afternoon, but who was otherwise honest, kind, generous, and hardworking, had been cast out of our community, stigmatized, and mythologized as a specific kind of female evil. She was Lizzy Borden, she was Medea, she was some sort of Kali with the cunt of a cow. Was it any wonder I wanted to excuse her? To explain away what she had done?

But no matter how hard I tried, or how I contorted my mental world, I could not make what Bunny had done right. No one could argue it was right to do that to Ann Marie. Yet I could not stop loving Bunny. I could not stop being on her side. I would continue to love her, even as she horrified me. I would continue to love her because she was mine.

One night in mid-January, when I was fully asleep, Bunny came into my room.

"Sorry," she said when she saw she had woken me. She already had my window halfway open. The window in the guest bedroom led out to a portion of angled roof, whereas her window opened onto empty air. "Go back to sleep."

"Where are you going? To see Eric?"

"Yeah," she said. "Sorry."

I went back to sleep. But she was not gone for very long. It was only an hour or two later when I heard the window grating open again.

"You smell like fucking gas," I said.

"Sorry," she said.

"Why do you smell like that?"

"I splashed gas on my shoe when I was gassing up the Jeep," she said. "Go back to sleep."

And I did.

The cops came while we were eating breakfast. Cheap bagels, the kind that are too sweet and never toast correctly, slathered in cream cheese. There was a knock on the door, and when I answered they swarmed inside, sliding past me and filling the space, at least six or seven police officers and a gaggle of crime scene techs.

"We have a search warrant and a warrant for your arrest," one of the officers told Bunny. "You're charged with the second degree murder of Ann Marie Robertson. You're also wanted for questioning regarding an act of arson at the construction project on 605 Grand Street. Please stand up and put your hands behind your back."

"I'll call your dad," I said. "I'll call Swanson."

Bunny nodded. But she didn't look scared. She looked somehow enlivened, bold, the way she did when she was on the volleyball court, about to slam a ball out of the sky on her new legs. As though she were proud of herself for the first time in a long time.

15

Bunny was taken away in a cop car, the house was searched, I gave a statement, and then I just sort of sat on the sofa. The statement had been remarkably easy to give. The detective, a different one from the detectives I had talked to in the hospital, was named Kirby, and she was the most tired-looking person I had ever seen. She questioned me like she had already reviewed the entire history of the earth and there was no longer one single thing that could surprise her. For every hyper-specific question about what we did the night before, what we ate, what we watched, when we went to bed, I told the truth. And then I simply omitted Bunny waking me up by coming through my room. It was some of the easiest lying I had ever done really. I don't know. I'd been lying to people about what I did and where I was going for so long, and maybe I should have been anguished, but I was calm.

The background questions were more difficult to field and so I opted for total ignorance. What did I know about those apartment buildings under construction? I said I thought they were going to be pretty when they were done. Did I know Bunny Lampert owned them? I said I had no idea and I asked how an eighteen-year-old could even get a mortgage. Maybe that was a mistake, but honestly I didn't care what happened to Ray. I hoped they found out that he routinely cheated his friends and neighbors, that he'd convinced the city council to change building codes not because it was better for the town but because it would be more attractive to the developers he had lined up. I hoped they found out he'd opened a credit card under his baby girl's name when she was only four. I hope they found out he'd destroyed her credit and she'd never get college loans now. I hope they found out every single dirty rotten thing that man had ever done.

No, she had never mentioned them to me. No, to my knowledge she had had no input on the construction process. Did I know what Bunny wanted to be when she grew up?

"Well, a volleyball player," I said.

The woman stared at me, then wrote this down.

I don't know, it seemed crazy to me, this woman was a North Shore police officer and Ray Lampert was one of the most visible citizens and his daughter one of the most prominent athletes, how could she not know?

"Has she ever talked about going into business with her dad?"

"No," I said. "I don't think it would really suit her."

"How so?"

I didn't feel she was trying to suss out some hidden truth from me so much as she was appalled by anyone not wanting to become a real estate agent when their daddy had it all teed up for them. "Well, I don't know. Bunny is not very good at being slick is all. She's a very genuine person, she's not a sales kind of person."

Just then there was a lot of shouting and then laughter, back-slapping. They had found her clothes soaked in gasoline.

Mainly I was worried about Bunny. What was happening to her now? Were they taking her mug shot? Were they taking her fingerprints? Were they being mean to her? On the worst possible day of your life, which is the day you are arrested, you would think people could be a little softer with you, but they aren't. It's like you're not human at all anymore. You got yourself into this and now it's just fucking funny or it's just fucking life.

"Was she seeing anyone?" the detective asked me, and I gained control of my facial muscles just a fraction of a second too late. She'd seen me tense up. If I lied now, she would think everything I'd said was a lie. If I told her the truth, she would be more likely to assume the rest was the truth, or at least this was my logjammed logic in the moment. Plus, I wanted to roll on Eric like the wheels on the bus.

"She was seeing someone, but it was a secret. Coach Eric, her volleyball coach. He's the assistant coach at the high school, but after she was suspended her father had hired him to keep her skill set up, and eventually things turned romantic between them. But as far as I know, this was only in the last couple weeks."

I suppose I had wanted Detective Kirby to seem surprised, or at least interested, but she just nodded and said, "We'll talk to him too."

"Is he going to be in trouble?" I asked.

"She's eighteen," Detective Kirby said, and gave me a look like I was crazy. "Is there some reason he should be in trouble that you know about?"

"I guess not," I said, fiddling with my ear.

"All right, well, let me get your phone number and we may ask you to come down to the station again later on."

"I'd be happy to," I said.

I called Ray again and got his voicemail. Where the fuck was he? The search had been going on for two hours now. I had watched them cart item after item from Bunny's room, her laptop, bags of her clothes, her school notebooks. There were two officers deep into digging through Ray's office, which perhaps explained why he was staying far away. One of the SWAT guys was smoking out by the pool. And I thought: Isn't that unsanitary? Isn't that disrupting the crime scene? I saw Detective Kirby go up to him. "Get the fuck out of here," she said.

"Let me milk this," he said, laughing. "I'm on overtime. Give me fifteen more minutes and I can buy my girlfriend a mani-pedi."

"Manicures cost more than you think," Kirby said, unsmiling. "Get gone."

I was darkly interested. I could remember the police from when I was small, coming when the neighbors called the cops because of the fighting, and they never failed to fill my small body with adrenaline. So I was interested to have the chance to examine them now with more adult eyes. They seemed like all right types. The men were loud, performing their masculinity so hard they waddled around, hips stiff as arthritic cowboys. Or maybe they all had injuries from playing high school football. Who knew? But I didn't hate them. Honestly, they reminded me of Jason.

When they finally left three hours later, there was black fingerprint dust everywhere and I was unclear whether I was even allowed to clean it up. I went outside and smoked a cigarette, then lay down on the couch and somehow fell asleep.

When I awoke, Ray and Swanson were in the kitchen, and from the light coming in through the curtains I guessed it was midafternoon. I was not sure why I had fallen so deeply and thickly asleep; perhaps it was some peculiar reaction to the adrenaline of the morning. When I stood my legs were stiff and I walked awkwardly. Swanson and Ray were sharing a bottle of white wine. I suddenly hated them so much that it seemed impossible to go on.

"I can't have them look into that building," Ray was saying. "They've got to drop that arson charge."

"They haven't charged her yet, we won't know what they're going to charge her with until arraignment," Swanson said.

"Swanson. Swanson. What do we do? What can we do?"

"Have you paid her bail?" I asked by way of hello.

"Not yet," Swanson informed me. "Look who's up."

"Why not?"

"We're trying to make a game plan," Ray said. "There's Thai food on the way."

"Are you not going to bail her out?" I asked. Ray avoided my gaze, took a sip of his wine.

"Bail is set at two million," Swanson said.

"But can't you get a bond, or like a—you don't have to pay all that."

"A bail bondsman would still need two hundred grand," Swanson said.

Ray looked out the kitchen window in a frozen way, pretending to ignore our conversation. I realized he was embarrassed that he couldn't pay.

"But I think the DA is going to charge the arson even if they don't have the evidence, Ray," Swanson started up again, touching his own face in a way that made me want to scream that he was going to give himself acne. "And arson is a serious charge."

"If they look at that building close, they're gonna find everything."

"How bad is it?" Swanson asked. "I don't want to know details, just give me an idea on a scale of one to ten."

"Like, a seven? A six or a seven."

I thought about what Bunny had told me about Ray stealing her identity, the credit card debt, the mortgage in her name, the bribed inspectors, the illegal fuse boxes. "I mean, I would say it's a nine at least," I said.

"Somewhere between a seven and a nine," Ray said, and without breaking eye contact with Swanson he got out another glass and poured, shoved it in my direction.

"I mean, the police are going to investigate," Swanson said. "There's no question about that."

"What if she copped to the murder charge?" Ray asked.

"What?"

"If she pled no contest on the second degree murder, do you think the DA would make the arson go away? I mean, if they charge her."

Swanson shook his head. "It depends. I mean, without the arson, I would say they never intended to go to court on second degree murder, and they're going to offer a plea bargain down to voluntary manslaughter. And they may still go down to voluntary manslaughter. But I'm not a criminal defense attorney, as I have told you many times. With the arson, it all depends how good their evidence is. I mean, if there's video cam footage from the construction site or something, if they have her doing it, then they're gonna have a lot of leverage. But it's also true, she only set those panels on fire. There was no damage other than that, so we're not talking about a conflagration here. And they were her property to begin with."

"They found her clothes that smelled like gasoline," I said.

"Not great," Swanson said.

But Ray wasn't having it. "There are no cameras down there, I never had cameras put in, there was no reason to. Ann Marie's mother is up the DA's ass about a murder charge, and he knows he can't win if we go to court. You know he can't win. No jury is going to convict a teenage girl of murder on what they have. My friend who's a doctor, a fucking brain surgeon, told me it was a freak thing, that it was one in a million Ann Marie died from that bleed. I bet we could even cast doubt—you know, maybe it was medical malpractice. Maybe her case was mismanaged by the hospital."

I did not believe this, but I tried to hold it in.

"It's also true," Swanson said, just rubbing and rubbing his greasy fingers over his cheek, "that juries don't like arson. Lots of boring testimony from experts. They don't understand it, and they don't convict well. They're not going to want this to go to trial, it's too expensive for one thing. But it's a lot, getting them to drop the arson *and* negotiating down to manslaughter. But second degree murder."

"You can't let her hang on the murder charge," I said, finally exploding. "I mean, she's your daughter!"

"No one's letting her hang," Ray said, angrier than I'd ever seen him. He took a step closer to me and his face was red-purple. He panted for a moment, glowering at me, then took a sip of his wine. "Better that she do six years for second degree murder than five years for voluntary manslaughter and five years for arson and meanwhile all our assets are seized and I wind up doing time so I can't help her! I'm trying to be smart here!"

"Maybe he should leave the room," Swanson said. "This was not wise. This was not wise at all."

"He's goddamn family, Swan," Ray said. "He's practically Bunny's brother. He's just as worried about her as we are."

While I was touched that Ray would count me as family, I certainly thought I was a great deal more concerned about Bunny than they were. I thought Ray wanted her to take the murder charge to save his own ass, but I also wasn't sure Bunny would really be better off taking both charges to trial, and I wasn't sure if Ray could pay Swan through two trials anyway, or if Swan could pull off a trial at all. He was a plaintiff lawyer for a firm that did mostly class action suits that settled out of court. Even talking about a trial here in the kitchen, he had grown moist with sweat.

"Ray, I have to tell you something," Swanson said.

"What is it, Swan?"

"Second degree murder. It's a minimum sentence of fifteen years. It's not something we want to take to trial even if we think we can win."

"All the more reason to plead," Ray said. "What I'm telling you, Swanson, is that it won't just be arson, it will be the beginning of a whole thing. And we can't do it. Trial isn't an option."

"I'll talk to the DA," Swanson said.

And then the Thai food got there.

I guess I had thought that Swanson would make an appointment with the DA's office, or that he would make a phone call, but he insisted that the best way to go about it was to drive to the Airport Courthouse and hang out in the hallway near a courtroom where the prosecutor handling the case was scheduled to be and then grab him on his way out. Ray and I were to stay out by the car in the parking lot and wait for him to come out and tell us what happened.

The Airport Courthouse was a building from the future, ten stories tall, with glass elevator shafts that made it look like criminals were ascending to the sky to be judged by the gods. I smoked a cigarette and leaned against Swanson's BMW. Ray got out of the car.

"Can I have one?" he asked.

I handed him a cigarette and lit it for him.

"I don't think I've ever seen so many dinged cars in my life," I said, surveying the parking lot. It was a sea of messed-up cheap cars interspersed with gleaming BMWs and Mercedes-Benzes. The accused and their attorneys. A minivan for the court reporter. A cluster of squad cars. And I thought that inside the building, the pageant of justice was being performed, as though the contestants had free will, as though anyone could blossom into a hero or a monster through sheer force of character. But out here in the parking lot, it was clear that if you were poor, your car simply had more dings in it. You were poor, you got a drug charge, you got a gun charge, ding, ding, scrape, scratch, because those were the problems that came from growing up in a poor neighborhood. They were not signs of individual moral turpitude.

These were problems that most kids in North Shore never even ran into. And I still believed that the fact that Ray and I were leaning against a BMW would be what saved Bunny. Not that she was innocent, not that she was worthy of love or dignity or mercy. Not that justice was blind or would be made manifest on earth as it is in heaven. I was counting on her rich daddy. I was counting on her milky-white, Aryan-wet-dream skin. I was counting on idiot Swanson and his correct sense of how to match a tie to a shirt. It was almost lavish, I reflected, the way Swanson was so obviously only quasi-competent. As a rich, white man, he could afford to let it show, the same way a skinny bitch with Kate Moss hips could wear unflattering avant-garde silhouettes. I trusted Swanson with Bunny's case when I wouldn't have let him run a girls' softball team. He couldn't have managed two toddlers at a mall. He was nothing but a floppy, spineless concatenation of wine trivia and pretentious sushi-ordering skills dressed up as a human man and walking around.

I didn't like Ray or Swanson, and yet I found myself allied with them and it was causing me to hate them more intensely than I might have otherwise.

"I just want you to know," Ray said, after taking a drag on his cigarette, "how much I appreciate you. It will not be forgotten. The way you've been there for Bunny."

"Thanks, Ray," I said, and prayed he would not continue talking. We were stuck here in this parking lot together, and I knew some amount of talking was unavoidable, but I hoped to keep it nugatory if possible.

"There's one thing I've been wanting to bring up," he began, and I felt my revulsion for him gathering in the base of my skull in a slow wave.

"That night," he said, "that terrible night, where we had the misunderstanding about gay schoolteachers," he said. "You mentioned about Allison driving into traffic."

"I'm very sorry for saying that," I began, thinking that what he wanted was an apology.

"No," he said and waved me off. "I understand—I mean, listen, if people are saying that, I get it. I think a lot of people hated Allison."

"Why?" I asked, aghast.

"Because she was beautiful and funny. She always dressed well. She had a kind of clique with the other mothers, and people could feel left out. If you weren't in their group. I know Ann Marie's mother often felt that way. And maybe there was a perception of Allison as being somehow cold. But she never meant to leave any of those women out, she just wasn't thinking about how things seemed. She was shy. She hung out with only the same four women because she was shy. She was a very gentle person. Anyway, her tire blew out as she was going around a curve and she swerved into oncoming traffic on PCH."

"Good god," I said.

"But the thing is, it was a new car, a Ford Explorer. Why would a brand-new tire blow out like that? That's how I met Swanson, actually. Well, we met in AA, but then during my share, I was agonizing about what I could have done, and maybe if I had taken it in for an oil change that week, they would have noticed something was up with the tire. I remember Swan interrupted, which is a big no-no, no cross talk, to ask what kind of car it was. I said it was a Ford Explorer and his eyes just popped out of his head because his firm was already handling the class action suit at the time. They were Firestone tires and Ford had lowered the psi on them to try and keep their SUVs from tipping—remember that? How they would roll in a sharp turn? They didn't want to do a redesign, too expensive, so they put these low-pressure tires on it. So it was kismet, basically. I never would have known. I would have thought it was some freak thing, maybe she drove over metal spikes or who knows what, but without Swanson I never would have known."

I believed him completely, even though I trusted Ray Lampert about as much as I would trust a talking doll on Halloween. It just made sense of too many things. I had known Swanson handled class action suits. He would always joke it was the only job where you could get paid millions to get your client fifty cents.

"And Bunny knows?"

"Oh god, yes," he said.

"Well, I'm really sorry I said that, Ray," I said. "I feel like a real turd."

"You're not a turd! You're not. Someone told you that. Not your fault you believed them. Makes me sad people are saying that, though. Still saying that."

"Did you at least get a big settlement?" I asked.

"Actually, yeah. I was a named plaintiff, and those get bigger payouts. For Swan it was a win because the story was just so perfect. Beautiful woman, a young mother, struck down in her prime. You know, no one was drunk, nothing to muddy the waters. And we work well together, and there's a lot of—if you're a named defendant, you're deposed and you have to attend the trial and make decisions."

"Wow," I said. I wondered what had happened to all that money.

"So that was when we decided to do the remodel of the high school," he said.

"You did that?"

"Well, yeah," he said, "how am I gonna get rich people to buy houses here if that school looked like shit? Smartest thing I ever did. Complete teardown. It was incredible, took years."

It was so complicated, the good and evil in him. They were so densely intermixed.

"Did you have a good marriage? With Allison?" I asked.

"Oh, absolutely. I worshipped her. I was like a lapdog."

I thought about Bunny telling me he would break one of Allison's vases or some other beautiful thing she loved on purpose and then keep her up all night, accusing her of loving the object more than she loved him, trying to torture her into confessing what he suspected all along.

"She was my one true love," he said, staring off into the distance.

We waited in that parking lot for a full forty minutes, and then Swanson appeared, and we could tell from his aggressive swagger that the news was good. We were practically jumping up and down by the time he got to the car. "What is it, what is it?"

"Huzzah!" Swanson proclaimed.

"Jesus fucking Christ, tell us what happened," Ray said.

"Bye-bye arson, three years on voluntary manslaughter. They're willing to support an OR at arraignment."

"What's an OR?" I asked.

"Released on her own recognizance," Ray and Swanson said in unison as they swung open the doors of the BMW. I scrambled to get into the backseat as Swanson turned over the engine.

We were blind with pleasure at his triumph. It would be years before I wondered why the DA's office seemed so eager to drop the arson and agree to voluntary manslaughter. They must have known they couldn't take the arson or the second degree murder to trial and win. Would a seasoned criminal defense attorney have been able to talk them down to involuntary manslaughter? A suspended sentence and three years' probation? What would Bunny's life have been if Ray had hired her a real lawyer?

I did not attend the arraignment the next morning, but Ray and Swanson swung by to pick me up on their way to Lynwood Jail to get Bunny back. We were giddy and it was a short drive with no traffic on the 105, but once we were there the process ground to a halt. Getting someone out of jail was as lengthy and boring a process as buying a car. Swanson and I wound up going to Carl's Jr. while Ray waited because Swanson complained he was getting low blood sugar. They needed to "locate the inmate," and for some reason this was taking hours. Didn't they know where she was? It made me anxious, but Swanson assured me it was always like this.

He ordered a Western Bacon Cheeseburger. I ordered a salad.

"So you met Ray in an AA meeting?" I asked.

He laughed. "Pretty ironic, huh?"

"It's like a meet-cute in a romantic comedy. Two alcoholic men, running from their financial and spiritual obligations . . ."

Swanson giggled and covered his mouth with his hands so his chewed-up burger wouldn't show. "Exactly, exactly," he said.

I punctured a little cherry tomato with my plastic fork. "But he said you helped with the lawsuit after Allison's death."

"I did, I did," Swanson said. "That's what bonded us, I think. He was trying to get sober after she died, and we met. Honestly, we met a few times before I put the pieces together. I'd heard him share multiple times, but he'd never gone into detail about the accident before, and as soon as he said 'tire,' I thought: I've gotta talk to this guy."

"Right," I said. "He told me. Because you were already working on a case against Ford."

"But we sure worked some magic on this one," Swanson said. "Boy." He took a big bite of his burger.

"So you think Bunny got a good deal?" I asked.

"Mmm—yes! Absolutely. The arson alone could have been up to three years. That was really very stupid. She should not have done that."

"Well, you know why she did it, right?"

"Angst?" he asked.

For a moment I could not speak, and the entire world seemed to me as sinister and sad as a fast-food restaurant, and even the beautiful photons of sunlight cascading through the air outside were nothing but extensions of the absurd and heartless Rube Goldberg machine that was the universe. I tried to speak with as little emotion as possible. "The panels weren't up to code. The inspector had been bribed. She was worried families would move in and one of the panels would malfunction and a real fire would start that actually killed people."

He laughed, a little uneasy. "Still illegal, however!"

"Moral, however," I shot back.

"The law of man has never been about morality," Swanson said, wiping his lips with his napkin. "Thank god!"

"What's it about, then?"

"Capital!" he cried, his face joyful, even resplendent. He sucked on his Diet Coke, and I saw the brown liquid come up through the straw and for a flashing moment I saw him as an ape. "Money is a more tangible thing than the Good, the Beautiful, or the True, right? I mean, I mean, money is about value, right? Whatever you value. Used to be, when you killed someone you just paid their family a lump sum, *Beowulf* and all that, right? A *wergild*. Man price. I don't know, don't worry too hard, Michael, everything's made up!" He giggled again. "It's all just made up!"

His phone buzzed. "All right," he said, "she's out."

—

On the car ride home from the jail, I felt so elated to see Bunny again, to have her in the car, that it was like being in love. We sat in the back of her father's car together, and held hands, and I remembered that first ride to Manhattan Beach together because Bamboo Forest's egg drop soup was too watery, and the way Ray had gotten drunk and rammed the light pole, and the way we had walked home through the salt air, bathed by the whooshing noise of cars and the ancient churning of the Pacific. How light our bodies were as we walked, how easy it was to begin to love her, how nimbly my tongue managed to tell her the truth. It seemed to me that it had been much easier then to know what the truth even was.

"Are you okay? Was it terrible?"

"Not terrible," she said. "I mean, I cried at night, which was embarrassing. But it wasn't like the movies, no one tried to beat me up or anything."

She knew, I presumed Ray had told her, that she was only temporarily free, that she would be remanded at her sentencing hearing. But it seemed indecent to speak of this, and we were all pretending that all of the bad part was over now, that she would never be parted from us again, that the two nights she had spent away were an aberration and that Ray and Swanson had saved the day.

I looked at her pink cheek as she watched the passing buildings through the window, and I wanted to gobble her up. I wanted to consume her. I wanted to tell her that I loved her and hold her tight. I wanted to smell her skin and close my eyes and beg God to let me keep her.

"Can we eat something?" she said. "The food in there was terrible."

—

That night I startled awake, certain that someone was trying to break into my room through the window. I fell off the bed, and for just a moment my kidneys and liver flared, every nerve lit up in agony, and I was certain I had exploded them within my body. It had been weeks since I had felt anything more than mild soreness, and the pain evacuated the air from my lungs.

"Are you okay?" Bunny asked, and she was kneeling over me. She was wearing red lipstick and she stank of perfume as sweet and synthetic as new plastic.

"Why are you in here?" I asked. I had never seen Bunny in red lipstick before, and somehow in the dim moonlight it made her unrecognizable to me. Like this was a dream and her face was trying to turn into someone else's face.

"I was going out the window," she said.

"Why?" I asked. I already halfway knew, but I wanted to make her say it. Somehow, fury had opened inside me like a parachute, when I had been previously unaware of harboring any rage at all.

"Eric's waiting," she said, pointing at the window.

"Don't go," I said. "Don't go fuck that shitbag."

She shook her head, like she didn't know what to say, tugged on her ponytail and turned away from me toward the window. I scrambled to my feet and put myself in front of her.

"Seriously. Don't. Bunny, don't go."

"I'm just gonna go for an hour," she **said**. "I'm coming back."

"It's not that I think you're running away—it's that you are *not* his two a.m. booty call. He can't just text and then come get you and get a blow job and then let you go to fucking prison!"

"I. Want," she said, saying the words slowly, with dramatic space in between each one, "To. See. Him."

"It's a bad idea," I spit back at her. But I wondered if I was just pearl clutching. Who was I to deny her the quick thrill of giving a blow job in a car, of gliding through a sleeping town, of feeling that one's life is one's own.

"It's *my* bad idea," she said, and she shoved me with her shoulder as she tried to get past me. I stumbled, but caught myself, and walked backward to keep myself between her and the window. "Bunny, Bunny, Bunny," I was saying.

"Get out of my fucking way," she said, and I could see the muscles in her neck widen and swell as she stood up taller, trying to intimidate me.

"Please don't. Don't go," I said, begging in a way that reminded me of my mother.

"I don't want to hurt you," she said. We were backed up to the window, I could feel the cool glass against my shoulder blades through my T-shirt. There was no farther to go.

"Get out of my way."

I didn't move.

"Get out of my way," she said.

"Bunny, Eric is a bad guy, he's not nice. He's not—"

"I don't want to hurt you," she said again.

"Just—there are going to be so many other guys. There are going to be so many other—"

"No, there's not!" she shouted in my face, and then she bent forward and I didn't understand what she was going to do until she heaved her shoulder into my abdomen and hoisted me like a sack of dog food and threw me hard across the room. I think she may have meant to throw me on the bed, but my velocity was such that I skidded across the satin coverlet and hit the floor beyond it. My organs screamed and I lost my eyesight. Then I started breathing again and I blinked and blinked until I could see the patch of carpet in front of me. I could hear the window scrape open. I could hear Eric impatiently honk like an idiot. I could hear her feet crunching along the roof. I could hear the thump as she jumped down into the yard. I could hear the car door open, a rush of music, then close. I could hear the engine and the tires on the pavement as he drove away, taking the stop sign at a roll and then making the right. I could hear the wind entering the window. I could hear the fibers in the carpet shifting underneath my face. I could hear my heart beating, a disgusting wet sound like the bag of innards in a chicken, but hot, pulsing. I could hear time unskeining like ribbon off a spool, and the fact that it would never stop seemed merciless.

But wouldn't I have gone if it were Anthony in that car waiting for me?

And I knew then why I didn't want her to go. It was because I wanted her to stay with me. I wanted our friendship to be enough. I wanted these last days together to somehow be about our closeness. I wanted her tragedy to belong to me.

16

The day Bunny was remanded at her sentencing hearing was a Tuesday. In the days between our late-night altercation and her court date we were quiet and formal with each other. She didn't apologize, and I didn't bring it up. I texted Anthony that I missed him, then immediately texted again saying I shouldn't have sent that and asking him not to reply. The morning of her court appearance, she knocked at my door. She was already dressed for court in a pink angora sweater and gray skirt that Swanson had picked out and dropped off at the house without anyone having asked. I didn't see what difference it made at this point, but we all supposed he knew what he was doing. As the doom of her court date came nearer, Swanson became ever more manically cheerful. Anytime anyone said the phrase "three years," Swanson would chime, "But she'll get half-time credits! Eighteen months, folks, eighteen months." He sounded like a game show host.

"Hey," she said, "I have something for you." She came in and sat on the edge of my bed. She was holding a thick manila envelope. "So I withdrew enough of the money from that account my dad has in my name and I paid off my Jeep. I'm signing it over to you. Here are the keys and the manual, and here's the pink slip. So all you have to do is take this form to the DMV to transfer the title, I've already signed it."

"Are you kidding me?" I asked. "Bunny, this is too much."

"How else are you going to get a car?" she asked.

"Does your Dad know? Is he going to be pissed it's not his?"

"I'll tell him," she said.

I felt badly about how happy and excited I was. This was my last day with her and I had prepared myself for the numb tragedy of it. Of driving to the courthouse in Ray's car. Of waiting for her appearance. Of handing her over. I didn't know what would pass over her face when the bailiff first put his hands on her and her body became not her own. It was the kind of terrible thing that was difficult to put into words, but I had watched it happen to my mother, and I knew what it was. I had prepared for bureaucracy and tragedy and tears, but I had not prepared for someone to give me a car. I kept trying not to smile, but pushing it down made it hurt.

"I'm sorry I was so mean about Eric," I said. "You can do whatever you want. It's your life. I don't know why . . . I—"

"No, I'm sorry. I don't know why I went. It was boring and stupid, but I just—I wanted so badly to feel like someone loved me. I always had this fantasy that—I have this tiny freckle, here," she said. "And here." She tilted her head so that I could see her neck. "See I have three tiny freckles in a row. And I have always had this fantasy of lying in bed with a man, and him noticing them and loving these three tiny little freckles. That only I have. That are me. And I thought—maybe he would see them."

"I've always loved those freckles," I said. They looked like the beginning of a dotted line. Like someone had marked where to start the knife when they cut off her head. I don't know why they always portended such violence to me, but they did.

"I don't know why I wanted *him* to see them."

"Did he?"

"Of course not. I mean, and obviously we were in a dark car, I didn't literally expect him to see them, it wasn't the freckles, it was the whole thing."

"You wanted to be seen."

"Yes."

Why did we want so desperately to be seen? I saw her. My eyes were full of her. But it wasn't enough, and I was no longer hurt by it. The way she loved me wasn't enough for me either. Maybe love would never be enough. Maybe it would never do what we wanted it to do.

The court was a buzzing, bustling place, and though our sentencing hearing was scheduled for eleven, Ray and Swanson and Bunny and I had gotten to the courtroom an hour early just in case. Our hearing was in Department 31 on the third floor, and even the hallway outside was crowded with people making deals or preparing or reviewing notes, lawyers and clients, street cops and detectives. There was a group of EMTs eating sunflower seeds and laughing. Swanson steered us to a cold granite bench, and we sat. "So once we go in, we can't talk. You guys want to chill out here, and I'll go see what case number they're on?"

We nodded dumbly. Even though there was no reason for me to be personally nervous—I would not even have to speak in the courtroom—I found I was so physically freaked out that my eyes didn't seem to be working correctly, as though my pupils were letting in too much light or not enough. I was incredibly distracted by this security guard who, while talking casually with an EMT who seemed to be his friend, had his hand on his gun and was gently fiddling with it. There were green tiles in a pattern with beige tiles, and I thought: Who designed this? What architect is tasked with determining the stagecraft of justice?

Swanson had returned to us. "They're ahead of schedule, so let's just go in. You need to go to the bathroom?" he asked Bunny. She shook her head. "Last chance," he said, which even in my stunted state I found to be a frightening thing to say.

But I was glad Swanson had us go inside, because the courtroom was like a bath and it was better to have time to adapt to its strange temperature. It was a large room with a curved ceiling like an airplane hangar, and at the front of the room the judge sat at the bench, the American flag and the California flag hanging limp behind him, flanking the seal of the State of California. These were the totems. These were the details that made this a real courtroom and not a dream. The judge seemed to be some kind of ancient mouse king, swallowed in his black robes, with a pointy face and bifocals. He still had all his hair and it was an unremarkable brown color, gray at the temples. His voice was a nasal, pointy instrument he used to poke holes in things. We watched a gun charge get dismissed, and the young man bounced out of there like he could barely keep his feet on the ground. His friend was wearing a crucifix so covered in diamonds it must have cost as much as a car. The bailiff was constantly hunting people secretly looking at their cell phones, the use of which was prohibited as many notices in the courtroom advertised, and whenever he would catch someone silently scrolling or texting, there would be titters as he confronted the person and confiscated their phone. The first time it happened, I didn't know what was going on, and he moved from the bailiff's box with such speed and emergency that I thought someone had drawn a gun.

Bunny and I held hands. Ray sat on her other side, and next to him Swanson sat, although Swan kept getting up, going outside, coming back in, and generally being in constant, agitated motion. We were watching a setting hearing where they were arguing over the date of a preliminary hearing, and the public defender explained she would be occupied for at least a month on a murder trial, and then would be taking a two-week vacation.

"Would you like to cancel your vacation?" the judge asked her.

"Excuse me?" the public defender asked.

"Would you like to cancel your vacation?" he asked again.

"No, thank you," the public defender said, very smoothly, but I could hear, we all could hear, the quaver in her voice.

"Very well," the judge said, and set the date of the preliminary hearing.

Watching all of this was absorbing and boring at the same time, much like a piece of theater. The case right before Bunny's, we were all on edge with the knowledge that we were next. The defendant was in custody, and when the bailiff brought him out, there was an anguished twist to his face, and it was plain he was on the verge of tears. He slumped as far down into the chair as he could.

A man got up and said that the defendant's lawyer had had a family emergency and he would be stepping in for her for the day.

"Sit up," the judge yelled at the defendant. "Sit up like a man at your own hearing."

The boy sat up more in the chair, but I could see his shoulders were shaking. I understood then what the man representing him was saying. The boy's lawyer had not shown up. She had a family emergency. And now this young man was at his murder prelim alone, and he was angry and terrified and crying very much against his will in front of the judge. I guess it was then that I understood how unsafe we really were. The judge did not have any tenderness or even any inclination toward civility for this young man. The fact that we would all be crying if our lawyer bailed on us during a hearing when we were accused of murder was not of consequence.

What it most reminded me of, in a way, was the haughtiness and control of a drag queen. I pictured RuPaul saying, "Sashay away." What was important to the judge was that the defendant maintain the decorum of the courtroom. That he control himself. Control was the matrix, was the soil, in which any kind of justice or rationality could grow, and if you did not carefully and rigorously maintain the atmosphere of control, then you would have no hope of clarity in anything. Or these were the thoughts that bubbled in my adolescent brain.

And then it was Bunny's turn. She and Swan pushed to the front of the room. Ray and I sat with the empty chair between us, the air still warm from Bunny's body. All I could see was her broad back as she stood before the judge. Swan had told her not to sit.

"I understand an agreement has been reached between the DA's office and the defendant," the judge said.

"Yes, Your Honor," Swanson said, and there was a murmured "Yes, Your Honor" from the prosecutor's side as well.

The judge looked at Bunny with a strange glint in his eye, as though she interested him. "Do you understand that by entering into this plea you are giving up your right to defend yourself with your own testimony?"

"Yes, Your Honor," Bunny said, her voice loud and ringing as a bell.

"Is this what you want to do?"

"Yes, Your Honor."

"Do you further understand that by entering into this plea, you are giving up your Fifth and Sixth Amendment rights, your right to refuse to testify against yourself, and your right to a speedy trial. By entering into this plea you are giving up very important, substantial, constitutional rights. Do you understand?"

"Yes, Your Honor," she said, and again her voice was a bell. I realized the entire court was hushed. They were all interested in this girl, in this girl murderer with the pink sweater and the crystal voice.

"Are you entering into this plea freely, voluntarily, and understandingly?"

"Yes, sir," she said. And I felt I could not breathe. *What if she copped to the murder charge?* Ray's voice was ringing in my memory. *Do you think the DA would make the arson go away?* And I worried we were making an incredible mistake. I wished this was like a wedding and the judge would ask if anyone had any objections, but it was not and he would not. It was too late for that kind of thinking.

"On the afternoon of October twenty-eighth, did you involve yourself in an altercation at North Shore High School wherein you attacked another student, Ann Marie Robertson, causing her to sustain injuries that ultimately led to her death on December tenth?"

"Yes, Your Honor."

"To the charge of involuntary manslaughter, how do you plead?"

"No contest, Your Honor," she said.

The judge looked at her for a moment more, then rolled on. "I find waivers knowingly intelligently made. I sentence her to three years state prison. Bailiff, please remand the defendant."

And then the bailiff handcuffed her and led her out a door on the side of the courtroom. There was a window into the hallway the door led to, so I could see them even after the door had shut on her. Her hands were cuffed in front of her and the bailiff was steering her down a hallway, and he seemed to be talking to her, and she seemed to be nodding, and then she was gone.

It took me about three days to understand that Bunny was gone, and when understanding finally overtook me, it was like breaching the surface of the water after a near drowning, desperately gulping for air. What was I doing in Ray Lampert's house? What was I going to do next? I began, haltingly, to claw myself toward a life.

I walked to Rite Aid, huddled into my sweatshirt, and every house I passed seemed ominous to me, as though there were people inside watching me. When I stepped inside the Rite Aid, I felt like I was home. Terrence let me into his little office, which had a one-way mirror so he could spy on the cashiers. It was all so straightforwardly Orwellian that it seemed a little sweet, from an older, more authoritarian time.

"Oh my god, oh kid," he said when he saw me. "How you doing? How's all your—guts?" He motioned around his own midsection.

"Well, a lot better. I mean, physically. I just—I'm so embarrassed, but I need help."

"Tell me."

The problem with telling him was that my eyes involuntarily produced tears, even though I was not sad about these things exactly. I explained that Jason had been one of the boys who beat me up, but that I hadn't wanted to tell anyone, and I hadn't told Aunt Deedee. I don't know why, but when I was talking to Terrence, it was easy to say it was Jason and to be sure. Everything was really very simple, there inside the Rite Aid manager's office. Maybe because I knew he would believe me. My questions and explanations came in little thorny bursts that were extremely physically painful in a way that bewildered me, but with each piece I got out, I felt lighter and calmer.

He immediately agreed to my request to come and live with his family. He immediately agreed to transfer me to another Rite Aid somewhere outside the orbit of North Shore. He hugged me so tightly my nose was smashed into his shirt and I smelled the sweet powdery perfume of some brand of laundry detergent I had never smelled before.

"You are such a good kid," Terrence said with a ferocity I had never heard in his voice except when talking about football. "Goddamnit, you're a good kid."

"Thank you, Terrence," I said. I felt like I was floating, like my body was weightless, the way it was in Bunny's pool. I wasn't sure if my legs would function well enough to carry me back to Ray's house to pack my things, but they did.

And so I moved in with Terrence's family, engulfed by his many noisy children who were charmed by the irregularity of my sudden appearance. "I think we are in a pretend world and someone is playing with us," his three-year-old said to me, her face inches from my own close to dawn in the gray-blue light of their living room. Breakfast time in that house was like Abbott and Costello on bennies but with a lot of farting, and by the time everyone left for school or preschool or kindergarten or wherever, I was usually slightly smeared with peanut butter from cuddles I would never have dared ask for. I loved it at Terrence's house. I cannot even begin to describe how safe I felt there. His wife bought me socks because she noticed I did not own any. I had never bothered to spend money on socks when I could just not wear them, but I found that I adored the soft black cotton socks she bought. They made my feet feel so chaste and clean. I tried to express my gratitude by doing laundry, vacuuming when the dog hair buildup became uncomfortable (they had an aged pug named Grinch), playing with the kids, and helping with their homework, and Terrence's wife, Olivia, was gobsmacked by this, as though no one had ever in the history of the world helped her, and so I became a most besotted suck-up, and she my sappy liege.

In February I turned eighteen, and my mother invited me to their new house, or new to me—they had been living there for over a year. She gave me a flask as a present, engraved with my name. "Did you think I was turning twenty-one?" I asked. "What? No!" she said, laughing and hurt. "Why would—I just—nobody waits to be twenty-one to drink."

"True," I said.

"Now you can seem like the cool guy at parties," she said. I don't know who she thought I possibly was. "Speaking of cool guys, I wanted to inform you: Surprise! There's a new member of your family!"

My smile was frozen. Was she saying she was pregnant?

"Me and James got married!" She squealed.

"Wow, when?" I asked.

"We went to Vegas just before you went into the hospital," my mother said. I always noticed how no one ever said "when you were attacked" or "when you were beaten." They always phrased it as my "going into the hospital," like it was a line of work, or like I was a nun entering a convent. Obviously, I had not been invited to their wedding.

"Gabby was my maid of honor," my mom said, smiling shyly. I knew that on some level my mother was embarrassed. As though she had no right to get married again, to wear a white dress and feel loved and important, no right to be happy. She held out her ring for me to admire, but then took it back too quickly. "It's not real," she said.

"Well, that's great," I said, but it was the most I could say and she could tell.

I was alienated by their house. I'd never been here before, the new house. I'd been plenty of times to the old apartment, and of course we often met at the beloved Denny's on Hawthorne Boulevard. Their house was so clean, much cleaner than our house had ever been in my memory. There were candles burning, even though it was still light out, which was very my mother, but the furniture was all new looking and matching and everything was gray and teal. The walls were a muted gray, the couch was gray, the rug was a lighter gray, then teal accent colors: couch cushions, coffee table items, candles, wall art, all teal. It was like the house had been decorated by a T.J.Maxx HomeGoods specialist. I had remembered my mother's taste as so much more bohemian, but then I wondered if perhaps our furniture had been mismatched and bizarre because we couldn't afford furniture that coordinated. I realized, too, that I was sitting in a house, albeit a small one in a not very nice part of Culver City, but it was a house, and I understood now what that meant. I didn't know if they owned, but even if they were renting, the feeling was different. I had been so overwhelmed by her new boyfriend's similarities to our father that I had failed to notice this key difference: He had money. Not a lot, but enough. And maybe that would change the way the story unfolded.

As we talked and ate (my mother had baked several different Trader Joe's appetizers, little spinach-and-feta cups, tiny pigs in a blanket, it was all very fancy), I kept finding myself evaluating the cost of the items in their home. I noticed Gabby was wearing socks that looked new, an unblemished snowy white with electric-orange toe caps. Her jeans seemed fashionable, with little rips in the knees. Her hair was cut in subtle waves that framed her face. There was a cookie jar in the shape of a French Bulldog in the kitchen. They had a spinning spice rack. While I had been living elsewhere, they had been buying things, acquiring things. Strolling through the aisles of Target or Marshalls and finding something they liked. I do not know why the idea of this made me so achingly jealous, but it did.

Now that my mother's boyfriend was my stepfather, I figured it was time to try to learn more about him. I knew that his name was James and that he worked in a garage as a mechanic, but I knew very little else. I guessed that they were still drinking because of the beers and box of wine I saw in the fridge, as well as a faux-rustic sign hung in the kitchen: DON'T TALK TO ME UNTIL I'VE HAD MY WINE. Maybe that was okay. Maybe I was wrong about everything. Maybe it was okay to just cast off one of your children, focus on the one you liked more, drink until you felt happy, and buy stuff. Hyena pups kill off their brothers and sisters until only one from the litter remains. The females even have pseudo penises with which to show dominance and rape each other.

But James was watching *Ancient Aliens* in the living room, and he did not feel any social need to engage with us. He had shaken my hand very warmly when I first arrived, and now he was a kind golem steadily absorbing the trickle of false information. I let my mother and sister take me outside to show me their yard.

"Show him the fairy garden," Gabby was saying.

"I will, I will," my mom said. She led me past some daisy bushes that were frankly thriving and much prettier than daisies had any right to be, and then held back the bladed leaves of a calla lily so that I could see a small clearing between plants. There I saw several tiny houses, their roofs painted to look like mushroom caps. There were tiny lanes paved with pebbles and some miniature white picket fencing. There was a small ladder that led up the trunk of a camellia tree with low branches so that it looked like a fairy had climbed up there to go about their fairy business. A little figurine of a hedgehog was swinging on a tiny rope swing behind one of the toadstool houses.

"Isn't it so, so cute?" Gabby was saying.

"Oh, he doesn't like it!" my mom cried.

"No, no, it's not that," I said. I didn't know whether I liked it or not. It struck me as both wonderful and very sad. The child part of me was enchanted, and also deeply jealous, while the adult part of me thought it was stupid and bizarre. The figurines were cheaply made, the colors garish. I didn't know what to think. "Whose idea was this?"

"I saw it on Pinterest," my mother said, "and the very first time I saw it, I just thought: I have to have that."

"So interesting," I said. "It's very cute."

"You think it's dumb," my sister said. Her brown eyes were hurt. She looked more like our father, and that had always been the family lore, that I took after our mother and Gabby took after our father, but now, seeing them standing side by side, their arms crossed against the cold, I could see the resemblance almost vibrating between their bodies, the similarity in the way they stood, the way they moved, the dark chocolate color of their hair, though my mother had several strands of silver coming in. I was overwhelmed. I was suddenly extremely upset and worried I would cry, but I had no idea why and it seemed so inappropriate that I was horrified by myself. I couldn't seem to breathe correctly.

"Michael, are you okay?" my mother asked.

"I'm fine," I said. "This is just so weird. I haven't seen you guys in a while, and then the house, and I . . ."

"I know," my mother said.

"Cause you're a traitor," Gabby said. She did a fake little ninja kick at my leg.

I stuttered, not sure what to say. "I-I'm not a traitor," I said.

"Well, you're the one who didn't want to live with us," Gabby said.

"Oh, Gabby," my mother said. "We don't need to talk about that."

"You never invited me to live with you," I said. I thought they meant the house, this house, the current house.

"Yes, we did," Gabby said. "Aunt Deedee said you refused. Said you wanted to stay with her."

"What? When? When are you talking about?"

"We don't need to bring all this up, this is ancient history," my mother said.

Was that what they thought? That it had been I who abandoned them? I tried desperately to remember exactly how it had all happened, how it had been decided, but it was so many years ago, and so many of the conversations had been had between my mother and Aunt Deedee that I had no idea what had been said.

"I don't know what to say," I said.

"He's not even sorry!" Gabby said.

"What? Sorry for what?"

"You were my big brother," she said. "And you just fucking abandoned me."

"You are twisting this. Mom didn't want me."

"Who said I didn't want you?" my mother said, her voice almost hysterical with emotion. "Did Deedee say that?"

"No!" I said, because I couldn't remember her actually saying that. "She didn't say that, it was just implied. Because—well, I mean, because I'm gay."

My mother clapped both her hands over her mouth in surprise.

"Michael!" she gasped. "You are not."

"I am," I said.

"You are not," she said again.

This conversation was getting so bizarre that I looked around at the grass, at the daisies, at the fairy garden, trying to find something to cling to, that was real, that made sense. "I thought you knew," I said, "when I was in the hospital—you just—I mean, why did you think I was there?"

"You were beat up!" she said. "Why would that make me think you were gay?"

"I was beat up because I'm gay," I said, though I didn't know if that was true either.

"I just want you to know that I accept you," Gabby said, which was such a one-eighty from her previous anger that I couldn't take it in as sincere at first.

"You're not gay," my mother said more confidently.

"I am definitely gay," I said. "Mom, I'm gay."

"I know you think you're gay," she said. "But you're not."

"Mom, if he says he's gay, he's gay," Gabby said, and I was grateful that she was my unexpected ally in this situation, but it did nothing to deter my mother.

"Trust me," my mother said, "I know you're not gay."

"How do you know I'm not gay?" I asked.

"Because you would get crushes on little girls!" she said, tugging her hands inside the sleeves of her beige sweater. "When you were little! You always loved the little girls. Listen, Michael, just being more sensitive, having taste, being interested in art, those things don't make you gay."

"I like to suck cock, Mom," I said. "I like to fuck men in the ass."

"Shut your mouth," my mother said, her fury instant and electric.

"I'm leaving," I said. "Thanks for the flask. I'll use it for all the drinking I don't do!"

And I turned and went back into the house. I looked for a second at the cake on the counter. They had gotten the bakery to write *Happy Birthday* and my name on it. The guilt was so strong it seemed to make my vision wobble, but I went into the living room where James was learning that aliens had visited the Old West and been seen by cowboys. "Bye!" I said, as I put on my sweatshirt.

"Oh, you leaving?" he said. "It was good seeing you!" He smiled.

"You too," I said, and I went outside, and I speed-walked to Bunny's Jeep, and I drove away.

17

I took my GED that February, after I heard that Tyler and the other boys I named had gotten one year of probation for almost beating me to death. One year of probation. It seemed so bizarre and useless to me. I had applied to ten colleges, all the state schools back in November, and some private colleges in January, and I agreed to let Ray Lampert help me with the admissions fees, even though I wanted nothing to do with him anymore. I drove Bunny's Jeep all around L.A. She had left her iPod in the center console and so I listened to her music. On some level, I was acting like she was dead. On some level, I thought she really was dead. I think I was pretending everyone was dead. Bunny, Ray. Aunt Deedee. Anthony. Gabby. My mother. Even myself. Every metamorphosis is violent, even disgusting. That's why you have to hide while it is happening.

I had applied to state schools, but I had no idea how I would afford even in-state tuition. My only hope, and it seemed like such a long shot I didn't like to even speak of it, was a scholarship to a private college. I applied to four of them, and I got into two, with a full ride to one. Pomona College. It wasn't Yale or Harvard, but it suited me to the ground. It was familiar and safe and free and even kind of fancy! When I moved into my dorm room, which I shared with a sullen young man named Trent, on the first day of freshman year, I felt like I had pulled off the most outrageous long con in the history of the world. And I was thrilled. I loved college. I loved every single thing about it. From the dining hall with its predictable, nourishing, bland food, to the library with its wonderful new-carpet smell, to reading Camus and studying calculus, college was for me in every way. There were free concerts, free lectures, there were art shows, there were barbecues. There were other out boys. I had never been so happy in my entire life.

I got a work-study job answering phones in the dean's office, and I excelled. "What a phone voice!" my boss, Mariana, said. She was an overweight perfectionist with absolutely unbearable carpal tunnel pain. She wore wrist braces every day. She loved me, and I accepted her maternal affection with gratitude, even if I didn't feel exactly the same way about her. She even liked my gayness and would bring all matters of aesthetics to me, as though I had some special expertise. Did I think the gray header or the navy header was more executive-looking for the budget memo? What did I think about this font for graduation name tags? On some level I found this insulting, she was stereotyping, but she was also not wrong that I was better than her at picking out which header looked good. Sometimes she bought me lunch, and she always tipped me off if she knew there was going to be free food somewhere around campus.

The first year living with Trent was somewhat miserable as he was frequently on drugs and prone to lapsing into slam poetry in regular conversation. He seldom bathed and never did his laundry so our room stank, not just of his sweat and crotch rot, but of a deeper, more earthy, troubling fecal smell. He also loved eggs, hard-boiled eggs, and he would boil a dozen and then eat them out of the pot of water as he sat on the floor, the shells and wisps of membrane scattered around him on the carpet. Still, early on in our rooming together, I had decided it was best to be straightforward and tell him I was gay and make sure he had no problem with it. I did not want to live with someone I felt unsafe around, but it took me several weeks into the fall semester to realize that I felt this way and to become sure that I had a right to it at all.

"I absolutely understand if you feel uncomfortable," I said, "and I'd be happy to switch rooms, no hard feelings."

"I think it's righteous," Trent said, and held up his skinny fist. "Gender is fluid and nonbinary, sexuality's a spectrum. I've had sex with dudes," he said.

"Oh," I said.

"I fucked a tree once."

"Did it hurt?" I asked.

"Not at the time," he said, "but later it was pretty brutal. Mr. Happy was scratched up like a Dionysian sacrifice."

"Wow," I said.

Still, it was a radical improvement over living with Jason. Trent was bizarre and ridiculous and very, very annoying, but at the end of the year he wrapped me in a bear hug I hadn't been expecting and whispered in my ear, "I will love you forever, homie, and always put light around you in my heart."

We rarely saw each other on campus, but when we did he would smile and nod at me. After that first year, I became an RA, which suited me perfectly, bossing people around, having a single room, getting paid a small stipend for making sure we had enough toilet paper. I was queen of that dorm and I ruled our floor with an iron fist in a velvet glove.

My sophomore year, I began dating a junior named Evan. He was a poet and he had handsome ears that were just on the verge of being too big but were instead distinctive. He lived off campus in an apartment because his parents were rich. He was lean and he had curly brown hair and a face that was delicate without being feminine. He had big fat lips like a little kid's. He was very good at being adorable. I'd never met someone who could make it seem cute to have failed at something. Once, he forgot to pay his electricity bill for several months. "Michael, I, like, forgot there even was electricity. As, like, a force in the universe. What *is* electricity, I don't even know!" He was a vegetarian. He was never mean to me. Not once. Not even in a single conversation was he once slightly mean. In fact, if he thought he had accidentally slighted me, he would apologize profusely. He often picked me wildflowers and gave them to me as a surprise.

Despite these things, I never managed to fall in love with Evan. I cared about him. I lusted after him. I loved his narrow buttocks and his delicate, ticklish rib cage. I loved the large oblong brown mole on his pale forearm. But I did not fall in love with him the way I fell in love with Anthony, and I wondered if maybe I was too happy to fall in love, too already fulfilled.

I did see Anthony again while I was in college. It was the summer between sophomore and junior year, and I texted him out of the blue, and said: *I just wanted to say thank you for our time together. I don't think I was grown up enough to thank you at the time, but I think in many ways you saved my life.*

We texted back and forth, and he mentioned he would love to get together for lunch nonromantically to catch up, and I said I was driving out that way to drop a friend off at LAX, which was true, and we agreed to meet in North Shore at a sandwich shop where they made their own bread that Bunny and I used to go to all the time.

I lied to myself that I was not nervous about this encounter, but I changed my shirt five times before taking my friend to the airport. I didn't want to reopen the romantic door with Anthony, and at that point Evan and I were still technically together, although I already knew it was mostly over, but I did want Anthony to be impressed when he saw me. Gone was my septum piercing, gone the black eyeliner. I had cut my long hair at Evan's insistence, but it was very chic the way the girl had done it, short on the sides and long and floppy on top. I had a tan. I had muscles. I was wearing shoes made out of actual leather. I was terrified.

It wasn't just seeing Anthony. It was being in North Shore again. It was being in a place Bunny had been. By that point, she had been released from prison, but I knew she wasn't in North Shore anymore, so it wasn't that I was afraid to run into her. I was afraid of the memory of her, but also the memory of who I had been. I found my own self unfathomable and grotesque. How had

I subsisted on so little? How had I lived hunched over in fear of my very self, scuttling about like a crab? I felt ashamed that I had ever been anything other than I was now.

I was also, on some level, upset that the town still existed. That people went on living here as though nothing had happened, which was absurd, obviously. I kept expecting to be recognized, but I met no one I knew. The town, I saw, had gotten richer. Its metamorphosis was almost complete. On every block there were only one or two of the old houses clinging to existence between the mansions.

The sandwich shop was exactly the same, its ambient air temperature as hot and weirdly humid as ever. I recognized the woman behind the counter, though I did not know her name, but she didn't recognize me. And then I saw Anthony at a table in the back, and I knew all of a sudden that I was wildly happy to see him. Just to look at his face produced ripples of joy in my solar plexus. It was involuntary. I walked over, and he looked up from his book. "Good golly Miss Molly," he said.

"I'm so happy to see you," I said. I was busy looking at him, and I was beaming stupidly as I took the chair across from him. He looked older, but it was hard to say why. Perhaps it was a softness in the jaw, a feebleness in the neck. He had lost some weight and his shoulders were narrower and more bowed. But he was still smiling at me with those wonderful, slightly crooked teeth. I had not known I would recognize his teeth. "I'm sorry," I said, "I can't stop looking at you."

"I can't stop looking at you either," he said.

"It's okay, it doesn't actually matter what we say."

"No, it doesn't," he agreed.

I suppose I had thought that I dreamed it. That I was so desperate for love back then that I was willing to project it onto even an old man who lied to me. But it was still here, whatever it was. I didn't know whether to call it love or joy or just connection, but it was all of those things, and it was generated by our proximity, like an electromagnetic field. I had never felt anything like it with anyone else, and the fact that it was still here—what did it mean?

"I brought this book for you," he said. He flashed me the cover. It was a book of Adrienne Rich poems. I liked Adrienne Rich, but I didn't have any of her collections, so I was happy. It seemed so amazing and wonderful. That he would bring me a present. As though he had known all along that it would be like this, exactly the same as it had been, only different.

"I don't know how to say this," I said, "and I have no intention of entering into a romantic relationship with you again, but this is weird. Is it just me?"

"No, it's not just you," he said.

"I still love you," I said. "But not like—"

"I love you too."

"Maybe we knew each other in a past life or something," I said.

"Maybe we knew each other in this one."

We ordered sandwiches and the bread was as good as I remembered. They came in red plastic trays with wax paper. There was a fly that kept buzzing our table. The air was hot and steamy. It should not have been the most incredible lunch I had ever had, and yet it was. He told me all about Hank and his wife and his retirement. They had recently been on a trip to Prague, which he said reminded him of me because he knew that I would love it, and he made me promise that I would go someday and think of him. I told him all about college and Evan and my mother, whom I had recently begun talking to again.

"How's Bunny?" he asked.

"I don't know," I said.

He was shocked. "Did you have a fight?" he asked. "You were so close."

"No," I said, feeling suddenly sick and unable to explain.

"Then what happened?" he asked.

—

I visited Bunny in prison exactly three times. The first two times were the first summer she was in prison before I started at Pomona. I was still living with Terrence's family to save money. I slept on the couch in their den and I lived out of a reusable grocery bag that I kept in their laundry room. I had my life pared down to the bare essentials. Two pairs of black pants, two black T-shirts, and two white button-downs for work, my laptop. Everything else I owned, my books, my mementos, the rest of my clothes, were in a box in Ray Lampert's garage, which in the end I never returned to get. It was just not worth it to have to look at his face.

I would have visited Bunny in prison right away, but being approved as a visitor takes time. It took time for Bunny to be assigned to a prison, time for her to go through the reception process, during which she was not allowed visitors, then time for me to fill out an arcane application, send it in, time to have my background check run and approved, time for them to notify Bunny and then for her to notify me. (Why couldn't they notify me? Why did it have to go through her? Such questions have no answers.)

When, finally, we had secured that much, I discovered that I had to schedule my visit with her specific prison and that visiting hours were booked for the next two months straight. The prison was open for visits only on Saturday and Sunday, as well as four holidays throughout the year, and it booked up well in advance. I made an appointment for the first Saturday in June, the earliest I could get, and waited, carefully reviewing the extensive rules Bunny had forwarded to me.

I did not remember rules like this when my mother was in prison and we would visit her, but perhaps I was not aware of them because I was a child. Any bag I brought must be made out of clear plastic. I was not to wear denim pants or a blue chambray shirt. I was not to wear an orange top, orange pants, or an orange jumpsuit. I was not to wear a red shirt. I was not to wear forest-green pants or a tan shirt. I was not to wear camouflage. I must dress modestly. I was not to wear hats or gloves. I was not to wear shorts that were two inches above the knee. I was not to wear jewelry. I was not to wear a layered outfit. My keys must be no more than two in number and on a key ring with no attachments. I could bring a small unopened pack of tissues. I could bring up to fifty dollars, but it must be in one-dollar bills. I could bring ten photographs. I could bring a document no more than ten pages in length. If I violated any of these rules, I would be turned away from the prison and not allowed to see Bunny for our visit.

While some of these were easy to comply with (I did not own nor did I desire to don an orange jumpsuit), there were still so many instructions of what not to wear that I felt anxious I would forget one and accidentally wear a blue shirt or green pants. The list made me very upset. The list signaled a kind of crushing bureaucracy and micromanaged oversight that I had last experienced, in a much more mild form, in school. I felt dread that Bunny was living inside such a place.

The day of our visit I was extremely anxious. She was at California Institution for Women, which was in Corona, a full hour's drive from Terrence's house in Carson. I had never driven that far before, and I was still a relatively new driver, so the drive alone was terrifying to me, let alone worrying I would hit traffic or be otherwise delayed and miss my visitor's appointment. If I was even ten minutes late, I would not be allowed to see her.

As I drove, I began to feel that this was insane. This level of scrutiny, of meaningless protocol. Why were visiting hours only on the weekends? What about people who worked on the weekends? I had had to get my shift covered by a coworker. Why were even the visitors of people in prison being punished? Because it was present in every communication from the prison I had received. This disdain for me. This weird fetish of control over me, and I was not even the one who had committed a crime.

And then I would think: She's in for murder. She's a murderer.

You're about to go visit a murderer. What do you expect, you friend-of-a-murderer. And she killed someone for you. In defense of you. It was only clear to me in retrospect that that was what happened.

By the time I reached the prison I was so anxious and my thinking so fragmented that everything struck me as surreal. The guards with Tasers. The metal detectors. The heavy locks on all the doors. The surveillance cameras in every room, in every hallway, on every corner, making sure that all spaces were universally seen. Nothing here could be private. Everything was monitored.

I was processed and then put in a waiting room where there were four surveillance cameras, and I sat and waited. There were lots of families, lots of other people waiting. No one was talking except the little kids. It felt very much like the DMV except there were no windows and an eerie feeling that we could not leave. The time for my visit came and went. About fifteen minutes after my appointment time, I went up to the woman behind a plate-glass window and asked if I had somehow missed my name being called, but she just said, "Sit down and wait."

"My appointment time was fifteen minutes ago, so could you check if maybe something is—"

"Sit down and wait and your name will be called."

"But you don't know what my name is, so how do you know it will be called?"

"Sit down or I will call security and have you removed."

I sat down. About thirty minutes later, a guard came in and called my name, then led me down a long hallway with blue linoleum and into the visiting room. Bunny was already sitting at one of the tables, and she waved at me in excitement until the guard chastised her. "You can hug for up to ten seconds, and after that you can hold hands, but no other touching, nothing under the table," the guard said when we arrived at the table. "When your visit is over, you may hug again."

"Oh, okay," I said, and Bunny and I hugged while the guard watched. She was so much taller than me that I felt like a child pressed up against her chest. She smelled like sweat. She was wearing a sky-blue, short-sleeve button-down shirt and dark teal trousers. Both items were bulky and ill-fitting, designed to mask any physical beauty that might accidentally become manifest. We sat down and looked at each other.

"Did you bring money?" was the first thing she said to me.

"I brought ten singles," I said. "Is that enough?"

She nodded. "Okay, I want an M&M's, a Doritos, a Sprite, and if there is any money left, then Sour Patch Kids."

"Can I get up and walk over there?" I asked, nodding with my head at the vending machines.

"I think so, just do it slowly."

I stood and the guard looked my way, I motioned at the vending machines and he nodded. I walked over and waited behind a woman and a five-year-old girl with sweet braids, who was getting Ding Dongs. I fed my sweaty dollar bills to the machine with shaking hands. What was I afraid of? Nothing in particular. But I hated this place powerfully.

I bought Bunny her treats. There was not enough left for the Sour Patch Kids. When I brought them back to the table she excitedly opened them and began eating and I felt that really she was more excited about the food than about seeing me.

"So how is it?" I said. "You look good."

She did not look good. Her skin looked dull and she had a handful of tiny pimples on the left side of her face. Her hair was greasy at the roots. "It's fine," she said. "I mean, I get by." She laughed.

"Do you have any friends?" I asked.

"A couple," she said, licking up a palmful of M&M's.

"It's just so good to see your face," I said, which was a lie. It was weird and sad to see her face. She didn't look the same. But then she met my eyes fully for the first time, and the eye contact was so intense I felt I was falling, that if I didn't concentrate I would lose consciousness. There was just her whole soul, right there. Looking at me. It was Bunny.

"I miss you every day," she said, still holding my gaze, flowing into me.

"Do you get all my letters? Because sometimes you don't write back," I said. "And I never know if you don't get it or . . ."

"Sometimes I'm too sad to write back," she said.

And I started to cry. I looked up at the ceiling, trying to stop. When I looked at her again, she was still there, looking frankly at me, her eyes dry.

"I couldn't tell you in my letters because they read them but I have a girlfriend in here," she said softly.

"Get out!" I said, wiping my eyes, grateful to recover myself.

"She's really cool," she said.

"That's amazing. What is she? I mean—what did she do?"

"She killed her stepfather because he was molesting her kid sister."

"Oh wow," I said, "I was kind of hoping you'd say drugs."

She laughed. "Us murderers gotta stick together, you know." There was a hint of a Jersey accent in her voice, and I had the impression this was a way the girls talked together to make each other laugh. Her attention was diverted for a moment as she opened the Doritos with holy reverence.

"I would offer to share, but my dad hasn't put anything on my commissary in like a month, and all the food here has saltpeter in it to keep you calm, it's disgusting. These chips taste like heaven."

"They put saltpeter in the food?" I asked.

"Well, I don't know if they really do, but that's what everyone says."

"So does everyone know you killed someone?"

"Oh yeah," she said. "Gives me massive cred in here."

"Weird," I said.

"I know," she said, "they call me the Knockout. Because for in here, I'm pretty. I know you may not think I'm pretty, like, I'm not pretty out there, but in here I'm pretty."

"I think you're pretty," I said, but I was so disturbed I didn't know what to say. "How's your dad?" I asked, even though I had consciously planned not to ask about Ray.

"Well, he had to sell our house," she said. "And he lost his business. But he's finally out of the last of the IRS debt, and he just bought a condo in Lake Forest and he's doing real estate down there."

"He still has his license?" I asked.

"He never lost it."

"It's just so unfair," I said. "Sometimes I can't get over it. That you're in here and he's buying a condo and probably drinking scotch with Swanson."

She shrugged. "Is what it is."

"Do you forgive him?" I really wanted to know. I did not forgive him. In fact, the more time passed, the more my heart calcified against him.

"Some thoughts are just too expensive to have," she said.

I didn't say anything, just looked at her. What a magnificent animal she was even now, all two hundred pounds of her, across the table from me, licking Cool Ranch dust from her fingers. "It's kind of like long-distance running," she said. "You have to keep your mind under control. You can't start thinking about when it's going to be over or what hurts or you'll lose it and your form will get sloppy and soon you'll be winded and you'll stop before you've given it everything you've got."

"So, like, you can't think about when you'll get out?"

"Exactly."

"You can't think about whether it's fair or unfair that you're here?"

"Exactly."

She was giving prison everything she had. She was determined to survive this. It seemed to me so honorable, to be committed to life in a place like this. I wasn't sure I would be able to do what she was doing.

"You're too good for this world," I said.

"No, I'm not," she said, and smiled.

—

The next time I visited her was in late August, right before I started at Pomona. We had an okay time. I knew what to expect from the prison protocol and was less freaked out. We talked, I bought her snacks. This time I brought a whole twenty-five dollars in singles and we both gorged on Snickers and Gardetto's.

"I haven't had an orange soda in years," I said.

I promised I would visit every month. Pomona was right next to Chino, it would hardly be a drive. I told her I would send her all my books I read, and it would be like she was going to college with me, and we could have a book club by mail.

But then I started college, and I did not visit her. I was absorbed by my new world. I also didn't want to go to the prison. It was as simple as that really. I didn't want to go, and so I didn't, even though I knew I should. Our pattern had always been that I sent two letters for every one she sent me, but now it dropped to an equal one-to-one ratio. And then it began to slip further, and I would wait sometimes a week or two weeks to write her back. I did not visit her again until the spring semester of my freshman year, on a Saturday in March.

The moment I saw her, I knew she was on drugs. Her eyes were glassy. The muscles in her face were slack. I didn't know what drug she was on, but I knew she was on something.

"What did they do," I asked, "put you on lithium?"

"What? No," she said, after hugging me.

"Seriously?" I leaned in and whispered, "You're not on drugs?"

"I swear," she said, "I'm not!" She laughed and I knew she was lying to me. Everything was different. The way she looked at me, the way she laughed, the way she talked, the way she held her shoulders. She had this new snicker that was near silent, just bursts of air through her nostrils.

"Well, how are you?" she asked, oddly formal. She was hostile, but she was smiling. I didn't know what to do.

"I'm fine," I said. "How are you?"

"Oh, I'm great, I'm fucking great, I'm taking this amazing course on Sartre and the existentialists."

"No, really?" I asked, leaning forward.

She laughed. "No. Get out. They don't have that shit here. That was straight from one of your own letters, you don't know your life?"

"I'm sorry I haven't been writing as much," I said.

"Oh, believe me, I get it," she said.

"I meant to," I said. "School is just really busy, and I have a job, and between the two—"

"No, don't apologize," she said, "I'm the one who should apologize. Everyone in here told me it would happen. They told me, eventually your friends, your family, they will stop thinking of you as you, and start thinking of you as a prisoner. The letters will stop. They won't put money on your books. Eventually, they will look at you just like the guards."

"Bunny, no," I said.

"And I thought maybe that would happen with my dad, and it did. Believe me, he stopped visiting long before you did. But I didn't think it would happen with you. Because I thought we were real friends. I fucking told people that. Whatever, I would say, you don't know him. But then you did what they all do. So it's me who should apologize," she said. "Because I was the one who was wrong."

We stared at each other for a moment. I didn't know what to say. I didn't want to have the conversation because she was high and I hated talking to intoxicated people. I had done enough of it with my own mother. You never got anywhere. They just got sort of stuck in a thought cycle, and if you were interrupting it or contradicting it, they literally could not hear you. They would do anything to just cycle through the thoughts again and stoke the anger and the hurt.

But that was only part of it. Really, I was so ashamed that I was almost unable to speak. I liked to think of her as hulking and invulnerable, but the truth was Bunny was a terrible victim. Ann Marie had been bullying her for years. The whole school had piled on the abuse. Ryan Brassard and the ear thing. And then what had lit the match of the whole powder keg was me. Was her love for me. Her defense of me.

And here she was, paying the price every day while I played around at college, examining texts and fucking boys and wrestling with the "big philosophical questions."

I wanted to throw up.

"I brought money for snacks," I said finally.

"That's cool," she said. "Buy me some Ding Dongs."

I bought an obscene armful of chips and cookies and candy and sodas, and carried them back to our table.

"I want to say something," I said, "that I've never said before, but I feel like we should really talk about it."

She raised an eyebrow, cracked a soda.

"Thank you for defending me," I said, my voice shaking. "When Ann Marie—thank you for defending me."

She looked at me for a very long time. Then she looked at the table. She peeled open the slippery, thin skin of a Snickers. "You're welcome," she said.

"And also, also: I'm sorry. I am so sorry that all this happened to you. I'm sorry you're in prison. I'm sorry Ann Marie died. I'm sorry for all of it. I'm sorry I didn't visit."

"Thank you," she said formally, as though I had presented her with a ceremonial gift.

We talked more easily after that, but I knew things still weren't right. I knew that the kind of transgression I had committed against her was large, was maybe the largest transgression I had made in my life. And I couldn't undo it.

Worse than that, I found myself disliking her. Disliking her new affect, her new slang, whatever was going on with her glassy eyes. We didn't have anything in common anymore, our worlds were so different. It was painful for me to hear about her world, and painful for her to hear about mine. Part of the social armor she had acquired to survive in prison was a nonchalant apathy that was anathema to intimacy. Every single thing I told her about my life she managed to imply was subtly stupid. Every single thing she told me about her life I was visibly troubled by. She told me about making pruno, about getting elastic strings out of the waistbands of underwear and making tiny woven rings with them, about tattoo guns made out of CD players, about some girl having an allergic reaction to calligraphy ink someone had snuck in. "Like, bitch, don't put that in your skin, that's for fountain pens and shit."

I wanted to love her again so I could forgive myself and I could not, so I could not.

That day I left, and I didn't go again. I didn't write her, and she didn't write me, except for one letter right before she was released, telling me I was her best friend and she hoped I still loved her. She signed it with a million x's and o's.

I did not know what to make of that letter. It was so saccharinely sweet that it was hard not to feel it was artificial.

I had always imagined that I would be there to meet Bunny when she got out. That it would be me and Ray, and we would take her to lunch and order the whole menu, and then go to Target and buy her all new clothes. I had imagined I would be part of her reentry into the world. But I was not. I didn't hear from Ray. I didn't know what her exact release date was, just that it was in October. I put my head down for midterms, and then before I knew it we were in December, and Bunny must theoretically be out in the world without me.

I started dating Evan that fall, and it was the following summer that I met up with Anthony and began a friendship with him that would last until his death from pancreatic cancer over five years later. I graduated from Pomona, class of 2015, and was accepted to the Graduate Program in Ecology and Evolutionary Biology at Cornell to do my PhD. My mother, Aunt Deedee, and Anthony all attended my college graduation, and there was no drama. It was as if none of it had ever happened. Anthony gave me a two-volume set of the *Oxford English Dictionary* in a special box with a drawer containing a magnifying glass, and I had never received a better present. I still have it to this day. I moved it with me to Ithaca.

I loved upstate New York immediately. I loved the snow. A fresh snowfall never failed to make me feel like Lucy when she is first in Narnia, as though I had accidentally climbed into another world.

I dated. I fell in love with a man named Conor, who was balding and a little fat and the most joyful being I have ever run across. He saw the world, he saw it clearly, but to him it was still good fun. Even the sad parts of being alive were beautiful. And mostly human beings cracked him up. He wasn't scared, scared of the darkness in others or in himself. He was so different from the other men I had dated. He was sane and capable. He was an engineer in robotics. He could cook only three things, but one of them was a delectable white chili. He had wide little feet and perfectly even toes.

It was after I had finished my master's and was burrowing into the long deep years of my PhD when I ran across a YouTube video of Bunny. I would never have even seen it if I hadn't been on Conor's laptop. He first started watching UFC fighting because of Ronda Rousey, and he was still a fan, watching her old clips on YouTube, and in one of the recommended to-watch-next videos on the sidebar, I saw a freeze-frame of a woman who could only be a grown-up Bunny Lampert. The video was titled "Watch the Knockout Queen Mop the Floor."

It was a boxing fight, in a ring instead of a cage. The fight lasted less than two minutes before the other girl was out cold. You could hear the fleshy slap of her body as she hit the mat. At the end, you could see Bunny go to her corner, and her trainer slapped her on the head with love, and then, clear as day, it was Ray Lampert standing there, smiling ear to ear, shouting at her, "You did it, you did it." In a feverish trance, I watched all her fight videos. She was undefeated, 12 and 0, with 5 TKOs. Numbers like a young Laila Ali, or so every commentator of her matches liked to say. The early videos were mostly grainy, without commentary, all crowd noise. The more recent ones were obviously higher production value, televised with commentators, and in them she was wearing what became her uniform: pink satin shorts and a pink satin sports bra–style top. The Knockout Queen. I bet Ray had come up with it himself. Her most watched video had over a million views.

"This is my friend from high school," I told Conor. "I know her."

"Wow, how cool!" he said. "We should go to one of her matches."

"They look like they're mostly in California," I said.

He laughed. "Oh, then we won't go to one of her matches."

"It's just so weird—she was my friend," I said. But I could not explain. I could not express what had happened and how formative it had been. "Her dad was really weird," I said. "He was an alcoholic."

"Oh yeah?" Conor said. "Where do you want to go to dinner?"

There was no one I could talk to about what had become of Bunny. Anthony was already very sick by that point; he would die just after that Christmas. I didn't want to bother him with this, and he didn't even know Bunny personally. I had kept in touch with none of our other high school friends, but I found myself curious about all of them, and I spent hours snooping through Naomi's Facebook page. She had a little daughter named Tara. It did not appear she had ever gone to the Olympics. That bruised me somehow. Without consciously thinking about it, I had always counted on her to go, as if in Bunny's place. But it looked like she had ripped off college's face and fucked the shit out of it, and law school after that, and it was clear from her selfies with her (extremely hot) husband, from her food pics at fancy restaurants, from her adorable daughter, that she was living the good life, and that made me happy.

I watched Bunny's fights over and over again. "This is unhealthy," Conor would chime in.

"I am well aware," I would say, "but I am in helpless thrall."

And then I would watch her knock out girls again and again.

There was one fight in particular that haunted me. Bunny had her hair in cornrows, which made her look less prissy, and her opponent was a particularly dumb-looking pinheaded girl. In the close-up before the match when they touched gloves, you could see they were both already drenched in sweat. The arena must have been sweltering. Bunny was looking at the other girl like she wanted to kill her, like she wanted to smear her on the sidewalk. The other girl disgusted her. But her look was not heated. It was a chilly disdain. She would take this pinheaded girl apart.

And she did. The match was four rounds long, two-minute rounds, and Bunny was methodical and relentless the whole way through, even though they were evenly matched—the other girl had a dogged persistence and ability to take blows to the head that boggled the mind. You could see the cool intelligence in Bunny's eyes as she evaluated the other girl's habits, found her weaknesses. Even as she got tired and staggered, you could tell she was in control. When she finally knocked the pinheaded girl out, it was exaggerated and cartoonish; the other girl swooned as though drunk, her mouth hanging open, and then fell to the ground. The camera zoomed in on Bunny, who was smiling around her mouth guard and holding her fist in the air, walking in tight circles, trying to burn off the rest of the adrenaline.

I must have watched this video of the pinheaded girl a hundred times. The pinheaded girl did not look like Ann Marie. Her hair was darker than Ann Marie's for one thing, and her eyes were not wide set. But it was the smallness of the head, and perhaps the way they were built, the angles of the shoulders, something. But I could not stop thinking of that pinheaded girl as Ann Marie.

"You are clinically depressed," Conor told me.

"Maybe," I said.

18

In the end, I finally called her. Obviously, it was all leading up to that. Calling her was the only thing that would break the spell and allow me to resume my life. And so I found her website, she wasn't on Facebook for whatever reason, and I sent her an email, very short and sweet in case she didn't read her own emails, and I got a note back, with her number, that appeared to be from her, and which said: *OMG, CALL ME!!! Xoxox.*

So I called her right then, afraid I would lose my nerve if I waited, and she picked up on the first ring and said, "Well, that was instant gratification!"

"I know!" I said. "I just got your message."

"I just sent it!"

"Modernity!"

"Or whatever," she said. "You serving up some academic realness now?"

I laughed. "I guess so."

"God, I'm so glad you called!" she said. Her voice sounded exactly the same. I felt seventeen again. It was truly surreal.

"I don't have long hair anymore," I blurted out.

She laughed. "How do you wear your hair now, Michael, my love?"

"God, I feel so stupid."

"Don't."

"So you're a boxer?"

"Yep."

"And do you like that?"

"I love it. It's like I was born to do it," she said. "I mean, I'd much rather do MMA because that's where all the money is, but I'm too big. The UFC's highest weight class for women is featherweight, which is like one forty-five, and I just can't cut enough weight to get down there and still, like, keep my eyes open."

"Oh yeah," I was saying, but I had instinctively withdrawn. I realized I was hoping that she would say she hated it, that Ray was making her do it. I didn't like the idea that she was born to do it. But on the other hand, boxing was a legitimate sport. What she was doing wasn't wrong. It was like a televised thing, not something to be ashamed of. She was an athlete, which is what she had always been.

We went on talking about the trivialities of our lives, catching up as best we could. In moments it would feel like everything was the way it used to be, and in other moments I would catch sight of a side of her I didn't recognize. She swore a lot. About her most recent fight she said she "dominated that binch."

"Ugh, binch. Don't say binch," I said.

"Why?"

"I don't know," I said.

"Wait, what were we talking about?" she asked.

Then we started talking about meeting up. She was going to be in New York City the following month for a match, would I come down? I said I wouldn't miss it for the world.

"I'll get you tickets to the match!" she said. "I'll book you a hotel! I'm writing a note so I don't forget!"

"Oooh, yay!" I said, even though the idea of watching the match live horrified me. But I agreed to meet her at a diner she particularly liked off Union Square on the Wednesday before her match. I would take the campus-run bus down. She would book us in the same hotel. It was all arranged.

—

I entertained fantasies of missing my bus accidentally/on purpose, or of standing Bunny up in some way, only because I was so nervous, but in the end I caught my bus, and I took a cab downtown, and I was a little bit late, but not too late, and when I walked into the diner, my heart dropped down to my stomach. Ray and Bunny were sitting in a booth in the back, and they both waved at me. She had said nothing about Ray joining us, and I was deeply unprepared. I had thought since I was an adult and no longer brought my parents everywhere, Bunny would be the same. I could not anticipate or control how strongly seeing his face made me react. Why was it easier for me to walk around North Shore and park in the same parking lot I had been almost beaten to death in than it was for me to look at Ray Lampert's face?

His nose was the dark raspberry of a true alcoholic, but his forehead lift had held up well. It was like my subconscious had simply stored all my animus from that time in his file, and now looking at him was allowing it to spill out and spread panic all over everything. But I walked over to their booth like a normal person, and did an impression of a normal person saying hello, sitting down, taking off my denim jacket, which was stupid to wear, it was too hot in the city in September.

I sat next to Ray, mainly so I wouldn't have to look at him, and he immediately put his arm around me and began slapping me with his giant, warm hands. "Well, look at you!" he crowed. "What a handsome queer you turned out to be!"

"You're not allowed to call me queer," I said, trying to say it in a friendly way.

"I thought that was the word now! It's not fag, is it?"

"No, 'queer' is a fine word, it's just you aren't allowed to call me that."

"I don't get it," he said. "Did I do something wrong?"

"Hey, Michael," Bunny said, as though I had just gotten there, and I thought she was just trying to end the mess I was in with her dad, and so I focused on her, and made eye contact, and I smiled, and for one long moment that's all we did, smile at each other, and it was good. She looked incredible. She was in peak physical form. Her skin glowed with vitality. Maybe boxing was good for her. Maybe I was just being a ninny. After everything, I marveled, Bunny Lampert was so damn beautiful. Part of it was that the world had changed around her, and people now saw Serena Williams and understood that she was gorgeous. Part of it was that her face had settled into itself somehow. Part of it was just the luster of extreme physical health. But she was a knockout. She took my breath away.

We ordered. Bunny requested seven egg whites and a side of broccoli and two chicken breasts, which caused the waitress to do some eyebrow lifting, which caused Ray to brag about Bunny's boxing record to the waitress. "She may even be," he said, "in fact she probably is, the best female boxer in the world." The dynamics were all very familiar, and at first that felt oddly good, who we used to be and how we used to act coming back to me so vividly, like I was rediscovering something I had lost.

"Have you heard from, oh god, what's her name? Oh, I know her name, it's right there, I just can't get it," Bunny said.

"Kelsey?"

"No. God, no, we were friends with her. She was black. It's right there, I just can't get it."

"Naomi?" I said, shocked that Bunny could forget her name.

"Yes! Naomi!" Bunny said. "Whatever happened to her?" And so I told Bunny everything I knew about Naomi from Facebook, and since Bunny was not on Facebook all of this was news to her. I filled her in on what I knew of the others, and told her about my life, but when I spoke too long about my work and my dissertation, I could sense her attention wandering. There was a lot we couldn't speak of with Ray there. Bunny didn't mention her time in prison, her girlfriend, or what any of that was like.

"Wait," she said at one point, "is my fight today?"

"No," Ray said, "it's tomorrow."

"I thought it was today."

"No, Bunny, it's tomorrow, I promise."

She loved boxing and she talked about it rapturously. "I just wish my mom were alive to see me box," she said, her eyes filling with tears. "I just think she'd be so proud of me."

"I bet she would," I said, even though I thought Allison probably would have preferred it if Bunny went to college or got married. But maybe that would have been wrong of Allison. Maybe it was wrong of me to have preferred that too.

"Did you ever think of going to the Olympics for boxing?" I asked. "They have that, right?"

She shrugged. "They do background checks, so I don't think that would work." I had meant to imply that she had achieved or still could achieve all her girlhood dreams, but instead I had stepped in it.

"Wait, is my fight today?" Bunny asked.

I looked at Ray, alarmed, but he answered calmly, "No, sweetie, it's tomorrow."

"Okay." She nodded, like she was deciding to trust him. "Okay."

What the fuck was going on here? Ray wouldn't look at me.

"Did it get rescheduled or something?" I asked. "All this confusion over the schedule?"

Ray didn't answer, took a huge bite of his club sandwich.

"Wait, what were you just saying?" Bunny asked. "Your train got rescheduled?"

"No," I said.

"Oh," she said, clearly confused.

When Bunny got up to pee, Ray leaned over to me. "Sorry about that," he said. "She's taken one too many in the head, if you know what I mean."

"What?" I asked, though I had heard him perfectly well.

"She's had a series of concussions," he said, "so she gets confused a lot. Her memory's bad." She hadn't been uninterested when I'd been telling her about my life, I realized, she'd been literally having a hard time following what I was saying.

"And she's still fighting?"

"We're doing this new therapy, that's part of why we're in New York, the doctor is the best, the best. They inject stem cells right into her brain, it's incredible!"

"Why is she still fighting?" I asked again.

"Ach," he said. "She's not that bad. Really, with the brain stuff. It's a very common problem, very common. She's at the height of her career, she can't stop now!"

Her brain was dying, and her father was fighting her anyway, like she was a racehorse who could win the cup and then be turned into dog food. Or maybe she would have stem cells injected straight into her brain (Was that even a thing? How could you inject something straight into the brain? It didn't make sense! Ray Lampert was insane!).

"What does her doctor say?" I asked. "Does he know she's fighting?"

"He knows, he knows," Ray said. "He advised against it, but they have to say that for liability reasons. What doctor is going to tell someone with brain trauma to go get in the ring?"

"Well, exactly," I said.

"You think Mike Tyson never fought with a concussion?"

"I think when Mike Tyson was fighting we didn't understand how bad a series of concussions was, and the whole joke of Mike Tyson is that fighting messed up his brain so it's just a really poor comparison."

"Touché," Ray said, and drained his mug of coffee.

When Bunny came back from the bathroom, I stood up and I hugged her and I said it was wonderful to see her. "Are you coming to my fight?" she asked. I told her of course I was, that I would see her later at the hotel but I had to run some errands. Ray wouldn't look at me and when I said goodbye, he was silent.

"I love you," I told Bunny, my arms still around her. I only came up to her neck. She looked down at me, smiled with so much sleepy love and joy that it physically hurt me.

"I love you too," she said. "Always have, always will."

"Okay," I said. "Take care. Be careful."

"I will," she said.

I walked out of the diner, and then I walked north for a few blocks, my heart pounding. I hailed a cab, and I had it take me to Port Authority, where I intended to take the next bus to Ithaca.

I didn't believe I could stop Ray Lampert. I could not avert the tragedy, but that didn't mean I had to watch.

But I didn't get on the bus. I didn't even buy a ticket. Instead I bought a pack of cigarettes, even though I had quit smoking my freshman year at Pomona. I stood outside Port Authority watching the frenzy of taxicabs and sweating in my stupid denim jacket in the September humidity, the hot smoke in my lungs like the city itself entering me.

I kept thinking of this joke Bunny and I used to have, where she would pretend to be what we called the "Love Monster." And she would talk in this strange Muppety voice, and she would say, "Love meeeee, love meeeee!" as she wrestled me and pinned me down so she could lie on top of me like a gigantic cat. "I do love you!" I would cry. "I do love you!" No matter what I said back to her, that's all she said. "Looove meeeeeee!" And once she had gotten herself arranged comfortably on top of me, she would begin to purr and pretend to fall asleep.

"You're crushing me," I would whisper.

"Love me," she would say.

I spent a few hours wandering the city before finally returning to the hotel. I didn't want to see them. But when I went to my room and passed by their door, I was somehow disappointed that it didn't open. I paused for a moment outside it, listening, and heard the low murmur of the TV. Then I kept walking down the long hallway to my own room, slid the key card, collapsed on the bed in a sweaty heap, and listened to the air conditioner singing some terrible robot madrigal until I fell asleep in my clothes, my shoes still tied to my feet.

Bunny's fight the next day was on the undercard of a fight between heavyweights Tony Barsotti and Mikhail Volkov in Madison Square Garden. When I looked at the ticket Ray had given me and it said Barsotti vs. Volkov, I thought he gave me the wrong ticket. I hadn't understood that women's boxing was just the opening act for the real boxing, the men's boxing. I had watched all of Bunny's fights, so I thought I knew what to expect, but I had been unprepared for the size of the spectacle itself.

My seat was, as I should have known it would be, right up front, in the second row next to Ray Lampert. "You made it!" he cried. "I've been backstage with her, how long have you been here?" he asked.

"Only a minute," I shouted over the noise of the crowd.

"She's ready, oh is she ready," Ray said, rubbing his hands together.

"Yeah?" I said. It seemed disgusting to me, the way that Ray was excited, like we were about to see a sex show instead of a boxing match. Maybe it was just that there was now something lewd about the cranberry-colored bulb of his nose. He could make eating a turkey sandwich seem indecent.

"This is what she loves," he said. "This is what makes it all worth it. She trains for months, and it kicks her ass, and it's hard and it's boring and it's hard. But then you get this." He gestured all around us.

On the screens above the ring Bunny's face was projected in pink pixels. A booming bass began, the hype music, and I could smell the fog machine before I saw the smoke rolling down the aisle, the ramp down into the arena. And then a figure pushed through the white wall of fog, and it was Bunny, but she was wearing a white satiny hooded robe, the hood pulled down low over her face. Her gloves were white, and not being able to see her hands or her face made her even more frightening and beautiful. As she walked to the ring, trailed by her coach and some assistants, she moved with a roiling, liquid power.

The announcer over the loudspeaker: "In one corner we have Bunny Lampert, the Knockout Queen, at one hundred sixty-six pounds, with twelve wins, five by knockout, undefeated." Bunny swept up into the ring and paced in a tight circle, then threw her hood back and the crowd roared. She ripped the robe off, and underneath she was wearing her pink satins. They were so tawdry. I wished Ray had picked a better color. She was spray-tanned a burnished tangerine that made her muscle definition look insane. It was like a twelve-year-old boy addicted to comic books had drawn her.

A new, different hype music began to play and fog rolled down the other ramp into the arena and then a beefy girl with frizzy brown hair in a ponytail pushed her way through. The moment I saw her, I knew she had no chance. She was jogging in a peppy way, but pep, I could already tell, would be inadequate to the situation.

"She doesn't have a chance," I said to Ray.

"I know!" he cried with utter glee.

The announcer: "Weighing in at one hundred sixty-two pounds, we have Courtney O'Day, with an eight-and-oh record."

"Look at how short her arms are," Ray said with scorn. I looked at the girl's arms but I could not detect any shortness in them, until I looked over at Bunny and then I understood. The other girl did not have freakishly short arms, but Bunny had freakishly long ones. The bell rang and the round began, and I worried that Bunny would just pummel her, but what happened was in some ways even worse. Bunny was calm and, most upsetting to me, playful. She would use those long arms to just sort of reach over to the girl and pop her in the face, the way a cat might reach a paw into a fish tank. There was such lazy power in that insane reach of hers, and every time it would surprise the other girl, who just couldn't seem to keep Bunny's absurd wingspan in mind.

When O'Day would go on the offensive, Bunny would hunch down behind her gloves and wait a few seconds, letting the girl get close enough to get in her combinations, a good deal closer than she probably usually had to get since she was having to punch up (Bunny was a solid six inches taller). And after a few of these ineffectual punches, Bunny would explode into a counterattack series, blows that landed hard, jerking the other girl's torso like she was a mannequin. Weirdly, this kept happening over and over again, and every time O'Day would take the bait, get Bunny backed up to the ropes, set about babyishly beating up Bunny's raised gloves, and then get surprised by devastating counterpunches. In between these little exchanges, Bunny just slowly followed the girl around the ring, reaching out those long arms every now and then to hit her in the face.

The rounds were only two minutes long, but the first round seemed to take forever. I was sweating like a sous chef. When the bell finally rang, I thought I might faint. Ray ran up to go see Bunny in her corner, but I was watching O'Day and her coaches. They were rubbing Vaseline on her face and talking to her the way you would as you put a dog down. The girl looked wild-eyed and slick with sweat, the skin of her chest and arms pale and covered in red blotches. I was so afraid Bunny would kill her that I actually said to Ray Lampert when he came back, "She's not going to kill that girl, is she?"

Ray laughed. "I hope not!"

The second round went along much like the first, and Bunny was clearly having fun. She loved doing a kind of bait and switch where she would let down a hand and create an opening, and when O'Day would go for it, she would duck the blow, move in close, and then explode into an uppercut. O'Day fell on her ass after one of these uppercuts and the crowd started chanting Bunny's name. They wanted her to finish it, to end the fight.

The bell rang.

"Three rounds," Ray said. "She should wrap it up." Bunny looked tired but radiant. She raised a fist at Ray while her trainer poured water into her mouth.

The third round was entirely different from the first two rounds. From the moment the bell rang, Bunny burst from her corner with a speed she had not displayed the whole match and she began a series of punches, all of them landing, that were so fast and beautifully syncopated that the other girl could not react properly or get away. If anything she looked like a movie being rewound, and then fast-forwarded, over and over. I saw the girl's nose break and the spray of blood that smeared Bunny's white gloves. The ref was dancing around them, and when O'Day turned her back to say she had had enough, the ref ended the fight.

I joined Ray as he rushed up to the ring, and we stood around while Bunny gave some brief on-cameras.

"I wanted to knock her out." Bunny was panting as she spoke into the microphone. "But unfortunately she didn't want any more."

"Who's the greatest?" the reporter asked, which struck me as a bizarre question. Ray let out a pleased laugh, then looked at his shoes, but I could tell he was listening for what she would say. I wondered if he had coached her on what to say. Or did all those hits to the head leave her uncoachable?

Bunny looked at him funny. "Me," she said. "But I mean, I was the greatest before the fight also."

"Oh god," I said, because to me her answer seemed psychotic, evidence of delusions of grandeur, as embarrassing as a turd on the carpet.

"What?" Ray said to me. "You shocked? She's literally the best in the world."

"What?"

"She is literally the best female fighter in the world. At least right now. And after the next few fights we have lined up, everyone will know it."

The man laughed. "Do you think O'Day knew what she was getting herself into tonight?" he asked.

"I always wonder what they think. They must not believe I am what I am," Bunny said. The reporter laughed and slapped her on the shoulder.

"What's next?" he asked.

"Oh, I'll keep handing out the thrashings," Bunny said with a rascal's grin.

Ray and I did not stay for the main event, but trailed Bunny back to her dressing room. We waited on a black leather couch while the doctor checked Bunny over. I was shocked to see that she kept spitting blood into a white coffee cup. I had not seen the other girl hit her in the face, certainly not hard enough to loosen any teeth. The doctor was fussing over her ear.

"If you don't want me to drain it now, just go in and get it drained tomorrow."

Bunny grunted.

He felt up and down her ribs. He palpated her kidneys, felt around in her abdomen, though how he could feel anything through her Ninja Turtle abs was a mystery to me. "Let me see the hands," he said, and Bunny gave him her hands, which were still wrapped, and he unraveled the gauze and tape as delicately as if her fingers were broken birds. I was watching, curious, then had to look away as I understood what I was seeing. Her knuckles were so swollen that the backs of her hands bulged, the skin pink as raw pork.

"Jesus," I said.

"That's probably fractured," the doctor said, feeling for the bones in her hand through the swelling.

"I know," Bunny said, "I felt it go."

"But the bone's still in place. Just a splint for now and then you can see in a couple days. Now, I saw you walk out of there, let's talk about your left foot."

"Are you thinking burgers?" Ray asked.

"Steaks," Bunny said.

"Steaks!" Ray cried, delighted. He began consulting his phone, clearly looking for a good steak house nearby, but he kept raising and lowering the phone to his face, like trying to scan a difficult bar code at the grocery store. "I can't fucking see," he said. "Can you look at this please?" and he handed his phone to me.

I found us a decent steak house in midtown and Bunny took an icy shower then had various parts of her wrapped. She hurt so badly that Ray had to tie her shoes for her, zip and button her pants. She was slow and impassive as a zombie.

"You won," I said. I guess I had expected her to be happy.

"Yeah," she said. "Wasn't much of a fight, though."

"It was a great fight," Ray said.

"There's just no one really," Bunny said. Her brow furrowed and she looked confused, but then I realized she was about to start crying. "There's no one," she said again.

Ray wrapped his arm around her shoulders and guided her out and down the hall. "Shhh . . . we just need to get you some food." He turned to me and said, "She's like this sometimes. All the adrenaline. She literally has no serotonin left in her little noggin."

The restaurant was a yokel's cheesy fantasy of a fancy New York steak house. Both Bunny and Ray liked it immediately, and I felt briefly proud of my choice. I knew them well, knew them still.

Bunny ordered two Long Island Iced Teas and a shrimp cocktail to start, Ray got a Seven & Seven, and I ordered a glass of Sauvignon Blanc. "Can I put in more food now, though?" Bunny asked anxiously. The server, a pretty redhead who was probably an actress, said of course. "Then I'll have the filet and can I also get the chicken breast, and can I also get a side of fries, and does it come with bread? Do you bring out bread?"

"Yes," the server said, "we bring out a basket of bread."

"Can you make sure they bring out two?" Bunny asked. Her right cheek was swelling, and the skin was stretched and glossy in the dim light of the steak house.

"Of course," the waitress said.

"Or you can just put double the amount of rolls in a single basket," Bunny said helpfully. "You're really pretty."

"Thank you," the waitress said, backing away from the table, her check pad held tight.

"Well," Ray said, "I'm just so proud of you, Bunny. That was an incredible fight. You've trained so hard. And now it's over, and it's done."

"Shut up," she said, and just looked at her swollen hands on the table.

"She doesn't really mean that," Ray said softly to me. "She can't help it."

"I said shut up!" she moaned.

Just then a busboy scurried over with a basket overflowing with rolls, and Bunny snatched one before he had even set it down.

"That's good," Ray said, "just eat."

"Shut up," she said with her mouth full.

So we didn't speak, and we just ate rolls. I had the sense that Bunny was concentrating hard on just trying to keep it together in the restaurant. Our drinks came. Bunny downed the first Long Island in a few gulps and after that she visibly relaxed.

"You feeling better?" Ray asked.

"Not yet," Bunny said, waving her hand at him as if to shoo him away. This was the first time I had seen her treat Ray badly in our whole lives, and to be honest I was enjoying it a tiny bit. She still didn't like to look either of us in the eye, and she didn't want us to talk either.

"Well, Michael," Ray said, keeping his voice down in an effort not to upset Bunny, "so tell me what it is you do again? I mean, you're getting a PhD, I remember that much, but what do you study?"

"I study evolutionary biology," I said, "which is—"

"Boring?" Bunny asked. "You're both fucking boring."

Ray looked at me apologetically and pantomimed zipping his lips shut. Even I, who had only the most pop-culture understanding of head injuries, knew that concussions could cause belligerence and temper issues. It seemed so obvious to me that Bunny's brain had been re-traumatized by the fight. Why had the doctor let her go? Why had he looked at her hands, at her feet, at her ribs, and not at this, this most obvious thing? We shouldn't be at a steak house, we should be at the hospital.

But after the shrimp, which Ray and I did not attempt to share with her, and about halfway through the steak, which Ray had to cut up for her, her hands were so fractured and swollen, Bunny seemed to come around.

"Did you see my fight?" she asked me.

"Yes, I did. It was incredible."

"Thank you. Who was O'Day training with again? Dad?"

"Dave McNair, or Mc-something?"

"I mean, I guess they really can't train her not to be stupid, that was the thing that was most frustrating about it, how stupid she was. She just kept walking into it again and again. I don't like that."

"I know," Ray said.

"Is it less of a challenge that way?" I asked.

"No, it's like, I just, I don't like them to feel like victims. And when they're stupid like that. It just makes me feel like I'm slaughtering animals." She drank the rest of her second Long Island.

"They're not victims," Ray said. "They're fighters."

"You've always hated fighting," Bunny said to me.

I paused, a bite of salmon halfway to my mouth. "Yeah," I said, wanting to go on and lie, to say something about how while I didn't prefer to fight myself, I admired her for fighting. I couldn't even think of a way of phrasing this. I worried I would gibber like a hostage to a gunman.

"I think," Bunny said, suddenly laughing, "that you would prefer to never have to act at all. To just passively let things happen to you. Like, blah. Like, I'm just a crying statue of pure suffering, wah."

"I wouldn't go that far," I said, flustered and wishing I had not drunk so much of my wine. I was such a lightweight that even a glass left me spinning. "Just because I don't like to beat people up doesn't mean I'm some passive crybaby."

"Not a crybaby," she said, "not a crybaby. But like . . . an artist that doesn't make anything. You study yourself. You study life instead of living it. And everything you feel is like a fine wine and you sniff it and swish it around and in the end you barely fucking drink it."

Around us the entire restaurant seemed dark and shadowy, as if we were in a massive cave with many chambers. I tried to remember that she was not right in the head, that I shouldn't take it personally, the things she said, but they were dangerously close to the truth and I could feel the muscles in my cheeks start involuntarily twitching.

"Like, on some level, don't you think you let those boys beat you up?" Bunny said.

"What boys?" I asked, incredulous. "Jason and Tyler and them?"

"You could have run into the Rite Aid," she said. "You could have screamed for help. The brewery was right there, someone would have heard."

"But I didn't understand what was happening until it was happening. I froze."

"You choked," she said. "I mean, isn't that the same thing?" Her left eye was now almost completely swollen shut. She had eaten her filet and her chicken and all of the rolls.

"You know what I think we should do," Ray said, "go back to the hotel and order a movie and just turn in and relax."

"Ugh," she said. "You're so fucking obvious, all you are trying to do is control me. That's all you ever try to do."

"Oh, that's not true," he said.

"Everyone's a victim," Bunny said. "Everyone is just fucking helpless."

Ray studied his watch. He seemed very tired. "I'm not trying to control you," Ray said finally.

"But you're gonna freak out," she said.

"I'm not going to freak out," he said.

She studied him for a moment. "Good. Then let's order another drink."

"I don't think another drink will—"

"Control. Freak out," she said.

"Fine, order the drink," he said, and she did.

"I'm sorry I'm being so mean," she said to me.

"Oh, it's okay," I said, though that wasn't true at all. I felt panicky and unclean, like I was in an early Harmony Korine movie, and yet I couldn't fully bring myself to blame her. As I always had, I found it much easier to blame Ray, who was encouraging her to do this to herself.

"Do you think everything means something?" Bunny said. I wasn't sure if this was a continuation of her earlier complaint, or if we were going in some new, terrible direction. I was done pretending to eat my salmon. Its skin looked sad and ruined on my plate.

"Like, it seems like you think everything means something and if you could only understand everything then it would all be okay. It's like thinking a map will change the size of the ocean. Do you have any gum? Dad?"

He handed her a piece of gum, then realized her fingers wouldn't work well enough to unwrap it, so he took off the foil for her. He motioned to the waitress for the check. They were both chewing gum, I could smell the spearmint over the odor of the steaks. Someone in the dark of the restaurant was laughing. I couldn't see him but it sounded like a big man was laughing.

"Even God can't understand everything," she said.

"I thought that was the whole point of God. That he could understand everything."

"Some things he chooses not to understand," she said.

"What do you mean?" I thought she was cracked, now truly and finally cracked.

"That's the whole point of hell, isn't it? A place to put the people God chooses not to understand?"

"Dear lord," Ray said, and rolled his eyes.

"Like, this one." She pointed at her father. "You would always ask me back in the day, ooh, what was his relationship with his mother like? That was what you thought would explain it. Like, if you knew why Ray Lampert was the way he was, then—what? Then what? What does understanding someone get you?"

"I don't know," I said.

"My mother was a fucking cunt," Ray said.

"Where's our hotel?" Bunny asked. "Is it near here?"

"It's downtown," Ray said. "We'll take a cab."

We said goodbye in the hallway without any fanfare, Bunny didn't even look at me, just shuffled into her and Ray's room saying, "Take off my fucking shoes, oh god, I need them off right this second," and Ray scurried after her. I took a long, hot shower in my room and called Conor and tried and failed to explain to him what had happened.

"That's such a tragedy," he kept saying. Was that the name for what it was?

"I wish I could teleport and just be in our house. I know what things mean in our house."

"Hotel rooms are terrible," he said.

"They really are," I said.

After we got off the phone, I turned off all the lights, but I couldn't sleep. The air conditioner kept clicking on and off, on and off. You could have run, she said. You could have screamed. You could have done something, but you did nothing, you let it happen to you.

I tried to think about a paper I was writing, to think about how I wanted to frame the abstract, and perhaps I was half asleep already because I realized I was explaining the paper to Anthony of all people. He was sitting right there before me, eight months dead, a newly minted ghost wearing a white hotel-style robe. "Essentially, the perceived risk of predation can affect melanin production and thus feather coloration in the nuthatch."

"Break it down for me," Anthony said, smiling.

"I played predator calls constantly to baby birds and their feathers turned out funny."

"A little more," he said.

"Fear can change you. It can change you on a physical level. It's not just feelings, it's chemical cascades."

"That's right," he said. And then I understood that he was going to give me a lot of money, it was like a prize that ghosts gave out to those who sincerely quested for knowledge, and he had been part of the selection committee even back when he was alive.

I became aware of a pounding on my door and I staggered through the dark, confused a little as to where I was. I wasn't entirely aware I was in a hotel room and that there was probably a peephole, so I just opened the door.

"I couldn't sleep," Bunny said. "Can I come in?"

"Of course," I said, because it is what I would have said when we were seventeen, even though now of course I did not want her in my room in the middle of the night. I did not think to turn on the light and she made no move to turn on the light, so we both just got into the bed in the dark. She smelled like liquor, like whiskey or something.

For a moment she said nothing, then she said, "Man, I really took her apart, didn't I?"

"Sure did," I said, terse and pissy, suddenly more awake.

"Do you hate me?" she asked.

"What? No, I mean, no. Why would you ask that?" Of course I hated her. She symbolized everything I most feared in the world.

"I don't know," she said. Her nose sounded even more stuffed than usual, and I wondered if it was from the swelling in her face. In the reflected light from the street, I could see that her cheekbone was still warped and shiny, like half an apple had been inserted under the skin.

"I can't believe you said I let those boys beat me up," I said. "I just can't believe you fucking said that." My heart was beating fast with how angry I was, and now I was entirely awake, scrutinizing her blue outlines in the dark.

"When did I say that?" she asked.

"At dinner."

"I'm sorry I said that," she said. "I don't remember saying that. But I know I've thought it before. I mean, couldn't you have run? Couldn't you have screamed?"

"Maybe I did," I said. "Maybe I did both those things."

"Did you?"

"No," I said, "I don't think so. It just wasn't—it wasn't like that."

"I don't get it," she said.

"You just don't know," I said. "You don't know what it is to be weak. You don't know how to be afraid. You can't even understand it."

"But you can't let things like that happen to you," she said. "You can't let things like that—those people, there are people, Michael, who are bad and who will hurt you and who will kill you, and you can't just let them because you are innocent and they are bad. You have to try to get away. You have to fight with everything you have." She was almost in tears, and I realized she was saying all of this because she wanted there to be some way to undo the beating, to avert it, to go back and make it not take place, to never let it take place ever again, and she felt that way because she loved me.

"Are you one of those people?" I asked.

"What people?"

"The people who will hurt and kill."

"People choose to fight me," she said. "They decide to get in the ring with me. It's different."

I didn't say it, but I think we were both thinking of Ann Marie, who had not chosen, who had not entered any ring at all, who had merely made the mistake of gossiping, of running that glossy little pink mouth of hers.

"What do you want me to say, Michael?" she asked. "Do you want me to hate myself? Do you need to hear that? I'm cold, can I get closer? You have the AC up really high."

"Yes," I said, and she scooted closer to me under the covers and then I could feel the heat of her breath and the warmth of her body.

"I want to put my arms around you, but my hands," she said.

"Here," I said, and lifted my head off the pillow so she could snake an arm under me without crushing her hand.

"Sometimes I do hate myself," she said. "Sometimes I do."

"I don't want you to hate yourself," I said.

"Sometimes I forget to hate myself. Or I hate myself for all the wrong reasons."

"You don't have to be good," I said.

"Is it okay that I'm in here? I forget how we got here, how I got in your bed, but I am so, so happy to be here," she said, nuzzling her face into my hair.

"It's okay," I said. "That you're here."

I loved her body so much. I loved her so much. She was exactly as good and exactly as evil, I thought, as a panther. As any of us animals. As me.

"Everything hurts," she whispered.

"Everything hurts," I agreed.

And then we fell asleep.

Acknowledgments

I owe the writing of this book to so many people. My kind and beautiful husband for his patience and support. My mother for her unfaltering belief in me, as well as her tireless willingness to read multiple drafts. My editor, Jennifer Jackson, who has toured the weirder warehouses of my mind over the course of the last six years—you always know how to say the thing that makes me see the book anew. My agent, Molly Friedrich, who is so wise, and who bore the brunt of my self-doubt more gracefully than I may have deserved. You are truly, sublimely kind on top of all the other things you are. I owe Lucy Carson, who makes me cry with the depth of her insight, and Kent Wolf, who makes me laugh with the depth of his. I owe Zakiya Harris and Heather Carr, both of whom keep the whole machine going and who are willing to explain things to me when I am being obtuse. I owe Decio Rangel, Jr., Esq., for his free and extremely jovial legal advice, and I owe the Airport Courthouse for putting up with my loitering and spying. Many thanks for all the medical advice and perverted dance moves of Dr. Bill Winter. I owe my salmon salad writers' group, who have buoyed me up and known when to knock me down. I am in debt to the kindness and editorial advice of Jeff Zentner and Kerry Kletter. I owe my copy editor, Annette Szlachta-McGinn; Maris Dyer; and my amazing publicist, Emily Reardon. I couldn't have written the book, done the work of the writing, without any of these beautiful people.

Acknowledgments

But then there are the ones who taught me the lessons in life that made it possible to write the book at all. Who taught me what friendship is, who taught me regret and heartbreak and love. This is a book, like so much that I write, about friendship, and I can't help but think about all the friends I have been lucky enough to have in my life. Simone Gorrindo, you are the best friend anyone could ever dream of, my first map of the world, and I am so proud just to know you. I can't imagine Jason Arold, Annie Bassett, Reina Shibata, Margaret Aiken, Sean Kazerian, Josey Duncan, or any of 9C will be able to read this book without seeing flashes of the way we used to spend our time, gloriously, masterfully wasting it. Here is to the stupid adventures, the passions of platonic love, the water bottles of vodka, the things we didn't understand yet, and all the things we knew too well. You have made my life so beautiful, and I fall on my knees in gratitude.

A Note About the Author

Rufi Thorpe received her MFA from the University of Virginia in 2009. Her first novel, *The Girls from Corona del Mar,* was longlisted for the 2014 International Dylan Thomas Prize and for the 2014 Flaherty-Dunnan First Novel Prize. Her second novel, *Dear Fang, With Love,* was published by Knopf in May 2016. She lives in California with her husband and two sons.

A Note on the Type

This book was set in the well-known Monotype face Bembo. This letter was cut for the celebrated Venetian printer Aldus Manutius by Francesco Griffo, and first used in Pietro Cardinal Bembo's *De Aetna* of 1495.

Typeset by North Market Street Graphics,
Lancaster, Pennsylvania

Printed and bound by Berryville Graphics,
Berryville, Virginia

Designed by Michael Collica